Cathy Williams can remember ~~reading~~
books as a teenager, and now th̶a̶t̶ ̶s̶h̶e̶ ̶i̶s̶ ̶w̶r̶i̶t̶i̶n̶g̶ ̶t̶h̶e̶m̶
she remains an avid fan. For her, there is nothing like
creating romantic stories and engaging plots, and
each and every book is a new adventure. Cathy lives
in London. Her three daughters—Charlotte, Olivia
and Emma—have always been, and continue to be,
the greatest inspirations in her life.

Jackie Ashenden writes dark, emotional stories, with
alpha heroes who've just got the world to their liking
only to have it blown wide apart by their kick-ass
heroines. She lives in Auckland, New Zealand, with
her husband, the inimitable Dr Jax, two kids and two
rats. When she's not torturing alpha males and their
gutsy heroines she can be found drinking chocolate
martinis, reading anything she can lay her hands on,
wasting time on social media or being forced to go
mountain biking with her husband. To keep up to date
with Jackie's new releases and other news sign up to
her newsletter at jackieashenden.com.

OUT OF OFFICE

CATHY WILLIAMS

JACKIE ASHENDEN

MILLS & BOON

First published in Great Britain 2025
by Mills & Boon, an imprint of HarperCollins*Publishers* Ltd,
1 London Bridge Street, London, SE1 9GF

www.harpercollins.co.uk

HarperCollins*Publishers*, Macken House, 39/40 Mayor Street Upper,
Dublin 1, D01 C9W8, Ireland

ISBN: 978-0-263-34460-8

04/25

This book contains FSC™ certified paper
and other controlled sources to ensure responsible forest management.

For more information visit www.harpercollins.co.uk/green.

Printed and Bound in the UK using 100% Renewable Electricity
at CPI Group (UK) Ltd, Croydon, CR0 4YY

HER BOSS'S
PROPOSITION

CATHY WILLIAMS

MILLS & BOON

CHAPTER ONE

'BEFORE YOU GO...'

Caitlin looked up from where she was busy trying to make sense of her desk, which looked as though a bomb had hit it. There were papers here, there and everywhere; two empty mugs, which she should have taken to the kitchen hours ago; three cute little pots with cuttings that Edith from accounts had given her; and her computer, which was demanding attention. She slammed shut the lid and looked at her boss who had sauntered out of his vast adjoining office and was now lounging indolently by her desk.

He'd caught her by surprise and her heart flipped over. The damned man always had that effect on her, even though she'd been working for him for over two years. He was pure, sinful, alpha-male perfection: six-two, dark hair, deep, dark eyes, lush lashes most women would have killed for and imperious features lovingly honed to perfection.

'Please don't tell me you've got something that needs to be done yesterday, boss.'

'Since when do you refer to me as "boss"?'

'Since I think that you're about to tell me that I've got to do overtime because something urgent's cropped up. I have to rescue Benji from the sitter.'

'He's a dog. He can wait an extra hour.'

'Angie might have plans.'

'Didn't you once tell me that all her plans revolved around her doggy day-care business? Or has her social life taken off since then? I can't wait to find out.'

Caitlin shot him a frustrated look from under her lashes and began doing something and nothing to sort out her desk because he was making her jittery, standing there and looking at her with lazy amusement.

He had no idea how much he rattled her sometimes because they worked so well together. They were at ease with one another, and so in tune that she could almost predict what jobs he was going to give her and when. Over the time they had worked together, he had given her more and more responsibility and had upped her pay accordingly in a cunning move that made it nearly impossible even to think about quitting.

Not that that thought had once crossed her mind, however much she occasionally railed against the pointless crush she had on him. A crush was a crush was a crush— manageable and, in a weird way, secretly thrilling. Plus, the work was everything she could ever have hoped for— challenging, stimulating, demanding and varied. She listened to friends drone on about how much they hated their jobs and was guiltily aware that it was impossible to join in the chorus.

'Well.' Caitlin gave up. 'What is it you want me to do?'

'Follow me into my office.'

'Should I bring my tablet? What files do I need to access?'

'No files,' Javier threw over his shoulder as he strolled back into his office, leaving her to gape at him with a puzzled frown.

Her boss lived and breathed work. He played hard, and she should know, because she usually ended up making all the candle-lit, romantic dinner-for-two bookings for him, along with all the theatre and opera tickets and expensive gifts of jewellery and perfume.

But, within the walls of his office, all that mattered to him was his work. When he issued a summons, it was always because some new deal had landed on his desk and he needed her to start working on it earlier than yesterday and faster than the speed of light. So what was going on now? She didn't know and not knowing made her uneasy.

She texted Angie about Benji and hurriedly followed him into his office, which was four times the size of hers and equipped with everything from a long, uncomfortable but very expensive sofa against one wall, to a drinks cabinet that housed any and every drink any client could possibly fancy after a long night hammering out a deal. The drinks cabinet was to ensure they were relaxed, he had once told her with a grin, and the uncomfortable sofa was to make sure they didn't outstay their welcome.

Through the bank of glass behind his oversized desk, guests had a bird's eye view of most of London. It was really magnificent. Caitlin never tired of looking down at the city and all the people, tiny and purposeful, scurrying through the streets. From where she had started in life, she'd reached heights she'd never thought she'd ever reach, and she always remembered never to take that for granted. This commanding view of the city from his magnificent office was a daily reminder of how far she'd come.

Right now, Javier had swung behind his desk and was waiting for her to close the door, which she did, before sitting on her usual leather chair slightly to the side. Her hands felt empty, because she was never in here without her trusty laptop or tablet.

'Well?' she ventured into the unnerving silence.

'I have something to discuss with you, Caitlin, that's of a somewhat…personal nature…'

Caitlin stilled. A rush of apprehension washed through her and suddenly she was catapulted through time, away from the happy-go-lucky, twenty-four-year-old woman and straight back to the kid in care who'd always known that discussions of a personal nature were never going to be pleasant. No family had come to adopt her. She'd had to understand that she had come late to foster care and that many people favoured a baby or toddler over an eight-year-old child. Maybe someday soon, she'd hoped, but times had been tough, and many people had found it difficult to make a conscious decision to add an extra mouth to their weekly budget.

She'd had to stop pretending to be Catarina. Her name was Caitlin—plain old Caitlin. There'd been no point getting above herself. And was it true that she'd busily concocted fairy stories about herself? Had told the younger ones that she was just going to be there for a short while because her family was abroad at the moment? She'd known she had to *live in the real world*.

'What's wrong?'

Caitlin surfaced with a jolt from her trip down memory lane, but she had whitened, and her blue eyes were huge as she stared at Javier in silence for a few seconds.

'Nothing,' she muttered.

'You're as white as a sheet. What do you think I'm going to say? Do you think I've brought you in here to sack you?'

'Have you?'

'God, Caitlin, what the hell would give you that impression?'

Caitlin lowered her eyes and clasped her hands on her lap. When she next looked up, it was to find that he had swerved round the desk and was now towering over her with a look of concern on his face. He dragged a chair across and sat down so close to her that she could breathe in whatever aftershave he was wearing.

'I…' She faltered. This man knew nothing about her, not really. No one could have known her better whilst knowing her less. He had no idea that she had been through the care system. Why would he? Why would the personal details of her life interest him? She was a great worker and that was the main thing.

'You look as though you're about to faint.'

'I… I suppose I jumped to the wrong conclusion…' she mumbled in a rushed undertone. 'You know, it's not like you to summon me into your office for anything other than work.'

When she looked into his deep, dark eyes she could see flecks of amber. Up close and personal like this, she couldn't escape the haughty beauty of his face, the bronzed column of his neck contrasting starkly with the pristine white of his shirt. Nor could she avoid the glimpse of hair on his chest because he had undone the top two buttons of the shirt.

She averted her eyes hurriedly.

'That's true,' Javier admitted. 'But, rest assured, I have no intention of sacking you. No, I asked you in here because…a situation has arisen and I need to know how you feel about taking on…er…some additional responsibilities.'

'I feel fine about that,' Caitlin said promptly, relieved

that her darkest fears had been dismissed, although she was curious as to why taking on 'additional responsibilities' required a chat in his office after work hours. Couldn't he just have given her a list of the clients he wanted her to add to her portfolio? She would almost certainly know what to do because she'd been at ground zero with several of them when it had come to putting the basics of several deals in place.

'Who do you want me to take over? If it requires much overtime…'

'These particular responsibilities will undoubtedly require a fair amount of overtime.'

'In that case, I'll have to make arrangements for Benji, and please don't say that he's just a dog. He gets very upset when I'm away from him for too long.'

'He's just a dog.' Javier grinned.

'When I left him for a week four months ago to go on holiday, it took him ages before he forgave me,' Caitlin murmured as she hived off on a tangent. 'Tail between his legs, doleful expression, barely looking at his food…'

'I'd never have guessed, judging from the dog I saw when you made up for lost time by bringing him into work for a fortnight. He seemed perfectly fine, making friends with every single person on the floor, and chewing his way through the Wilson Partners paperwork which you'd left on the table in my office.'

'I could never thank you enough for allowing me to bring him in, Javier.' She meant that as well. Javier could be a stern taskmaster but he could also be oddly thoughtful and empathetic. She thought of the way her tiny little mutt had clamped his teeth into his expensive trousers, and winced. He hadn't uttered a word of complaint. 'I might have to do the same if I have to work overtime here and can't get cover for him.'

'I re-read your CV and saw that you have some basic grasp of Spanish, as well as law and accounting courses you did before you joined me.'

Caitlin frowned at the change of topic. She thought back to her days studying Spanish, loving what she'd learnt at school, finding the language so wonderful and romantic. At the age of fourteen, she'd whiled away many a happy hour daydreaming about being a swooning, Spanish princess with trailing dark locks and soulful dark eyes—as opposed to a plump, blue-eyed blonde with ridiculously untamed hair who'd been placed into foster care because her mother had died from a drugs overdose and who didn't have a clue where her father was, or even *who* he was.

She'd actually thought about going to university to study Spanish, but in the end hadn't been able to bear the thought of not earning money for years on end. She'd done night courses in basic law and accounting. She'd dabbled in Spanish because it appealed to her whimsical heart.

'I can speak a little,' she told him cautiously. 'My week in Barcelona with Jannah and Ivy was good. I thought I'd forgotten how to speak it, but I picked it up again pretty quickly. I'm not saying I'm going to be able to understand loads of technical stuff, though.'

'You won't have to.'

'What client are we talking about?'

Javier raked his fingers through his hair and shot her a wary look. Accustomed to exerting control over all aspects of his life, he'd lost sleep thinking about the chain of events now awaiting him. A chain of events that had come ahead of schedule, and would be dealt with, but which would certainly change things up considerably in his life.

Strangely, he'd also lost sleep when he'd thought about asking his PA to take on duties that went beyond the call of what comprised her working duty. He appreciated her probably more than she thought, although her frequent huge pay rises should have given her a clue. She was keen, obliging and never balked at taking on extra responsibilities. The last thing he wanted was to put her in a position where she might feel uncomfortable with what would now be asked.

His lack of immediate response instantly made Caitlin suspicious. She narrowed her eyes and looked at him in silence.

'You'll find out soon enough,' he eventually said, glancing at his watch. 'The reason I called you in here is to try and explain what this job will entail before…er… Isabella arrives.'

Again, he felt that sickening lurch as plans made crystallised into shape, form and substance. It was one thing to lay the groundwork but quite another when that groundwork finally came to fruition and he then had to take action. And it made no difference that the action had been considered well in advance.

It also made no difference that this was the right and only course of action in more ways than one. He'd fancied himself in charge of the situation and yet, as he gazed briefly into Caitlin's cornflower-blue eyes, he had the oddest temptation to let go of his control and succumb to a vulnerability he hadn't had since he'd been a kid, wrapped up in the trauma of his mother's premature death. He had a sudden urge to *open up*. Crazy. He was a guy who always relied on his head and never on emotional responses—never. He shut his mind off from memories of a time when he'd seen first hand where raw emotional responses could get a person. He refocused.

'Isabella? What's her surname? I don't remember any Isabellas on your client list.'

'"Client" might not be quite the word I would use to describe her.'

'Javier, this is driving me crazy. What are you trying to say?'

'Isabella is going to be my wife, Caitlin, and your job will be to show her the ropes here in London, because this will be where we will be living.'

Caitlin's mouth dropped open and she stared at her boss with huge, incredulous eyes. Since when was he engaged to be married? The whereabouts of his last girlfriend might not be known, but what *was* known was the fact that her departure from the scene had only happened a little over a month ago! How fast a worker was he?

'You're *getting married*?'

'I understand that you might be a little surprised…'

'It's none of my business how you conduct your private life, Javier, but your last girlfriend—I forget her name—was around only a matter of weeks ago! An engagement now does seem a little hasty. Unless…'

'Unless?'

'Unless,' Caitlin said quietly, as her heart constricted and her stupid girlish fantasies about her boss began to dissipate like mist on a summer day, 'you were in love with Sylvie and have now decided to rush headlong into a committed relationship in an attempt to recover from a broken heart.'

'I would stay away from trying to analyse my personal life, Caitlin,' Javier said gently. 'But, just for the record, I was far from being in love with Sylvie. Also, I thought you couldn't remember her name?'

'It came back to me.'

Their eyes met and Javier held her stare for a few seconds as he tried to organise his thoughts into something that would make sense to her before Isabella arrived, which she would do in roughly half an hour. He could see her utter bewilderment and was surprised at how much it affected him. He'd become used to her easy-going predictability. Was she shocked, disappointed?

He realised he wanted to see neither of those on her face. Caitlin was by far and away the best PA he had ever had, and that included his previous one—a tough-as-nails battle-axe who had inconsiderately decided to emigrate to Seattle to be closer to her grandchildren. She was attuned to him in ways that he occasionally still found a little startling. Not only was she highly competent at what she did, but she was intuitive. She could pick up the nuances of what people said, and arrive at conclusions about what they thought, which was very handy when it came to reading the direction of many deals that hung in the balance.

Javier lived life in the fast lane and having Caitlin by his side was a blessing he had become accustomed to over the months and years. Not only did he manage his family's vast business concerns, but he also ran his own highly successful hedge fund, and a specialised acquisitions team that sourced promising tech startups and bought them. It paid to have someone who worked to his incredibly high standards and was always willing to put in overtime.

The fact that she was sunny-natured, that she countered his ferocious drive with humour and that she could tease the stress out of him were benefits he was often barely aware of her bringing to the table. Was that why her questioning, puzzled gaze twisted something inside him?

For all that she knew about the superficial aspects of his private life, they kept their respective distance when it came to anything really personal. He knew when she went on holiday, and the broad strokes of what she did at the weekend, but he didn't know what she thought about anything that wasn't to do with work. She'd never mentioned a boyfriend, so he assumed that there wasn't one on the scene, but had there been? Was she looking for love or just interested in furthering her career? Was she even into guys?

She knew who he dated, and when he broke up, but nothing about what he felt about any of those women he dated and broke up with. She certainly would have been caught on the back foot at the revelation that had just been tossed at her. He belatedly thought about what she had said, about his last girlfriend and the fiancée he had now pulled out of the hat.

'This isn't a rebound situation,' he said with discomfort at the intensely personal suggestion coming from someone who had never commented on his life before. 'I've known Isabella since I was a kid. Our families go back a very, very long way, and for some time now it's been a given that we would marry and join our families' two powerful Spanish houses. It works for both of us.'

'She's a childhood sweetheart?'

'I wouldn't exactly put it that way,' Javier admitted. 'At the risk of destroying whatever romantic notions you may have of love and fairy-tale endings, our marriage will primarily be a business deal, and a highly successful one at that. Her family run a prestigious string of international hotels which will slot in nicely with the leisure side of my family's business interests. There are benefits for Isabella, marrying me, and for me there are likewise advantages.' He paused, on the cusp of saying more, but then retreated from the temptation.

That speculative remark about rushing headlong into a committed relationship in an attempt to recover from a broken heart... For the first time, Javier wondered about the deeper places in his PA that he had never glimpsed. Was she into love and marriage? Was there a boyfriend in the background, someone she'd never mentioned? Maybe there was a string of boyfriends. Maybe his PA was a dutiful employee by day and a pole dancer by night.

Dark eyes rested on her for a few seconds, taking in the unruly vanilla-blonde hair, curly, fly-away and currently restrained by a large glittery butterfly clip that wasn't doing the job it was paid to do because escaping tendrils of fair hair framed her heart-shaped face. Her wide, blue eyes somehow managed to look smart and oddly innocent at the same time. She might not be head-turning glamorous, but there was something about her that got under the skin. Was it the fact that she looked as though she was always ready to smile, to laugh, to tease? The impression that there was a whole lot more there than met the eye?

He knew there was. He knew how sharp she was, how expert at reading situations and how fast her brain worked when it came to solving problems. The fact that she revealed little about herself, that she ran deeper than she chose to put on the table, said a lot.

He went for leggy brunettes who were as transparent as glass: soothing after-work enjoyment, women who didn't challenge him intellectually and who knew from the get-go that he wasn't in it for the long haul.

He lowered his eyes and dismissed suddenly intrusive thoughts about the woman staring at him in silence, the woman with thoughts he wanted to know and who was distracting him from the reason she was in his office in the first place.

He picked up the thread of the conversation. 'Like I said, Isabella speaks reasonable English, but she would benefit from your help in showing her around London in preparation for our wedding. Taking her to various shops…showing her how life works in the city… The fact that you speak Spanish will help matters.'

'You want me to be a tour guide?'

'In a manner of speaking. Arrangements for our marriage have been a little more rushed than might have been expected, so you may also have to pick up the slack on that front as well.'

'Pick up the slack on that front?'

'I've compiled a guest list—close friends and family. At a later date, something bigger will be held in Madrid for business associates in both companies, and all our relatives over there, but for the moment I expect the event to be attended by no more than fifty people.'

'When is all this supposed to happen?' Caitlin asked faintly.

'In a month.'

'A month? That's impossible.'

'There's no such thing as impossible, not when money is no object.'

'Any halfway decent venue might disagree with you on that, Javier. Nice places get booked up sometimes years in advance. Can I ask what the big rush is?'

Javier hesitated, but of course she would be curious, and she had every right to be.

Isabella... That was a story with so many twists and complications, and he knew that he would have to avoid touching upon most of them. Beautiful Isabella, his close friend from childhood, and the secret she carried about her sexuality. He was the only person who knew that she was gay. She'd always been too scared to confide in anyone, despite his encouragement over the years. She was an only child from a deeply traditional family and, like him, she had lost her mother when she'd been young. How could she ever confide her secret to her father? So she'd kept it to herself. And he was free, single and disengaged, playing the field but knowing that he would have to settle down before his thirty-fifth birthday.

An eccentric clause in the family inheritance would only release two beautiful vineyards into his safekeeping if he married as stipulated. Javier wanted those vineyards. He could remember playing there as a child, when his mother had still been alive. He could remember the sound of her laughter and the look in her eyes as she'd stooped and held a fat grape in her hand and told him how it became wine. He longed for those vineyards for the memories far more than for their potential for huge profit.

Years ago, he and Isabella had shaken hands on their marriage of convenience. He would get his wife and she would get the useful cover she felt she needed. They liked each other. What could go wrong? Those were details he would keep to himself. In truth, Isabella's story was not his to share.

Now the time had come, for reasons neither of them had expected, and he needed his PA to fulfil duties way out of her orbit. Isabella was an only child, without a mother figure to navigate this rushed marriage with her. She needed to be here, because this was where she would be living; and, whilst her English was perfectly passable, she needed someone to metaphorically hold her hand while she was in London, at least for a few weeks, until she found her feet. He didn't have the time to devote to hand-holding and he couldn't think of a single woman he knew who could do the job without being a liability in the process.

'Isabella's father has had a major health scare,' he began heavily, and this was certainly the one thing he could tell her. 'Problems with his heart. He's not out of the woods yet. Isabella has been called in to take charge of the entire show in his absence, to make decisions she isn't yet entirely confident making. She's an only child, and of course there are people to guide and advise, but the buck stops with her. Even though she's been geared to head the company, she's not quite there with the experience.

'Aside from that...and whatever her credentials...the business world can sometimes be an unfairly chauvinistic place, and as it stands shareholders are beginning to get the jitters at the thought that things might not be as under control as they would like. At the moment, the word is out that Alfonso is making hearty progress, but alas, that is far from the case, and it'll just be a matter of time before the market responds to the uncertainty and the share prices plummet.'

'Which is where you come in,' Caitlin murmured.

Javier looked at her with appreciation, seeing that she had grasped the situation without him having to explain further, but he did anyway.

'Which is where I come in.' He wondered how he hadn't noticed before just what a good listener she was. Smart as a tack, yes... Talkative, yes... Upbeat in a way he personally found baffling, yes... But, when it came to listening, she was making it strangely easy for him to expand an explanation she hadn't asked for, and made him feel almost regretful about the confidences he had no intention of sharing.

'Like I said, this union between us has taken shape over a number of years. We've both been free to do our own thing, knowing that our destinies would eventually be entwined. It's something...eh...something that suits us both in equal measure. Lots of reasons, but let's just say that it's not only because it might be desirable to merge our powerful interests.

'The fact is that our grandfathers go way back. They were two friends who founded their own fledgling companies with the unspoken agreement that they would always be there for one another—blood brothers, so to speak. An antiquated concept in this day and age, I guess, but a powerful one back then, and that's something that's run true through the generations. There was an occasion decades ago when my family's empire ran into huge problems, and Isabella's family stuck to their word and bailed us out. Now the time has come for the favour to be repaid, hence a wedding a little earlier than either of us had predicted. We marry, and I will steady the ship until things settle into place. It's nothing that hadn't already been on the cards, although it's now been accelerated.'

'It all sounds very…sensible.'

'Excellent description.'

'But what about love?'

'What about it?'

'Don't either of you want…believe…?'

Javier made a sweeping gesture with his hand and smiled crookedly. 'We have an understanding. So, moving on, you'll naturally be compensated for taking on these additional responsibilities.'

'Wouldn't your…er…fiancée rather *you* took on the job of showing her around and making sure she settles in okay and finds her feet?'

'Of course, I'll do the best I can, but I have three deals on the go, so my time is going to be limited, and I think she'll quite enjoy having another woman with her. I'll be honest, there are quite a few things on the list I can't say I'll be that interested in doing.'

'Really? Such as?'

'Shopping for wedding paraphernalia… Sorting out the venue, the food, the décor…'

'Right…pretty much everything, if I'm reading this correctly?'

'You'll have to take some time off work during the day to attend to certain things, I imagine, so I've made sure to get Tricia Bell on standby to cover for you.'

'As long as I have a job to return to,' Caitlin returned lightly.

But she didn't look away when he raised his eyebrows and said with genuine sincerity, 'No one can replace you, Caitlin. She'll be on loan and then routines will be re-established as soon as the wedding is out of the way.'

He tapped into his phone and pushed it across to her. 'I have in mind financial compensation along these lines.

Let me know what you think. No need to say anything now, because Isabella will be here momentarily. Go away and think about the package and then we can talk tomorrow.'

His phone buzzed, then he spoke rapidly in Spanish and vaulted to his feet.

'Stay here.' He looked at her as she half-rose to her feet. 'I'm going to get Isabella to meet you.' He smiled. 'Don't be apprehensive. I know this is a little out of the ordinary, but look on it as something of an unexpected break from routine. One that will be financially very rewarding for you. Isabella is a lovely woman. You'll like her.'

Caitlin watched him vanish through the door and remained where she was in a state of numb shock.

What had just happened? Had she just hallucinated this whole bizarre episode? Her boss was getting married, as cool as a cucumber as the world order collapsed around her. Was she due to blink and wake up any time soon?

No such luck. She dialled Angie about Benji and told her to hang on to him overnight, if she could, because she wasn't sure when she could collect him—emergency at work, blah, blah, blah...

Her mind was reeling from a series of revelations she certainly hadn't expected. Her boss...married in a month? A fiancée she'd never known existed? A union sealed with consent from both of them over the years? Had she suddenly been transported to a parallel universe?

No. The bottom line was that she just didn't know her boss half as well as she thought she had because she'd always assumed that he was predictable when it came to women. They came and they went. She booked restaurants and theatre tickets, and then bought elaborate bouquets of flowers when their time was up. None lasted. She'd never thought anything of it, and had happily and guiltily nurtured her secret crush on the guy who was unattainable—the player who would never settle down.

But he was settling down now, and had always planned to settle down with a woman who made sense in his life—a woman chosen from his part of the world, with the sort of wealth and power that matched his. An aristocrat of Spanish descent just like Javier.

Suddenly her innocent crush felt like a mortifying lack of judgement. What on earth had she been playing at? Had she subconsciously thought that there could be something between them, once he'd finally grown bored with his revolving door of gorgeous catwalk models?

She was twenty-four years old; it was time to grow up and get past the one disastrous relationship she had had three years ago. Time to forget the trust she had placed in a guy who had cheated on her with not just one girl, but four, and counting. He had made big promises in the hope of getting her into bed, and she had believed that he was so strong and so devoted, to have resisted the temptation to push her into sex. In fact, there had been no need for him to do anything of the sort, because he had had his needs met behind her back.

Why had he bothered to stay with her? Because he'd wanted to see what it would feel like to sleep with a virgin? Because she'd done all his coursework for him on one of the courses they'd been doing together? Because she'd been useful, adoring, convenient and happy to do all his boring chores when asked, from ironing his shirts to keeping his cat when he was on holiday with his buddies?

She'd so longed for the safety of a committed relation-

ship after a life in care that she had pinned her hopes on
a guy who had been the last thing from *safe*. She'd broken up with Andy and had filled the vacancy with a guy
who *had* been safe because she could never have him: her
beautiful boss. Who was about to be married.

It hurt, and she was angry with herself for hurting, and
angry for not quite knowing why it hurt like it did when
it was nothing but a harmless crush. Maybe it was the
thought of getting back into the dating scene—a place
she had never really been to, if she was honest with herself. She had lots of friends and did things in groups.
Andy had been a juvenile mistake, but it had reminded
her that fairy tales weren't for people like her—girls who
had taken hard knocks in their lives and had had to wake
up to harsh reality when they'd still been kids. She could
dream, and dream she did, but she was pragmatic enough
to know the difference between dreams and real life. Real
life was waiting out there for her and, in the meantime,
dreams were all about her boss.

Lost in her thoughts, musing on her stupid crush and
wondering whether there was some rogue gene in her
that inclined her towards pointless fantasising, she was
only aware of Javier returning when she heard the soft
whisper of the outside door being pushed open.

She half-rose as he entered the office with his hand
gently propelling a tall, elegant woman ahead of him.
Caitlin's mouth dropped open and she managed to make
it to her feet with her hand outstretched, even though she
was gaping. Her wildly colourful summer dress didn't
make her feel cheerful and filled with the joys of a balmy
June evening. It made her feel like a cheap, tacky toy
from a charity shop. She self-consciously tugged it down

as the tall brunette walked towards her with a broad, friendly smile, hand reaching out to take hers.

Isabella… There wasn't a woman on earth who could have looked better with Javier than the one standing in front of her. The models he dated were all stunning, but the woman now reaching out a hand to her was exceptional. Not only was she beautiful but her proud, finely chiselled features were stamped with that veneer of the aristocrat. She was as bronzed as Javier, her eyes as dark as his, and her hair was cropped short, framing a face that could easily withstand the severity of the cut.

Introductions were made and Caitlin heard herself mutter the usual pleasantries.

They really cared about one another. It was there in the softness in his eyes when he looked at his bride-to-be, and in the smiling trust on her face when she gazed back at him.

Caitlin felt the pang of jealousy and swallowed hard. *This* was who Javier de Sanchez was destined to marry: someone as stunning, as elevated socially, as *Spanish* as he was. The last fragments of her idiotic, escapist crush fell away and she forced a smile back at Isabella.

She was probably in her late twenties, perhaps early thirties, and Javier had been right—she was an easy woman to like. Her smile was warm and genuine, reaching her eyes. The hug she gave her now was spontaneous and generous.

'Javier has told me much about you.'

'All good, I hope!' Caitlin exclaimed.

'Of course! You speak some Spanish?'

'I can struggle by at a push.' She smiled as Isabella leant down and pulled her into a conspiratorial, girlish huddle.

'Is good, because this man of mine is not interested in the shopping, and there will be a lot of that to do, I am thinking.'

Caitlin glanced at Javier and shrivelled inside just a little bit more at the warm indulgence on his face.

Isabella began listing off the various things that they could do together: finding flowers for the wedding; a venue; the food. Her brow had knitted, as though she'd been trying to think of what else could be added to the tally... She said the invitations were all in such a hurry because of...

At this point she faltered and looked to Javier for support, then relaxed when he said something very fast in Spanish, the tail-end of which Caitlin managed to grasp, which was that he'd explained about her father.

'Will he be able to attend the...er...big day?' she asked politely. 'Your father?'

He wouldn't. It was regrettable but, however, needs must. He insisted on the marriage going ahead without his attendance. There would be some relatives there holding the fort, and of course there would be a big event in due course when he was back on his feet.

In the meantime, Isabella was here to acclimatise to life in London, and would travel back to Madrid every weekend to visit her father.

Caitlin could tell that, however much Javier had told her that this was a business arrangement, a marriage of convenience, it was also a love match. She could see it in their easy familiarity and in the way they looked at one another. The thought of arranging their wedding made her insides knot and she ventured to ask whether a professional might not do a better job.

'Out of the question,' Javier told her as he rested his

hand gently on Isabella's back, urging her to the door with Caitlin trailing behind them. He glanced over his shoulder. 'I want the personal touch.'

'As do I,' Isabella agreed, glancing back with a shy smile.

'I trust you,' Javier told Caitlin, pausing at the door so that both women could brush past him. 'I know you'll do a good job, but it's more than that.'

He paused and Caitlin tried to stamp out the flutter of crazy, utterly inappropriate *awareness* that swept through her as their eyes met. With her silly crush truly dead and buried, surely there was no room for physical awareness of the guy?

'Oh, yes?' she just about managed.

'Isabella knows no one in London, do you, Isabella? So we're both hoping that you're more than someone who's around for a few weeks to help with the wedding. We're both hoping that you might become…a friend.'

CHAPTER TWO

CAITLIN HAD NEVER thought that friendship could come with such big downsides, and the biggest downside was the fact that, after two weeks, she could say with hand on heart that she really liked Isabella. Not only was she beautiful and smart, but there was a kindness there that Caitlin would never have expected, given the other woman's elevated status.

Shouldn't stunningly gorgeous women born with silver spoons in their mouths be horrible and snobby? Shouldn't they enjoy giving orders and lording it up over the riff-raff? Or had she succumbed to stereotyping? Maybe it was time to change her reading habits.

She'd spent precious little time in the office, just a handful of hours over the previous fortnight, because she had been out and about with Isabella, visiting various venues which seemed magically to have space when the fee they would get fell squarely in the 'eye-wateringly generous' category.

They'd been to florists. Then, just because it was such a nice day, and because Isabella had wanted to see more of London than just do stuff to do with the wedding, they had gone to Kew Gardens. They had strolled around, chatting in Spanish and English, laughing and correcting one another, and had had lunch there with the sun on their faces surrounded by people enjoying a day out just like them.

In the evenings, Isabella duly returned to her fiancé, and Caitlin returned to her small, rented apartment in West London where she caught up on work. The fact that she and Javier's fiancée got along so well, the fact that the guy was going to be married and that he had found love whether he chose to admit it or not, should have completely put paid to all inappropriate attraction. But, much to Caitlin's frustration, her body still continued to do its own thing.

She no longer saw him daily for hours at a stretch, but she still found herself treacherously looking forward to those snatched times when she came into the office to catch up with some of her work. He would walk in and her heart would do what it always did and skip a few beats; her pulses would race and her mouth would go dry. She kept it all to herself. She made sure to plaster a smile on her face when she told him about some of the things she and Isabella had done. Of course, Isabella would be confiding in him as well, sharing news of where they'd been and what they'd achieved in terms of progressing the wedding arrangements, but he asked and she replied. She hadn't talked to him at all of certain concerns she had about the whole wedding scenario because it wasn't her business.

Right now, Isabella was back in Madrid for four days, and she was back in the office and pleased to be back in the routine. Tricia could only handle so much, and there was tons to do. She was busy writing up a report when Javier strode into the office and paused in front of her desk.

Caitlin looked up, eyes travelling along faded black jeans and the black V-necked tee-shirt that clung lovingly to his muscular abs. He had a casual jacket looped over one shoulder.

'You're not in your work clothes,' she remarked.

'Shocking, isn't it? I decided to take the afternoon off to see two of those venues you and Isabella narrowed down on the list of possibilities.'

'Oh.'

'One more to see before the day is out. I intend to make a decision by the end of the evening.'

'Oh.'

'Are we going to get more than just a monosyllabic reply to all my statements?'

But he was grinning, his dark eyes lazy, amused and doing all sorts of unwelcome things to her nervous system. This was an expression she had seen before, one that feathered along her spine and made her shiver. Did he even know that the way he sometimes looked at her— lazy, intense, dark eyes lingering for a second too long— always put thoughts in her head and kept her fantasies alive? Her lips thinned at her own weakness in reading signs that weren't there.

'But Isabella isn't in the country.' She frowned.

'Duly noted.'

'You'll decide without her input?'

Javier shrugged, his expression shuttered as he looked at her. 'I don't think she'll mind whatever I choose. I am, after all, a fifty-percent shareholder in this arrangement.'

Which, said like that, brought back those concerns that had been wafting around in Caitlin's head for the past two weeks since she and Isabella had begun putting the wedding plans into effect. She hesitated, tempted to say something, but instead held her tongue and looked at him in silence.

'About to say something?'

'Which of the two have you narrowed down?'

He pulled out a couple of creased brochures that had been stuffed in the back pocket of his jeans and held them out to her.

'Good choices,' she murmured approvingly. 'Out of the four, these would have been my top picks, and I think Isabella would have agreed with me. And with you, of course. It's good that you're on the same page.'

She paused and mentally reminded herself that having any kind of physical response to her engaged boss was one hundred percent taboo. 'Because it shows that you think alike, which is so important in a healthy relationship.'

'Thank you for that observation. And out of the two?'

'I don't think that's for me to say,' Caitlin told him politely.

'Nonsense. You must have an opinion. You always have opinions. At any rate, you can share it with me, because I want you to come with me to the next venue. A little female input would be welcome.'

'Javier, this is the sort of thing you should be doing with Isabella.'

'Who is currently in Madrid, so that's something of a non-starter.'

'Can't you wait until she gets back?'

'The sooner the place is booked, the better. Time marches on. Come along; it's Friday, and that work can wait until Monday. I'm sure Tricia can help out on whatever needs doing, anyway.'

'I thought that would involve shepherding your fiancée around and acting as translator when necessary. I didn't think I would be taking on the role of dedicated wedding planner.'

But he was already moving towards the door, expecting her to spring into action and follow him. The thought of looking at a wedding venue with her boss felt scarily intimate. The sight of him in casual clothing, crazily sexy and way too macho for anybody's good, made her pulses leap just a little bit faster as she reluctantly gathered all her bits and followed him out of the office. She was slipping on her cotton cardigan as the lift doors pinged open and he stepped aside to let her slide past him.

'How have you been finding Isabella, and showing her around and introducing her to life in London?'

'She's absolutely charming. I can see why you two are so close.'

'We understand each other, I suppose. As an only child, like me, she's always been geared to taking over the family business, even if many of the nuts and bolts were handled by other trusted CEOs. She studied business and law at university in Spain, and her exposure to outside influences has been less than you'd expect, given her family's high profile.'

Caitlin had been staring fixedly at the brushed matte doors but now she slowly turned to look at him. He was lounging against the back of the lift, although he eased away when the doors opened to the busy foyer.

'She's clearly very smart. She's talked quite a bit about the family business and what's involved, not that I followed every word she said.'

Truly, Caitlin reflected, Isabella and Javier were both so business-like. To her, it seemed crazy that any bride-to-be would be happy to miss something as vital as choosing her wedding venue. But perhaps this was just the necessary ceremony, and the main event would happen when her father was there along with all their relatives in Spain.

As for Caitlin, she had her own daydreams, but in her heart she knew that they were only daydreams. The rich, handsome boss was never going to gaze into her eyes with sudden adoration and get down on one knee. She would meet a nice, ordinary guy one day who would give her the security she needed—the same security she had thought Andy would give her.

Her life wasn't going to be the fairy tales she had spun in her head as a kid. But for Isabella and Javier? They had all the makings of just the sort of grand romance she read about. They weren't two ordinary people leading ordinary lives. They would never have to make prosaic decisions about paying gas bills and mortgage repayments. They were *meant* for the 'swept off feet' thing. And they weren't even bothered about taking advantage of it!

'I did tell you that you would like her.' Javier broke into Caitlin's reverie, snapping her firmly back into the present.

Soon, they were strolling out into the busy, warm summer streets where his driver was waiting for them in a sleek black Range Rover. It was blessedly cool inside from the air-conditioning. Caitlin relaxed back and half-closed her eyes as the car moved smoothly towards the venue they were going to inspect.

She knew where it was, and knew how long it would take to get there, and the answer was 'not very'. Not very long to get to a place she shouldn't be going to because the woman he was going to marry should be the one going there with him. The woman *he loved*. She had seen it shining in both their faces. The memory of that suddenly cut her to the quick and she shot him a fulminating, rebellious look from under her lashes.

'I don't get it,' she said abruptly.

'Don't get what?'

Caitlin felt hot and bothered at this departure from the usual easy-going working relationship they enjoyed. Suddenly, there was an urgency to say what was on her mind. Yes, she was being paid a small fortune to undertake this mission, but still…

She looked at him coolly and seriously. 'I don't feel comfortable making any kind of decision about something as big as a wedding venue on behalf of your fiancée.'

'Since when was I asking you to?'

'Input should come from Isabella. She would care if you chose something she didn't want.'

'I think you're going beyond your brief here, Caitlin. Just a mild word of warning—I didn't pay you for your observations and conclusions about something you don't know about. You say you think looking at a venue with me is out of your scope, but it's a lot less out of your scope than lecturing me on the dynamics of my relationship with Isabella.'

'Point taken.'

'But it's better than you sitting next to me in sullen silence, so go for it.'

'What about the brief I'll be crashing through?'

'If I'm honest, I think I can handle the directness. It's one of the things about you I happen to like.' He smiled and looked at her for a couple of seconds in silence, eyes assessing and amused. 'Even though it's never applied to my personal life. So…spit it out.' He looked away, shielding his expression.

Caitlin drew in a sharp breath and balled her fists because she had a crazy urge to turn him to look at her to see what was in his eyes. Why did he keep doing this to her—making her think that there was an electric charge there, resting untapped just beneath the surface? Was it her yearning for romance getting the better of her, even though she tried hard not to let it?

She breathed in deeply. 'Isabella is just lovely, but she really doesn't seem at all interested in the exciting business of wedding preparations. I understand she doesn't have a mum being enthusiastic behind the scenes, and that this is all rushed, but still…she's a lot more curious about restaurants and things to do in London than she is in hunting down an outfit for the big day, or even picking which caterer she wants for the reception. She hasn't once mentioned a photographer. I talked about having those disposable cameras on the tables for guests to use and she honestly looked at me as though I was nuts.'

Caitlin grinned ruefully at the memory. 'It's as if she doesn't care one way or another whether there are pictures of the ceremony. Who doesn't want a record of the big day?'

Javier shrugged. 'It's going to be a subdued day, a small affair, with her father still in recovery. An elaborate photo shoot would feel a little overblown.'

'It might be subdued but it'll still be significant.' Caitlin thought about all the daydreams she had had about love, marriage and weddings. None of those daydreams resembled what she was helping out with. 'It's not as though you two don't really love one another. If you love someone why wouldn't you want to celebrate properly? I know you say it's all about business, but it's obvious that's barely half the story with you two.'

'Okay, Caitlin. You've now left all goalposts behind, and that's a step too far.'

His voice had cooled and Caitlin felt that coolness like

a slap on the face. This wasn't *them*. But then, these circumstances were far from normal. The separation between them had dangerously blurred because she was
now involved in his personal life.

Her feelings were compromised. She knew that. The
innocent crush was being tested to the limit and it wasn't
going away. He had his wife-to-be on the scene, a woman
of whom Caitlin was genuinely fond, a woman he clearly
loved—and yet she still felt the dangerous pull of attraction when she was with him.

Such as right now. The dark eyes resting on her flushed
face did all sorts of wild things to her body she didn't
like. Instead of this intrusion of his personal life slam-
ming shut the door between them, it had opened it wide.
It had engineered a curiosity inside her and had allowed
her imagination to take flight. Right now, she felt faint
as she imagined just reaching out and gently touching
this guy who was totally off-limits.

She lapsed into tight-lipped, resentful silence.

'You're right,' she muttered eventually as the silence
stretched and stretched until she could have heard a pin
drop. Thank goodness he had closed the sliding partition
so that his driver couldn't eavesdrop on the most awkward conversation on the planet.

She suddenly longed for the easy familiarity to be
back, for this edgy tension to melt away. She would put
all her intrusive curiosity into a box and return to the
cheerful, upfront girl he knew and liked. She knew she
could do that. If there was one thing she had learnt in foster care, it was the value of compromise and the wisdom
of saying as little as possible that could be held against
her at a later date. To survive, she'd had to know how to

pretend and toe the line even if, as in this case, toeing the line involved a whole lot of pretence.

They arrived at the venue, which was a glasshouse set alongside a National Trust property. The glasshouse was perfect for drinks and the room inside the beautiful property was perfect for the reception. It was just the right size. Caitlin caught herself imagining the dining area filled with flowers spilling over elegant columns…pink-and-white vintage roses…candlesticks on crisp, white linen tablecloths…the background fading tones of a violinist welcoming the guests…

She abruptly snapped out of the daydream and chatted about the venue, comparing it to the far more modern one, which was the other option.

'And which do you prefer?' Javier asked, when they had both duly looked around.

'Like I said, that's not for me to say.'

'Very restrained for a woman who's never been shy at voicing her opinions.'

'I'm just remembering those goalposts that I accidentally knocked out of my way,' she said truthfully, and he burst out laughing.

'You have a gift when it comes to making me laugh.'

'I suppose that's a compliment?'

Their eyes tangled and now Javier wasn't smiling when he looked at her. She really was something else, wasn't she? Oh, it wasn't as though he hadn't looked at her before. Now, though, with barriers a little askew, looking had a different kind of feel to it, and he shifted to adjust a sudden stiffening of arousal that took him by surprise. This was dangerous territory. This marriage might be a

sham but that didn't give a green light for him to start
wondering about his PA.

'Of course it is,' he said gruffly. 'You're cheerful and
good-natured and smart. Those qualities count for a lot.
And, as far as offering an opinion about a venue goes,
it's work of a sort, wouldn't you agree? Goalposts will
remain firmly in place. I'm curious as to why you're so
tight-lipped about a straightforward question, anyway.'

'Because it's important that you two decide this sort of
thing between you, as a couple.' She sighed and he raised
his eyebrows, although there was no return of the unwel-
coming coldness that had been there before.

'So I'm taking it that you're into the romance of the
situation?' he murmured as they climbed back into the
car, he giving his driver instructions to Caitlin's flat,
which he had the address of on his mobile. 'Red roses
and a harpist in the background? Confetti and tossing
the bouquet for someone to nab it and join the queue to
walk up the aisle?'

'Red roses would be way too obvious, if you really
want to know.'

Javier grinned and cast his dark eyes over her, lingering on the fullness of her mouth and the clean, satiny
smoothness of her skin. He shifted. 'I'm guessing your
parents got hitched in a village church with white petals
scattered along the aisle and a horse and carriage to take
them away, wherever they got taken away to, for the req-
uisite honeymoon of a lifetime?'

Caitlin looked away. She felt a sudden sting of tears prick
behind her eyes and she had to breathe in long and deep
to find some self-control from somewhere.

'What's the matter?'

His voice was surprised…soft…urgent…his hand on her arm gentle but insistent. Still looking away, she shrugged, but her eyes were still glazed as he reached to place a finger gently under her chin, urging her to look at him. The touch was soft and brief and it shot through her body like an exploding firework. His dark eyes had gentled and he was staring at her with his head tilted to one side.

He dropped his hand but she could still feel the heat of his finger on her chin, hot and unsettling.

'Nothing's the matter,' she muttered tightly.

'Something's the matter. What is it? What have I said to upset you? You can tell me anything. I hope, after all the time we've worked together, that you know that.'

'I said *nothing's the matter*,' Caitlin told him sharply. 'So please could you just *lay off*? I'm not the only one who can travel past the brief!'

The silence that greeted this outburst was shocking, unheard of. She rushed into instant apology, her words tripping over one another.

Meanwhile, Javier continued to stare at her with undisguised curiosity. Well, well, well… In all the time she'd worked for him, he'd been presented with someone who was cheerful, easy-going and bright. There was depth, for sure, but no dark side. Yet, now, he had seen something in her eyes, heard the sharpness in her voice, and had known that beneath the surface swirled a lot more than he had probably suspected.

Fascinating. It was obvious that she and Isabella had got on like a house on fire, but she disapproved of the way the wedding was being approached, even though he had explained that the situation was simply something that made sense, a business arrangement.

She seemingly disapproved because she was an incurable romantic, yet when he tried to quiz her on that, half-teasing, half-curious, her reaction had been extreme. Why? Was there a story of a broken heart somewhere? She had stronger feelings about his wedding than *he* had, but then he had reason to be jaded by the whole business of love and marriage.

He thought of his father and the way he had been paralysed by his wife's premature death. Javier had understood then, as a young child, that pain and love were interlinked. If someone lost their heart to a person, and the person they loved was then taken away, they couldn't cope. And, when he'd been still a kid, the loss had hurt even more.

Javier shut down that line of thought and returned to the intriguing present. He was suddenly overwhelmed by the urge to find out more about Caitlin.

'I never asked and maybe I should have…' he began softly, lowering his eyes yet alert to every nuance in her.

'Asked me what?'

'About whether all this business with Isabella is getting in the way of your private life. I realise you've had to juggle things around the dog, but is there someone in your life you're also having to juggle things around?'

'Someone in my life?'

'A partner? Boyfriend?'

'No boyfriend.'

Javier glanced at her to see that she was blushing, defiant and challenging, and her lips were tight. His curiosity deepened. When it came to women, he couldn't remember a time he'd ever been curious about any of them. The women he'd dated had been transitory flings. He'd enjoyed them, just as they'd enjoyed him, and getting deep and personal with any of them would have been unthinkable. Even when it came to Isabella, there was no real curiosity, because he knew her so well.

But Caitlin, with her suddenly fluctuating moods, guarded expressions and skittish retreat whenever he seemed to get too close to something she wanted to keep hidden… Well, he was curious now.

'You surprise me,' he murmured, his dark eyes alert to her physicality and absently appreciating what he saw.

'Why?'

'You're young, you have an active social life, you're outgoing and attractive…you should have a queue of men lining up to ask you out.'

'I think you might be living in the past, Javier. These days, women are equally concerned about their careers. Anyway, I've never had a queue of boys lining up to ask me out.'

'Funny. We work so closely together and yet I'm realising that Isabella might know more about you than I do after a couple of weeks.'

'What are you talking about?'

Javier shrugged but he could sense her wariness. 'I think I'll arrange venue number two.'

'Yes.' Caitlin nodded approvingly. 'Since you've made the choice, I'll admit that I prefer it. It's less harsh. Venue one looked expensive, but it also looked quite cold in the brochure, I thought, even though it was beautiful with the high ceilings and the marble columns.'

'Your apartment.'

The driver was slowly pulling up in front of a functional sixties apartment block and Javier watched as she hastily began to unbuckle the seat belt. He'd been here once before, a flying drop-in on the way to the airport to collect a hard copy of a file he'd unexpectedly needed to take with him to New York. He hadn't made it past the communal entrance because she'd met him at the front.

This time, he wanted the tour. 'I'll show you in.'

'There's no need.'

'I wouldn't be a gentleman if I didn't.' He leapt out of the car at the same time as his driver opened her door. Their eyes met and he grinned.

He noted a barely suppressed sigh of resignation and his grin broadened. He was enjoying his PA in a way he hadn't before. He sauntered behind her into the apartment block and up the two flights to her flat, where they were greeted with yelps of barking long before the key was inserted in the door.

'I've never understood why you have a dog. Isn't it more trouble than it's worth, considering you work full-time?'

When Caitlin spun round, it was to find him closer to her than she'd expected and she shuffled a few steps back.

'Angie said she'd drop him back on the way to get some stuff from the pet shop.'

As to why she had Benji... How could he begin to understand her joy at Benji's unconditional love? How could he ever get that, when she'd grown up with nothing to call her own, a dog was something that filled that void and healed her? She spent a good amount of her salary on him and she wouldn't have it any other way.

She was wired. She'd been insanely conscious of him next to her during the entire trip out to see the wedding venue. Why had he insisted she come? She didn't know;

she wasn't sure whether it was her imagination, but there had been an atmosphere between them ever since they'd left the office.

And then that shocking outburst! She'd snapped at him for the first time ever and with a sinking heart she'd seen the astonishment on his face.

He was right: he knew very little about her. And now this situation had added a layer of intimacy to their relationship that was unnerving. It made her behave out of character but some gut instinct told her that acting out of character wasn't going to rouse his anger or even his irritation. It was going to rouse his curiosity and she decided that she didn't want her boss to be curious about her. If he started digging, what would he find? He was so astute when it came to reading people and she had a feeling that he could probably give a masterclass in reading women.

How long would it take him to find out that she had a crush on him? The thought of that made Caitlin fidget with embarrassment. She almost wished she'd fabricated a boyfriend to keep any unwanted curiosity at bay, but then wondered what would happen if he asked to meet said figment of her imagination. The tangled web wasn't worth thinking about.

She opened the door, and on cue Benji flew out with frenzied delight, acrobatically leaping into the air and planting his furry body against Javier's legs.

'Benji, stop!' But she was smiling and Javier glanced at her with raised eyebrows.

'Stop!' he growled and the dog instantly pulled back and gazed up at Javier's towering figure with eager eyes, small body vibrating with excitement at an unexpected visitor.

'Thanks for delivering me to my door.'

'May I have a glass of water before I go? Looking at wedding venues is thirsty work.'

He smiled and she stood back as he swept past her into the one-bedroomed flat which she rented. She saw him looking around, glancing at the optimistic posters on the walls of exotic holiday destinations, the bookshelf stuffed with wonderful romantic fiction, the liberal scattering of Benji's toys and the dog basket by the telly in the small living room.

Like having Benji, having a place to call her own was something else she cherished. She couldn't have shared a house even if the rent might have been half what she paid. She'd longed for her own space way too much. It was what came from having a legacy where the only thing that had really been hers and hers alone was her imagination.

He followed her into the kitchen. She poured him a glass of water and watched, standing back, as he swallowed it down, looking at her over the rim of the glass.

She took in the surroundings: the sticky notes on the fridge; the old-fashioned calendar by the little dresser; the weathered pine table she had bought for a song when she'd first moved in...

He was here...in her flat...eating up the space with his overpowering masculinity... She shivered and felt a tingle of sexual awareness zip through her body like quicksilver. She would have to get a grip. She held out her hand for the glass and gritted her teeth when he shot her a look of knowing amusement.

Benji had calmed down and she reached to pick him up and buried her face against his soft fur.

'That dog has issues,' Javier said, grinning broadly.

'I realise Isabella is in Madrid, so couldn't do the final

venue check.' Caitlin ignored his teasing remark, deposited Benji on the ground and continued tersely. 'But…'

'But…?' He scooped Benji up and stroked behind his ear, gazing at her, hip propped against the kitchen counter.

'But next week is wedding dress week,' Caitlin told him flatly. 'You should be around for that.'

'Isn't that supposed to be bad luck? Groom seeing what the bride has in store for him on the big day?'

'It's not about actually *seeing* the dress. I've sourced a couple of places and you could come and collect Isabella when she's finished. It's a special day, and I'm sure Isabella would appreciate the gesture.'

'She said so?'

'Not in so many words, but I've done the maths, and you've been to precisely zero places with her that have anything to do with your upcoming wedding. Surprising her by showing up after the wedding dress appointment would be a nice gesture.'

There was steely determination in her voice. They had it all, she thought bitterly. They were glamorous, aristocratic, wealthy and beautiful. They had the world at their feet. They cared for one another. And, with all those things in place, instead of celebrating the marriage that would unite them for ever they were indifferent and blasé.

While she could only dream of big, white, frothy affairs that belonged to a world she would never inhabit. She didn't even know whether her time would ever come. Would the background she'd never asked for deprive her of a stab at finding true love? Was she destined to have another Andy experience and end up trusting the wrong guy because she was so desperate for security?

Javier lowered Benji back to the ground and watched

as, calm now, the small ball of fur padded underneath the table and settled down among the chair legs to peer at them with interest, head resting on his front paws.

'Let me know when and where and I'll try and be there.'

'Aren't you interested at all in what you're going to find when you show up to get married?'

'I'm not really into choosing flowers, and I already know what I'll be wearing: trousers and a shirt. A jacket might be thrown on for good measure.'

'I suppose if the real big event is happening in Madrid later on when Isabella's dad is back on his feet...' Her voice was strained as she took the conversation back to safer waters.

'Correct. These are just the formalities we're going through, with sufficient icing on the cake so that it passes muster with various friends and business associates.'

Javier knew the complexities of the situation were beyond her. He had filled her in on the barest bones of the marriage he was about to willingly undertake. A marriage that was a little ahead of schedule, although he was thirty-two and knew there was only so long the pair of them could defer the inevitable. He'd known for years that he had a deadline when it came to getting married. The knot would have to be tied by thirty-five for that sliver of his inheritance to pass into his hands, with all its memories and back stories.

He wondered whether he'd expected Caitlin to be as business-like about the job she'd been given now as she'd always been when tasked with doing something that involved his personal life. She'd never made any judgements about the many women who came and went in

his life. He'd lazily fallen into the habit of getting her to
buy stuff for them—to book outings and send flowers.
She'd never once ventured any opinion that he lacked
the romantic touch. She'd never once said that it might
have been an idea for him personally to have chosen an
item of jewellery for whatever woman he happened to
be dating at the time instead of routinely delegating the
job to his obliging assistant. No wonder he'd lulled himself into thinking that his PA wasn't the romantic soul
he now realised she was.

'I should be heading off.' He half-saluted Benji, who
instantly sprang to his feet, alert to the possibility of an
unexpected run out.

As he headed towards the door, Javier glanced around
him one last time. 'Places you want to see?' he asked idly,
taking in a couple of the posters she had neatly stuck to
the walls in the sitting room.

'Some of them.'

'You have a list?'

He turned to her with a smile and Caitlin looked back at
him with a serious expression. She was relieved that he
was leaving and yet part of her wanted him to stay because his presence was electrifying. She'd never realised
how alive she felt around him until now, when everything
was changing and being around him, and feeling that
pleasurable tingle, was no longer appropriate.

'I haven't travelled much,' she now confessed, following his eyes to the bold poster of turquoise seas, white
sands and a jetty disappearing into deeper blue.

'No school trips? Annual holidays with parents you
wanted to swap for friends, because they wanted you
home by ten?'

He grinned, moving towards the door, and Caitlin felt that tension again as a past she'd always kept to herself began to nudge its way to the surface.

'Not exactly,' she said vaguely. 'How about you, Javier? Home by ten and bunking down with twelve other classmates on a ski trip in France?' How she'd longed for the normality of that when she'd been a kid, but those trips had been out of reach for her. So she'd had to make do by weaving enjoyable imaginary scenarios in her head about what it might feel like.

'That might have been nice.'

Caitlin paused at the momentary wistfulness in his voice and breached the mental 'don't go there' sign in her head without even thinking.

'What do you mean?'

He had half-opened the door but now stopped and looked down at her thoughtfully.

'A life that's set in stone from birth doesn't allow much freedom of movement,' he murmured. 'As an only child, and heir to a historic family fortune, responsibility was never far away.'

Caitlin knew that at this point she should say something light and teasing, something to release the sudden electric charge, but instead she said, thoughtfully, 'It must have been tough. But still...you would have had some adventures. I know you've travelled extensively.' She smiled wistfully. 'I can't think that having lots of money prevented you from seeing as much of the world as you wanted to.'

'Maybe you have a point, but money can take as much as it gives.'

'What do you mean?'

'I had everything money could buy given in one

hand…and in the other, I had childhood normality taken, the small things that money can never buy.'

Her breathing hitched and she blinked at him, not wanting to let go of this moment, but knowing she had to because there was something dangerously intimate going on between them.

She laughed shakily. 'However restricted your life was, Javier,' she breathed huskily, 'I'm betting it wasn't a patch on mine.'

She was riveted by their conversation…by the thoughtful depths in his dark eyes…by the way he was looking at her, a little awkwardly, but with an intensity that was setting her senses on fire.

'Anyway…' She stood back. 'Please don't forget about coming to surprise Isabella after the dress appointment. I'll email you the details. She's such a wonderful woman; it'd be a nice gesture…a nice surprise. It's…it's the sort of…of surprise any woman would really love.' She paused and took a deep breath to get a grip. 'You might be doing a duty, but from what I see you couldn't want a lovelier partner in crime.'

She sidestepped him to open the door and her heart beat like a drum inside her. She only breathed a sigh of relief when the door was shut and she could hear the faint echo of his steps growing fainter as he descended the two flights of stairs to where his driver would be waiting patiently outside.

She needed to get her act together.

As she lay in bed much later, trying to court sleep with thoughts of her boss swooping and swirling in her head, all she could think was…*this feels like losing control…*

CHAPTER THREE

ISABELLA WAS A NO-SHOW.

'I am so sorry, *mi querida*,' she said on the phone, when Caitlin had been at the boutique patiently waiting for twenty minutes, making lively conversation with the young girl with whom the appointment had been made for a personal run-through of what they had.

'What do you mean, you can't come, Isabella?' she asked, half-dismayed and half-irritated. She'd rolled her eyes and smiled grittily at Anna, the twenty-something tasked with helping them.

'Something very important has come up. I am at the airport waiting to board a plane to Madrid. Caitlin, *mi querida*, I would have called earlier but I forget about the wedding appointment until I looked at the calendar on my phone.'

'How could you forget, Isabella?'

Caitlin was genuinely stupefied. Yes, levels of enthusiasm had been running below average when it came to the wedding arrangements, but to *forget* your own *wedding dress appointment*? She had a moment of complete anger, because how often had *she* dreamt of walking down the aisle with a guy who loved her, who wanted to be her husband and take care of her? Isabella and Javier cared deeply for one another, so how could she remove herself to Madrid on such an important day?

'Caitlin, *mi amiga*, I have things on my mind.'

She'd sounded close to tears then and Caitlin reluctantly went into sympathy mode, asked her if her father was all right and if he'd had some kind of relapse. She thought not, because surely Javier would have said something this morning when she had popped in to the office to catch up on her work?

'Have you told Javier?'

'I have to run, Caitlin. I hear my flight being called. I… I have not managed to get through to him. Anyway, he would be working. He probably would not know that today we had to go and see some outfits. You know men, *hermana*—that is not their thing, and for sure not Javier's!'

Caitlin didn't say anything to that because she hadn't mentioned to Isabella that Javier would be coming to collect her post-appointment to take her out for dinner. She'd wanted it to be a surprise for the other woman. What woman wouldn't be tickled pink by that gesture? But maybe she'd just been projecting what *she* would have wanted onto a woman who really wouldn't be that bothered anyway.

'Well.' She ended the call a minute later and turned to Anna with an apologetic expression. 'You heard all that. Isabella, the bride-to-be, isn't going to be coming after all.'

Caitlin looked around the gloriously well-stocked boutique, beautifully laid out on two floors with racks upon racks of froth and lace, and every style of wedding dress any bride-to-be could possibly wish for. The top floor was for fittings, and the dresses there were all designer labels with eye-wateringly expensive price tags. On the ground floor were the less expensive but just as gorgeous dresses, including outfits for mothers of the bride. She could have spent a day there just touching all the lovely lace and silk, and gazing at the veils and tiaras and losing herself in the daydreams she'd had growing up.

'I'm sorry. I think we'll have to make another appointment. Although, at this rate,' she mused, 'I wouldn't be surprised if the excited fiancée doesn't get me to choose something for her to wear. It's just a simple ceremony until the main event later in the year, but even so, something gorgeous in cream silk... A little flared skirt with a matching jacket, perhaps, and some fabulous shoes... I would have even added a hat—just something simple but exquisite, although I'm not sure that's Isabella.'

'Some brides take more of a back seat than others,' Anna said sympathetically. 'Some are just really busy with their careers and simply don't have the time. You'd be surprised at how many last-minute cancellations we get.'

'What a nuisance for you.'

'I have an idea. I mean, you're here now, and I can see how disappointed you are and also...how thrilled you are to be here.'

'Well, it's all so beautiful...'

Anna burst out laughing and winked.

'I'm here on my own before closing and it's not as though I can sign out early. My boss has eyes in the back of her head. Don't know how she does it. So, as we're both here and I have no client to impress, why don't you be naughty and choose your favourite dress? I can measure you and fit you, just like the real thing. I mean, who knows, you might be back here one day to buy something for yourself! Trust me, I'll make sure you get a healthy discount if you come back for your own dream wedding dress.'

Caitlin's mouth fell open. Suddenly she was Cinderella—a guilty one.

'Wouldn't you get in trouble?' She glanced around just in case 'trouble' happened to be lurking in a corner somewhere.

'My boss would never know that you weren't my client,' Anna said drily. 'And it's not as if I'll be cutting any fabric or sending anything off for alterations. A few pins here and there... No one will know and, if you like, I can even take a picture of you in your perfect dress on your phone, for posterity. Just make sure you don't show your fella!'

'I don't currently have one of those,' Caitlin said absently. She grinned. 'But, if you're *sure*, might be fun. Hey, a girl can dream, can't she?'

For the next forty minutes, the time allotted for the non-appearing fiancée, Caitlin pretended. She was back to being a kid, losing herself in a make-believe world that had always been a lot more fun than the real one; dreaming big dreams she sadly knew would never come true.

She chose a flamboyantly romantic wedding dress, chattering all the time to Anna, who was as careful and meticulous as if she were the real deal.

Standing on the chair in front of the full-length mirror, Caitlin's eyes were shining as she breathed in the frothy aroma of a wedding aisle lined with flowers...faces turned in her direction...an avuncular vicar smiling and ready to join her in holy matrimony. Somewhere, there would be a little choir of children with their pure voices singing one of her favourite songs, or perhaps violinists.

She would have written and memorised a special little speech for her husband-to-be. Someone would be walking her up the aisle—identity to be determined at a later date, but probably one of her girlfriends. And, waiting for her, turning slowly to face her, her dream groom...who looked suspiciously like her tall, dark, handsome boss.

It was a wonderful feeling. She was Cinderella for the very first time in her life and in that moment, everything was forgotten: the sadness of foster care; the eagerness to forge a life of independence; that juvenile broken heart; her improbable crush on her unavailable boss; the topsy-turvy mess of helping to sort out a wedding for a woman she liked to a guy she fancied...

She lowered her eyes, blushing and smiling, and did a little awkward twirl on the chair. When she opened her eyes...there he was: the guy in her wild imagination waiting by the altar for her to sashay towards him.

Javier—her boss.

Except, this wasn't a convenient figment of her imagination. This was *her boss*, standing at the top of the narrow staircase, looking at her in a wedding dress. Caitlin broke out in an instant cold sweat. Sheer panic combined with paralysing mortification.

She literally couldn't move a muscle as he strolled towards her, his dark eyes resting on her burning face, giving a once-over of the extravagant dress that barely contained her abundant curves—way too many curves for something as elaborate as this. She agonisingly avoided glancing down at her breasts which were bursting out of the snug, heart-shaped bodice.

'Not exactly what I was expecting,' he drawled, coming to a dead stop in front of her.

Caitlin was lost for words. In the heat of the moment,

she'd forgotten about Javier; she had somehow assumed that he would be politely waiting outside for Isabella to join him.

He couldn't have looked more devastatingly handsome. He'd come straight from work. His white shirt had been impatiently rolled to the elbows and he'd undone the top two buttons so that she could just about glimpse the dusting of dark hair on his chest.

'I... I...' she spluttered, but before her addled brain could come up with something suitable Anna stepped in front of her and held out her hand.

'I'm Anna.'

'And I'm surprised.' Javier continued to look at Caitlin with amusement. 'Where is my fiancée? Last I knew, you and I weren't engaged to be married, were we?'

He made a show of looking around him for Isabella while Caitlin stood there, desperately wanting the ground to open up and swallow her whole, and not disgorge her until she was very, very far away from her boss.

Anna filled in the blanks. 'Your fiancée unfortunately couldn't make it.'

'So...?' he prompted in a long, lazy drawl.

His eyebrows shot up and Caitlin finally found her voice, although what could she say—that she'd been swept away on a tide of wishful thinking, to the guy who'd probably never crossed paths with wishful thinking and so wouldn't have a clue what she was on about?

'So,' she hedged, 'I thought that...'

'I persuaded her to try on her dream dress,' Anna piped up. 'Good for business.' She winked at Javier, one business person to another. 'If I can get Caitlin to fall in love with a wedding dress from the shop, then I've got a potential customer in the not-too-distant future!'

'I'll get changed,' Caitlin muttered huskily and self-consciously as Anna helped her off the stool and Javier lent a hand, steadying her. She'd gone from feeling on top of the world in her fairy-tale, fantasy wedding dress to feeling like a complete fool.

She burned up as she hurried towards the fitting rooms, having to gather great swathes of fabric as she walked because the dress had been far, far too long for her.

Javier watched Caitlin hurry away, cheeks pink. The petite girl standing next to him was chattering away, obviously trying her best to smooth things over in an awkward situation. He barely heard a word she was saying. This wasn't what he'd been expecting. When Caitlin had told him that it would be a nice gesture to surprise Isabella by showing up post-wedding-dress fitting to take her out for a meal, he'd acquiesced, largely because it hadn't been worth the debate.

He and Isabella communicated daily. She'd chosen to stay at one of his penthouse apartments in Knightsbridge rather than share his house, and he got that. They had an understanding of which Caitlin was unaware. But could he be bothered to argue the toss about whether or not to meet Isabella this evening? No. It had become apparent that his PA was the epitome of romantic. Why disappoint her? She was already utterly confused by his arrangement with Isabella. She'd no doubt been raised on a diet of the traditional fairy stories, where the fair maiden always ended up walking up the aisle to the handsome suitor.

So here he'd come, fully expecting his fiancée to be waiting for him. Instead, he'd rung the doorbell, pushed open the door and headed up the stunted staircase to find… Just thinking about what he'd found made his mind go into instant meltdown.

Of course, he'd noticed those lush curves before, hidden underneath the bouncy but unrevealing work outfits. But to find Caitlin standing on that chair, her face radiant and shining, her body barely contained in a wedding dress that was all pinched-in waist and deep neckline, had been mind-blowing.

'Lush' didn't come close to describing her body. She was the perfect hourglass—slender waist with rounded hips and breasts that were several sizes more than a handful.

He'd felt faint. His libido had duly risen to the occasion and he'd only managed to control his body by focusing on the fact that finding her standing on a chair in full regalia was a shock. He'd kept his eyes fastened to her face, but how could he have missed the push of her breasts against the tight-fitting bodice? There'd been so much cleavage on display that he'd struggled to breathe properly.

And, when she walked off, the sway of those generous hips kept him nailed to the spot, unable to move or even take in what the girl next to him was jabbering about.

Javier didn't do instant lust—not like this. He liked to be in control. Maybe it was because he had been brought up to respect the obligations that came with his family's standing. Maybe a life led on the straight and narrow just didn't allow for anything *but* control. But there were times when he knew that the explanation for the man he was just wasn't so simple.

The loss of his mother had inserted a shard of ice into his soul, and it had only grown as he had matured. Had he ever tried to pull that shard out? Ever tried to see what he could be if he came down from his ivory tower?

No. He liked things the way they were because he could never be hurt the way he had been all those years ago, not if he controlled everything and everyone around him. Just as he controlled this marriage, getting just what he wanted from it, and knowing that Isabella was as well, which was a bonus.

He was attracted to women; he dated them, slept with them, got bored and moved on. He had never been so physically bowled over that breathing became difficult but he had been just then.

She emerged in record time, back in the knee-length flowered skirt and the loose green top with buttons down the front. He wondered what it would feel like to undo those buttons one by one and then scoop those magnificent breasts out of whatever bra might be struggling to contain them.

She couldn't meet his eyes, and he had a sudden, primitive urge to tilt her chin so that she had to look at him and tell her that it had been a pleasure seeing her in that dress. He knew that somewhere deep inside she was uncomfortable and embarrassed. Weirdly, so was he. His control had taken a knock.

'Okay,' she said vaguely to no one in particular, before turning to Anna and offering a few stilted remarks about her client who had gone AWOL.

'I'll rearrange,' she said, moving towards him, and yet managing not to catch his eyes.

'I should apologise,' she said, still not looking at him as they made their way down the stairs with Anna following a discreet distance behind to lock up for the evening. She was saying something about being remiss in not making sure the front door was locked while she'd been upstairs. Javier barely heard. He could breathe in the heady floral scent of the woman keeping her distance slightly behind him.

'Apologise for what?'

'I lost track of the time.'

'Apologise for what?' he repeated.

'For… Isabella didn't show up… Well, she called, actually, to tell me that she had to fly back to Madrid. She didn't say why, so…'

'You're stammering.'

'Can you blame me? I feel uncomfortable about this!'

'I booked a restaurant. Since Isabella isn't here, why don't you join me for dinner?'

'Aren't you bothered that your fiancée has disappeared off to Madrid without telling you?'

'I expect she'll call me later to explain.'

'This is crazy!'

Javier raked his fingers through his hair and paused briefly to look down at her. Her face was pink and angry and he wanted nothing more than to push back her tangled blonde curls and kiss her full, pouting mouth.

'I think your concern is misplaced,' he said softly.

'What do you mean?'

'I live in a different world to the one you're accustomed to.'

'You're not kidding. Don't get me wrong, Javier. I see that maybe you've had an arrangement in place with Isabella for a long time because you're both from the same background, and your families go back a long way, but I don't get why you're both so indifferent about the details when you care about one another. It's not like one of these cases of two people only meeting a week before they tie the knot.'

'Neither of us is romantically inclined.'

'You don't have to have stars in your eyes to want a photographer at your wedding or to show up for an appointment for a wedding outfit with just a week to go before the big day.'

'Modestly sized day.'

'And I'm not having dinner with you, Javier!'

'The table's booked. It would be a shame to waste it. Besides, we can call it a working dinner.'

'What do you mean?'

'Fill in the blanks.'

'What blanks are there to fill in? Hasn't Isabella kept you in the loop about the practical details of what's been booked?'

'Okay, we can fill in other blanks.' He glanced sideways at her and grinned, hailing a black cab and ushering her in before she could protest.

Javier was playing a dangerous game, he knew that, but he couldn't resist the temptation to spend a little longer in her company and find out a bit more about her. His body had betrayed him with a physical reaction that had shaken him to the core and he'd liked how that had felt, danger or no danger. He'd *liked* having a taste of what it felt like to be a little out of control.

What was so wrong with wanting to find out more about her? With this situation in the melting pot, wasn't it natural that he would want to find out a bit more about her? He'd always thought of her as an open book and, now that he'd discovered that she wasn't quite as open as he'd thought, wasn't it only human nature to pursue his curiosity? Wouldn't it actually bring more depth to their working relationship in the future if he knew a little more about her? That seemed a reasonable conclusion and he was happy to stick to it.

* * *

'I'm not dressed for a fancy dinner,' Caitlin protested tightly and with impatience.

How had she found herself in the back of a black cab with her boss? She knew. She'd been hot and bothered, seeing him there, staring at her in a damn wedding dress of all things. What on earth had possessed her, twirling around and completely forgetting the time? Had it been sad for her to want to reach out and touch some fairy dust for once? Or had it just been human? Caught on the back foot, she just hadn't been thinking straight. Now she'd followed Javier out and straight into a taxi, her thoughts all over the place.

In between those thoughts of how embarrassed she was, there was also a crazy urge to try and second-guess what had been going on in his head when he'd seen her. Just for a second she thought she'd seen something there, a flare of *something* and, however silly it was to harbour that thought in her head, she couldn't resist pulling it apart and dissecting it.

He was engaged... What on earth was she thinking?

'You're more appropriately dressed than if you'd come out in what you were trying on.'

'Can I ask you to let that go?'

'I'm sorry, it's just that, well, it was quite the surprise.' Javier grinned and, not for the first time, Caitlin wished the ground would open up and swallow her.

Once they arrived at a fabulously Michelin-starred restaurant she could remember having read about a few months back, Caitlin groaned. Could things get any worse?

She glanced down at her work outfit and imagined how much more fitting it would have been for Javier to walk into a place like this with Isabella on his arm. Isabella was like one of those impossibly beautiful heroines she used to read about in teenage romances—the sort she'd pretend to be before returning to planet Earth.

'Hey.'

She raised her blue eyes to his and their gazes locked. Her breath hitched, and she parted her mouth and watched as he automatically looked at her lips before guarding his expression.

'There's no need to be self-conscious,' he told her in a roughened undertone.

'I'm not,' Caitlin returned quickly. She was tense as a bowstring as he reached across to open her door. She had felt the brush of his arm against her breasts, just a brush, and her body had gone crazy in response.

'Sure?'

'I'm just not sure what I'm doing here, aside from filling up a reservation you happened to make.' She sighed. 'I guess we could spend some time talking about work.'

'Or we could leave work chat for another day.'

Typically, with effortless self-assurance, he paid absolutely no attention to any of the looks the other diners gave them. She, on the other hand, couldn't help but wonder whether those curious eyes were trying to work out what a guy like Javier was doing with a girl like her.

When they were seated at one of the tables at the back, he said thoughtfully, 'Isabella has discussed all the things that are already in place. You might not think that I'm that interested—and maybe I'm not as interested as you might expect me to be—but I'm satisfied that you've been efficient in sorting everything out. I realise there wasn't a lot of time, and you've had to do a lot of tricky co-ordinating, and I appreciate that.'

'Thank you.'

'It's nothing less than I would have expected.'

'I'm the consummate professional.' Caitlin grinned reluctantly. 'Plus, I love organising.'

'It's an excellent trait in a PA and, on a personal level, good practice for you—like trying on the dress.' He lowered his eyes, shielding his expression.

'That was stupid and I don't know what you mean.'

'Like the girl said, you're preparing for when it's your turn. I've realised that you're not quite as blasé as I thought you were when it comes to a situation like the one I've thrown you into. When I assigned you to this... project... I had no idea you would find it so difficult.'

'I don't find it difficult.'

'You keep trying to work out why it's not obeying the ground rules you have in place when it comes to relationships.'

'I...' Caitlin opened her mouth to deny that she had ground rules about anything but she knew that that would be a lie. She had tons of ground rules when it came to the sort of lasting commitment that went with marriage.

'You're a hopeless romantic.' He smiled. 'And it's hard for you to understand those of us who aren't.'

'I guess you're right, although not in the way you imagine. I suppose...'

'How so?' Javier was looking at her carefully. 'What do you mean, not in the way I imagine?'

'I mean that, whatever restrictions you grew up with, you still had advantages most people could never imagine in a lifetime.'

'Like I said, money is not the answer to everything.'

'It's actually the answer to quite a lot, except you

wouldn't know about that, because you've never known what it feels like to do without.'

'Is that what you were talking about when you mentioned that your life was as restricted as mine? Tell me about that. Did you grow up with financial hardship?'

Menus were placed in front of them, along with the bottle of wine Javier had ordered, and Javier stared at Caitlin. She fidgeted and lowered her eyes, keen to change the topic.

'So you remembered that.' She flushed.

'When it comes to remembering, elephants and I have a lot in common. Still, I repeat what I said to you, that money comes with its own limitations. Our lives may have been very different from a money point of view but I'm betting we still both had to deal with our own private struggles, big or small. Anyway, when you're young, everything feels big.'

Caitlin was very still as she listened to Javier. Restrictions? She felt tears of self-pity spring up inside her. He might have lived his life in a gilded cage, but she'd lived in a cage as well, and it made a big difference when the bars of the cage weren't made of gold. She thought of the longing she had had for a 'normal' family. She remembered her daydreams, silly make-believe fantasies of things she would never have and places she would never get to go. How *dared* he pry into her life and somehow try and make out that his privileged life had been anything like hers?

'I feel so sorry for you, Javier—prisoner of wealth and privilege with loving parents who only wanted the best for you. So you had your future mapped out,' she said bitterly. 'There are worse things in life than that, believe me.'

'And what are those *worse things* that you're talking about, Caitlin?'

Caitlin's heart hammered. Javier couldn't possibly understand. So, he had had a few despondent moments gazing from his castle at how those carefree kids on the other side of the tracks got on with life. Well, it all felt hopelessly patronising, given her own background. She had done her own gazing, but through the windows of a foster home, just longing to have a family of her own; just to have somebody who really cared whether she did her homework or not. She wished he'd let this go but, like a dog with a bone, he wasn't going to give up asking her questions, and the more she retreated, the further he would delve.

'You really want to know?' Caitlin said shortly.

'I'm all ears.'

'I was raised in foster care.'

The silence stretched and stretched until it became unbearable. For a few seconds, Javier wasn't sure he'd heard correctly. Foster care? It wasn't a revelation he'd expected and, caught on the back foot, he could only stare at her in growing silence.

'You look shocked,' she said defensively.

'I am.' Why bother beating around the bush? He was truly shocked. He'd always prided himself on being able to read people but he hadn't read her. Sudden sympathy flared inside him and he felt as though parts of a jigsaw puzzle had slotted into place, parts he hadn't even realised had been missing in the first place: that curious mix of innocence and robust, streetwise savviness; the apparent openness even though he had always sensed something guarded just beneath the surface, an element of there being more than met the eye.

The image of her in the wedding dress leapt into his head and he drew in a sharp breath. Had that been a lonely child's dream?

'You don't get how Isabella and I could be so casual about something so big as a marriage,' he murmured softly. 'Shall I tell you what *I* don't get?'

'What?'

He waited until oversized plates of food had been set in front of them with flourish, and until more wine had been poured, and then he leant forward and met her wary gaze steadily.

'I don't get how you could be so romantic, be such a believer in love, when you were brought up…in foster care. Didn't you develop a hard shell? Something to protect yourself from the slings and arrows of circumstances you couldn't control?'

'Of course I have. I do believe in love, and I have dreams, but I'm realistic. Because I had a tough childhood doesn't mean it's killed everything inside me. But I look at you and Isabella, with your privileged, cushioned lives behind you—two people who love one another—and I can't believe you would be so casual about your marriage. You treat it as though it's just going to be another day in the week, no big deal.

'Do you know how lucky you are to have found someone who loves you, someone you love back? To have lots of family wishing you well and looking forward to you both tying the knot? So what if there's an element of practicality in getting married? So what? It's still going to be something special, something you should both want photographs of, to look back on down the years.'

She was bright red and her blue eyes were wide and urgent.

Looking at her, Javier had never felt more out of his comfort zone. She looked as though she was about to cry, and he wanted to reach out and rub the tears away before they fell.

She'd put all those dreams she'd woven into a lonely childhood into the idea of some kind of dream, fairy-tale wedding between himself and Isabella. He'd told her that it was a marriage of convenience, but she had translated their mutual affection as some kind of unacknowledged, burning love that was just there waiting to burst free. It was way off target, but oddly incredibly touching.

'I developed a hard shell,' he admitted, thinking back to a background that had been immensely privileged and yet circumscribed. His parents loved him, but it had been a regimented life, and a series of nannies had done most of the graft when it had come to the nuts and bolts of his day-to-day life as a kid.

'To protect you from what?'

Javier said softly, 'To protect me from anything that might have been out of bounds, be that friends from different social circles, hobbies that weren't suitable or risk-taking adventures that were deemed too dangerous.' He hesitated. 'Fairy tales are built on the concept of falling in love,' he said roughly.

'Yes, they are, and...'

'And that's not the case for Isabella and myself.'

'But...'

'Yes, we care deeply for one another, but we're not in love—neither of us. Caring deeply about someone is all I'm capable of, Caitlin.'

'What do you mean?'

'I lost my mother when I was young,' he confessed, 'and, while foster care may have kept your dreams intact against all odds, losing my mother put a torch to mine. When she died my father went off the rails…fell for a younger woman who fleeced him of a fortune. He couldn't handle his grief, and it made me realise that love and loss go hand in hand.' He shot her a crooked smile. 'Affection,' he said, 'is doable, however, and that's what Isabella and I share.'

'Javier, I'm so sorry…'

'We all have our stories to tell,' Javier said drily. He looked at her for a few seconds then said in a quiet voice, 'I think it might be sensible to close the lid on any more personal details, don't you? And one more thing—thank you for sharing a part of your past with me. I wouldn't have pried if I'd known just how private you may have wanted to keep it.'

Their eyes met and he thought, *I've said things here that I've never said before to anyone… The lid will definitely have to be closed on this because this urge to confide stops here and now…*

CHAPTER FOUR

CAITLIN NODDED SLOWLY at Javier's offer to bring up the drawbridge of privacy between them again. 'That sounds good to me.'

'And,' Javier continued, 'if you feel too uncomfortable dealing with the details of the wedding, then you can devote your time to showing Isabella around London.'

'It's okay, and actually there's not much time to do that, anyway. When she gets back to London, it'll be all systems go until you both get married.' She looked at him thoughtfully. 'And, now that I know a bit more about everything, I'm definitely going to be taking a more practical approach to what's left to be done. I can't imagine how the venue is going to cope with such little notice, but I'll give them a call first thing in the morning.'

'Leave that to me. I am very good when it comes to persuasion.'

'Money can talk,' Caitlin agreed, laughing. She'd ordered an elaborate salad but her mind was only half on the food on her plate as she dug in.

What Javier had told her were confidences, and she could never have foreseen him sharing them in a million years, because he wasn't that sort. Yet he had let her into an intensely private part of his life, and that made her feel...*special*. Their normal working arrangement had shifted and deepened into something more substantial, something that was more personal and more intimate. When Caitlin thought about what he had said about never being able to love anyone because of the loss of his mother, and the collapse of his father in the wake of that, she could feel a swell of tenderness and compassion.

She understood. Experience had a way of carving out which road a person ended up going down. It truly wasn't all about how much money a person had. She'd been blazingly angry when he'd tried to compare the nuisance of living in a gilded cage to the sadness and deprivation of her own foster-care background, but now...

He had suffered his own tragedies and they had scarred him. He had felt the basic structure of his life fall apart when his mother had died, and she couldn't imagine how pitiful it must have been to realise that the one person he should have been able to turn to had removed himself to handle his own grief in a different and destructive way.

Next to her compassion and sympathy, though, was another emotion that wasn't quite as straightforward... He really wasn't in love with his fiancée. Maybe he was truly incapable of dropping his barriers and really *loving* anyone, but this marriage was really one of convenience. She didn't feel quite so bad about the crush that wouldn't budge.

She looked at him from under her lashes, taking in his hard-edged masculinity that she had always found so impenetrable. 'Once you're married,' she ventured into the lengthening silence, 'how is it practically going to work? I know you've just said that we have to close the lid on talking about anything personal, but I'm curious whether you'll still be based here all of the time or not.'

* * *

When Javier looked across the table to her, all good intentions of returning to their relationship being strictly business with some light-hearted banter went down the plug hole. He was still shocked at her confession and was seeing her in a new light. He wanted to close his eyes and breathe in deeply when he recalled seeing her on that chair in the wedding dress of her dreams, twirling to some imaginary scenario she'd probably had in her head since she'd been a young girl. At the time, he'd been amused—amused and turned on, because her voluptuous curves were just so unbelievably, unexpectedly sexy.

Now, he wasn't amused. Now, he wanted to take her in his arms, and it was such a crazy feeling that he didn't know what to do with it. He told himself that it was natural to feel sympathy and maybe even a little pity for her story. Life wouldn't have been easy for her. He would probably have felt the same about any one of his employees if he'd found out something about them of that nature. He would have to be a monster not to want to...hold her.

Who was he kidding? If he'd found out the very same thing about Tricia, the bubbly brunette currently covering for Caitlin, he would have been sympathetic enough, produced some tissues from somewhere and given her a bracing pep talk about painful experiences making you stronger. He would never have been tempted to take her in his arms and soothe her back to her usual good-natured self. He would never have gone down the road of saying anything about himself.

Where had that come from?

She'd gathered herself and was looking at him with polite curiosity, which made the logical need to return to normality even less tempting.

'Probably not all the time, at least not to start with. I'll have to be physically present to oversee the technicalities of taking over the business, but I don't anticipate having to relocate there for any period of time. Isabella's family concerns are less significant than my own, bearing in mind I have my own empire that's quite separate from my family's.' Javier was barely aware of their plates being cleared as he looked into her eyes.

Caitlin laughed with genuine amusement. 'When you say stuff like that, I really see what a different world you live in compared to the rest of the human race.'

'There are lots of other people as wealthy as I am.' He was smiling and sat back so that coffee could be put in front of them. His eyes were lazy and amused and sent shivers racing up and down Caitlin's spine.

'But they don't exactly grow on trees.'

'True.' Javier laughed and didn't say anything for a few seconds, although he kept his dark eyes fastened to her face until delicate colour bloomed in her cheeks.

Caitlin licked her lips and sipped some coffee. She felt his eyes on her as she drank and she wondered whether he could see how flustered she was. She hoped not.

She carefully placed the cup on its saucer and kept her eyes lowered for a couple of seconds before looking at him. 'Isabella loves London but she seems quite hesitant about living over here. I hope I'm not out of order telling you this.'

'You're not.' Javier sighed. 'She's going to have to learn to adapt over here, as this is where I'll be based, but that's not to say that she won't be free to come and go as she pleases.'

'Won't you miss her company at all?'

* * *

Javier took some time before he answered because the one answer he could have given her that would have been truthful was something that it was not within his remit to do. He and Isabella would discreetly lead their separate lives, respecting one another, while she continued to see the partner she had secretly had for nearly three years.

It was ironic to think that, if she'd had the sort of ordinary background the woman sitting opposite him had probably longed for, she would have had fewer restraints when it came to declaring her sexuality. As it was, her privileged background and the traditional circles in which her family moved had made it hard for her.

He produced the least contentious answer he could think of.

'You know me well, Caitlin. I find work is very successful when it comes to filling in the gaps.'

'And I suppose if you have to flit between Spain and London, you could always time your visits there to coincide with hers. But what about when a family arrives?' She looked at him thoughtfully over the rim of her cup. 'I'm guessing, even if it's a business arrangement, that you'll both want to have a family?'

'We'll have a family.' Javier looked down, played with the handle of his cup and nodded to the waiter for the bill. 'We both have a responsibility when it comes to that.'

'Well, that'll really mean you'll have to be in one place without too much flitting going on.'

Caitlin looked past him to the ideal family she had always had in her head: four kids, maybe five. She knew that she would have plenty of love to go round. She also knew that she would be there for every one of them, seeing their first steps, hearing their first words, going to the first parents' days... Doing all the things no one had ever done with her.

'That's your background talking,' Javier said gently and Caitlin blinked and looked at him.

'What do you mean?'

The bill had arrived but they were still sitting at the table. Caitlin didn't know about him, but for her there was no one around them. She felt oblivious to everything and everyone but for the man looking at her with his head tilted to one side. Was she the only one aware of an electric charge between them?

'Would you like a liqueur?'

'A liqueur? I wouldn't know, because I've never had one.'

'Maybe it's time we remedy that.'

'I really need to go and fetch Benji.'

'Okay.' Javier shrugged and Caitlin immediately decided that Benji could wait a while. Angie was used to her erratic timekeeping. They were friends and they had fallen into a routine of sharing him.

'I mean...'

'Limoncello is very user-friendly.' He beckoned to the waiter and ordered two, but his dark eyes remained pinned to her face.

'Why did you say what you said, Javier?'

'About your background dictating your views on family?'

'Yes, because I don't think my background has anything to do with it. Most people share my views when it comes to bringing up children.'

'Maybe you're right.'

'Why do you sound surprised?'

'Because Isabella and I led a very different life when it came to family bonding. There was bonding but not quite in the way you'd probably understand.'

'What does that mean?'

Javier shrugged. 'What you would expect of most rich dynasties: nannies, help and then even more so after my father's expensive divorce, which brought him to his senses. He never tried to replace my mother again, but he buried himself in work, and I can't say I saw a lot of him over the years. I was, it has to be said, boarding for quite a number of those years.'

'And Isabella... I suppose you'll tell me that her experience mirrored yours?'

'As did quite a few of our mutual friends'. It's a very small world when you live at the very top of it.'

'Can I say something?'

'Why not?' Javier grinned, his seriousness dissipating into amusement. 'I'm not sure I could stop you at this point.'

'I'm guessing that all those women you've dated in the past...' Caitlin sipped the limoncello and winced, although on the second sip it somehow tasted a lot better.

'Go on. I'm eager to hear where you're going with this.'

Javier watched her with brooding intensity, watching the way she delicately sipped the liqueur and the way her eyes flitted to his face and then flitted away just as fast. He'd never had a conversation like this before in his life. His interaction with women tended to be pleasant, fun and superficial. They flirted and he responded and a nice time was had by one and all. He was a generous and considerate lover. He just wasn't a committed one and, when the time came for him to walk away, he could do it without any feelings of guilt because he'd never promised anything. He didn't encourage the sort of deep conversations such as the one he was having here and now.

Actually, he'd never been tempted to. He hadn't thought himself capable of going down that road or even being interested in it. But he was. He couldn't take his eyes off her face and every muscle and sinew in his body was engaged in what she was saying.

'Well?' he prompted.

'I reckon you've gone for a certain type,' Caitlin said quietly, 'because you've known that you would never be tempted to form an attachment to that particular type.'

'And what type is that?'

'Well...not that I've met them all...but I suppose the type of woman who enjoys being pampered and being seen hanging on to your arm at openings and functions.'

'Tut-tut. Why can't a guy be tempted to form an attachment to a woman like that?'

Caitlin raised her eyebrows but she was smiling because his amusement was infectious.

'Lots of guys can, but my theory is that, even if you and Isabella had never had any kind of arrangement, you would only ever want to settle down with someone like her. Someone from the same social circle you belong to...someone who knows how the ritual of living a life of privilege is handled. And I don't mean a rich life, I mean one that involves tradition and expectation and duty and all that stuff.'

She breathed in sharply and then held her breath, because now that she had said what she'd said she could feel herself hanging on for his answer.

Was she right? Would he only ever seek to settle down

with a woman from the same privileged background? It made sense, especially in the light of everything she'd seen and heard. He and Isabella were matched and, if not Isabella, someone like her, someone with the same acceptance of a life of old money and ingrained tradition.

For just a second, Caitlin looked at the place she'd come from and felt like the matchstick girl standing outside in the cold and looking through the windows to where people from a very different world enjoyed a banquet of the finest food. The differences between Javier and someone like her couldn't be more stark, and it was something that had really only crystallised in her head when Isabella had come on the scene.

It didn't matter how he answered her question—of course it didn't!—but she was still hanging on, pretending to smile and be amused while her heart thudded like a drum inside her.

'You're right. I've never given it much thought, but maybe you have a point when you say that I've been having fun with women I never had any intention of settling down with, because I already knew the sort of woman I was always destined to wed.'

Caitlin forced a laugh. 'Understandable.'

'Not that it matters, because I already have my bride waiting in the wings. Which reminds me… I'll be in touch as soon as I hear from her. Everything's in place as far as I can tell so all that's needed now is…'

'Something for the bride to wear.'

'Excellent. Now…' He stood up, glanced at his watch and stepped back, waiting as she followed suit and scrambled to her feet. 'My driver will be waiting outside. I can get him to deliver you back to your house.'

'No need.'

* * *

'How did I know you were going to say that?'

He gazed down at her thoughtfully. She was wearing the sort of outfit no woman he had ever dated would have been seen dead in: loose, lots of clashing colour, not even a token nod to a designer. Her hair was all over the place. And yet the pull he felt was intense because he had connected with her on a basis that went far beyond the superficial appeal of how she dressed.

Javier was uneasy with this. He'd never opened up to anyone and he couldn't understand how it was so easy to do so with her. Was it because they weren't involved in any kind of physical relationship? Over the years, Isabella had confided in him, and considered him one of her closest friends, and yet, he realised he had never opened up to her the way he just had to Caitlin.

He had never shared his feelings about his mother and her premature death, and had never voiced how those feelings had changed him for ever. Isabella knew all about his father's lapse of judgement, the way he'd gone off the rails for a while, but had she known anything about how he'd personally *felt* about all that? When Javier thought back to that time, he didn't think so, yet somehow he had shared it with Caitlin. He wasn't guarded with her; that was why. He had always been guarded with women, always watchful for prying questions as a way into trying to seduce him into the sort of relationship he wasn't interested in.

The thoughts were like a low, persistent buzzing in his head as Caitlin hailed a cab, just as his driver eased in front of them and drew to a stop.

'Thank you for inviting me out to dinner, Javier.'

Javier shook his head, frowned and looked down to meet her blue eyes. She gazed steadily back at him.

'Was it as torturous as you'd thought it was going to be?'

'I never thought it was going to be torturous.'

'I had to drag you here kicking and screaming.'

'That's an exaggeration—mildly protesting. I was caught on the back foot because it was a dinner you should have been having with your fiancée.'

'But now you see why the situation may not be quite what you had in mind...'

'We'd said...' Caitlin looked away and took a deep breath before continuing. 'We'd said that we wouldn't do the whole *personal* thing, Javier.'

'So we did.'

'But I just want to say that I have a much clearer picture of your situation and I apologise for falling into the trap of romanticising it.'

As Caitlin ducked into the cab, Javier leant down till he was level with her.

'When it comes to me,' he drawled, 'the best advice I can ever give any woman is to never romanticise about me. I can do flowers and jewellery and tickets to the opera, but romance? That's way beyond my scope and always will be.'

He straightened and stood back just as she turned away so that he missed the expression on her face. He watched as the cab eased its way into the traffic and eventually disappeared left after some traffic lights. He'd enjoyed the evening. Maybe he'd been wrong in assuming that spontaneity wasn't his thing. *Or*, a little voice in his head said slyly, *maybe you've only discovered the joys of spontaneity since your PA has shown a side to her that's got your curiosity going...*

He pushed the voice to one side, preferring not to dwell on that, and began to think about the nature of his arrangement with Isabella. It had all seemed so straightforward when they had talked about it a couple of months previously. They had both recognised that, as only children—both from family dynasties that were bound with ties that stretched from duty into friendship, both with the unspoken agreement that they belonged to family lines that would always protect one another when it came to safeguarding their respective dynasties—marriage was always going to be the desired final destination.

And, as it turned out, one that suited both of them. Within that marriage, they would discreetly lead their own separate lives. There would never be a lack of pleasant companionship and deep affection, and those were powerful bonds that could easily unite two people in a lifelong committed relationship.

As for kids, they would find a way. Medical intervention would achieve the desired result. They cared deeply for one another. There would never be any acrimony between them, wherever their paths led. Whatever their unusual situation, they would make good parents. What could go wrong?

Javier's gut currently told him that there might be more hitches with their well thought-out plan than he might suspect.

He took the car back to his house, resisting the urge to contact her immediately. As soon as he was back at his place, he punched in her number, moving to the kitchen to pour himself a stiff whisky. It was late, but not too late for a nightcap, and he had a sinking feeling that a nightcap was necessary.

Isabella answered on the second ring and he could tell

from the stilted, stressed tone in her voice that whatever she was about to say was probably not going to be what he wanted to hear.

It was not yet nine in the morning when Caitlin yawned her way out of sleep and groped towards her phone which was beeping next to her on the bed. She nudged Benji aside, eyes half-shut, debating whether to answer or not, because eight-fifty-three on a Saturday was way too early for her to take calls. Benji edged his way back to his original position at her side and resumed snoring.

Which was precisely what Caitlin wanted to do. Her weekend stretched ahead of her completely empty of social engagements. It was a blank canvas waiting to be filled with absolutely nothing in store but pottering, heading to the nearest park to enjoy the weather and have an ice cream, and then watching telly in her most comfy clothes with a bowl of pasta on a tray on her lap while she caught up on trashy programmes.

Guilty pleasures after an evening that had left her nerves jumping. She'd felt bonded to her boss in a way she never had before and suddenly her crush felt dangerous—something she could no longer write off as a harmless fantasy. And it was especially dangerous because, even though he wasn't in love with Isabella, he'd made it abundantly clear he was never going to fall in love with anyone else...especially not someone like her who had zero understanding of what it meant to live in his rarefied world.

She reluctantly took the call and then bolted upright when she heard the dark, sexy familiar strains of Javier's voice at the end of the line. Benji gave a yap of protest and then watched her balefully as she listened to her boss tell her that he needed to have a word with her as soon as possible.

'You're not still in bed, are you?' he asked as an afterthought.

'Of course I'm still in bed!'

'It's nearly nine in the morning.'

'It's also a Saturday. Can I ask what this is about?'

'My driver's on his way to get you, Caitlin. I'd make the journey over to you myself, but I have to take care of a couple of things before I see you, and I can't do that in the back of a car.'

'Your driver is on the way to get me?'

'I'm sorry to have sprung this on you, Caitlin, but... there was no choice. He'll be with you in half an hour.'

'Javier, has it occurred to you that I might have plans for the day?'

'It hadn't, now that you mention it. Have you?'

'No, but...'

'Then that's good news for me. You can bring the dog.'

'Bring the dog where, exactly?'

'My place.'

'Javier...'

'Caitlin, I have to go. I have an incoming call. I'll see you in under an hour and, trust me, if I didn't have to disturb you at the weekend then I wouldn't. I hope you know that.'

She was already hopping out of bed, followed by Benji, whose tail was wagging in keen anticipation of an unexpectedly early start. Javier sounded bright-eyed and bushy-tailed and she knew that he'd probably been up since five. He'd once let slip that he worked out in his basement gym no later than five-thirty as often as he could because by six-thirty he liked to be on the move.

That included weekends. She'd privately thought that that must be a big ask for his partners who might prefer someone who didn't leap out of bed at the crack of dawn come rain, hail or shine. But then, not many men could match up to Javier, whether he flung off the bed-covers at five sharp or not.

She showered and dressed at the speed of light and was groggily waiting for his driver at the allotted time. He'd barely given her time to breathe, far less debate what she was going to wear, so she had chucked on a pair of jeans, some plimsolls and a white tee-shirt, with a logo of a famous rock legend, which had shrunk in the wash but was soft and comfortable.

There was no time to take Benji for his morning walk so she packed some food for him and, like it or not, she would have to walk him as soon as she got to Javier's place, whatever urgent situation happened to have arisen.

Still sleepy, she dozed against the car door as she was delivered to Javier's house which, unlike nearly every property in the capital, sat completely within its own grounds with a courtyard at the front that was barely visible behind high black wrought-iron electric gates. The pavement outside was broad and peaceful because all the houses had their own parking spaces behind similarly forbidding gates. Perfectly pruned trees interrupted the pavements, neatly set in equally perfect circular beds. The electric gates eased open and then quietly closed behind them as his driver stopped, killed the engine and then leapt out to open the passenger door for her before she could do it herself.

Benji had been sitting on her lap, tongue lolling out as he eagerly absorbed the passing scenery, and as soon as the car door was opened he leapt out and bolted across the courtyard, tail wagging, sniffing everywhere before leaving his mark on one of the car tyres just as Javier emerged through his front door.

'Sorry,' Caitlin apologised, glancing at Benji before settling her gaze on Javier, who had begun walking towards her. 'But he hasn't had his morning run. I'm afraid he's going to have to run around here till he does what he has to do.' She waved a roll of poo bags at him. 'But I'll clean up, don't worry.'

Her eyes were helplessly drawn to him. Like her, he was in a pair of jeans, but instead of the rock tee-shirt, he was in a loose-fitting white linen shirt that hung outside the waistband. He was wearing very expensive tan loafers. He was the very essence of sophistication and she had to peel her eyes away just to make sure Benji didn't embarrass himself too much on the pristine courtyard.

'Come inside. Have you eaten breakfast? I could get my driver to pick something up from the local deli.'

'I'm fine. I just want to know what's going on.'

It was a wonderful, crazily enormous house with three floors above and one below. It must have been at least ten thousand square foot, with towering vaulted ceilings and a sweeping staircase that travelled upwards in glass-sided spirals so that the magnificent interior downstairs was showcased from every angle. There wasn't a single element to the house that wasn't bespoke.

She'd been here before, in a flying visit to get some stuff for work, and had even joined a couple of clients for a celebration drink post signing a deal, but she still had to be reminded where the nearest downstairs cloakroom was and then how to find her way to the kitchen. Benji was nowhere in evidence and she could only pray that he wasn't discovering the delights of leaving paw prints on white furnishings.

But Javier and Benji were waiting for her as she entered the kitchen and for the first time she noticed that there was a grimness to Javier's expression that she hadn't noticed before.

'What's wrong?' she asked, suddenly very concerned, moving towards him instinctively. 'You're scaring me, Javier. Are you okay?'

'Thanks for the show of concern but I'm okay. I've brought you here because there's been a slight hitch in proceedings.' He'd had his back to her as he fiddled with his coffee machine and now he turned to hand her a cup of coffee, which she took without really noticing, because her eyes were on him.

'What kind of hitch?'

'The wedding is off.'

CHAPTER FIVE

'SORRY. WHAT ARE you talking about?'

'I spoke to Isabella yesterday and, to cut a long story short, the wedding is off. That's why I wanted you here, Caitlin. I didn't think it was a conversation we could skim over in a phone call.'

'How could the wedding be *off*, Javier? We were only planning things out up to a few days ago! I know Isabella has been a little indifferent about proceedings, and I can understand why now that you've explained the situation, but to call the whole thing off? I thought you said that it was an arrangement that suited both of you. Why would she call it off? Are you sure?'

She tried to remember the last time she and the other woman had been out doing wedding stuff. Things had been fine then, hadn't they? As she'd told Javier, the general level of interest might have been well below average, with no noticeable excitement on show, but that was how it had been from day one! She'd become used to it. Had Javier had any kind of hand in this? Could it be anything to do with the heart-to-heart they had had the evening before?

Caitlin looked at him from under her lashes. She could recall every word he'd said to her in the restaurant, every confidence shared. Had that sharing of thoughts and feelings roused something in him? Had it broken through the hard granite behind which he kept his emotions and freed him to want more than just a business arrangement with a woman with whom he wasn't in love?

'I'm very sure,' Javier said gently. 'It's hard to make a mistake when someone tells you that they no longer want to get married to you.'

'I'm so sorry, Javier. I know that it wasn't a traditional sort of situation...'

'That's a very diplomatic way of putting it.'

'But you must still be disappointed.'

Javier said nothing. He'd known that things weren't proceeding smoothly for the last few days, of course. Isabella had been vague and evasive with him and, when he'd prodded her for an explanation, her eyes had skittered away and she had mumbled something and nothing about everything being fine.

However, that had been far from the truth, as he had found out the evening before when he had called her. Her partner, Maria, who had originally been sympathetic to the situation, had issued an ultimatum. Isabella had realised that to proceed with the marriage would end her relationship with Maria, so she had made her choice.

For Isabella's and Maria's sake, Javier was quietly pleased. The burden of carrying such a big secret would eventually have had consequences. Besides, her fears were unfounded. She might be scared of upsetting the apple cart but how would she ever know if she didn't dive in at the deep end and find out?

Although...the decision did screw with all the plans he had in place. On an immediate level, a deal was in progress for her company that would require a conclusion and, even though he would no longer be involved in the running of her family's business empire, it was only right that he finish what had been started. He had called Caitlin to his house urgently because that was where she would be needed. Not that she had any clue about that.

Then there was the annoying inconvenience of arrangements that had been put in place which would have to be *un*-put. On a much more pressing level, though, was the fact that, with Isabella's withdrawal from the bargain they had agreed, he would now be up against it to find himself a suitable bride before the clock ran out. Isabella had been perfect. Now he was left with a problem. He intended to get those vineyards. When he thought about losing them because of a stupid inheritance clause, he felt sick and his heart tightened up. He wasn't an emotional man, but he had memories of a time of joy and innocence, and he intended to do what it took to have that piece of the puzzle slotted into place in his life.

But he wasn't going to be shackled to anyone who wanted to lay claim to his heart. He couldn't envisage a future of trying not to disappoint a woman who wanted more than he could give.

How many women would fit the bill of the wife who was happy to lead a life of duty without making demands on him? How many women were there out there who weren't romantics at heart, like his PA? How many women would be able to get on board with a marriage that would bring everything they could possibly dream of…except love?

The thought of searching for a suitable bride threatened a headache. He roused himself from his depressing train of thought and considered Caitlin's observation that he would be disappointed.

'Very much so,' he said truthfully. 'Look, Caitlin, I'm sorry if I've sprung this on you,' he said a little awkwardly, 'but as you can imagine there are a number of things in motion that will have to be sorted. Of course, Isabella offered to do that herself, but if I'm honest I think you would be more efficient when it comes to sorting that out.'

'Yes. Of course. Er…can I ask what brought about the change of heart?'

'You can ask, Caitlin, but that wouldn't be a question I would be prepared to answer.' *Or qualified to divulge.*

Caitlin stiffened. When she had been summoned to Javier's house, she hadn't known what to expect. It hadn't crossed her mind that he might have a health issue. She'd never known him to have an hour off work in his life. So she'd immediately thought about some deal or other that was time-pressured and about to collapse. He could be a tough taskmaster when it came to work and would have thought very little of rousing her from her beauty sleep if he needed something urgently.

She'd been knocked for six when he'd told her that the marriage was off. And underneath the shock was just a little thrilling thread of hope that perhaps she'd got to him. Would it have been that impossible? He'd told her things she just knew he would never have told anyone else. She conveniently discarded all the bits of the conversation that didn't tally with the sneaky, treacherous thought that something might have stirred inside him, something that had made him call it quits with Isabella.

That single cool answer to her question brought her right back down to planet Earth and those bits of conversation she had conveniently discarded—the bits that involved a description of the sort of woman he'd seen himself destined to marry had Isabella not been on the scene.

'Understood. I have details of everyone involved in the preparations and all the contact details of the guests. What shall I give as a reason for the cancelled event?'

'No need to give any reasons to anyone. It's off and that's the sum total of it.'

'People will naturally be curious. What if they ask questions?'

'People are entitled to be curious but that doesn't mean their curiosity has to be satisfied. It's a personal situation; maybe you could tactfully imply as such.'

'You're so cool and collected about this,' Caitlin murmured and Javier relaxed enough to half-smile.

'What's the point getting worked up over something that can't be changed?'

'That's true.' The man she'd had dinner with the night before was very different from the guy she was talking to now and she wanted the dinner guy back. She wanted to have that low, sexy voice tell her things he'd never told anyone before. She wanted to feel special and, much as she knew it was wrong and stupid, she wanted to feed the crush that hadn't managed to go away, however hard she'd tried to make it.

She was desperate to see behind the polite mask and the polite words. She *wanted* to play with fire, and that was heady, because she'd never been someone who wanted to do anything dangerous, and this urge felt dangerous.

Andy had messed her around and made her withdraw into a place of guarded caution when it came to her heart. She had trusted what she had seen and hadn't looked deeper at all the stuff that hadn't been visible on the surface. He'd been the safe bet who had pulled the rug from under her feet. She'd turned her attention to her boss because his absolute inaccessibility made him safe, but he was the least safe man on earth when it came to women and their hearts.

He'd said so himself. He'd been honest and straightforward about what he looked for in any woman who might end up occupying a place in his life for longer than ten minutes. Yet the desire to stick her hand out and get it close to the fire was overpowering.

'I knew that growing up in foster care,' she said quietly. Somehow it felt liberating to look back on the past and open up a bit with someone, which was something she'd never done. She looked down and realised that she wasn't doing this to encourage confidences from him, to try and bring some of his walls down. She was doing this because she wanted to.

'Caitlin...'

Caitlin fell silent. When she glanced at him, his dark eyes were urgent, but the second he met her quiet gaze he looked down. The only sign that he had heard what she had said was the tic in his jaw and a certain tension in his body language.

'Talk to me.' Javier's voice was low and ragged and her breathing hitched as their eyes met.

'I'm sorry. This isn't about me.'

'Isn't it? It's not like you're not involved here.'

'What I mean is...'

'I want to hear what you have to say.'

'I guess, when you said that you just had to live with what you couldn't change, it took me back. It was lonely being in care. It's not like anyone was cruel, because no one was. I suppose, looking back, they all gave the best they could, but most of them had families of their own. We were just a job, all of us.'

'I can't imagine what that must have been like for you.'

'Learning to resign yourself to what fate had dealt you was key to surviving intact. I mean...' Caitlin smiled '... I had my fantasy life in my head, but reality, well, that was always a very different thing.'

She looked at Javier thoughtfully. 'So I understand why you're dealing with this calmly. Still, I can't say that I've always been so stoical when it comes to matters of the heart.' She grinned and shot him a teasing look from under her lashes.

'What happened?'

'Oh, the usual: girl meets boy, girl falls for boy and thinks marriage is on the cards, girl finds out boy's been having a bunch of affairs behind her back and only kept her around to help with his coursework. I was upset and it wasn't as though there was anything like a ring on my finger!'

'That's why I find it helps to steer clear of emotional complications, as you know. So, to recap, I'll leave you to make suitable excuses for the non-event but it's all going to have to be done very quickly. At least there are no presents to return to anyone.'

'I'll make sure you approve of the wording before I send anything formal out.'

'No need, Caitlin. You've been working for me long enough and dealing with enough situations out of your remit for me to trust you completely when it comes to matters like this. I'm sure whatever wording you use will be perfect.'

'Okay, if you're sure. On another note, there might be

some trouble recovering deposits paid to various people—the venue, for instance, also flowers and the caterer.'

Telling Javier about Andy had opened the door between them even wider for her. As for him, he was still
all business, wasn't he? She almost resented the detach-
ment of the conversation they were having, even though
to have considered anything else only a few weeks ago
would have been unthinkable.

'Pay every single person involved the full amount
owed to them as if the wedding had taken place, and
add a ten percent bonus to what they would have received
from me. They'll have had their noses put out of joint,
and it would hardly be fair for them to take the hit with
such short notice. Call it a goodwill gesture from me.'

'I'm sure they'll appreciate that.'

'So…moving on to something else.'

'Yes?' Caitlin blinked and dragged her wayward
thoughts in line. 'If it's about work, then naturally I can
come in first thing on Monday. And… I know you paid
me a huge amount to finish this process and now that…'

'Forget about the money.' Javier waved his hand.

'In that case, thank you, Javier. It's been an amazing
bonus and it'll help with the deposit I'm getting together.'
She paused. 'I'm betting that Tricia will be pleased to
get back to her routine. I've been keeping in touch with
her, making sure that all the deals on the table when I
handed over have been going in the right direction. I can
deal with all the stuff with the wedding first thing and
be ready to start back by lunchtime.

'Also, if I can bring Benji in, I'm happy to work as
much overtime as you need me to. Angie is one of my
closest friends, and we pretty much share Benji between
us, which he loves, but she refuses to take any money

from me for all the cover she provides and I don't want
take advantage of her. I'm actually planning to use some
of the money you've given me to help her with some building work she needs to house dogs she wants to rescue.'

Javier saw the softening of her features when she talked
about her friend and the way she automatically reached
down to rub Benji's ears.

For a few seconds, he stared in brooding silence at her
far-away expression, thinking about what she could do
to help her friend. She had come from a background of
hardship but none of that had dented the soft generosity of
her nature. She had no examples of loving parents to have
provided guidance with what a successful relationship
might look like, but she still believed that they existed.
She'd had a learning curve with a partner who had used
her, from the sounds of it, and yet she still hoped that she
would still find love. She was the essence of the hopeless
romantic, whatever hard edges she might have. He felt as
though he was looking at someone from a different planet.

'Very laudable.'

She burst out laughing. 'Not really. I'll tell her that she
owes me big time.'

Their eyes tangled and she flushed and fidgeted.

'So...is that all? I can start straight away on cancel-
ling stuff.'

She readied herself to leave but Javier held up his hand.

'Not quite.'

'Okay.'

'Isabella and I were due to go to the French Riviera
after the wedding for a week...'

'Right. Wow, that's such a shame. I don't remember
booking the flights and hotel...' She frowned.

'You didn't. I did it myself. Neither of us was entirely sure how to play that angle and, when we did agree, I handled the arrangements personally.'

'No problem. Add it to the bundle of things to be cancelled and I'll handle it.'

'It's not as simple as that.'

'What do you mean?'

'This was a busman's honeymoon. We discussed what we could combine it with and chose the French Riviera because that's where one of the hotels in her father's chain is being finalised for planning. It was a toss-up between there and Lake Garda. I have a deal nearing completion there, so that would have worked as well.'

'Very…er…practical.'

'Ideally, Isabella would have been there to cast her eye over the architectural drawings—make sure she was one hundred percent satisfied with the finished product, bearing in mind she has a stake in the place—but *c'est la vie*. I've already told Jean Michel, the head guy in place, to supervise everything once work begins and that she won't be coming along with me as anticipated, for unforeseen circumstances. Phoned him before I phoned you, as a matter of fact. Everything's been cleared for me to sign off on the project.'

'Okay, well, that's a result, I guess. If you and Isabella parted company on an amicable basis…um…couldn't she just have gone with you as planned?'

Javier thought of what Isabella was gearing herself up to do—to have the biggest conversation with her father of her life.

'No,' he said flatly. 'But a sense of honour and duty means that I still have to see this deal through.'

'That's so wonderful of you, Javier. I know you two

go back for ever, and there's a lot of family history, but many guys would have been tempted to walk away in your situation.'

'I'm not many guys.' He wondered if this was her background kicking in. She dreamt her dreams but her experience with her last partner was probably where her expectations lay when it came to men: hopeful, optimistic, but realistic.

It felt good to think that she didn't include him in that category, which was understandable, considering he was and always had been a pretty fair and generous employer. Nevertheless, he enjoyed the warm approval on her face as she smiled back at him.

'This might have been an arrangement rather than a marriage, in the sense that you understand marriage, but I have and always have had a strong sense of duty.'

It was almost possible to forget the repercussions of the marriage being called off as he basked in her admiring smile. 'But moving on from that…' He reluctantly changed the subject. 'It's not just about the arrangements that have to be cancelled. I called you here because this situation involves you.'

'I beg your pardon?'

'I would have got one of the PAs at Alfonso's head office to join us in France to handle the details of the deal.'

'Alfonso?'

'Isabella's father. He has his own bank of people who could have come into play.'

'Okay…'

'But, with the marriage called off, that no longer seemed appropriate. Still leaves me with the small matter of having someone by my side over there to wrap up the details and format it for signing off. You know the way I work and you can come with me.'

'Come with you?'

'It's the perfect solution. To be honest, it would have slowed things down having to make sure someone knew how to keep up with me. You know I can sometimes be impatient.'

Caitlin stared at him, mouth open as she digested what he had just said. *She didn't want to go on a work trip with him.* She could smell the danger of that a mile off but he was looking at her with a neutral expression, fully expecting her to comply.

The fact that they had breached the boundary lines between them wouldn't have registered with him. He might have opened up to her, but he wouldn't be dwelling on that, tearing himself apart as he analysed what it might mean. He might have surprised himself but he would not have gone down the road of thinking that it meant anything other than a lapse in his usual rigid self-control, brought about by the suddenly unusual nature of their circumstances.

'I don't think I'll be able to put things on hold without a bit more advance notice,' she ventured and he frowned.

'What would you have to put on hold that requires a lot of notice?'

'I…well, Benji… I've barely seen him recently.'

'I gathered from Isabella that the dog went with you nearly everywhere.'

'Well, be that as it may…and I wouldn't actually say *everywhere…*'

'Do you have an up to date passport?'

'Yes.'

'And no personal obligations that can't be dealt with while you're away for a week?'

'No.' Caitlin sighed.

'Then it's just a matter of packing a case. No need to take care of flights and the hotel is already booked. I'll email you the details.'

'When?'

'A week on Monday morning. Most of the days there will be occupied with work-related issues but you can do your own thing in your spare time.'

'Right.'

'And don't look so worried. I know you've had a hell of a lot sprung on you over the past few weeks, and not much by way of explanation but...' he absently scooped up Benji with one hand, tucked him against his chest and looked at her '...but, once this is out of the way, life will return to normal. Count on it.'

Javier broke eye contact.

Having her there for work was the best outcome but he uneasily remembered how far their working relationship had travelled in the space of just a few weeks. At the back of his mind, there was the unsettling thought that she might have read too much into the confidences he wished he hadn't shared. There had been an intimacy in some of their exchanges; he'd seen her in a different light and had been turned on.

But she hadn't flirted. He was used to women who flirted. If he'd caught the occasional look, well, nothing had been encouraged. In fact, he had made it clear that he was just the sort of guy a girl like her should stay far away from. And she would know that. She knew what he was like first hand from the number of women who had come and gone over time.

He wasn't sure whether asking her on the trip had been the right thing to do but, the sooner their relationship was returned to the box from which it had been temporarily removed, the better. He'd told her that things would return to normal as soon as the deal in France was completed and he'd meant it.

Caitlin didn't feel *normal* as she waited for Javier's driver to collect her on the day of the trip—not unless 'normal' meant jittery, apprehensive and treacherously excited.

There had been no undercurrent of anything when Javier had explained the situation. She would be going there to work. When he'd told her that life would return to normal once that job was done, she'd got the message loud and clear: boundaries, temporarily shifted, were back in place.

She'd packed a compact case with sufficient boring clothes to last her the week. It was going to be hot. She assumed the hotel would have the usual stuff—a pool, a couple of bars, a restaurant or two, and the all-important conference room. So she'd packed one black one-piece swimsuit, a few nondescript work clothes—largely to remind herself that whatever door had been opened between her boss and her would now have to be very firmly shut—and some sundresses, because if she had any free time then she would explore as much as she could.

His car collected her promptly, driver leaping out to carry her case to it, and then holding the door open for her to find that the back seat was empty. She was told that Javier would be meeting them at the airport.

It was a beautiful day and Caitlin relaxed back against

the tan leather seat and let her mind drift. She'd never, ever been spoiled by anyone. Care had been practical and regimented in her foster home. She'd always had to pull her weight, help out and then, when she was older, keep an eye out for the younger ones.

Then she'd met Andy, started dating him and had seamlessly moved back into the caring zone, doing stuff for him, and pretty soon he'd accepted that that was her role: to *do stuff for him*. Why should he have lifted a finger when she'd been happy to do all the lifting on his behalf?

Now, as she relaxed in the back of the car, she felt spoiled for the very first time in her life, as much as she tried to tell herself that this was a work trip and nothing more.

Was that how all those women had felt—spoiled and special? Had he made the same effort with Isabella? Or had it been more practical without any need for Javier to go overboard with the courtship?

She gazed off through the window at a cloudless summer day but, although she expected to find them heading towards the congestion of an airport, she realised after a while that they were heading away from London. By the time she'd marshalled her thoughts back to the present, the car was swinging away from the main road and following a winding route to an airfield that was busy with all manner of small planes. Under a milky blue sky, people excitedly hung out behind a sturdy wire fence that was interrupted by gates. Small planes were stationary behind the gates, waiting as one of them taxied its way out into the blue sky to replaced by another.

Javier's private jet was waiting for her, black, sleek and streamlined, and dwarfing all the other tiny single props around it. This was beyond opulence. This was a declaration of untouchability: who owned this beast owned the world. She was aware of eyes curiously following her as she walked towards the jet.

Javier was lounging by the plane, chatting to someone she assumed was the pilot, and she paused, heart hammering, just to stare at him for a few seconds. In cream trousers, a black polo shirt and a cream linen jacket he was utter, masculine perfection. He was wearing dark sunglasses and before she could peel her eyes away he turned to look at her and then sauntered towards her.

'You're here.'

'Mmm. Wow, Javier…is this yours?'

'Everyone needs a toy.'

He grinned as she shielded her eyes from the glare and looked at him.

'It's a very expensive toy.'

'I have a lot of money. Besides, it's very convenient for getting from A to B very quickly, and it's easy to work on board. You could almost say it pays for itself. Did you get the reports I emailed you about the hotel?'

He had spun round and stood back so that she could precede him into the jet and, on the verge of answering, Caitlin stared around her in silence. Very pale, tan armchair-style seating complemented an arrangement of smooth walnut tables that could be used for dining or working. There was a concealed bar to which Javier went, also in walnut, producing two bottles of sparkling mineral water.

'Short flight,' he said. 'So no one will be serving us food, although there's champagne if you prefer it to water…'

'Water's fine,' Caitlin said hurriedly as they both went to sit, facing one another with one of the low walnut tables separating them. She launched into some spiel about the reports he had sent, on top of her game as always. Her voice was breathless and it was an effort not to just keep staring around her and soaking up the unspeakable luxury.

'We can catch up with all this when we get to the hotel,' Javier said as the plane began pushing back. 'We'll only be in the air for an hour and a half, maybe a bit more.'

Javier noted the way she clutched the arms of the chair and shot him a frozen, glassy smile. He felt a kick of satisfaction at introducing her to something that was obviously so wildly out of her comfort zone. He knew that was a purely masculine reaction, a juvenile instinct to impress, and he could almost smile at the passing weakness because it wasn't something he had ever recognised in himself.

'You can relax,' he said soothingly. 'The leather isn't going to survive that vice-like grip for very long.'

'I haven't been on anything like this before,' Caitlin confessed.

'In which case, you should sit back and enjoy the experience.'

The roar of the engines diminished when they gained height and he could hear himself think. For a few seconds, he was immersed in the moment as he looked at her.

'I used to dream of travelling.' Caitlin half-smiled. 'The furthest I got with that was travelling on a normal plane to a normal place surrounded by normal people going on a normal package holiday. You would have collapsed with shock when I went to Spain. There wasn't a single free seat, and when the guy in front decided to recline his chair I spent the rest of the flight pinned to my headrest.'

Javier's lips twitched and he smiled back at her, relaxing for the first time since he had spoken to Isabella.

'Can I ask you something?'

'Sure.'

'How is it that there's no eager guy in your life? Did one bad experience put you off men for good?'

Caitlin hesitated for a couple of seconds. She thought of the unattainable guy she had pinned her innocent fantasies on, the guy sitting opposite her with the curious expression, head tilted to one side, dark eyes capable of seeing too much for her liking. 'There *is* an eager guy in my life. He may not make the sort of demands on me that keep me from doing this or going on holiday, but he's really and truly my one great love.'

'Who?'

'Benji. He's very, very eager. Sometimes way too eager, if I'm honest. There's only so many times a girl wants her chap jumping up on her and getting dirty paw marks all over her trousers.' Her heart was thudding as his eyes remained on her, lazy and amused. She felt he could see straight into her soul and pick out the thoughts she wanted to hide, thoughts about him and how he got to her.

'Tell me where we're heading and what's on the agenda when we get there,' she said abruptly as she broke eye contact and fumbled for her laptop. 'I can start getting to grips with the details I'll need to know before the first meeting...'

She didn't want to look at him. She was going to have to get herself together before they landed and remind herself that, whatever confidences they'd shared, she was still his employee and he was still her boss.

Things no longer felt harmless for her and it was time she began moving on.

CHAPTER SIX

CAITLIN HAD NO idea what to expect as the jet swerved lower to a view of the blue Mediterranean, curling in an arc with trees and the cluttered town sprawling behind it. Even from above, the sight was breathtaking, the absence of impersonal skyscrapers promising the old-fashioned charm of history, old architecture and atmosphere.

'You'll see why it seems like a natural place for a hotel,' Javier murmured as the jet began its descent to the airport. 'It's taken a long time for all the planning to go through, hence the importance of signing off at this last stage.'

'What would happen if you decided not to follow through and finish the deal right now?'

'It wouldn't be the end of the world.' He shrugged. 'But it would be seriously delayed and then, of course, if the fortunes of the company took a blow with the marriage falling through and news of Alfonso's ill health hitting the headlines...' He gave another shrug. 'There might have been cold feet and, with all the planning that's gone into this, it would be a very costly waste of time. Alfonso was keen to get a stake in the leisure industry here in this historic slice of Europe and, like I said, I feel duty-bound to hold my end of the bargain.'

The jet sped down with the force of a rocket landing because of its size and Caitlin gritted her teeth and regulated her breathing. She wasn't expecting Javier to reach for her hand, which was balled into a fist. He gently unclasped her fingers and linked his fingers through hers.

'Relax.'

As a ploy, it worked insofar as she was no longer focused on the jet as it dropped down at a sharp angle. How could she focus on anything but the feel of his cool fingers against hers? She stared glassy-eyed at the dark hair curling round the metal of his watch and her breath caught in her throat.

'You can give me back my hand.' She breathed. 'I'm fine.'

'I'll return it when the plane's landed.' His thumb absently rubbed hers. 'Sometimes one person's energy can rub off on someone else and I've flown on this jet a million times. I'm very calm. Are you beginning to feel a bit calmer now?'

Caitlin thankfully managed a response as her blood pressure shot through the ceiling and her eyes travelled from his wrist along his bronzed, lean and sinewy forearm.

As the jet made a soft landing, he turned to her with a smile and gently patted her hand.

'Safe and sound. You okay?'

'Perfect!'

'Good.'

He dropped her hand, sat back, and Caitlin forced herself to try and breathe normally.

Her skin burned from where it had been touched and she surreptitiously rubbed her wrist with her hand, trying to erase the tingling sensation of being branded. Her whole body tingled, as if that brief touch had ignited nerve endings everywhere inside her. She barely noticed the black four-wheel drive that waited for them as they were ushered from jet to car like royalty.

'What will you do when we get back to London?' she asked breathlessly, as soon as they were seated and the car was pulling away at a sedate pace. Nerves propelled her into speech because silence would have felt too intimate. Her body was telling her something, asking questions that she didn't feel prepared to answer.

How had this innocent crush become so overwhelming? Why hadn't it just fizzled out when Isabella had turned up, when harsh reality had intruded? How innocent was it, really?

He reclined back against the seat, his legs spread wide, one hand draped loosely over his thigh.

She licked her lips and then smiled politely when he shifted so that he was looking at her.

'Do about what?'

'Well, if your original intention was to handle Isabella's interests so that her father's illness wouldn't affect the share prices, what will happen now that the marriage has been called off? Will you still take over?'

Past him and through the window, Caitlin could see the calm, attractive panorama of palm trees fronting the sea with a deep blue sky as the backdrop. All around, there was a lack of urgency that made her feel as though she might be on holiday but, before that could take root, she killed it dead because the last thing this was, was a holiday.

'To be decided.'

Javier looked at her thoughtfully. Her skin was shiny from the heat, even though the car was air-conditioned, and her hair had gone wild. Corkscrews curled in tendrils round her heart-shaped face, her mouth slightly parted, as though she was on the verge of gasping at the scenery flashing past them. She was wearing a short-sleeved shirt, patterned with pale flowers and buttoned down the front, and a loose skirt that fell to mid-calf. It should have killed all hope of sex appeal but, the second he had seen her, her sex appeal had knocked him sideways.

He wondered now whether he had always been drawn to her on some crazy subliminal level. Had she been like a background song in his head that he only recognised now that their working relationship had shifted on its axis?

Because shifted on its axis it had, whether he wanted to admit it or not. He'd opened up to her. It was a disquieting and unsettling thought. He'd opened up to her, and had that somehow brought to the forefront an attraction he was now forced to acknowledge? A sexual pull that couldn't be indulged?

Had the different dimension to their relationship opened up a Pandora's box filled with things that couldn't be countenanced? What Caitlin wanted from life was very different from what he wanted and what he knew he would aim for. She wanted all the things he would never be able to give any woman and would never be inclined to *try* to give any woman—not to mention the small but important fact that she worked for him. Still, his eyes lowered and lingered on the fine blonde hair on her arms, her short unvarnished nails, the curve of her breasts underneath her shirt.

Aside from anything else, his days for playing the field were coming to an end. He would have to find a suitable wife, one who fitted the only lifestyle he would be able to offer, and he had a deadline. There was no Isabella around who could step up to the plate without notice, because marriage would have suited her as well and, in many ways, the later the better. He would have to spend some time finding the right woman. It wouldn't be easy.

Content with a powerful line of reasoning that was steering him away from an unacceptable temptation, Javier cast his mind back to what they were talking about—something about working in the Albarado empire. His mind wasn't on it. His mind was still trying to get off the urge to keep looking at her luscious body.

'Won't it be a little awkward?'

'Come again?' Javier frowned and dragged himself back to the present while trying to stifle the sort of tightening in his body that might be awkward to conceal.

'Even if your split was amicable, won't it be a little awkward working in her company?'

'Why would it? We're all very close to one another and always have been. The only tricky bit will revolve around a proportion of ownership. As Isabella's husband, a percentage of the shares would have devolved to me, hence there would have been more motivation on my part to make sure I had significant input into company decisions.'

'I get that. And now?'

Javier wondered what it would feel like to trail his finger over her full mouth. The feel of her small hand in his had been a powerful turn-on. Taken a couple of steps further, how much more powerful would the turn-on be? He almost groaned aloud at the disobedient tangent his mind was going down.

'Now,' he managed, 'now I'll do as much as I can and keep a close eye on Alfonso's health. He's already making small strides so that's a positive.'

'Isabella must be so relieved. Has she told him about the marriage being called off?'

'She's waiting until he's a little stronger.'

'I hope he won't be too shocked, especially considering so much was riding on your union with Isabella.'

Javier thought that the shock of the marriage being called off would take a definite second billing to the other news his daughter would soon be imparting.

'I'll continue to help out.' He brought the conversation back to its original starting point. 'But not indefinitely. I'll just paper things over until Isabella gets a handle on the nitty-gritty.'

'Can I ask you something?'

'I feel I should say no at this point.' But he smiled and continued to look at her, his eyes lazy and indulgent.

'Are you angry at Isabella for what she's done?'

'Angry?' Javier thought about it. Anger, and the loss of control it entailed, was an emotion he seldom indulged. His father's loss of control over his emotions when his wife had died had been a powerful lesson in the dangers of losing it—the dangers of letting oneself be pummelled this way and that by *feelings*. He should have been angry because, to some extent, his future had been derailed, but anger was not an emotion he could summon.

'Angry.' Caitlin half-smiled. 'As in, wanting to punch something or shout from the rooftops.'

'What would be the point of getting angry? It's not as though anger would change the circumstances. I don't do anger. And add to that list jealousy, envy and need. A life spent without those things is a richer, more rewarding life.'

'I'll bear that in mind, moving forward.' She grinned and her heart skipped a tiny beat as their eyes collided.

There was amusement in his expression and something else—something that set up a slow burn inside her, just like the burn she had felt when he had linked his fingers through hers. She was struggling to move past the warm gleam in his eyes and a tenseness in the atmosphere that gave her goose bumps.

'I mean...' she said a little weakly.

'You mean...?'

'Everyone gets angry now and again, and jealous and envious, and everyone sometimes longs for stuff they can't have but feel they need...'

'Repeat—I'm not like everyone,' Javier said softly. 'My experiences of seeing how my father reacted to my mother's loss was a lesson enough in letting emotions guide your decisions. You allow that to happen and your decisions are always going to be wrong.'

He was so close to her, Caitlin could reach out her hand and brush it against his cheek.

'Stop looking at me like that,' she whispered.

Caitlin knew what he was going to do. She felt it in her bones. He was going to kiss her, and she wanted him to, just as she had wanted to get away from talking about work and dig into his head to try and find those deeper parts she had started glimpsing. She wanted to lean against him so that she could feel his hardness against her and the steady beat of his heart under the palm of her hand pressed against his chest.

This was something that had been simmering under the surface between them for a while. She had felt it and had ignored it but it had been there, now unlocked because she was no longer just his PA. The door between them hadn't just opened for *her*. It had opened for him as well and maybe that was why she hadn't been able to kill the crush on him. Maybe she had *sensed* a spark there waiting to be lit.

Her breathing hitched and she willed him to do what she wanted him to do: kiss her; settle his mouth against hers; let his hand find the heavy weight of her breast, because her nipples were pinching against her bra and she wanted him to stop that pinching.

She should have been shocked that her beautiful boss was staring at her with hot desire, eating her with his dark eyes, but in some part of her she wasn't. Gut feeling was pushing through any sense of surprise and telling her that this was something that had been gathering momentum. If Isabella hadn't broken off the marriage, it would have come to nothing, but it had been there even when Isabella had been around because Javier hadn't been in love with his fiancée. So his eyes had wandered and she had *sensed* it.

Excitement coursed through her. A legacy of uncertainty had left her craving stability and safety when it came to any relationship with a guy. Javier was as safe and stable as a hand grenade.

But she felt an urge to see what adventure tasted like. It was one thing to read about romance and have adventures in her head but what would it really *feel like* to touch this man and have him touch her back?

Fire… She'd be putting her hand in an open flame and she would end up burnt—badly burnt.

She pulled back from the brink but she was shaking.

'This place…the scenery…amazing.'

She turned away to gaze through the window, taking in a place bathed in the last rays of early-summer sunshine. Nestled between the sea and the mountains, and curving round one of the finest bays in the country, Nice was a seductive melting pot of elegance, vibrancy and charm. The sea was very blue. As the car swerved through the streets and her mind began to calm down, she could appreciate what she had missed, the graceful architecture of some of the grand, ochre-coloured buildings. If aristocrats had flocked here once upon a time, she could understand why.

She did her best to ignore Javier's dark, disturbing presence next to her and the tingling from her near-brush with a situation she had only just about managed to swerve.

All was forgotten as the car swept towards the hotel. It was a magnificent curving masterpiece of cream fronted by a glass-panelled arch guarded by two uniformed men. The courtyard was huge and bordered by perfectly manicured lawns on either side. Even the trees and flower-beds looked as though they had been individually seen to by a top coiffeur, not a single leaf out of place. She automatically sifted her fingers through her unruly hair and absently wondered how trees and bushes could look more precisely trimmed than *her* hair.

The people milling around were the last word in glamour, perfectly tanned with big sunglasses and designer clothes.

'This is amazing…' she breathed at yet another opulent experience.

'Not too shabby, I suppose.'

'Of course,' she said, as the uniformed guards held open the doors for them, and they left the warm sunshine to step into the cool of the white marble-and-glass foyer, 'it wouldn't be my personal choice for a honeymoon hotel. It's not exactly brimming over with romance, is it? But then, I suppose, neither was your courtship.'

'"Courtship" is a rather old-fashioned word, and there was nothing like that anyway. Can I have your passport? I'll need it to check us in.'

Caitlin reached into her handbag, handed it to him and gazed around her. Huge, ornate marble pillars intersected the expanse of cream, white and pale greys. Clusters of white upholstered chairs formed seating spaces around glass tables, and in turn were loosely partitioned off by long, oblong walnut dressers, some of which were dressed with enormous vases of white lilies.

She was vaguely aware of Javier talking to the girl behind the desk in rapid French before he turned back to her sharply.

'Right. Off we go.'

How to break the news? Javier wondered as they silently rode the lift up to their floor, because he had a feeling she was going to freak out when he told her that they would be sharing a suite of rooms, especially after their drive to the hotel. Just thinking about the sexual tension that had stretched between them made him break out in a sweat.

He'd never wanted any woman so badly in his life before. He'd known that, if he'd touched her, she would have melted in his arms, just as he'd known that giving in to that temptation would send their reliable working relationship into territory best left unexplored. She'd pulled back but he'd seen how shaky she'd been. She'd come as close as he had to turning their relationship on its head, in the grip of something as pointless as lust.

'Here we are.'

As Javier swiped the key card and stepped back, Caitlin stepped into a glorious expanse of living area. He saw her gaze past white sofas, a pale Persian rug and little glass tables, through to a veranda with yet more seating, and beyond that the fading colours of the sky that melted into a panoramic view of the sea.

She strolled towards the French doors that were flung open onto the veranda and stepped out into the balmy fresh air. There was a stupendously impressive view of a rectangular pool surrounded by neat rows of white deck chairs and white umbrellas overlooking a drop down to the ocean beneath. People were still there, drinking and being served by waiters, elegant figures in floaty sarongs and wide hats.

'Wait…' She swung round. Javier was almost directly behind her. 'Are we *both* going to be here?'

'I'm afraid so.'

'You're afraid so? I'm not sure your fear is going to help here! How is this going to work?'

'No need to look so horrified, Caitlin. It's going to work because it has to. I did ask at the desk whether two rooms would be available because of a change of circumstance but, unfortunately, the place is sold out—very popular time of year.'

'I can't share a room with you!'

'Look around you, Caitlin—this is hardly *a room.*'

'I'll stay somewhere else. It's not a problem for me. I'm not fussy.'

'Everywhere is going to be booked up.' He raked his fingers through his hair and stared at her. 'There are two bedrooms. There are two bathrooms. Our paths need not cross until a designated time in the morning when we can spend an hour or so doing our due diligence before we meet the various CEOs in the conference room reserved for us here.'

'Javier…'

'What's the problem?' His dark eyes challenged. 'What do you think is going to happen, Caitlin?' What so nearly happened between them in the back of the car hung between them, unspoken.

'Nothing's going to happen. I just...think it might be a slightly awkward situation, given it was supposed to be your honeymoon suite.'

'Isabella would have been in a separate room. This would have been a work base. You'll be in a separate room, this will be a work base. So, again...what's the problem? Because I'm comfortable with this arrangement. If an alternative had been possible, fine. But there was no alternative.'

'Isabella would have been in a separate room?'

'I told you, ours was a business arrangement in every sense of the word. So back to your objection—do you feel somehow unsafe sharing this space with me?'

Again, cool challenge was in his eyes, daring her to voice what she had no intention of voicing.

'Absolutely not.'

'Then that's nicely settled.'

He spun round on his heels and headed to the cases which had preceded them. 'Now, why don't you have a look around and settle in? I'm going to stick my case in whichever room you don't want, head downstairs, and start some preliminary liaising with the guys we'll be meeting tomorrow and confirm arrangements for the conference room. The sooner I get this wrapped up, the better.

'Isabella and I were going to meet Don, the site manager, for dinner. There's no need for you to join us but you're more than welcome, although it won't be a business meeting as such. He's an old friend of the family. You can stay here and order up food or go wherever you want to—up to you. You have the company card. Use it on whatever you choose.'

'Okay.'

'Okay to which part of what I just said?'

'Okay to being very happy to stay put and order up something to eat. Or maybe venture out. I'm not sure, but yes, I'll let you catch up with your friend and, as for the rooms, I don't mind which I get.'

'Tomorrow we can convene on the veranda at eight-thirty. I'll have breakfast brought to us.'

'Sounds good, and I'll make sure I do some final work on the deal before then.'

'Feeling a little better now about the horror of sharing this suite with me?' Half-turning to her as he strolled to retrieve his laptop from the sleek, expensive case, he raised his eyebrows, but his expression was unreadable.

'I don't remember saying anything about being horrified to share this enormous suite of rooms with you, actually.'

'Splendid, because…' he captured her gaze and held it so that she could hardly breathe '…despite what very nearly happened between us in the car, there's nothing at all to worry about.'

'I have no idea what you're talking about.'

'Of course you do.'

Caitlin felt anger roar through her because he had raised something she wanted to forget; because that brief moment, which had been earth-shattering for her, had not touched him in the same way. Her stupid crush made her vulnerable and she hated that.

'I think that's best left forgotten,' she told him coldly. 'Nothing like that has ever happened before and nothing like that will ever happen again.'

'Of course,' he murmured into the lengthening silence.

He headed for the door and repeated his invitation to

spend on whatever she wanted—whether it was clothes or food, because she was doing him a favour by coming here with him—and left with a half-salute and no backward glance.

Caitlin didn't relax until she knew that Javier would no longer be in the hotel, at which point she scarpered to one of the two enormous bedrooms and firmly locked the door behind her.

She took in her surroundings, but distractedly. There was an enormous bed with crisp white linen, an enormous white sofa and a huge walnut desk, with sufficient plugs to ensure no one who wanted to work had to hunt around for charging points, and beautiful abstract paintings. The television was wafer-thin and large enough to ensure a theatrical experience. Everything was so huge and so beautiful that it was almost a shame to think about ruining it all by actually being in the room and doing stuff like going to bed or just sitting on the sofa. She could see the ocean sparkling beyond through the floor-to-ceiling French doors. Unsurprisingly, the bathroom was the size of her flat, and she and Benji could have slept in the bath with room for him to have a run.

How could she ever have foreseen this? And how could she ever have predicted that her childish crush would morph into this great, big thing she was finding difficult to handle? She'd been hurt after Andy, and had retreated to lick her wounds, but now she could see that, even when the wounds had been well and truly licked clean, instead of getting back out there she had been lazy. She had turned her attention to Javier and idly whiled away two-plus years living in cloud cuckoo land instead of doing what any other young woman would have done—

namely replacing her dead-beat ex-boyfriend with some-one more suitable.

The arrival of Isabella on the scene had knocked her right back to planet Earth, but instead of propelling her into hitting the singles scene it had plunged her into the confusing place where her secret crush had grown shoots and shot up like the beanstalk in the fairy tale.

What a mess. She didn't want to be up and about when Javier returned. She needed to gather herself and take heart from the fact that they would only be here for a week. London would restore everything back to where it should be. Open doors could be shut.

With the prospect of Javier bouncing up earlier than expected from his dinner, she hurried the meal she'd or-dered, which had arrived with pomp and ceremony, lots of silver domes and starched linen. She was well and truly bathed and in bed, with her door locked and only the bedside light on, when she heard the sound of the outer door being opened.

The rush of forbidden excitement, the sudden tingle of absolute awareness that he was just in the same space as her, filled her with dismay. As she switched the bedside light off, she vowed that tomorrow was another day and she would make sure to stifle all the inconvenient feel-ings that had no place in her relationship with her boss.

Forget about that crazy almost-moment that had nearly overtaken them. It was all in the past. And, as soon as they returned to London, she would hit the singles scene and destroy the parasite that had taken her over and was eating her up.

She just had to last out her time here and focus on the reason she had come in the first place: a missing fiancée and a deal to be delivered.

CHAPTER SEVEN

CAITLIN HAD THE day off after five days of intense meetings, with barely time to pause and think about what had turned out to be a less awkward situation than she had expected.

As arranged, they convened for breakfast first thing every morning, during which they briefed each other on what would be happening during the day, what needed to be done and what issues had to be dealt with before signing off.

On the first morning, after a restless night's sleep and with butterflies in her tummy, she had emerged from her bedroom to find Javier sitting in front of his laptop on the veranda. He'd barely glanced in her direction as she'd sat alongside him and pulled out her laptop. There'd been coffee, to which she'd helped herself, and ten minutes later various pastries and breads had been trundled in.

But for the magnificent scenery and the warmth of the sun, they could have been in his offices in London. Out of the corner of her eye, she'd glimpsed the elegant pathway below, lush green gardens on either side and the stone steps that led down between swaying palm trees to the beach in the distance. How could she not have noticed before?

Easily, she had discovered, because Javier had moved at breakneck speed through so many files and folders that she'd almost struggled to keep up with him and then, breakfast done, they had headed straight to the conference room to carry on the rest of the business at hand.

She had cleverly brought the sort of work clothes she would have actually thought twice about wearing in London—because she preferred bright, casual stuff—but, predicting an uncomfortable ambience, she had rustled up a couple of drab outfits which made her feel a bit like a fool in the balmy, laid-back surroundings.

The evenings were spent on her own while Javier did his thing with the people who would be working on the completion of the hotel deal. Five times he had issued the invitation to accompany him and five times she had politely declined, telling him she preferred to have a look around a place she'd probably never visit again.

She duly did some light exploring. She was keen but anxious, and always eager to return to the hotel before Javier so that she could avoid any conversations over a nightcap. She didn't want any more of those heady heart-to-hearts because they were too catastrophic for her nervous system. She wanted to distance herself from temptation so that things could be normal once they returned. She was desperate to bury what had happened between them.

Caitlin knew that all of that was needless worry, because Javier barely paid her a scrap of attention, reverting very easily back to being the boss and away from the guy who had linked his fingers through hers to calm her on that flight. Away from the guy who had looked at her with scorching sexual intent in his eyes.

What had been earth-shattering for her had barely registered with him as anything out of the ordinary. He might briefly have been attracted to her, but the circumstances had dictated that passing reaction more than physical lust. If he'd ever seen her in that light before then, she would have known.

It was just as well that she had pulled back from the brink of doing something both of them would regret. One touch, and he would have known that there was no way she was as casual as he was about physical contact between them.

Today, he had removed himself to have lunch with some old acquaintances who lived in Châteauneuf-du-Pape and were extensively knowledgeable on the wine grown there.

'I have a small-scale hobby on some land in southern Spain,' he had drawled, halfway out the door and before the usual breakfast routine. 'Thinking I might take it further, so a little basic info on wine growing might be in order. Don't wait up.'

'I'll try my best,' Caitlin had told him drily.

'Turn of phrase.'

She had reddened as his dark eyes had rested on her, opaque and unreadable.

'What sort of time…?' she had prompted, mentally calculating how her day would pan out in his absence.

'Very late. It's a long drive, and I intend to spend some time enjoying the company and the town. Weather's good, and there's nothing more relaxing than gazing up at a ruined mediaeval castle with a glass of the best red waiting to be drunk. So, in short, I won't be back before ten tonight.' He'd spread his arms wide in an expressive gesture and half-smiled. 'Seize the day, as they say.'

He'd given her a mock-salute and left, and she'd breathed a sigh of heartfelt relief and got on with doing exactly as he'd instructed.

Nice was famous for its museums. She took one in and

then strolled in the mild summer warmth, enjoying the sights, smells, chatter in different tongues and the rapid, romantic French accent as people strolled past her. She grabbed lunch but was too eager to carry on sightseeing to sit still for long and, by the time mid-afternoon rolled round, she had managed to explore Old Nice with its narrow cobblestone streets and buildings in pale pastel hues, enjoying all the cheeses and breads spilling from stalls and the huge array of flowers that filled the air with an aroma that was fragrant and seductive.

Never in her wildest dreams, in foster care, had she thought that the experience of being somewhere else could feel so wonderful and so alien at the same time.

Once she became tired of walking, the hotel pool became irresistible, perched up above the ocean with its elegant array of shaded loungers and precision-straight umbrellas. People were lazily sunbathing, but there were many empty loungers, and it was bliss to while away a couple of hours soaking up the sun.

Javier wasn't going to be back until very late. She'd actually checked how far the place was, and he'd be several hours on the road, never mind sipping red wine and catching up with old friends while gazing at a mediaeval castle. All that stuff took time. He would be very lucky to be home by midnight, she reckoned.

Caitlin had never envied the lifestyle of the rich and famous—the opposite, if anything. She had occasionally seen some of the women Javier dated, and had often wondered—how much time went into the business of being impeccably groomed? How much time was spent hunting down the perfect outfits to grab the attention of a guy who was never going to be in it for the long haul?

What effort was involved in trying to impress the world? It must be exhausting.

But, here, she guiltily saw what serious money got a person when it came to sheer luxury: poolside staff jumping to attention; a list of cocktails as long as her arm served with melt-in-the-mouth snacks; loungers she could fall asleep on; and the quiet hush of very expensive people who never did rowdy things such as yell, shout or dive into the pool irrespective of whether they splashed anyone.

It was bliss, quite frankly. She was a couple of mojitos down by the time six o'clock rolled round and she headed back to the suite. Pleasantly relaxed, and relishing the freedom of being able to strip off and walk around in the buff safe in the knowledge that Javier wouldn't be around for hours, Caitlin reminded herself that she was really going to commit to embracing her singledom just as soon as she returned to London. For the moment, however, as she flung on a thin, sheer sarong—which was just about okay for sitting on the veranda, because there was nothing at all underneath—she had not a thought in her head except for the mindfulness of the moment.

The intensity of the sun was fading. Down below, if she was to look over the railings of the veranda, she would see the very pool she had just left, but from here, half-dozing with a bottle of water in one hand, all she could see from the cushioned chair was the blue sky and ocean and the fine, dark line dividing the two.

She nodded off to the pleasant background sound of the breeze and the distant sea and the even more distant sounds of people below, thinning out at the pool as the light began to fade.

When she started at a sudden noise and looked at her phone it was only just seven—loads of time to take it easy before she catapulted into fifth gear and made sure she was in her bedroom by the time her boss returned.

And tomorrow would be the perfect time to get round to all her good intentions.

Javier let himself into a silent space. It was a little after seven-fifteen and he still wasn't entirely convinced as to why he had changed his plans for the day. He'd set off with great intentions to enjoy some downtime whilst also quizzing his grizzled, humorous friend about vineyards and wine production. He would inherit his vineyards by hook or by crook and, once he did, a little useful information would come in handy.

But he'd been filled with a vague restlessness as soon as he'd left the hotel. The past five days had stretched his willpower to breaking point. He was in the unique position of knowing that a woman wanted him, knowing that he wanted her just as much, yet powerless to do anything about the situation because Caitlin was out of bounds.

Much more than that, though—she was complicated. He thought of her having been in foster care…all the sadness that would have gone with that…the faith in love and romance that it had engendered against all odds, the desire for security.

The last guy she needed was someone like him, whether he was her boss or not. He was not going to go there, whatever erotic fantasies he had going on in his head…was he?

With all sorts of problems looming on the horizon— from marriage plans going down the plug hole, to an expiry date on his freedom if he was to get control of the vineyards he was so desperate to have—there was more than enough to worry about. Instead, the only thing he was able to think of was whatever was going on between Caitlin and himself.

He hated to think that he was the sort of guy who could crave what he couldn't have but, ever since that almost crazy moment, he had watched her out of the corner of his eye, watched her every movement, and had gritted his teeth against a libido that threatened to rocket into the stratosphere.

When he lay in bed at night, he practically groaned aloud at the thought of her lying in a bed within touching distance of him. How was he supposed to have talked wine, drunk wine and whiled away several hours in the sun without itching to get back to the hotel? Which was why he had met Jean-Paul halfway, enjoyed a light lunch with him, caught up on news, while only glancing at his watch four times, and then made his way back to the hotel earlier than intended.

Last day in Nice... He'd planned to avoid all temptation, but something had got the better of his usual impeccable judgement, and now here he was, in the suite...

Javier drew in a sharp breath as he moved towards the veranda just as she lazily stood up with her back to him.

What was she wearing? What was she *not* wearing? Where was the attraction-killing work garb she had been keen to wear for the past few days? The thin wisp of fabric swathed around her showed everything he'd fantasised about for the past five days: round backside, shapely legs, narrow waist...

She was moving back inside, staring at her phone, and smiling as the sarong blew open. Javier went rock-hard in seconds. He felt his urgent erection pushing against his linen trousers. He couldn't have peeled his eyes away from the luscious sight in front of him if he'd tried. Her breasts hung like ripe fruit waiting to be tasted, her nipples large orbs, pink and perfectly defined, begging to be sampled.

Dios mío!

Caitlin was moving forward towards a sound that had barely registered, smiling at the picture Angie had sent her of Benji, until she glanced up, and for a few seconds her mind went blank.

She had a sluggish déjà vu, a flashback to standing on that chair with a wedding dress on, but this time, as reality returned in a rush, she knew that it was much, much worse.

She stared down and saw the nakedness of her breasts and the panties that barely covered anything. She felt every inch of her body; felt the rush of blood through her veins, the tickle of wetness spreading between her thighs and the sensitive tightening of her nipples as they scraped against the thin sarong.

'What are you doing here? What the *heck* are you doing here?' She scrambled to get herself presentable.

'I...' Javier raked his fingers through his hair and glanced away, but not for long.

'You shouldn't be here!' Caitlin screeched. 'And... *don't*. Just...*don't*!'

'Don't what?'

'Don't you *dare* look at me like that!'

'Like what, Caitlin? Tell me! No, you don't have to tell me. You don't want me to look at you as if you're the only woman on earth; as if I want to do nothing more than rip that flimsy bit of cloth off so that I can do what I've been wanting to do for too long now.'

'You don't mean that!'

'Damn right I mean it—every word. Wanting to touch you has been driving me crazy.'

'You're my boss! I'm not your type. *You're* not my type… We've all but *agreed* that!'

Silence fell, an electric silence thrumming with everything that was unspoken, charged with *want*.

'In that case…'

Javier began turning away and, in that split-second, Caitlin had a soaring insight into her life, her choices, her past, her present and her future. She saw all the dreams she'd had in her foster home: romantic dreams of frothy weddings, babies and happy-ever-afters. She'd lost herself in those dreams. They had been her escape and, for a while with Andy, she'd projected those dreams onto him and pretended that he could be 'the one' for her. Her disillusionment had pulled her into a place of safety. She'd looked at her boss and taken refuge in a crush that had never been able to come to anything but, in doing so, she had removed herself from real life with all its complications, dangers and chances that she could have taken.

Somewhere in her head, she had decided that chances weren't for her. But here she was, and she was suddenly driven to take the biggest chance of all.

What would it feel like just to give in to temptation? Could she live in the moment without looking ahead to regret? With Javier, she knew what she would be getting into, and that would be nothing—nothing at all. Wasn't that safer, in a way—taking the plunge without spinning castles in the sky about a future that was never going to happen?

'Wait…' Heart in her mouth, she reached out and circled his wrist with her hand, while she clutched the sarong tightly together with the other.

* * *

Javier stilled.

Every muscle in his body froze at the branding touch of her fingers on his skin and the hesitant tone in her voice. He looked at her with hunger. If he'd ever thought for a single moment that he'd known what it felt like to play with fire, then he'd been wrong. *This* was playing with fire.

'What am I waiting for? Tell me!'

'I'm not sure! I'm confused! I don't understand. I'm so attracted to you but I know that it would be stupid to do anything about it. *Dumb!*'

'You think I don't know that?'

'I don't know what to do! This is all your fault!'

'You think *I'm* not confused?' He raked restless fingers through his hair.

'We should walk away from this. It doesn't make sense.'

'If we do, will what we feel, this charge between us that's come from nowhere, conveniently leave us alone? Or will curiosity never let either of us go? And, if that's the case, how will it impact our working relationship down the road? Think about it.'

Javier half-turned away, because if he carried on looking he knew that he would find it impossible not to reach out…smooth those strands of hair from her cheeks…trace the delectable hollow of her cleavage…reach down and kiss her full mouth…

'I'm trying to think, Javier, but you make it pretty hard to keep a clear head.'

'Okay, so how about this?' he said shakily. 'Whatever happens tonight happens or doesn't happen. That's your call. Either way, we leave tomorrow and, once we're back in London, whether this thing is still there between us or not, we will never talk about it again—ever.'

'Okay.'

Okay? *Okay?* Frustration tore through him, but there was no way he would do anything to make her feel uncomfortable or to jeopardise the terrific relationship they had fostered over the years. He respected her too much for that, even though he'd never felt so turned on in his life before.

When he harnessed his wayward thoughts, it was to find that she had turned away and was heading towards her bedroom, closing the door on him.

He wanted her!

Caitlin lay in bed with her eyes wide open, staring up at the ceiling as the minutes and hours ticked by. She played and replayed every word of what he had said and analysed every expression on his face she remembered until her head was spinning. Her whole body ached from the desire she was desperate to subdue, because of course they were both right in acknowledging that this...*thing*... between them had to be ignored. So what if curiosity ate away at them? If they mutually agreed never to mention it again, then curiosity would surely fade over time.

Except, what would happen to all these feelings that had been unleashed inside her? It would be easy for Javier to move past a brief attraction generated by the unusual physical circumstances in which they found themselves, with her a heartbeat away in a honeymoon suite. But would it be equally easy for her?

He had no idea of the fantasies trapped in her head about him, fantasies woven over time, carefully nurtured while she'd foolishly avoided the singles scene. Would those fantasies become more strident when they returned to London, when her eyes followed him as he moved in the office? Would her body yearn to take what was on offer here, an offer which would no longer be on the table the minute they returned to the reality of the outside world? Would sleeping with him finally kill off an inconvenient desire?

She had hours to decide—less. She knew that he would respect whatever she chose to do because that was the kind of guy he was.

As the thoughts buzzed in her head like angry insects, she wished that she could be better prepared to handle a situation like this but, whilst making her resilient in many ways, the strange world of foster care had left her curiously vulnerable in others.

It was a little after ten when she decided that checking the fridge for something to eat might be a good idea. She couldn't stay lying on the bed a minute longer. She was overthinking and needed to move. She knew that the fridge was ridiculously well-stocked with chocolates, biscuits, bottles of water and interesting packets of various French cheeses.

But how did her feet manage to pause outside Javier's bedroom door en route to getting something from that fridge? How did her hand end up pushing open his door—a door that had been left invitingly ajar? And how did her feet softly pad to where he was turning in the bed?

Her heart was thudding and the feverish thoughts had coalesced into one, overpowering realisation: *she was going to do this. She had to do this.*

The life in her imagination had always been colourful, but that had never mirrored reality, and the reality was that she had always been risk-averse. She had always thought that daring adventures of the heart were meant for other people, but not for her.

She'd always assumed that her need for safety was too ingrained for her to jeopardise it by taking chances—especially after Andy, who had been a terrible error of judgement.

But with Javier... The error of judgement would be to deny what her body wanted and shy away from this driving need greedily to take what he offered.

'You came.'

Caitlin hovered. She was a lot more covered than she had been when she'd worn her sarong—she was modestly attired in a baggy tee-shirt and long pyjama bottoms—yet she felt more exposed now than she had with less on. She felt stripped bare under the hooded gaze of those dark eyes—stripped bare and unspeakably excited.

'I came.'

'I'm glad you did.'

'Were you expecting me?' Her voice was shaky and barely a whisper.

'Come a little closer and I'll tell you.'

Should she confess to him just how innocent she was when it came to sex? That was a thorny conversation she had never rehearsed in any of her make-believe scenarios.

He was now sitting up, watching her with lazy interest as she came closer, and he patted the space next to him.

'I wasn't expecting anything, I was hoping—hence I left the door ajar.'

'To tempt me in?'

'Should you be passing,' he murmured with a crooked smile. 'To give you something to think about. Come, climb in. It's a lot warmer under the covers with me than it is standing there.'

Her inexperience roared through her like a gale-force wind, filling her with a tremor of apprehension, but she shuffled towards the bed, took a deep breath, half-closed her eyes and did as he'd asked. She slipped under the soft duvet which he had raised obligingly for her.

Oh, good heavens...

The feel of his nakedness sent her blood pressure soaring and she gasped and closed her eyes. He slowly ran his hand over the tee-shirt, then under it, and she trembled when his fingers found the stiffened bud of her nipple and began to stroke. She was in the moment and yet outside it, looking down at herself in wonderment at what was happening.

It was surreal. The wetness between her thighs was shocking, as was the raw need for him to put his hand there and soothe the restless, demanding tingle that was driving her crazy.

He pushed up the tee-shirt and she opened her eyes a crack to watch as he straddled her with his big, muscular body, absently touching himself before easing down to suckle on a tender nipple.

Caitlin groaned. Pleasure exploded inside her. She could barely breathe as a new world was unleashed, a world of dizzying sensation and mind-blowing excitement.

The adventures in her head were tame compared to the tumult of sensation racing through her, igniting every corner of her responsive body. She arched up, wanting more of his mouth on her. She didn't want him to take his time. She wanted him to be in a hurry so that this weird, wonderful, crazy craving was satisfied immediately! Instinct made her reach down to touch herself but he didn't even lift his mouth from her nipple as he stayed her hand.

She felt him murmur something against her breast and groaned. By the time he rose from his thorough exploration of her breasts, she could barely contain her escalating pleasure, and it took just one touch from him, just the slide of his fingers over her clitoris, for her whole body to burst into orgasm.

She cried out and spasmed, not caring a jot that his eyes were on her, watching her come.

'Oh, Javier!' She gave a long, shuddering moan.

'Good God, you're so damned beautiful.'

Caitlin reached to squeeze him tightly as he subsided next to her on the mattress. 'So are you. God, so was *that*. I've never... Oh, Javier... I'm sorry.'

'For what?'

'For...not lasting a little longer but...but...'

'But what, *querida*?'

Caitlin squirmed from where she had burrowed against his neck and looked at him anxiously. Her body was calmer but she could still feel the heat inside her, ripples of sexual awareness making her warm and tender.

'Javier, I don't want you to freak out.'

'Just saying that is making me freak out. What is it?'

'I... I've never done this before.'

'Never done...*what*?'

Caitlin looked at him defensively. 'I knew you'd freak out. I knew you wouldn't want this!'

She began turning away, humiliated in advance at the prospect of doing the walk of shame to the bedroom door, dishevelled and semi-undressed. Why had she said anything? She could have faked it and he would have been none the wiser but, as it stood, why on earth would he want to make love to someone with zero experience? How would that be a good time for him?

'Caitlin...'

'Don't say anything,' she ordered shakily. 'I know it's not what you expected...'

'You're a virgin.'

'It's not a crime.'

'Look at me.'

Caitlin raised cautious, challenging eyes to his. In the semi-darkness, there was amused tenderness in his gaze and something soft fluttered inside her.

'You're not…disappointed?'

Staring deep into her eyes, Javier realised that he couldn't think of a single word further removed from 'disappointed' to describe how he felt right now.

A virgin. He had never sought one out and, if asked, would have said that the prospect of sleeping with a virgin would have him running for the hills, because it smacked of the sort of complications he would never touch with a bargepole. Now, though, as he looked into her hesitant, defiant, hopeful gaze, he wanted her with a ferocity that shocked him.

'Far from it,' he murmured huskily, an understatement to beat all understatements. 'It makes me want to show you everything, *querida*. It makes me want your sweet, responsive body in ways I can't even begin to describe—and, trust me, I'll be gentle with you. When I enter you, you'll open up to me like a flower, and I promise to take you to heights you can't begin to imagine.'

'That's a lot of big promises.' There was a shaky smile in her voice.

'And I intend to keep every one of them…'

True to his word, Javier took it slow. He stripped her with the delicacy of someone handling priceless porcelain and, when she was stretched out in front of his devouring gaze, naked and breathtakingly beautiful, he forgot his own needs and devoted every ounce of attention to making this the best experience of her life.

He linked his fingers through hers, held her hands above her head and explored her breasts, revelling in their lush abundance, lathing the orbs of her nipples with his tongue until she was wriggling and moaning.

He delighted in the little mewling noises she made as he traced a sensuous contour along her ribcage with his tongue, moving lower to circle her belly-button. He took his time, even though it was agonising, because his body was on fire.

He reared up as his wandering mouth, tongue and fingers reached the sexy crease of her womanhood. She was flushed, eyelids trembling, her mouth softly parted on an expectant sigh.

For a few seconds, Javier was overwhelmed. His life had been prescribed for so long that this felt like an adventure—a thrilling, dangerous adventure with no signposts to follow.

She made a tiny urging sound, and he smiled then levered himself in just the right position to swing her legs over his shoulders. He breathed her in, nostrils flaring at the musky feminine scent. Delicately he slid his tongue between that damp crease and found the throbbing bud of her clitoris with no trouble. He was determined that the next time she orgasmed it would be with him inside her, deep, hard and moving at just the right pace to take her over the edge.

He did things slowly, teasing her with his tongue, getting her high on *want*, and then, when he knew that he would come himself if he didn't do what his body clamoured for him to do, he reached for protection, sheathed himself and took her.

CHAPTER EIGHT

JAVIER LOOKED AT CAITLIN, who was moving around the bedroom in search of clothing that had been scattered earlier en route from door to bed. It was a matter of a few paces but after an excellent meal, that had gone on for way too long in his opinion, they had been so desperate to rip each other's clothes off that there were items of clothing everywhere.

Worth the haste, though, he mused now with intense satisfaction as he watched her hold a sock in one hand and her bra in the other. He'd propped himself up on one elbow, all the better to appreciate the swing of her heavy breasts as she padded naked across the room. Her hair was dishevelled and he clocked the sway of her peach bottom... Incredibly, he could feel himself hardening again.

They'd prolonged their stay. That first night had been amazing, explosive, revelatory and, more to the point, not enough for either of them.

She'd lain in his arms and he'd stroked her hair and been tickled pink as she waxed lyrical about how fantastic the experience had been.

They explored the city to within an inch of its life. She'd barely travelled, and he enjoyed showing her around the famous museums, strolling through the old town, with its charming streets and colourful buildings, and pausing for lunch on the promenade surrounded by tourists with the warm sun pouring down on them like honey, making them lazy and hot for one another.

For Javier, life was on hold, and he was enjoying it. Why not? Problems lay round the corner and there would be time enough to deal with them when this madness was over: Isabella; her situation; the company that would need at least some steering whether he was her husband or not; and of course the timeline for his own marriage, which wasn't going to go away, because he wasn't ready for it.

He thought of Caitlin—her joyous innocence, her sweetly responsive body that was always eager for his touch...

He wanted to lose himself in a holiday from reality and enjoy what he would never have again because his journey now would be with another suitable wife to replace the empty spot left by his vanishing fiancée.

Of course, he'd been astute enough to remind her that this was just time out for them, nothing serious, just fun. He'd sidelined any concerns that had sprung to mind when she had confessed that she'd been a virgin. He'd buried them under the fact that she knew him, and knew what he wanted in a woman, because he'd made it clear over the time they'd been here.

She'd met Isabella, so she would be in no doubt that the woman he eventually sought for his wife would be of a similar mould. She'd said as much, unprompted by him.

If he'd omitted the fact that there was a timeline governing finding this woman yet to appear on the scene, then that had simply been a courtesy. He fancied that she was enjoying him, and enjoying the bubble they were in, and would hardly want it burst before its time.

He fancied that he was doing her a favour, when he got

right down to it. With him, she was preparing herself for the reality of life in which sex and lust didn't necessarily lead to love and marriage. She would emerge tougher and stronger, more capable of protecting herself against men like the boyfriend who had broken her heart.

His thoughts did what they always seemed to do when he was with her—strolled off in the opposite direction. Lying back just as he was now—naked and stirring into pleasant arousal, appreciating her voluptuous curves—he would suddenly catch himself idly imagining the sort of guy she should end up with. And found the whole idea of it vaguely distasteful.

'Is it just me or are you getting a little bored here?'

'Here, as in the bedroom, right now? I'm…not bored, no, but I'm a little hungry.'

Javier glanced at his phone on the bedside table and realised that it was now a little past seven-thirty in the evening. They'd been in bed for a staggering amount of time. How had *that* happened? he wondered. He frowned and swept aside a stirring of unease.

'Now that you mention it, so am I. It's later than I thought.'

'I guess we've been busy.'

Their eyes tangled and again he felt something stir inside him, something a little bit unwelcome, a tenderness that seemed to leave her and find a connection in him.

'It's time to get out of here,' he drawled. 'And no need to go with the bra, by the way. I like the weight of your breasts in my hands. I like being able to touch and feel your nipples harden.'

He grinned with wolfish intent and enjoyed the way she went red and was momentarily lost for words. His addled head cleared.

* * *

'Get out and go where?'

When she looked at him, she felt that familiar surge of sexual charge, but this time it was mixed with a flare of sudden panic because she knew that she was living on borrowed time with this beautiful, wonderful guy.

One night! That was all it was meant to be. She had crept into his bedroom, nerves shredded but overcome with the sort of mad desire she'd never thought herself capable of feeling, and they had made love. She'd been scared that her lack of experience might turn him off, but it had been just the opposite. The minute he'd touched her, her body had burst into flames and now…? Now she knew that he held her in his hands like a puppet master. The crush had turned into something fierce and raw, and it was more than physical. He'd captured every bit of her, from her body to her soul. She'd fallen for him, and she wondered whether she hadn't fallen for him a long while back, because he was just so much more than the sum of all his parts. Barriers had been broken down and, in this wonderful bubble, he had become her world. It didn't matter that he had warned her off wanting more than he was prepared to give.

As she glanced over her shoulder, she could see that what she'd felt for Andy had been a pale shadow of what she felt for Javier. But, then again, working for him, alongside him, getting to know him in a million different, little ways… Her heart had been lost a long time ago and she hadn't even realised it.

Of course, she couldn't carry on working for him when they returned to London, so this time here was precious. The longer they extended their stay, the happier she was.

She would deal with the chaos of her emotions when it ended and she walked away from him for good.

It was a struggle to meet his intense, dark gaze without giving away her thoughts. She didn't dare raise the topic of returning to London. If he raised it, then fine, but she wasn't going to pre-empt anything.

She found that she was holding her breath and, at risk of going blue in the face, she hissed it out slowly.

'No need to look so worried, but I think it's time to move on.'

'Oh, really?' Her heart sank but she kept her cool and maintained his stare.

'We've done the cafés and the jazz club and the museums, and exclaimed sufficiently at the ocean and the scenery.'

Caitlin maintained a mute silence whilst surreptitiously gathering her clothes from the ground and trying to shield her nakedness. Naked and serious, life-altering conversation didn't seem to go hand in hand.

'Change beckons,' Javier drawled, flinging the covers aside and treating her to the magnificent sight of his bronzed, muscle-packed body.

'So it does,' she said faintly.

'And I know that there's frankly a ton of work waiting to be done, amongst other duties too many to mention.' He strolled towards her, relieved her of the bra, held it up while maintaining eye contact and grinned. 'Tut, tut. What have I said about not liking you wearing a bra?'

'And back in the day, when dinosaurs ruled the world, that sort of macho talk might have meant something...' Her voice was more tart than she'd intended.

'Don't tell me you don't love it when I do this...'

Caitlin breathed in sharply and shuddered as he

reached to cup her breasts and then roll his thumb over her stiffened nipple. She flung back her head, felt wetness begin to spread between her thighs, and her arms went limp. She could *feel* his hot satisfaction as he stroked her nipple between his fingers, while with his other hand he reached down to cup her wetness.

He slid fingers into her and teased a devastating response. Caitlin dropped everything she'd been clutching and clutched him instead as her whole body quivered. She barely recognised the guttural moan that emerged as his rhythm got quicker and firmer over her throbbing clitoris until she could no longer contain the orgasm splintering through her.

She arched back and groaned, eyes squeezed tightly shut, and the high colour of sexual gratification scorched her cheeks.

He caught her as she subsided like a rag doll against him, their naked bodies pressed hard against one another. She felt his hardness against her and reached down to circle it. It was his turn this time.

He'd taught her well. When she glanced down, forehead pressed against his chest, she thrilled at the sight of his impressive brown member and the slightness of her pale fingers circling it. She could feel the pulse of his arousal and, as she worked her own magic, she never took her eyes off him as, like her, he came to a shuddering orgasm.

'I think we're both due a bath,' he rasped into her hair, and she looked up at him and blinked, already careering into the conversation they'd left behind when touching had become more urgent than talking.

'Why are you looking at me like that?' he asked with a frown.

'Like what?'

'Like you're worried about something.'

'I always get worried when I'm hungry.' Caitlin glanced down to escape the penetrating intensity of his gaze. 'One day I'll get to grips with a rigid diet, and then I'll be able to laugh in the face of semi-starvation.' She was keeping it light but her heart was pounding like a sledgehammer as he drew back from her, held her at arm's length and just looked until she reluctantly returned the stare.

'Promise me you'll never do that,' he said seriously.

'Do what?' Her voice was bewildered.

'Go on any diet, rigid or otherwise. You're beautiful just the way you are.'

'If you say so.'

'I do. I love making love to you, feeling your body under my hands, your curves… I think I've already proved that. In fact, I'd say that particular record is on permanent repeat.'

Caitlin thought that 'permanent' was an adjective that couldn't be further from the truth. 'Permanent' was the one thing he'd reminded her more than once that he would never do.

She turned, breaking the connection, and walked towards the en suite, aware of him padding softly behind her.

'I'd go for the bath option,' he said with lazy amusement, reaching to turn on the waterfall shower which, in its vast wet-room space, was easily big enough for both of them and then some. 'But I think we both need to eat. I can hear my own stomach protesting from lack of food.'

They showered together. It wasn't the first time. But

this time her head was cluttered as she tried to make sense of what was going on.

Was he going to try and persuade her to carry on what they had when they returned to London? She would, naturally, decline the kind offer if that turned out to be the case but no way would she hint about the resignation she was determined to hand in. Or maybe he was going to call it a day. That being the case, he was very upbeat, but then again he wasn't emotionally involved. She was just someone else who'd come along in the void left by Isabella.

Tension made her stomach tighten as she flung on some clothes. She'd bought some stuff in a couple of the little independent shops. Javier had tried to urge her into some of the more expensive boutiques, but she had laughed and turned down the offer.

'Where will we go for something to eat?' She broke the silence as they headed out.

'Somewhere small and quiet so that we can talk.'

'We do need to do that,' Caitlin said tensely while her heart continued to beat a frantic tempo and her brain scrambled over possible scenarios, none of which had a happy ending. 'There's a ton of work stuff piling up, as you said. I've actually tried to clear some emails over the past couple of days.'

'As have I. We can get to the work chat later. Right now, let's try and find somewhere to eat.'

'You…mentioned that it was time to move on,' she forced herself to say as they stepped into another balmy evening and walked out towards the bustling shops and cafés.

'I did. Like I said, I think it's time to move on from Nice, and I have a proposition.'

'No.'

'Come again?'

Caitlin was warming up to what was coming. She carried on walking briskly but then slowed up when he tugged her to his side, pulling her to a stop.

'Let's find somewhere to sit so that we can have this conversation,' he said quietly.

The minute he'd uttered those words about having a proposition, she'd known where he was going. She'd worked alongside him long enough to be wise to his dating habits. He enjoyed women, and treated them like queens just until his interest started to wane, at which point they were politely but firmly ushered out. Isabella might be no more, but Caitlin would stake her life's savings on her boss returning to his previous lifestyle.

Was she going to be like all those other women? No. Her heart just wouldn't be able to stand it. She lacked their experience, and the line between fun and misery would be an easy one to cross. She intended to have her say before he could use any persuasive tactics on her. She was weak around him, but being weak wasn't going to do. She had to assert authority over the situation or risk even greater heartbreak by being persuaded into ditching the resignation and continuing an affair with the guy she worked for.

How easy it would be, working by day with the slow build of excitement racing in her veins as she anticipated a night with him...the accidental brush of his hand on her arm...dark eyes lingering just a little too long. It would be clandestine, thrilling, decadent...

And way too dangerous for someone whose dream had always been to be safe in a relationship.

She had no regrets about making the choice she had

made. How could she? But she couldn't afford to layer it up with complications she would find impossible to deal with.

'So...' Javier mused, just as soon as they'd found a suitable restaurant, having strolled there in silence. 'You're suddenly very serious, *querida*. You haven't heard what I'm going to say and you've decided that you want no part of it?'

'I know what you're going to say.'

'Really? I'm shocked. I had no idea you were gifted in the art of mind-reading.'

'Work calls,' Caitlin said wryly. 'And it's time for us to return to London. In all the time I've worked for you, I've never known you to take spontaneous time off, so I'm guessing you've got itchy feet. How am I doing so far?'

'I'm curious to hear where the story is going.'

Caitlin's heart fluttered. Why did he have to be so stupidly gorgeous, so incredibly clever, witty and perceptive? So *unavailable*?

'You and Isabella are no longer together...'

'Ten out of ten for observational accuracy.' He grinned, raised his eyebrows and slid a glance at her. 'What comes next?'

'And we've had a good time here. Unexpected—not a good idea, but...'

'Agree on all counts.'

'I won't continue this situation once we return to London. It would be untenable.'

There, she'd said it. She thought about walking out of his life for good and gritted her teeth. Tough situations demanded tough choices. Would he miss her—the person he'd grown to know aside from the employee without the back story? 'You're not the kind of guy I'm looking for as a partner and, whilst this is fun, it's really opened my eyes to the importance of getting on with my life.'

'Getting on with your life?'

'Finding the guy who's right for me. You were my adventure, and it was good that I…that we… It wasn't a mistake, put it that way.'

'That's very gratifying, and should I be flattered that you considered me a stepping stone in your ambition to find yourself Mr Right, or offended? Or *insulted* even?'

Caitlin reddened. Was he teasing her? Was he less bullet-proof than she'd always thought?

'I've hurt you and I'm sorry.'

'I'm kidding, Caitlin. Of course you haven't hurt me, so don't worry about that. I'm thicker skinned than you think. No, I get what you're saying one hundred percent.' He leant forward, elbows on the table, and steepled his fingers. 'We've already established that when it comes to longevity you're no more my type than I am yours. You want all sort of things a man like me could never provide, aside from which…'

'Aside from which…?'

Javier hesitated. He'd already told her enough about himself—too much. Why launch into his need to get hold of vineyards, what he had to do to get them to fulfil his dream of owning a slice of his past tied up in memories of joy and happiness? Why repeat what she already knew? That the lessons from his past could never be undone. That he would tie the knot with someone who understood his limitations.

'You had a rough time growing up, and I can understand why you've invested so much in finding love with the right guy, and that's fine. If I'm your adventure on the way to getting there, then that's also fine.'

'Will you…?' Caitlin hesitated but what did she have to lose? They'd already crossed a million lines, and besides, she would be handing in her resignation as soon as she got to London so there would be no repercussions from anything she might decide to ask him now. No awkward moments.

'Will I what?'

'Will you still have a business-like marriage, with some other suitable candidate?'

'Yes.'

'How can you be so sure?'

'I know myself and I know what I want and what I need.'

He'd said that before and yet she still felt a stab of pain because she was forced to accept what her heart didn't want: his casualness; his affection that was only skin-deep; the fact that she was disposable, however much he liked her, and however many laughs and confidences they shared.

'What I meant—' she smiled stiffly '—is whether you think you're destined to marry someone else who has a company you would like to merge with yours.'

'No immediate candidates spring to mind. Why are we talking about this?'

'I don't know how we got there. I suppose I'm curious.'

'Well, if it satisfies your curiosity…' He dropped his voice, topping up both glasses with wine and leaning towards her in a way that was confidential and intimate, making her skin tingle. 'I'm not completely ruthless when it comes to choosing a woman I'd want to spend my life with.'

'What does that mean?'

'It means I would never marry any woman because of her financial holdings.' He grinned. 'I have plenty of my own. Isabella and I had something that went beyond that. We had family loyalties and tangled duties and a shared history, along with the weight of familial expectations, not to mention a list of other reasons all vying for airtime.'

'So then what on earth would you be looking for?'

'Let's stay in the present,' he drawled. 'This is a dead-end topic.'

'It's only dead-end because you don't want to talk about it.'

'It's dead-end because it's not relevant to what I want to say.' He sighed, impatient and indulgent at the same time. '*Querida*, you know the sort of woman I'll end up with. Someone who doesn't need of huge amounts of attention. Someone who will be able to ease comfortably into a lifestyle of making sure everything is running efficiently on the home front, and also being able to effortlessly deal with the socialising that will come with the terrain.

'It would also help, I suppose, if she came from a similar background to mine. Spanish high society is slightly different than its equivalent here, and as and when I take over my father's business interests I expect I'll end up splitting my time between London and Madrid. There won't be much time for on-the-job training.'

'Perhaps you might need a training manual of sorts for whoever gets the job,' Caitlin said. 'I could get one put together for you.'

How could he say all this stuff, utter sentiments that couldn't be further from what she expected out of life, and yet capture her heart and soul without even trying? Eager to get away from this diversion, she dug into the prawn salad, made suitable noises about it being delicious and then reconfirmed what she had earlier said about having no intention of continuing what they had just because they still happened to be attracted to one another.

'This…all of this…' She drank some of the wine and looked at him evenly. 'Is wonderful.'

'Got it—your personal adventure before you find the real thing. No need to labour the point… And yes, it's been good, I won't deny that.'

'Well, that's sorted, then. We agree.'

Javier looked at her steadily. 'I agree,' he told her flatly. 'About London. When we return, it would be difficult for us to return to the right balance if this continued— too many blurred lines. Which is why I'm not proposing that we do any such thing.'

'You're not?'

'I'm not.' He smiled slowly and sat back, pushing his plate to one side and looking at her for a few seconds in contented silence. 'What I'm proposing is this: we leave here and head somewhere else. This was a work destination, after all, and the work's been concluded. We've had fun here, but I want us to go where we won't be interrupted. Somewhere where we can make love whenever we like and get this thing we have between us out of our systems before real life beckons.'

He made it sound so simple. As if what they had between them was no bigger than a passing infection, easily killed off with some antibiotics, never to resurface again. They couldn't have been more on different pages.

'What are you suggesting?' she asked carefully.

'Maybe a week or two on my yacht.'

Whilst Caitlin knew everything there was to know about the company holdings, she knew next to nothing about his own private possessions. Yes, he owned several priceless paintings. She had once had to renew the eye-watering insurance on them, because his private fund manager had been in hospital, but for the rest she had not a clue, really.

'Your yacht...'

'Which is conveniently moored at the moment off Monaco. We could do some perfunctory sightseeing there and then decamp to the yacht which, let me assure you, is far from ostentatious. You could say it's in the same league as a handy run-around car when you don't want to bring out the Bentley.'

'I doubt it's the equivalent of my run-around car.'

Caitlin was already thinking ahead to a few more snatched moments with Javier. She gazed off into the distance and rapidly worked out pros and cons. It was all pros and no cons, as far as she was concerned. She'd committed to this wonderful bubble for as long as it continued. She'd accepted that she would resign once the bubble had burst because there was no way she could continue working for a guy she was madly in love with, watching while he picked up where he'd left off with other women; arranging dates for him to fancy places with his trademark catwalk-model girlfriends. Until such time as the perfect accessory came along, suitable for marriage and living the life expected of Spanish aristocracy.

But in the meantime she was on this adventure. She would pick up the pieces later and she knew that, when she did, she would be all the more determined that safety was what she wanted, but at least she would have got the heady adventure out of the way. She was only doing what most girls did! She'd just taken her time getting there and had had to jump one enormous hurdle along the way.

'You're looking thoughtful.'

Caitlin blinked and focused on Javier, who was staring at her with an expression she couldn't quite read.

Capturing her thoughtful blue gaze and holding it in brooding silence, Javier realised that he was in the grip of something seldom experienced: uncertainty.

Why was she looking thoughtful? Why hadn't she jumped at his offer? What was there to think about? They still wanted one another, neither of them was in this for the long haul and they had to let it run its course or risk it interfering with their working relationship when they returned to it.

And, from a more personal perspective, Javier could see that once they returned to London his hunt for a wife would become serious business. This was his window, probably his last window, of carefree sexual pleasure.

And, more than that, this was... He frowned and didn't follow that thought. Instead he focused on her thoughtful expression. Neither of them wanted complications and that was the main thing. So where was the problem?

It was an effort to sit in silence and wait for her to say something. Always in control of events, Javier was unsettled at the way he now felt out of his depth and controlled by something over which he had no say. He had a moment of wondering whether this was the right thing. It made sense on paper. He still wanted her so badly it was overwhelming, and yet...

He had this weird feeling of not being in control... Should he be wary of it? Had he somehow become vulnerable because his deadline was now set in stone? Vulnerable to the need to snatch fun while he still had the chance?

'Well?' he finally prompted in a voice that was a lot heartier than he was actually feeling.

'I think it's a good idea.'

Javier hadn't realised that he'd been stressed out waiting for her to respond until she actually responded, and then he half-smiled with relief and satisfaction.

'I'll have to sort stuff out with Benji.'

'If it's a problem, you can bring him over,' Javier said magnanimously.

'*Bring him over?* I didn't think you were that fond of dogs.'

'You'll miss him, and I have no problem with arranging transport for him.'

'A yacht might be a little much. I'm not sure how good a swimmer he is. Plus, there are loads of formalities involved when it comes to getting a dog from the UK into Europe.'

'You hardly have to worry about such things with me.' He clicked his finger and shot her a smile of utter satisfaction. He was the magician pulling rabbits out of the hat and impressing his audience. 'Put it this way, I wouldn't want you to spare a thought for shortening our time together because you're missing the dog. He's old and, trust me, there's sufficient room for him to stretch his legs, and we'll disembark on a regular basis. He can come with us and explore the wonders of the second-smallest country in the world.'

Their eyes tangled and Caitlin lowered her eyes as a thought flashed through her head.

Surely this was more than just sex for him? The fact

that he was prepared to dump work, enjoy what they had and, furthermore, do what it took to make her day complete by getting Benji over—wasn't that above and beyond? He might laugh off what they had as just something physical that he had to get out of his system…but maybe he didn't see that there might just be something more lurking just beneath the surface.

'Okay.' She smiled and was flooded with warmth. 'I would love to see Monaco, and I'm pretty sure Benji would as well…'

CHAPTER NINE

MONACO WAS A SMALL, busy city on steroids. It reeked of wealth. This was where the rich came to play and frolic, and there was evidence of that everywhere—from the decadent casinos, where the stakes were high, to the eye-wateringly expensive designer malls and the opulent bars and clubs. Under glittering blue skies, beautiful people drifted by, carelessly swinging their designer totes and hiding behind oversized sunglasses.

The atmosphere was lazy and decadent and Javier told her a few facts about the place that made her eyes widen. One in three people living in the city, he'd said, were millionaires, and most of them were not natives of Monaco at all but there to take advantage of the generous tax breaks.

'Would *you* live here?' she'd asked on day one as they'd sat people-watching outside one of the smart cafés with a couple of ice-cold cocktails in front of them.

'I'd die of boredom!' He had laughed in response and his eyes had lingered when he'd added in a wicked undertone, 'Unless you were living here with me. The hot sex might make it worthwhile.'

The common-sense, down-to-earth part of Caitlin knew that those were words thrown out there in the moment, meaning nothing, and yet she couldn't help herself from storing them up and reading into them feelings that might run deeper than he was prepared to admit.

So what if he and Isabella had embarked on a marriage of convenience? She had no idea why Isabella had called it off at the last minute; perhaps she had had cold feet at the thought of marrying for business and not love. She knew women could be sentimental in ways that men sometimes couldn't fathom.

And maybe, deep down, Javier himself had longed for something more than a contract to unite two powerful families with ties that went back for decades. He cared deeply for the woman, however he categorised it, and Caitlin felt that maybe, just maybe, he was capable of love...*wanted* love...even if that was something he would never voice in a million years.

Had she come into his life to find him in a place where he was actually ready to fall in love, even though he made so many noises about not believing in it? Caitlin knew that it was crazy to speculate but, with every passing second, she just knew she could see evidence of a guy who felt more for her than he was prepared to say out loud.

This was stolen time, but when that stolen time came to an end would he look at her and realise that she was indispensable? Realise that she had crept into his heart, the way he had crept into hers? Would he realise that arranged marriages that made sense were not what they were cracked up to be? Would he realise that he might talk the talk till he was blue in the face but he couldn't actually walk the walk now that he had invited her into his heart?

The fact that he'd brought Benji over said a lot. Caitlin had no idea what Tricia would be making of their prolonged absence but she knew that he remained on top of everything, waking before five to kill a load of emails. She, too, had fallen into a routine of catching up on stuff, working with him as she always had, but free to touch him because there were no curious eyes on his yacht.

Largely, they had a routine. Javier had managed to employ someone to take Benji out first thing for an hour and after that, while Benji snored his way through most of the day, they worked, talked, worked, made love, and had breakfast and lunch, sometimes in the nude, just for the hell of it.

The yacht was pretty amazing. It was not the biggest moored in the crystal-blue water, because there were a few far bigger ones bobbing here and there in the distance, but it was big enough, and kitted to the highest standard. There were three en suite bedrooms, staff quarters, an amazing kitchen and living quarters with pale leather seating. Two circular pools were perched on the upper deck, one with a Jacuzzi, and there was a fully stocked bar with bar-stools and tan leather seating against the sides, along with deck chairs and umbrellas.

And, in the bowels of the yacht, was lodged a six-seater black-and-red motor boat perfect for covering the distance between the yacht and the shore. Caitlin didn't know who was more impressed by the speedboat—Benji or her. They hopped on board, with Javier at the helm, and eyes closed, she enjoyed every second of the experience as they sped towards the city.

Right now, encased by a moonlit night, Caitlin was as relaxed as she could possibly be on one of the loungers by the pool with Benji in his bed next to her on the deck. She heard the rustle of Javier behind her, and turned lazily to watch as he shoved a deck chair close to hers and settled on it, handing her a glass of wine.

It was still very warm and he was in a pair of faded swimming trunks and a white linen shirt cuffed to the elbow, which was flapping open, affording her a fantastic view of his hard, brown torso with its sprinkling of dark hair. She was in her bikini bottoms, a new purchase from one of the boutiques in Monaco, and had discarded the top at some point in the evening, probably just before they'd made passionate love after dinner.

It was a struggle, resisting all his attempts to lavish her with *stuff*, but she remained savvy enough to know that accepting presents from him would do nothing for her self-respect when everything came crashing down. So she'd dug into her savings and added 'poverty' to the tally of all the things she would have to deal with when the inevitable happened.

It was worth it. Deep inside her, she knew that.

'Beautiful night…' she breathed, sitting up and shamelessly enjoying the sight of Javier.

'I'd forgotten how impressive the landscape here is,' he admitted, gazing out to sea, his arm lightly touching hers as he sipped the wine.

'Who uses this yacht when you're not on it?' Caitlin asked curiously, twisting a bit so that she was looking at him.

'Family members. Occasionally my father and his cronies. Some of them enjoy time out from their better halves.'

'You've told me a bit about your family,' Caitlin began. 'I know you were devastated when your mother died. I would be as well in your shoes. I suppose I had years of my mother failing to be a mother, so by the time she died I had already grieved for her in some ways. How did your mother die?'

'I'm thinking this isn't subject matter for a beautiful evening.'

'Guess not.'

Caitlin immediately backed off. He'd said so much about himself but would he want to be reminded of it?

'Cancer,' he finally said heavily. 'It was quick. Not a lot of time to say goodbye.'

'I'm so sorry...and you're right; this isn't the sort of conversation to have when there's a bright moon in the sky and we can hear the sound of the water lapping against the side of the boat.'

'I was away at school at the time. I boarded from a young age. Arrangements were made and, by the time I returned, my mother was already dangerously close to death. It was...shocking how gaunt she'd become. I think she may well have known that something was wrong, but she wasn't a complainer. She would have laughed off the weight loss and the tiredness until she couldn't any longer. At any rate, I was with her for a handful of weeks, by which time she was too weak to engage.'

This was the most Javier had ever said to her about the details of his mother's death and Caitlin felt a bloom of tender satisfaction as yet another small window opened up, letting her inside.

'I know you said that your dad went off the rails a bit after she died because he couldn't cope with the loss...'

She wanted to pursue this conversation, even though she knew that she was treading a thin line, because if those shutters slammed harder then she might be shut out for good, but she was greedy to see more of him.

Javier shifted. She was prying but he'd already told her so much about himself and he couldn't understand how that had happened. Her questions were so lazy and gentle, and opened up a side to him in a way he couldn't quite get a grip on.

Did he want to have this conversation when touching her would have been more than plenty? It jarred, didn't it, sitting out here and talking about things he'd spent his adult life burying, yet again?

Yet, he was uncomfortably besieged by memories that filled his head like marauding wasps. He remembered how his father had cocooned himself and then emerged to have a catastrophic, short-lived fling with a gold-digger who had ended up conning him out of millions. The depth of his pain, hurt and bewilderment hit him with the force of a sledgehammer.

'Not the time or the place, Caitlin.'

'Understood.'

'What we have…here and now…isn't about this.' The lines of what exactly they had in the here and now formed a blurry smudge in his head and he frowned.

'About what?'

'We've talked…we've had to, given the circumstances…but that doesn't mean that the talking has to continue. Caitlin, when we return to London, all this is forgotten. Personal conversations of this nature will have no place in a work environment.'

'Honestly, Javier, I didn't mean to barge past any "keep out" signs. I guess, growing up in foster care, I spent a lot of time imagining what life was like for other kids. Not that we didn't meet other kids, we did, but I always felt like an outsider.'

'A lonely life.' Javier felt the treacherous swirl of a current under his feet, dragging him back to the very place he had just closed off. 'But,' he said bracingly, 'loneliness can make a person strong.'

He was relieved when he heard the buzz of his mobile next to him. It gave him an excuse to stand up and head indoors, excusing himself while staring down at the phone.

Caitlin watched as he strode away into the bowels of the yacht. Every shared confidence fed the love inside her and watered the hope that wouldn't listen to common sense and go away.

Suddenly the void that had opened up at the thought of returning to London and handing in her resignation started to close. For the first time there was light at the end of a dark tunnel. First, he'd extended their time together. He'd wanted more than just sex, because if it had only been about sex, then he would never have confided in her, opened himself up. Yes, there had been times when she had caught some fleeting expression on his face that was soft and unguarded and had struck right to the core of her.

Then, he had personally arranged to have Benji flown over. That had been a giveaway because, as thoughtful and considerate as he was as a boss, getting Benji over had been well beyond the call of duty, and lust.

She idly stroked behind Benji's ear and relaxed back in the deck chair. She could hear very distant sounds coming from the shore and, looking across, the glittering lights were like stars studded against the shoreline. The air was balmy and carried the fragrance of the ocean, salty and fresh.

She wondered how she could broach the subject of trying to make this wonderful thing they had together work.

How could he contemplate walking away from what they had so that he could embark on finding a woman who met a checklist but with whom he would probably have nothing in common?

Maybe if he hadn't confided in her… But he had, and he was a clever guy—clever enough to understand that, if he'd been affected by the past, it didn't mean all doors were closed. His head might say that, but she'd seen his heart, and his heart wouldn't agree.

Lost in swirling thoughts, but feeling ever more excited and hopeful with each passing moment, Caitlin was barely aware of Javier padding back across the deck until he subsided onto the lounger. When he looked at her there was a smile of satisfaction on his face. With only subdued lighting on the upper deck and the radiance of the moon, his beautiful face was all shadows and angles and thrillingly sexy.

'Good phone call?' Caitlin smiled and reached out to cover his hand with hers, moving to link their fingers, and for once not hiding the tenderness in her eyes.

'Excellent phone call. Isabella.'

'Really?'

'There's something you need to know, Caitlin.'

'What's that?' Her voice was wary and, as their eyes met, he smiled.

'Nothing for you to worry about, no need to look as though I'm about to tell you that the sky is falling down. It's about Isabella… There are certain things I omitted from the story, certain facts that… Okay, how shall I put it… were not within my remit to tell you, but I can tell you now because they've finally and terrifically been made public.'

'I'm intrigued.' She liked the sound of 'nothing for her to worry about'.

'As you know, for both myself and Isabella, our marriage was something that made sense and suited us both equally.'

'A marriage of convenience. Literally a business partnership.'

'Beyond the business practicalities, it suited us emotionally. Friends but not lovers, and so no emotional complications.'

'I'm still intrigued.'

'It suited Isabella because she's gay.'

Silence stretched between them, and Caitlin knew that her mouth had dropped open because this was the last thing she'd been expecting.

'As in…'

'As in the normal definition of the word,' Javier said wryly. 'She's had a partner for nearly three years and I've always known about her preferences. I was probably one of the first and the few she shared that intimate secret with, and I've obviously been duty-bound to keep it to myself, hence I've said nothing to you earlier.'

He was smiling now and looking into the distance. 'I've encouraged her over the years to come clean but she's been scared stiff at how her father might react and, when his health began deteriorating, even more apprehensive. There was also the matter of an extremely traditional board of directors who would have had to accept something they might have found a little unexpected, although I personally thought that she was over-apprehensive on that count. Time's moved on since the bad old days. But, largely, it was her father's possible reaction that pushed her into accepting our marriage of convenience.'

'What happened to change that?'

'Her girlfriend gave her an ultimatum, and Isabella

took a deep breath and did what she knew she should have done a long time ago—she told her father who, incidentally, is recovering extremely well and is already itching to get back to work.

'By the way, she sends her love and apologises profusely if you thought that she was messing you around. When she disappeared without warning on that wedding dress viewing day, it was because her girlfriend had run out of patience and contacted her to return to Spain to sort things out or else she wouldn't be there waiting in the shadows.'

'Wow.'

'You're shocked?'

'Surprised at you choosing to marry Isabella under those circumstances. That…that must have been a sacrifice for you, Javier. I know family bonds mean a lot, but still…'

'Oh, the marriage also suited me, quite aside from the family bonds, strong as those were.'

'How so?'

'Long story, Caitlin…' He hesitated but only momentarily. 'I inherit vineyards in Spain when I turn thirty-five, but only if I marry.' He grimaced. 'Getting hold of those vineyards means a great deal to me. Isabella would have been the perfect solution. As it stands, I have to find another suitable wife, and my timeline isn't exactly generous.'

'Another suitable wife…'

'Well, my parameters for marrying still stand, and now there's a sense of urgency to my search because time isn't going to stand still and wait for me to catch up.'

Caitlin stared. What a fool she had been. There was no door opening in his heart. What planet had she been on? He still wanted, and would only ever want, the sort of woman who would never make demands on him. Isabella would have been perfect, but in her absence he would find a suitably high-born Spanish woman who knew the rules of the game and would be content to be mistress of his empire without demanding love and attention.

Without demanding heart-to-heart chats…and giggling and laughter. And maybe just having sex to make babies, although clearly even that wasn't a prerequisite. He and Isabella would presumably have left the baby-making part to the doctors.

The simmering euphoria she had felt just moments before, when she had been so convinced that what Javier felt was more than just lust, evaporated like dew on a hot summer's morning. He'd told her that he wasn't into commitment, that what he wanted would always be a manufactured business arrangement without the complications of emotion. Instead of listening, she had eventually chosen to play with the fantasy that he didn't know himself as well as she knew him.

She had interpreted his behaviour and jumped to conclusions, but the hard truth was that all he wanted from her was the hot sex. He might have confided in her, they might have laughed together and she might have built her castles in the air based on those things, but Javier lived in a black-and-white world and love was never going to intrude. He was never going to be open to persuasion.

'You've gone quiet on me.'

Caitlin blinked and focused. 'It was very brave of Isabella to face up to her sexuality and tell her dad. It couldn't have been easy. I can understand why you're proud of her, because you care about her.'

'Why am I getting the feeling that something's going on under the surface here?'

Caitlin took a deep breath and grappled with a way forward. 'I guess I'm a diehard romantic after all,' she said quietly. 'I never thought your marriage was *that* much of a cold business arrangement.'

'Far from cold.'

'For you to be prepared to face a future without…without…a future without any semblance of… Where you'd be both living separate romantic lives…'

'Where are you going with this, Caitlin?'

'And then,' she murmured, 'to hear that the deal suited you because you want to inherit some vineyards when you already have wealth beyond imagining… And to hear you say that you're now time-pressured to find a candidate to fill the role of your wife—someone who doesn't expect anything other than to run your households while you go about your business having fun on the side, because fun on the side would never involve any emotional involvement…'

'Tell me what's going on here. I thought I was being honest with you.'

'You are. I just thought…'

'That somewhere along the line I was going to fall in love with Isabella and live happily ever after? Even though I told you that love and everything that goes with it wasn't for me?' He tilted his head to one side and looked at her narrowly.

Caitlin saw it. She saw the light bulb going off in his head as he joined the dots and worked out what was going on with her. The silence gathered around them as they stared at one another and Javier hissed a sigh and raked his fingers through his hair.

'Caitlin…'

'So, I was a fool.' She snatched the top she had earlier discarded and shoved it on.

'I thought I'd made it clear…'

'You did. Like I said, I was an idiot. I… I never thought in a million years that we would ever end up sleeping together, Javier.' She was as tense as a bowstring. What happens next? she wondered.

She hadn't originally planned to pour out her heart, but then again she hadn't expected to be confronted with information that challenged everything she'd clung to. She gritted her teeth and stuck her chin out at a defiant angle.

'But,' she said tightly, 'we did and, yes, you did warn me off, but I just didn't have the good sense to protect my heart.' She lowered her eyes because she didn't want to see his expression: appalled horror; mouth slack with dismay; frantic glances towards the nearest escape route…

'No,' she said with wrenching honesty. 'Maybe I didn't want to protect my heart or, if I did, I wanted you more for whatever little time we had together.'

'This is a conversation we shouldn't be having, *querida*.'

'Why not? And *don't* call me *querida*! *Querida* is the last thing I am to you!'

'Caitlin, let's not go there!'

'Why not? Because it's a scary place? Where's the point in not being honest with yourself?'

'I can think of a thousand reasons off the top of my head.'

'When we were together, Javier, I felt I saw something in you, *sensed* something in you—something that made me think that there was more between us than you're probably willing to admit.'

'I don't do emotion.'

'I have no idea what that means. You've never explained exactly what that means! How can someone not *do emotion*? You're not a robot!'

'Let's drop this.'

'It's time for me to hand in my resignation, Javier.'

Like an unstoppable train gathering momentum, there was no way she could stop now, and she didn't want to. She'd always planned to enjoy what she could of the guy she loved before walking away with her pride intact, but then the minute she had seen chinks in his armour everything had changed. She'd started to entertain the thought that she could change him. She'd started to believe that he would be able to see what they had as something deserving of a shot, as something more than just the fling he'd told her it was.

Surely no one was *immune* to emotion, the way he said he was? But he'd been prepared to marry Isabella and live a life devoid of any chance of real love. He was now prepared to marry some unknown, suitable woman and happily live his life in an emotional vacuum. Because he'd really meant what he'd told her about wanting a particular sort of woman—a woman who made sense, with no hearts and flowers attached to the relationship.

'Clearly, I was foolish. I thought you'd just never fallen in love with anyone before but that maybe, just maybe, what we had had changed that. When you offered to bring Benji over, I jumped to the conclusion that you must feel more than just lust, because you really wanted to do something you knew would make me happy. I couldn't have been more mistaken!'

It was cleansing, having her say after all this time bottling up what she felt. She could feel the weight lifting off her shoulders and realised that somewhere deep inside, when she got past the 'living in the moment' philosophy, she'd been terrifyingly aware of the day of reckoning lurking round the corner.

'It's a bit difficult to storm off when you're sitting on a yacht in the middle of the ocean, but I'll leave as soon as humanly possible.' Her voice was flat and hard.

Javier felt as though he'd just been hit with a sledgehammer when he'd least been expecting it. He'd been pleased with Isabella's news. She'd faced down her demons; every fear she'd had had proven unfounded and she'd been over the moon. He hadn't thought twice about sharing the news with Caitlin. Left to him, he would have told her from the very start, but of course it hadn't been his story to tell.

Now, when he reflected grimly, he could see that he hadn't been thinking *at all* when it came to Caitlin. He'd made a few perfunctory remarks, laying down his ground rules, but he'd been so busy enjoying himself, enjoying *her*, that he'd taken his eye off the ball big time.

He cast his mind back now to the way he'd dropped his guard, and paled, because it was almost as though he'd learnt nothing from the past. He'd lived in a ridiculous, manufactured bubble and forgotten all the principles of self-control he'd always lived by. He hadn't been himself, and he couldn't understand *why*, but the one thing he *did* understand was that she'd mistakenly read all sorts of things into his behaviour and he couldn't blame her.

He was man enough to accept the blame for the mess in which he now found himself. He'd drifted and, if he could pinpoint a moment when that drift had started, it was when he had seen her in her full glory twirling on a stool in a wedding dress for a wedding that wasn't to be.

The sight had knocked him for six and had lodged in his head like a burr, like something waiting to be released the minute the opportunity came along, and along had come that opportunity when the wedding had been called off.

And since then he'd ignored all alarm bells and red flags. He'd played truant from work for the first time in his life. He'd opened up about himself in ways he couldn't remember doing. *Was it any wonder that she had begun to feel all sorts of things about a relationship that had been a lot more casual for him?*

He thought back to the flash of consternation he had felt when he'd found out that she was a virgin, and the ease with which he had dismissed any concern that she might have been a lot more vulnerable emotionally than she'd stoutly announced. She'd implied that he wasn't her type, and he'd decided to go along with that, and not once had he bothered to reflect on whether that continued to hold true once they'd become truly intimate.

'Caitlin...' He raked his fingers through his hair and shifted.

'You don't have to say anything.'

'You made it clear that I wasn't the sort of guy you were looking for.' To his own ears, the protest sounded pathetic.

'You still aren't, but I've found out that hearts don't always play by the rules. I'm going to head in now.' She stood up and backed away from him. 'I'll get my things from your room and pack. I'll need to know about arrangements for returning to London.'

'I would say that I don't want you to resign but...'

'I was going to before I told you how I felt. I was going to walk away because it would have been impossible for me to carry on working for you.'

'You would have left me in the *lurch*?'

'Yes.'

'If I could promise you what you want…'

'I wouldn't believe you anyway,' Caitlin told him sharply. 'I know how the cards stack up now. Good luck finding whatever it is you're looking for so that you can get your vineyards.'

'I can arrange everything for tomorrow. No need for you to wait for a flight; my man will take you in my private jet. If you'd rather, I can even arrange an overnight stay in a hotel on the mainland should you find our arrangement here…er…somewhat uncomfortable.'

In a flash, Caitlin knew with biting bitterness where Javier was going with this. She'd outlived her usefulness by confessing that she loved him. That wasn't part of the game and never had been. Now he wanted her out as fast as possible. That hurt—really hurt.

'Good idea,' she said tightly. 'How long do I have?'

'I'm not rushing you off my yacht…'

'Of course you are,' Caitlin snapped dismissively, scooping up Benji and burrowing against him as she stared at Javier with simmering, edgy hostility. She lowered her eyes and gathered herself because he hadn't asked for this, and just because he wanted to get rid of her now didn't make him a monster. He just couldn't return her love and was dealing with what she had thrown at him the best he could.

She turned away to feel his hand circling her arm, tugging her gently back until she wanted to pass out from the nearness of him.

'Caitlin.' His voice was ragged, barely audible. 'You don't have to do this…'

'Do what?'

'Go. You don't have to go. We can pretend this conversation never happened.'

'Of course we can't,' she said flatly. 'And I wouldn't want to.' But there was a flare of triumph inside her because she knew then that, even if he didn't love her, he really, really *wanted* her. Maybe she wouldn't fade from his head as fast as all the others who had preceded her. It was scant comfort, but it was some.

She tugged her arm free and backed away, still looking at him, while Benji threatened to let the side down by leaping out of her arms and making a fool of himself by wanting to play with the guy staring at her.

Javier broke the silence. 'I'll arrange a hotel. And someone to take you to the mainland in the speedboat. Won't be longer than an hour at most.' He flushed darkly.

'Perfect.' Caitlin smiled tersely. 'And then you can move on with your life, Javier, and thank your lucky stars that you successfully dodged a bullet.'

'And you?'

'Believe it or not, when you've lived the life that I have, you can overcome anything.'

What a lie, but she left him with that thought as she spun round on her heels and walked away.

CHAPTER TEN

JAVIER STARED OUT of the window of his vast office down to a crowded London street several storeys beneath him. The office was empty. Why wouldn't it be? It was Saturday, it was a little past five on a sunny afternoon and most people with anything resembling a life were out there enjoying what passed for the great outdoors in London. The parks would be crammed, the cafés would be heaving, the pavements spilling over with crowds drinking and enjoying the ongoing fine weather.

He missed her. For a few days after she'd left, he'd gone back over what she had told him and had picked apart every word spoken, every admission of how she felt, every valiant declaration of love. Then, for a few more days, he'd told himself that she'd been spot on when she'd said that he'd dodged a bullet because the last thing he wanted was the sort of love and romance that was always riddled with complication and disappointment.

Javier grimaced now as he thought back to the optimistic dates he had set in motion—potential candidates. They'd been easy to source, because he knew almost everyone who belonged to the elite social set in which he'd always mixed in Spain. He'd had one conversation with Isabella and the rest had been a matter of the grapevine. It didn't matter about the marriage that had never been.

All that mattered was that the most eligible guy in Europe was single and ready to settle down.

He'd been on one date and had backed off after an hour of surreptitious watch-looking and thoughts of Caitlin that wouldn't leave his head. He'd told himself that he just needed a bit more time. He knew what was good for him, knew that love was not something he wanted, or indeed was even capable of subscribing to. It was good that she was no longer in his life because that inevitably would have led to demands for things he couldn't give her.

What was the point of lessons learnt if they got thrown down the drain just because he got caught on the back foot? He wasn't built for love and that was the end of it. So it wasn't a case of any genie let out of any bottle, no wayward emotion that accounted for his restless nights and lack of concentration at work. It was just that he needed a bit more time.

But how he remembered the way she smiled…the way she laughed…the way her blue eyes had lingered on him…the flush in her cheeks after they'd made love and the way she could touch him so that in seconds his body went up in flames.

And he also remembered stuff he maybe wanted to forget: the way he'd felt comfortable talking to her; the way they'd lain in bed in the warm afterglow of good sex and he'd talked to her about anything and everything.

He'd intellectually accepted the sort of woman he would need to replace Isabella—the wife who understood everything he had to offer and accepted it. It was the same mental picture he'd planted in his head from a young age, when he'd understood the dangers of loving too much, loving so much that it made a person weak instead of strong. She would be wealthy in her own right, able to manage the life he led without need for guidance, because his work life would have to remain uninterrupted. She would be happy to enjoy the fruits of his vast fortune without nagging for attention, clinging or needing validation. She would be as emotionally independent as he was. The last thing she would want was *romance*.

But, rubbing alongside that mental image was the reality of a woman who was the complete opposite to that. A woman who wanted and needed love and devotion. A woman who hugged, cuddled and snuggled, and did all the things he'd always made sure to discourage in past relationships.

And even before they'd become lovers…

She was a woman who grounded him and could tease him out of his stress. He'd accepted it all as part and parcel of her proficiency at her job but it had been a whole lot more than that. While he'd been busy thinking about the boundaries he'd set down, supposedly never to be breached, he'd failed to realise that she'd spent the weeks, months and years slowly breaching every one of them in small, incremental steps.

He thought of the times when she'd worked late, when they'd shared a takeaway and she'd somehow managed to convince him not to do an all-nighter. Thought of the anecdotes about Benji, the softness in her voice when she'd talked about him, the way that softness had pierced into the heart of him and lodged there.

And then later, when he'd found out about her childhood…everything had come together. The warmth had flooded him then; he'd felt tenderness. Realisation came slowly because he fought it tooth and nail. He didn't want to admit, even to himself, that love had crept up on him, ambushing all the self-control he had thought would always protect him.

But all those dots being joined up would not allow him the luxury of pretending that he felt nothing for her. What he felt was the despair of denying the love that had blossomed inside him, eating up all his objections and turning him into the kind of guy who closed his laptop and stopped caring when he next opened it.

Javier stared down blindly at the busy roads below and felt a sickening churning in his stomach, the pain of turning his back on something he should have grabbed with both hands.

What the hell happened now? That was what he was thinking. How did he approach the situation? Did he leave it? Climb back into his ivory tower and tell himself that it was for the best?

Nearly a month had gone by! She'd said her piece and disappeared off the face of the earth. He hadn't even had a company contact him for a reference. Was she looking for another job? Was she still living in London, come to it?

Had she turned her back on him for ever?

He had her mobile number, and he knew that he could simply call, but he hadn't...*had he*? He'd lost count of the number of times over the passing weeks when he'd looked at that number in his phone and backed away from calling it while he'd stupidly carried on the pretence that he was still in charge of his emotions.

For the first time in his life, Javier was scared: scared of opening up to her about how he felt; scared of *not* opening up to her about how he felt; scared of emotions that were so big he barely knew how to handle them or what to do with them; scared at the thought of a future without her in it.

And, most of all, scared of making a move only for her to turn her back and walk away from him as he sickeningly suspected she would. She'd laid her cards on the table, and so had he, and he doubted she would want anything to do with him, having been firmly knocked back and shown the door.

He had never been a guy to succumb to creating scenarios in his head but Javier now found that creating scenarios in his head was just about the only thing he seemed capable of doing. He had no idea how to approach her and he knew that, with every passing day, the chances of her listening to a word he had to say became more and more remote.

Fed up with the state of indecision which had been his state of mind for weeks, Javier swung round, picked up his mobile and began scrolling through it while walking to the door.

It felt good to take charge of the situation and, in the end, what would be would be...

Caitlin hit Kensington Gardens at pace because she'd been held up every step of the way, and it had sounded urgent when Angie had made the arrangement for them to meet. Which, frankly, wasn't like her friend at all. She was the most laid-back person on the face of the earth. So, when she had called the day before and asked her in a hurry whether they could meet at a designated spot in the park at a designated time, and that *it was important*, Caitlin had been instantly concerned. She'd asked questions, but in the background she could hear dogs barking, so she hadn't been surprised that few of her questions were answered because Angie was in a rush.

Anyway, she'd been glad that the conversation had

been brief. There'd been no time for Angie to pry into how her time out had gone because Caitlin wasn't sure how good she would be at pretending it was all fine and dandy in the world.

It wasn't. The past few weeks had been hell. Like an addict with the supply of the love drug she had overdosed on severed without warning, the withdrawal was agony; no other word for it. She hadn't even been able to get her act together to start job hunting. She was relying on her savings to get her through the temporary apathy which was all-consuming.

It made her desperately sad to think that this was the sort of time when a daughter might flee back to her mum, but in the absence of any family all she could do was try and fix herself with no shoulder to cry on.

She tried to remember every passing expression that had crossed Javier's face when she had blurted out how she felt about him. When her memory refused to play along, she became adept at filling in the gaps herself: horror; dismay; probably revulsion, which he had hidden well, because he would have been conscious not to hurt her feelings. Still, he had swept her out of his life like some debris he'd needed to clear asap, and that hurt, however much she tried to rationalise it.

Had she made a mistake in pouring out her heart? That had not been the original intention but, the minute she had got it into her head that his feelings for her ran deeper than he thought, she had thrown caution to the winds and started building all sorts of stupid fairy-tale castles in her head. She had been so blinded by her own love, and so heady at the thought that what they had was the real thing, that she had conveniently forgotten everything he had said about the sort of person he wanted in his life until that call from Isabella had come through. That person was not her. He had to marry, but never to a woman like her, because his emotions she'd thought she'd tapped into had been a mirage.

She hadn't heard a peep out of him since leaving his yacht and that hurt. Yet why would he contact her? What would he say? That he was sorry she'd misread the situation, and *have a good life*?

She sprinted from the bus across the busy road, tugging Benji, who was looking around him with ears cocked, tail wagging, tongue lolling and a sprint in his ageing step. The change of scenery had got him going and he was looking madly around as she stooped to let him off the lead. He would follow her; he always did.

At five in the afternoon, it was still hot and the place was packed. And she was late, by ten minutes. She kept looking around as she headed to their meeting place, making sure Benji didn't decide to start exploring their new, exciting environment.

She knew exactly where to go because she and her friend had met many times in the same spot over the years, Angie for her dog walking, and she with Benji, because the company was great. But when she peered through the crowds, there was no sign of Angie, and she frowned, tapping into the message on her phone to make sure she'd got the place right, when she heard someone calling from behind her.

They were calling for Benji. And it wasn't Angie's voice. In fact, it took a couple of seconds for Caitlin even to realise that it was a man's voice, and even longer for her to realise who the man in question was.

She turned around slowly. Shock made her numb. She could barely breathe and her thoughts clouded over as she balanced a fine line between disbelief and dawning realisation.

Javier. After no word from him for weeks—radio silence. She'd poured out her heart to him and, not only had he politely sent her on her way, but he hadn't seen fit to send so much as a text to ask her whether she was okay. It was obvious that he hadn't given a jot about her in the end. He'd cared *a lot* about the sex, and he'd been affectionate enough when they'd been together, but that affection had been generated by the physical relationship they'd shared and, when the physicality had ended, so had the affection.

She felt the colour mount in her cheeks as she looked at Javier in the distance, her treacherous dog bounding towards him like a long-lost pal. He wasn't walking towards her and he was dangling...*were those sausages?...* to tempt Benji, who would have needed next to no temptation, because he had developed a shameful attachment to her ex-boss.

Caitlin felt the shock and disbelief coalesce into white-hot rage. How dared he, after all this time, seek her out via her *lily-livered dog*? How dared he *just show up* without warning? How dared he ambush her when she was still fragile and hurting and desperate to forget all about him?

Yet, on one very important level, she was aware of that dark current of excitement underneath her anger, an excitement that had continued to simmer, unabated, all through her sadness and disillusionment. Which only made her more furious.

As she looked, he dangled a sausage before tossing it to Benji. His eyes were fastened on her. God, it was unfair how drop-dead gorgeous he still looked. Couldn't he have gone downhill in the interim—stacked on some weight, lost all his hair? Could he have done anything, become *anything*, that could no longer hurt her the way he was hurting her right now?

Why was he here? That was the question that raged inside her as she remained glued to the spot for a few seconds. Had he come to try and get her back into bed? Or maybe her replacement wasn't living up to expectation and he actually thought that, with some time now between them, he could woo her back into her old job and they could both pretend that nothing had happened between them. Either way, she was going to put him straight on both counts!

That would mean walking over there on her leaden feet. Benji was showing no sign of returning to base camp. He was zooming around Javier with crazy fervour and Caitlin lacked the nerve to yell for him to come back, mostly knowing that there was a good chance she would be ignored. Besides, people would stare. A lot of people were already surreptitiously staring at Javier. He had that effect on other people, male and female alike.

Caitlin propelled herself forward and, the closer she got to where Javier was reaching into a bag to produce another treat, the more her heartbeat quickened. Seeing him again was like seeing him for the first time—the time when she had walked into his office for the interview that would change her life and had forgotten how to breathe because she'd never seen anyone so beautiful.

'What are you doing here?' were her opening words as she pulled to a stop in front of him and glared, first at him and then at Benji. 'How did you know where I would be?'

'I phoned your doggy friend.'

'She had no right to tell you!'

'It's a public place, and besides—'

'Besides *what*? And stop giving Benji those sausages! He's not allowed them! Did you purposefully come here armed with treats for my dog because you knew he wouldn't be able to resist? That I would have to come over here and talk to you? Because I don't want to talk to you, Javier. I've done enough talking to you to last a lifetime!'

Caitlin looked away quickly because she could feel tears begin to prick the back of her eyes. She stooped, reached for Benji's collar and began putting his lead back on. She was only aware of Javier stooping to her level when she felt his shadow on her and the warmth of his body so close to hers that she could have reached out and stroked his beautiful face with no effort at all.

She looked up and her blue, glassy eyes collided with deep, dark ones; she felt a jolt of agonising awareness.

'I was afraid that, if I called you, you would refuse to see me,' Javier murmured in a low, shaky voice. 'And, Caitlin, I needed to see you.'

'I'm not falling back into bed with you, Javier, and I'm not returning to work for you as though nothing's happened because you miss my skill set. I said that when I walked away weeks ago, and nothing's changed since then.'

She forced herself to stand, to break the electric connection between them. He remained where he was, stooping at her feet and idly rubbing behind Benji's ear, who dug in his canine heels when she tugged the lead.

Javier, playing with Benji, could feel her hostile eyes on him and he couldn't blame her. She hadn't asked to see him and, now that he had shown up, she wanted him gone.

Would it have been easier if he hadn't been such a blind fool for so long? If he had tried to see her sooner? Was it possible even to begin to fill the hole left behind in those weeks of stubborn silence on his part? And how could he begin to explain to her that, when he'd lived a lifetime being rigid, it had become the only thing he knew?

She'd fallen in love with him, but love could turn to hostile resentment at the flick of a switch, and he had deliberately flicked that switch weeks ago when he had scurried away from her declarations faster than a rat leaving a sinking ship. How could he begin to explain just how much things had changed for him? He could barely look at her.

'Tell your mistress,' he half-whispered unsteadily to Benji, who was panting in anticipation of something more exciting than conversations, 'that I love her.'

He remained where he was but raised his head to look at her.

Caitlin drew in a sharp breath. What could she read in those dark, fathomless eyes? She was scared to trust her instinct, which had spectacularly let her down before, but she had stopped tugging at Benji's lead and she found it hard to tear her eyes away from Javier. He said something to Benji in such a low voice that it was a strain to hear, and whatever he'd whispered was gluing her to the spot.

'What did you just say?' she asked tightly. Her blue eyes were narrowed and suspicious as he slowly stood up so that now he was gazing down at her, his handsome face darkly flushed. 'Because I'm done with you feeding Benji sausages.'

'I said that I love you.'

Caitlin loosed a laugh of pure disbelief. In the space of

a few weeks, he'd gone from the guy who'd been relieved to see her walk away to the guy who suddenly *loved* her?

'And pigs fly,' she shot back. 'I don't need this. I don't want to talk to you!'

She spun round and, damn it, tears pricked the back of her eyes again. She yanked at Benji and began striding off, half-dragging the stubborn, resistant dog, knowing that Javier was following her and not quite sure how to deal with that.

Why was her reluctant heart yearning to hear what he had to say? Was she a glutton for punishment?

'Please, my darling, please let me talk. I'm begging you...'

'Don't!'

She stopped dead in her tracks.

'There's a tree over there. Let's go sit under it for five minutes. Let me say what I have to say and then, if you tell me to go, I'll walk away and you'll never be bothered by me again.'

Of course she was going to walk away! She refused to let her heart get the better of her head this time...

'Five minutes, then,' she said warily, turning round and walking at speed to the shady tree, while her heart picked up pace and her pulses began to race. She sat down and tried to focus on Benji while Javier sat at a respectable distance.

When she reluctantly and finally looked at him, her heart constricted, because he looked miserable and uncertain, and those were two things she had never seen in his repertoire before.

'I let you go,' Javier said hoarsely. 'And I should never have done that.'

'Because you miss the sex?' Caitlin mocked, but her

heart was doing it again—beating like a sledgehammer and sending stupid thoughts racing through her head.

'Because I love you, *querida.*'

'You don't love me,' she said fiercely. 'And I told you *not* to call me that!'

'I understand why you might not want to believe me...'

'I poured my heart out to you and you were nothing but embarrassed for me—and then you got me the first ride back to London—so no, I don't believe a word you say.'

'Caitlin...'

'Are you going to deny that?'

'Like I said, I was an idiot. I... I didn't believe in love. That was something meant for other people, fools who got taken in by fairy tales only to wind up disenchanted and a hell of a lot poorer. My father rushed into a relationship that cost him dear. He wasn't there for me when I needed him because he got lost in his own grief, his own uncontrollable emotions. He never saw a son who was hurting. I vowed I would never let my emotions blind me. Duty and eventually a marriage of convenience was what was in store for me, and I liked the predictability of something that made sense.'

He raked his fingers through his hair.

'Marrying Isabella made sense. It killed two birds with one stone. It sorted out her dilemma and it gave me the wife I needed to get the vineyards I wanted—which by the way I wanted because they hold happy memories of my childhood with my mother. I know it sounds ruthless that I was pursuing an inheritance but...most people aren't like you. Your childhood experiences... Somehow they didn't make you hard, bitter, I don't even know how—'

'If I could have had that protective covering,' Caitlin

snapped through gritted teeth, 'do you think I would have ended up where I did?'

'I like where you ended up. I like where *we* ended up. I like the softness inside you, the honesty, the lack of guile. I think I always did. I just never acknowledged it.'

'Don't you *dare* say anything you don't mean,' Caitlin warned shakily, and Javier reached daringly to stroke her cheek, encouraged when she didn't push his hand away.

'I'm not. Everything I'm telling you is coming straight from my heart. From the start, you appealed to me in ways I never consciously registered. When Isabella broke off the relationship, it wasn't my intention to sleep with you but, looking back now, it feels as though fate had finally decided that I need to wake up and start seeing what it felt like to jump into the thing called life.'

'Fate came for me long before,' Caitlin haltingly responded. 'I always had a crush on you and it just didn't go away, even when Isabella came on the scene. I kept thinking that you getting married would open my eyes up to how stupid I was, but I still couldn't look at you without my whole body going up in flames.'

'I wish I'd known…'

'Why?'

'Because we might have started this thing between us, this amazing, wonderful thing, long ago—and maybe I wouldn't have wasted my time with women who came and went, in a mindset where the only relationship that seemed feasible was one that made sense. Nothing makes sense about the way I feel about you, *mi corazón*, and I never knew just how much I like it that way. When we were together… I forgot everything.'

'Even work.'

'Especially work. All I wanted was to be with you. I

kidded myself that it was all about the mind-blowing sex, but there were times, so many times, when I looked at you and in my gut I knew that there was so much more to what I was feeling than lust.'

Every ounce of hesitation in Caitlin vanished at the utter sincerity in Javier's eyes and she reached forward and leaned into him. The cool feel of his mouth against hers ignited an explosion inside her that went straight from her head to between her thighs, and she sighed into his mouth before pulling back to trace the outline of his lips.

'It's what made me say what I did,' she confessed, hand flat against his chest. She stared past him thoughtfully. 'I thought that common sense would protect me from you, but I was wrong, and I realised that pretty quickly after we became lovers. And then… I sensed more than just lust. Maybe I was picking up some of the vibes you didn't know you were giving off, but the minute you offered to bring Benji over… Well, my imagination went into overdrive.'

'You came out with everything you felt.'

'It was a very comprehensive confession.' Caitlin grimaced.

'And my knee-jerk reaction was to run away.' He sighed and, when he kissed her, it was slowly and tenderly and their noses touched when he next spoke, voice low and quiet. 'But over the past few weeks I began to read all the writing that had been on the wall for so long, began to realise just how much I'd fallen in love with you and just what a fool I'd been to deny what was in my heart. I had no idea how I was going to get up the courage to come and see you, but then I figured that Benji might work as my intermediary.'

'He seems to have been a cheap trick when it comes to sharing his allegiances!' Caitlin laughed.

'So what I want to say…' Javier pulled back and looked at her gravely.

'What you want to say is…?'

'Will you marry me?'

Caitlin felt the damned tears again but this time tears of joy. There was no holding her back this time. She flung her arms around his neck, buried her face into him and whispered against him,

'Yes! Yes, yes, yes! My darling, wonderful Javier, for ever…'

* * * * *

NEWLYWED
ENEMIES

JACKIE ASHENDEN

MILLS & BOON

A day may come where there will be
a car chase in one of my books, a day of gunfights
and explosions and all the side characters,
but it is not this day.

CHAPTER ONE

FLORA MCINTYRE WANTED nothing from life.

Nothing except the total ruination of Apollo Constantinides.

She stood on the other side of his vast antique oak desk—placed in lordly splendour near the window of his London office—and watched with some satisfaction as he stared at the photos she'd laid down in front of him.

They were all grainy images—she'd made sure they looked grainy—of his office, of him and her in various positions. Compromising positions. In some he had his hand on her waist, as if he was holding her, while in others he was bent over her, looking as if he was kissing her. In one she was sitting on the desk and he was crouched in front her—one stilettoed foot on his knee—while his hand cupped her bare calf, as if he was stroking it.

The images told the tale of a torrid affair they'd been having with each other, which was exactly what Flora had hoped.

Eventually, after an aeon of icy silence, Apollo lifted his head and looked at her, his dark green eyes blazing with barely contained fury. 'Where did these come from?'

He was the most coldly controlled man she'd ever met,

so for him to betray anger meant he was truly in a titanic rage.

How satisfying.

Flora schooled her expression to show nothing but concern. 'I was sent them anonymously.'

Apollo looked back down at them for a moment, muttered a curse, shoved back his chair and stood. He turned his back on her, staring out the windows to the London skyline beyond.

It had taken her six months of careful planning to get the photos, and then another couple of weeks to choose the ones that looked the most incriminating. The ones that would appear to indicate that Apollo Constantinides—billionaire investor, Nobel-nominated, well-known philanthropist, winner of various awards for his ethical business practices, including landmark sexual harassment policies—was having an affair. With his PA.

Apollo Constantinides, who'd just got engaged to Violet Standish, head of a global charity aimed at helping women who had survived such crimes as domestic violence, sexual violence, trafficking and drug abuse. Violet's charity had won awards, too, and the news of their engagement had been the subject of much positive press.

Sadly for Apollo, Flora had just torpedoed said engagement, and she didn't feel a single shred of regret about it. Especially when she knew for a fact that it wasn't a love match, but a business arrangement. In fact, Flora had often wondered if Apollo was even capable of such a soft emotion as love.

He was a hard man, blunt to the point of offensiveness—his commitment to honesty was total. He was also cold, ruthless and utterly determined to get what he wanted. Really, she was doing Violet Standish a favour, even if the engagement was purely for strategic business reasons. Violet would soon learn that she'd married a shark, not a man, and Flora wouldn't wish that on her own worst enemy.

She glanced down at the photos again and gave herself a mental pat on the back.

The photos were all part of the plan she'd put into motion years ago, after her beloved father, David, had taken his own life, having lost everything in an infamous Ponzi scheme run by Apollo's own father, Stavros Constantinides.

That Stavros had been sent to jail and died there wasn't justice enough for Flora. Not for the pain her mother, Laura, had endured, after David had selfishly taken the easy way out. Not for the years of living on the poverty line, because her mother had refused all offers of compensation, calling it 'blood money'. Not for how she'd been left alone—physically, due to the two jobs Laura had to take on, and emotionally, due to her mother's grief. Laura had eventually died of cancer far too young. Cancer she'd ignored the signs of because she was too tired and too broken to care about her own health.

Not for the powerlessness Flora had felt after her father's suicide, then watching her mother slowly get sicker and sicker, knowing there was nothing she could do to help her.

Not for a life bled dry of hope, happiness and the promise of a better future.

No. The only justice for Flora was the total and complete annihilation of everything Apollo Constantinides cared about.

Because while Stavros might be dead, his son was still alive, and his son was the man who'd convinced Flora's father to invest in Stavros's scheme in the first place. It didn't matter that Apollo had turned his father in. It didn't matter that subsequently he'd given compensation to all those affected by the scheme, and then tried to rehabilitate the family name with his ethical business practices, and philanthropic donations. It didn't matter that he and Violet had been jointly nominated for a Nobel Peace Prize, for their charitable work in human rights and, most importantly, the rights of women globally.

As far as Flora was concerned, the only thing that mattered was never feeling that sense of powerlessness, of helplessness, ever again. And she would do that by channelling every ounce of her rage into making sure Apollo lost everything. His engagement to Violet would be the first casualty.

Flora stood quietly before his desk, watching his tall, powerful form as he directed the full force of his fury to the cityscape beyond the glass, and allowed herself a small, private smile.

She'd spent three years at Helios Investments, his investment company, initially as a junior secretary in the HR department, before steadily working her way up the chain, until she'd finally landed the position she'd been aiming for. Apollo's PA.

She'd been in that position for a year now, gaining his trust, making herself indispensable. He had no knowledge of her links to Stavros's scheme. He didn't know who she was—her parents hadn't been legally married, so she'd kept her mother's name as her own legal surname—and she'd make sure he never would.

Hiding those links hadn't been difficult, despite him being a very sharp, astute and intelligent man. After all, no one was particularly interested in the family history of one of his employees, even if that employee was his personal PA. She'd passed all the stringent background checks he ran on all his staff, signed the NDAs that were mandatory, and no one had said anything to her.

It had been easy.

There was, however, one small problem with Apollo Constantinides. One teeny, tiny issue she'd never completely managed to solve. And that was the fact that he was literally the hottest man she'd ever had the misfortune of meeting, and every time he got close—every time he even looked at her—her heart would beat fast and her mouth would go dry.

She hated it.

She hated his beauty.

She hated him.

Six foot three, with short black hair. Eyes the colour of a deep, dark jungle, with winged soot-black brows. A straight nose that harkened back to his Greek heritage, and a mouth that haunted her dreams. He was also intensely charismatic, with the sort of authority that made emperors kneel. He held the whole world in the palm of his hand and he knew it.

And that had made every one of those compromising photos she'd taken an enormous trial, because of how near she had to get to him. It had been a test of both her resolve and her ability to dissemble, but she'd aced it, if she did say so herself.

Not that there was any doubt. Working with him as closely as she did was its own form of exposure therapy and, after those photos, she could safely say she was now fully inoculated.

Apollo turned abruptly from the window and, despite herself, despite all her bracing thoughts of how impervious she was to him, her breath caught as she was pinned by his intense green gaze.

He was in her favourite suit today—dark grey wool, tailored perfectly to his powerful figure—and a plain white shirt. His silk tie was a myriad of different greens, reflecting the colour of his eyes.

'This is unacceptable,' he said, his normally cool, deep voice hot with leashed anger. 'I want a full investigation as to where they came from.'

Flora made sure none of her considerable satisfaction showed. 'Don't worry,' she said smoothly. 'I already have that in hand.'

'What about online? Have the pictures reached the wider public yet?'

'I have the tech department looking into that right now.' She adjusted her expression, so it showed the appropriate amount of concern. 'Unfortunately I think some of them have made their way into online spaces.' And they had. She'd posted them on various platforms herself. 'And once it's out on the web...'

A muscle in the side of Apollo's impressive jaw twitched. 'Get IT onto it. I want the pictures taken down. All of them. Immediately.' He turned back to the desk again. 'How is this even possible?' He leaned forward, hands gripping the edge of the desk, staring at the photos as if he was trying to light them on fire with the power of his mind alone. Which, given his ruthless determination when he wanted something, could very well happen. 'These were taken in this office.'

'It seems so,' Flora said carefully. 'Perhaps they used

a telephoto lens or planted a small camera somewhere. Those things are pretty small these—'

'What are people saying?' His gaze came to hers once more, a laser focus that always managed to steal her breath away. 'What about the media? What's PR doing?'

He did not, she noted, ask how she felt, which, considering she was also in the photos, was yet another black mark against his name.

'I've informed them.' She kept her tone cool and controlled. 'I also made sure they knew that, despite the photos, there is nothing going on between us.'

And there wasn't. Apollo was a model employer. He'd never crossed any boundaries with her, never betrayed the slightest hint that he was even aware she was a woman, let alone anything else.

It was almost disappointing in a way. Ever since she'd started work at Helios, she'd been looking for hard evidence that he was the same man who'd convinced her father to buy into Stavros' scheme, yet she hadn't found any. That didn't mean it wasn't there though.

David had always been looking for get-rich-quick shortcuts, and had been convinced by Apollo that Stavros's investment scheme was legitimate, no matter how much it had looked too good to be true.

But then that was Apollo Constantinides. He'd made an art out of looking too good to be true. When his father had gone to jail, Apollo had somehow avoided a sentence himself. He'd acted contrite in the interviews he'd given in the news media. Portraying himself as also a victim of his father's lies, garnering sympathy with his blunt honesty and his willingness to offer compensation.

Flora knew the truth though. The only thing he really

cared about was his reputation, and that was it. People were there to either be used to help polish that reputation or they were seen as hindrances and got rid of. She'd personally seen him fire a man who'd been using the company credit card to pay for a few little treats of his family. It had been wrong, yes, but the amounts of money spent had been small, and the man had confessed. In fact, he'd pleaded with Apollo to let him stay, but Apollo had fired him with the same cold indifference with which he treated most people.

'There is nothing going on between us whatsoever,' Apollo agreed, glancing down at the photos scattered over his desk, dark brows drawing down into a scowl. 'Inform Violet,' he added. 'She needs to—'

He broke off abruptly, dug into his pocket and pulled out his phone. His scowl deepened as glanced at the screen, but he hit the answer button all the same. 'Violet.' His tone softened as he said her name. 'Yes, I've seen the pictures. You must know that Flora and I have nothing to do—' He stopped, sent a furious glance at Flora, before turning to the windows once again. 'What?' he asked.

Flora moved over to the desk and began to gather the pictures up slowly, keeping half an ear on the conversation with Violet.

'I realise what people will say,' Apollo was murmuring. 'But my PR department is excellent, you know that. It'll all blow over and… Yes, I understand the media is harder on women. Which is why I'll… What?' He was silent, but Flora could feel the rage emanating from him like an icy breeze straight off a glacier. 'We can change the optics,' he went on after a moment. 'You can't possibly let this—'

Flora stole a glance at him.

He stood gazing out of the windows, his face in profile, as perfect as that of a king on a coin. But that muscle jumped again in the side of his jaw.

'Yes,' he bit out, his tone now icy. 'I see. Well naturally I wouldn't want anything to compromise the integrity of your business… Fine. Will you let me do the honourable thing at least? You can play up the part of being the wronged woman. Yes… Yes… Good. I'll send over the press release beforehand.'

Flora couldn't resist another private smile. Sounded as if Violet was breaking things off, which was exactly what she'd hoped. The world needed to see just how cold and ruthless he was, and she would expose him.

She'd make the world see the truth about Apollo Constantinides if it was the last thing that she did.

Apollo couldn't believe it.

Violet had broken off their engagement.

Their wedding was supposed to be the icing on the cake, the crowning achievement of all the work he'd put into rehabilitating the Constantinides name. Marriage to Violet Standish, head of one of the world's leading philanthropic institutions, was going to be the perfect union of two pillars of the global community.

When they'd announced their engagement—after the NDAs and other contracts had been signed, naturally—the press had had a field day. His PR department had told him that faith in the Constantinides name had never been so high and Helios's stocks were through the roof. Everyone was totally for their 'ship', sharing opinions and photos and memes on every internet platform there was. Apollo had been thoroughly satisfied with the optics. He hadn't even minded the press calling their partnership 'ViLo'.

But now…

Violet had been adamant that their union could not possibly go ahead. Associating herself with a 'cheater' would irreparably damage her charity's brand, and considering it was a charity dedicated to helping women from all walks of life and in different situations, he couldn't blame her.

Except right now, he very much wanted *someone* to blame.

And then that someone to *pay*.

His jaw ached from clenching it, all his muscles tight with fury. He didn't know how those pictures had been taken from inside his office—someone must have sneaked in a camera somehow—but all of those images were totally innocent. The strap on Flora's shoe had broken, so he'd told her to sit on the desk. Then he'd kneeled in front of her to try and fix it, that was all. His hand cupping her calf was to steady her because she'd been ticklish, it had *not* been a caress.

Then, that one of him sitting back in his chair while she bent over him… She'd said there had been a spot on his shirt, and he'd let her double check the cotton was clean, because he'd been busy talking on the phone.

All the pictures looked compromising, yes, but they weren't. He hadn't touched her like *that*, and he never would.

Someone had set him up.

Apollo bit back the growl that formed in his throat as he furiously went over possibilities. An employee with a grudge? Could be. He was a demanding boss, and plenty of people didn't like that, even though they were paid handsomely for it. A spurned lover? Probably not. He hadn't indulged in lovers since his engagement, and even before that he only slept with women who wanted what he did—sex and nothing more.

A business rival? That was very possible. Helios was, after all, a global company, and there were those who still remembered his father transgressions.

Not that the question of who or even why mattered in the greater scheme of things.

He'd worked too hard, for too long retrieving the Constantinides name from the gutter his father had thrown it in, and he wasn't going to let some nameless fool use clumsily staged photos to throw it back.

Taking a couple of silent breaths to get his fury under control, he turned from the window.

Flora was gathering up the photos on his desk with careful hands, her expression, as usual, impassive. Over the year he'd had her as his PA, he'd found her not only to be cool, calm, collected, but also extremely competent. An excellent employee, who never complained about the amount of work he gave her—and it was a lot of work, he was a very busy man.

Today she was in her normal PA uniform of a plain black pencil skirt and plain white blouse, buttoned all the way up. Her black hair was smooth and sleek, coiled into a neat bun on the top of her head, and she radiated no-nonsense competence. He'd never seen her with a hair out of place or look flustered in any way. She was as serene as a swan, the best PA he'd ever had.

Even now, even with those pictures of herself in all those positions, she seemed unflappable. No doubt she'd weather it with her usual calm.

It was different for him. He had more to lose than she did.

'We will need to draft and send a press release,' he bit out. 'Violet has called off the engagement.'

No expression of shock moved over Flora's delicate features. She was, as ever, perfectly composed. 'I'm sorry to hear that, sir,' she said. 'How quickly will you need a draft?'

She'd always called him 'sir', even though he'd never insisted. It had never bothered him, but today, for some reason, it got under his skin, as did her entire cool manner.

Wasn't she concerned about those pictures? Didn't it matter to her? Not even for her own sake?

'As soon as possible.' He kept rigid control over his own tone and expression. It would not do to betray just how furious he was. His emotions were kept under lock and key; as he'd learned, there was no room for them in business. 'You do not seem unduly concerned, Flora,' he noted coolly. 'And you should be. This is a serious problem, and it involves you.'

'Yes, I understand that, sir.' She gave an elegant little shrug. 'But there's not much I can do about it. The photos are in the public arena and it will be next to impossible to get them all taken down.'

Again, she said it all with zero emphasis, as if her own reputation and his good name were of no importance to her.

'I don't care how impossible or otherwise it is,' he snapped icily, trying to keep the lid on his temper. 'I want them gone.'

'Of course, sir,' she murmured, long black lashes veiling her gaze.

Was she placating him? If so, that was a mistake. He hated being managed. 'I will not have the Constantinides

name dragged in the mud,' he said, insistent. 'I want whoever is responsible for these pictures found.'

'Naturally, sir.' She collected the photos into a neat
little stack, then began sliding them back into their en-
velope.

Every moment was precise, calm and controlled, and
for some reason he found that extremely aggravating.
'Leave them,' he snapped. 'I will be handing them on
to the police.'

'I'm quite happy to—'

'No, I will do it.' He really was having difficulty keeping the annoyance from his voice, which was concerning.
Normally he had no problems mastering himself. Then
again, the potential crumbling of the Constantinides good
name was not a normal situation. 'Since the pictures concern you and I,' he continued, 'we'll need an explanation
for them as soon as possible. Now, in fact. Violet and I
have agreed that I will break off the engagement, and I
won't have her waiting.'

Flora's eyes, the dark charcoal grey of river stones,
gave nothing away. 'What do you suggest regarding ex-
planations?'

'Denial will only stir up more fuss.' Which was true.
He'd observed that when his father's investment scheme
had collapsed. Stavros had kept up his protestations of
innocence, that the scheme was perfectly legitimate, all
the way to court—and then all the way to jail. It had made
the media circus of the trial more intense, the sensational
suicide of one of his victims adding more fuel to the fire.

Apollo would not make the same mistake. He was
adept at manipulating his public image—he'd learned in
a hard school after all—and the best way to deal with a

media blaze was to deprive it of oxygen. Either that, or encourage the wind to turn, so the flames burned in the opposite direction.

Unfortunately, Flora was likely correct, the pictures would be impossible to take out of circulation, and attempting to do so now would only make things worse. No, the only way to play this was to not deny what the photos implied, but to take the speculation and turn it on its head.

That meant he'd have to admit that he and Flora *were* in fact involved. It would be a complete and total fabrication, which went against everything he believed in, but there was no help for it. His reputation and that of his company was more important. Helios was supposed to be a model employer, and it would not do to look as if he'd thrown one of his own employees under the bus. Which meant protecting Flora from any blowback was also vital.

So, how to make all of this sympathetic? He couldn't say it was a passing affair, that wouldn't help his cause, especially since he was her boss. His rigorous sexual harassment policies had been lauded around the globe as an example of new, progressive business practices, and having such an obvious affair would label him a hypocrite.

He couldn't stand that. He'd never crossed the line with his employees and never would, and he believed totally in those policies. He'd drafted them himself.

However, there might be those who didn't like his management style, who might see this as an opportunity to take him down peg or two. They might use it as an example of his behaviour to bring spurious claims against him.

So, no affair then. He'd have to claim that Flora was something more than merely his PA, and that their affair was more than merely an affair. It would have to be a grand passion, a meeting of soulmates, or something along those lines. All nonsense, of course. Love was a vice he'd never be guilty of, but it was the best way to save the Constantinides name.

People loved a romance, they were gullible like that, as he would know, since his father had taught him all about how gullible people were. How to prey on their little weaknesses, their little vulnerabilities, and turn them to his advantage. It wasn't manipulation, he'd told Apollo. It was merely business, and where business was concerned anything was allowed.

Of course, he'd soon learned that his father's 'lessons' were nothing but Stavros manipulating his own son, but Apollo had learned them all the same.

Now, though, he went still, as his brain offered him a solution that would allow Flora and himself a modicum of respectability, not to mention a way out for Violet also. A way that would limit the damage of the pictures as much as possible. It wasn't the most elegant of solutions, since it would involve a lie. But it was a harmless lie, which would hurt no one and, most importantly, would potentially rescue the Constantinides name.

'Then what else do you suggest?' Flora asked, her expression still unruffled.

'I suggest that we don't deny it,' he said, holding her gaze. 'In fact, I think the perfect solution is for me to marry you instead of Violet.'

CHAPTER TWO

AT FIRST FLORA thought she'd misunderstood him, because seriously, marriage? To *her*? Was he insane?

Then, when the intense laser beam of his focus didn't relent, the lines of his perfect face unyielding, she understood that, yes, he was serious. And, no, he likely wasn't insane.

The idea was so preposterous, though, she almost laughed. So near to almost, in fact, she could feel her mouth begin to curl into a smile without her express permission. Which was not acceptable. She *had* to be on her guard with him.

She'd managed to get away with the photos only because he treated her as an extension of himself, and so didn't pay much attention to her specifically. Which was exactly what she wanted.

What she did not want was him looking at her the way he was doing so now, as if he was a scientist and she an interesting specimen he was examining through a microscope.

He couldn't be interested in her. He couldn't be curious about her. Because, if he looked too closely, he might find out who she really was and she couldn't allow that to happen. She had to be as unexceptional and boring as possible.

Forcing her shock aside, Flora tried to maintain her usual calm manner. 'I don't understand. How is marrying me a solution?'

Apollo came back to his desk and stood behind it, suddenly seeming much too tall and much too powerful for her comfort. She hated how sometimes her awareness would zero in on him, noting all the things about him that she liked. It was all physical—her body was inexplicably drawn to his in a way that she couldn't seem to shake off.

Even now, at the point of achieving the first step in her revenge plans, she couldn't help but notice the breadth of his wide shoulders and chest. The light coming in through the windows behind him and turning his black hair glossy, shadowing the hard planes and angles of his face. The deep jungle green of his eyes, glittering like dark emeralds.

He was the most physically perfect man she'd ever met, and if he was any other man she'd be dazzled. But he wasn't any other man, he was the man who'd destroyed her family, and the only thing that should dazzle her was her own genius at managing to stay hidden from him all this time.

'As I mentioned,' he said, 'denial will only make the situation worse, as will ignoring the issue. Admitting that we're having an affair is our only option.'

Which was not what Flora had been expecting. At all. His anger was right on target, but she'd thought the damage control would be denial. He hated a lie, and she'd counted on his outrage at being accused of something he hadn't done to dig in and, yes, that *would* make things worse. She wanted it to be worse.

The last thing she'd anticipated was him deciding to embrace the lie.

'W-what?' she said, unable to help the slight stutter.

His gaze pinned her to the spot, sharp needles of green glass holding her in place. 'We admit that we've been seeing each other. We won't call it an affair, though, as that implies something casual and sordid, so we'll have to go with calling it a grand passion instead. One that we tried to resist and failed, and then I ended up asking you to marry me and, naturally, you said yes.'

Flora blinked as her brain tried to get a handle on what he was saying. Not an affair, but a grand passion that ended in a marriage proposal?

The calm, which came with feeling totally in control of the situation she'd engineered, began to dissipate, and that could not happen.

She was going to have to recalibrate her entire plan.

'I see,' she managed.

'You have doubts?' His deep voice carried the familiar tone of faint impatience, which he used whenever someone questioned him. 'This will mitigate the damage of the photos, and perhaps even garner some public sympathy, especially if it looks like we're desperately in love with each other. It will also allow Violet an opportunity to be magnanimous and noble in allowing us our happiness.'

He wasn't wrong—even she could see that. It would allow everyone some dignity, a dignity that she'd been counting on him *not* having.

You should have expected him to come up with the perfect solution. He's far too smart not to.

Yes, she should have, damn him. Her intentions had been to set him on the back foot, not herself.

Flora tried to moisten her suddenly dry mouth. 'We're not in love with each other, though,' she said, the statement more to buy herself some time to think than any kind of protest.

His black brows twitched. 'No, of course we aren't. This isn't about reality, Flora. It's about optics.' Alarmingly, he rounded the desk and headed straight for her, and it was all she could do not to take a step back. Getting close to him was always an issue since it was difficult to disguise her physical reaction to his nearness, just as it was difficult to think clearly. Yet she couldn't give ground. He would note it and wonder why, and he was already asking too many questions as it was. Allowing him to ask more would be a mistake.

He was a man who took charge of any given situation, and if she wasn't careful he was going to take charge of this too.

She couldn't let that happen. She had to act before he did.

Flora held her ground as he came to a stop just in front of her, tilting her head back so she could meet his intent green gaze. 'Of course, sir,' she said with a calm she didn't feel. 'Optics are important.'

'Indeed,' he said. 'In which case we will need to be seen in public together. You will also need a ring. The wedding will have to be a circus, there's no escaping that, but if it's big enough people will soon forget about those photos.'

He was far too close for comfort, his nearness making her thoughts feel like they were coated in warm honey, slow and thick. The warm, woody scent of his aftershave was the most delicious thing she'd ever smelled, and she had the almost overwhelming urge to lean in and inhale him.

'We can stay married for six months,' he went on. 'Or perhaps a year. Then we'll get a divorce once all the fuss has died down. No harm done.'

Get it together, fool! You can't go sniffing him when he's in the middle of ruining your revenge plans!

'Well? Are you listening, Flora?'

Flora gritted her teeth and wrestled her recalcitrant awareness back into submission. What had he been talking about again? A ring. A wedding. They can stay married for six months, a year…divorce.

He is *taking charge of this, and you're letting him.*

'Yes, I heard you,' she said, by now holding on to the calm by the skin of her teeth. 'A ring and a wedding. Divorce. This will all be just for show, I hope?'

Apollo's dark brows twitched again. 'It will be a paper marriage, naturally, but from a legal standpoint it will be absolutely real. I abhor a lie, Flora, you know this.'

'Yes, I do know that, actually.' The words escaped without her conscious control, as did the edge of sarcasm.

His gaze narrowed. 'You don't seem to be treating this situation with the appropriate amount of concern.'

Damn him. And damn herself for letting him get under her skin so badly. This attraction to him was a problem, and she should have found a solution by now. She'd hoped that ignoring it would make it go away, yet it hadn't. If anything, it seemed to have got worse.

It was stupid. She'd basically ignored men in her quest to get herself to where she was now, and that had been made easier since she'd never met a man she wanted. Now, though, it seemed some kind of karmic joke that the one man who'd ever affected her was the one man she hated, who she hoped to bring down.

Ugh.

'I'm very concerned.' She kept her tone cool. 'But surely we don't have to go through with an actual marriage. You can break up with me or something—'

'No.' The word was hard and flat, the weight of his authority turning it into an anvil dropped from a great height. 'It will be a pretence both emotionally and physically, but legally it must be real. I will not have it discovered later that the whole thing is a lie.'

Great. There went the idea of her leaking a pretend marriage to the press.

'No, of course not,' she said soothingly.

He frowned down at her. 'Don't placate me, Flora, I won't have it. Just as I won't have the Constantinides name attached to some sordid headline or nonsense soap opera. These photos, wherever they came from, are likely a setup, and I will not be held to ransom by them.'

Of course he'd already thought this through. And once again, she should have anticipated that he'd move quickly and decisively. He'd never been a man to sit around wringing his hands when faced with a seemingly insoluble problem, after all. He made decisions and took action.

God, why couldn't he have been more of a wet blanket?

'I'm not placating you, sir,' she said, adjusting her tone a touch. 'I actually agree with you. Denial would look bad, and it would likely only encourage more gossip. Perhaps, though, an actual wedding would be overkill?'

Apollo's gaze became intent in a way she wasn't expecting. 'Why? What does it matter to you whether the marriage is real or not?'

Her heart thudded, suddenly loud in her ears, and for no reason that she could see. He did this sometimes, turn his attention onto her like a predator spotting prey, and it always made her breath catch and her adrenaline spike.

She'd been so careful the whole year she'd been working for him, always appearing calm and cool and in control. Never questioning him. Never talking about herself. Never doing anything that would draw his attention. She'd been so pleased with herself at the way she'd managed to keep hold of all her secrets, that perhaps she'd become complacent.

'It doesn't matter to me,' she said carefully. 'But... Well. I might be seeing someone, or have a partner.'

He didn't even blink. 'And are you? Seeing someone, I mean.'

'No, but...'

'But what?'

'What about the expense? A real wedding is a waste of money.'

'I don't care about the expense.' He frowned down at her. 'I'm trying to protect you as well, Flora. You do see that, don't you? I'm your boss, don't forget. Which makes the optics on this whole situation look even worse, especially since Helios is supposed to be a world leader when it comes to employee relations. Then there's the Constantinides name to consider, and I will not put that reputation in jeopardy. Which means this has to be as real as it humanly can be.' He folded his arms across his broad chest. 'It will be better for both of us if it looks like a passionate public love affair and ends with a fairy-tale wedding. That will make the public forget there were even photos of us in the first place.'

Oh, he was clever. She really, *really* should have known he'd find some way to spin this, even that bit about protecting her. He was wasted as a CEO. He should have gone into politics instead, since he had the power to make even the devil himself look good.

Perhaps the photos were a stupid idea. You should have just gone with the insider trading stuff.

The photos, of course, weren't the whole of her plan. She had a bullet-point list of all the things she was going to do to ensure his total and utter destruction, only one of which involved incriminating photos. Aiming at the monolith of his personal reputation was the first of her targets and the easiest one to undermine—at least that's what she'd thought when she'd first taken the job as his PA.

She'd considered a seduction initially, but then had discarded the idea, since he seemed to be an entirely passionless man, and she certainly wasn't experienced enough to generate any kind of response from him, despite the response he managed to generate in her. So, she'd gone with engineered photos instead.

You were far too satisfied, far too soon.

Yes, she had been. And now the damage control she had to undertake was for her own plans, which had suddenly become a whole lot more complicated.

It wasn't insurmountable, however. She could still salvage things. She had to keep her cool, stay in control and not betray just how badly he'd rattled her.

'Very well,' she said with what she thought was admirable calm. 'Shall I add all this to the draft press release or would you like to do it?'

Flora gazed back at him, one dark brow arched in polite enquiry, and he found it…irritating. Normally her calm and unflustered manner was the thing he appreciated most about her as a PA, but not today. Especially when he was seething inside that someone had dared think they could try to ruin him, because that's clearly what was happening.

It wouldn't work, though. He'd make sure of that. He'd turn around and marry the woman they'd used to try and ruin him, and he'd come out of the whole affair smelling like roses.

Violet wouldn't mind. He'd entered into a marriage agreement with her initially for the cachet her name would bring to him and to Helios, and also to add a further layer of insulation for the precious crystal that was the Constantinides reputation. His father had shattered it into glittering shards, but Apollo would put it back together, piece by piece, if it was the last thing he did.

It wasn't purely for his own sake. He had thousands of employees around the globe who would lose their jobs if Helios collapsed, as well as all the charities that benefited from his money. And last, but certainly not least, for the memory of his mother, Elena, who'd believed totally in Stavros, and who'd been left heartbroken after Stavros had gone to jail.

She'd died a few years ago of complications due to pneumonia, and the last words she'd ever spoken to him had been to request that he rebuild the family name. She'd left unsaid the role he'd played in his father's downfall, yet he'd heard her loud and clear all the same.

This was all your fault...

She was wrong, of course. His father's scheme had been doomed from the start, and someone would have turned him in eventually. That it had been his son was something neither of his parents had been able to get over, but that had been their problem, not his.

Yes, he'd told the police about his father. Yes, he'd turned Stavros in.

He'd gained immunity from prosecution in return, but that wasn't why he'd done it. He'd done it because a man had died after hearing the scheme was illegal—a man Apollo himself had brought on board, and turning Stavros in had been the right thing to do. He hadn't felt guilty about sending his father to jail, not then and not now, not one single shred. Not when his father hadn't felt guilty about all the people he'd been duping, and all the lives he'd destroyed.

Stavros had sold it to Apollo as some kind of glorified Robin Hood scheme, that what they were doing was merely taking from the rich and giving to the poor. Apollo had loved his father, and working in the family company was all he'd ever wanted to do. However, that love had blinded him to the truth. It hadn't been an enterprise to invest money in new tech that would allow impoverished communities to access clean water and cheap power. It had been a scheme that allowed Stavros to take all the investors' money for himself to clear his own debt.

His father had told him, just before they'd locked him away, that all he'd wanted was to make sure the company survived for Apollo and Elena's sake. He didn't say anything about how his own financial mismanagement had run Helios into the ground and he had no one to blame for his jail sentence but himself.

Which was why Apollo had decided, early on, that the only way he could mitigate the damage his father had caused was to get Helios back on its feet again, and make it as profitable as he could, so he could then offer his father's victims some decent compensation.

Luckily, he had a gift when it came to finance and investing, but, even so, it had taken a lot of hard work and determination to earn back the trust Helios had commanded before his father had ruined it, and then more work to get it making money again.

At that stage, though, he'd realised that nothing less than the total and complete rehabilitation of the Constantinides name would do. That not only was compensation for the victims not enough, but spearheading a movement to overhaul company business practices worldwide, especially when it came to protecting staff, was also necessary.

There were ways to be ethical and honest when it came to investing. There were ways to be transparent. There were ways to prioritise people's wellbeing that didn't impact the bottom line, and, in fact, you could have both.

He didn't want anyone else falling for charlatans like his father either, so he'd dedicated one arm of Helios to investigating and exposing Ponzi schemes and other illegal, unethical business practices. He also gave away a significant portion of his wealth. He was what his father wasn't, a true Robin Hood. Taking from the rich—himself—and giving it to those desperately in need.

He was also not a man who compromised, and he would not compromise on this. Just as he would not compromise on ways to scupper the plans of whoever it was who was trying to ruin him.

He had, however, expected more objections from Flora.

She'd seemed shocked at his initial suggestion—he'd definitely caught a flicker of it in her eyes, which was of note, since she was always unflappable. Then his curiosity had been further engaged when she'd protested the idea of them having a real marriage.

She'd never questioned one of his decisions, not once, and he'd accepted that, because he was of the view that a PA should make everything he did smoother and easier, not more difficult, with lots of questions. He had other people to do that kind of thing and she was not one of them.

He'd never wanted to know her as a person or have her tell him details about her life. He wasn't interested.

Yet, now, he found himself intrigued by the fact that, out of all the decisions he'd made since she started working for him, she'd been so unusually vocal about this one. He wanted it to be a legal marriage, yes, but only on paper, nothing more, so what was really the issue here?

Did she think he meant it? Did she think that he really felt something for her? Or was it something else?

He took a moment to study her.

She wasn't beautiful, not typically so, though her face was possessed of a certain...interest. And her PA uniform did accentuate a lush, womanly figure, which wasn't perhaps fashionable, but now that he was looking it was... well, again, interesting.

But he shouldn't be looking, not when he was her boss. He liked to lead by example, and whoever had set him up had known that, since they were hitting him where it would do the most damage.

Colour had risen to her cheeks, which was odd. He'd looked at her a thousand times like this and she'd never blushed before, or at least not that he'd noticed. Had it been the mention of a grand passion between them? Had it embarrassed her? Or was she merely uncomfortable being studied?

Why are you even being curious about her? She's just your PA.

This was true, he'd never been curious about her before. He needed to stop.

'You can add it to the draft,' he said after a moment. 'But first, we'll need to agree on what story we give to the press about our love affair.'

She nodded calmly. 'As you said before, we met at work, obviously. And after a few months of working together—perhaps after a few late-night strategy sessions?—we gradually realised our love for one another.'

The whole sentence was delivered in the same dispassionate tone with which she delivered everything she said. Which would not do, not if they were going to act as if they were the love of each other's lives.

He gave her a severe look. 'We're supposed to be talking about irresistible passion, Flora, not giving a Power-Point presentation.'

Again, there was that flicker in her eyes, and the dark brow she had arched, arched further. 'Oh? I didn't realise we had to fully enact our irresistible passion right now.'

Apollo narrowed his gaze at the faint hint of sarcasm in her voice.

He was adept at reading people—it was what his father had taken advantage of, back when Apollo had been younger and still thinking that his father's idea for an investment scheme was a marvellous opportunity. He'd been the public face of the scheme, had read the files of all the potential investors his father had sent his way, noting any frailties or vulnerabilities. He'd enjoyed showing off his gift to Stavros as much as Stavros had enjoyed using it.

Even these days, even though he knew where it had the potential to lead, he'd found himself using it to his own advantage in the boardroom. Though—and he had to remember this—it was all in service to furthering good in the world rather than duping people. He wasn't like his father. He wasn't.

'This is not a game,' he said repressively. 'This is about Helios's reputation, and the thousands of people we employ. I am this company, and if I fall, so does everyone else.'

If she was chastened by this, she gave no sign, except for a minute tightening of her full lips. 'Very well. How else would you like me to talk about it then?'

He ignored the question for a moment, caught by that almost imperceptible sign of annoyance. Was she angry with him? Or was it the photos? She hadn't seemed upset by them, and yet surely she had to be.

'You don't seem put out by these photos.' He met her steady stare, noting another flicker deep in the charcoal depths of her eyes. What was it? Another emotional response? And if so, why was she hiding it?

Her lashes fell, veiling her gaze. They were thick, those lashes, and a deep, sooty black. He couldn't recall noticing them before, and wasn't sure why he was noticing them now.

'I'm startled by them,' she said evenly. 'But they're in the public domain now. There's nothing I can do about it.'

'And you really don't know who sent them to you?' he asked, noting yet another tightening of her lips. 'Or do you have any idea who might have?'

Her gaze remained veiled, which he found frustrating. He didn't like not being able to read people. It made him feel as if something was being hidden from him, and he didn't like that either. He wasn't the gullible fool he'd been back at twenty, when he'd thought everything his father said was the God's honest truth. These days he questioned everything.

Reaching out, he put a finger beneath Flora's determined chin and tilted her head back. 'You know something about them, don't you?' His fingers closed on her warm skin. 'Tell me, Flora.'

CHAPTER THREE

FLORA'S BREATH CAUGHT abruptly, every inch of skin pulling tight. She couldn't seem to move, all her awareness zeroing in on the firm press of his long fingers holding her chin. Warm and strong. She had the impression that, even if she'd wanted to, she wouldn't have been able to pull away.

His gaze pinned her to the spot and she realised that his eyes weren't the simple dark green she'd always thought they were. It was as if someone had taken an emerald and shattered it, with some of the pieces glittering a lighter, grass green, while others were darker, spruce and pine. Many shades, like his tie, and all perfectly framed by thick, black lashes.

The last time she'd been this close to him was when she'd leaned over him as he'd sat behind his desk, on the pretext of checking a non-existent spot on his shirt. He'd continued talking on his phone, paying no attention to her, while she'd been thinking about the phone she'd hidden on one of the bookshelves, hoping she'd set the timer correctly and that the photos would come out okay. She been so anxious about it, she hadn't had time to even consider their proximity.

Now, though, every bit of his intense focus was on her and she had nothing else to distract her.

She'd slipped up somehow, betrayed some kind of response that had caught his attention. Stupid fool that she was. She couldn't afford mistakes, not with a man like this one.

It was only that he'd been staring at her as if he could read all her thoughts, and she'd had to protect herself somehow. She shouldn't have looked away, that was clear. Well, she wouldn't make that mistake again.

She had to remember that she hated this man. He was the direct cause of the destruction of her family, and all the years of misery after it, and she could *not* let him get under her skin simply because her idiot female hormones found him unbearably attractive.

After all, she knew where that led. Her mother had been a hopeless romantic who'd thrown everything away to follow her father, his easy charm going straight to her head, like good French champagne. Flora had been the same. She'd idolised her happy, optimistic, fun-loving father. He'd hung the moon and all the stars in the sky for her, and she loved him. And he loved her. As he'd told her so often, he would protect her. He'd never let anything bad happen to her.

But he'd lied.

He hadn't loved her at all, because if he had, he wouldn't have taken his own life, leaving her and her mother alone.

Nowadays she wasn't like her mother, a romantic fool with a head full of dreams. Love didn't sustain anyone and those dreams dissipated like smoke at one hint of reality.

The reality was a rundown flat above a chip shop, and nights alone, eating baked beans from a can, because her mother was out at her second job pulling pints in a pub, trying to earn enough money just to keep the lights on.

The reality was watching her mother slowly succumb to a slow and painful death.

Love was a lie, and she would never believe it again.

This wasn't love though, this was only physical attraction. Yet she couldn't let herself be ruled by it. She couldn't let any sign of her susceptibility to him show either. Already he saw too much, all that shattered emerald roving over her, looking for weaknesses, probing for vulnerabilities.

Bracing herself, Flora stayed where she was, blocking the delicious scent of his aftershave from her mind and ignoring the warmth of his body. She gave herself a moment to regroup, then she said, fighting to keep her voice calm. 'I don't know anything, sir. I assure you.'

This didn't seem to satisfy him as his focus only intensified, making an odd heat sweep unexpectedly through her. She could feel it in her cheeks, glowing just beneath her skin, and before she knew what she was doing, she'd pulled her chin from his grip and taken a couple of steps back, putting some distance between them.

Apollo said nothing, but his gaze had turned speculative, making her heart beat faster.

Good God, what was she thinking? Pulling away from him so suddenly was only going to make him even more curious than he already was. She'd seen that happen before, when someone interested him. He'd ask them all kinds of questions, never seeming to be bored with the answers. He might not have a charming bone in his body, but people seemed helpless to resist the concentrated beam of his attention.

She, on the other hand, was terrified of it. She'd always wondered if she'd be able to keep up her facade of smooth, capable and not at all interesting if he ever turned it on her.

Apparently not.

She smoothed her skirt and fussed with a button on her blouse, trying to hide how badly he'd flustered her.

'Perhaps it's a disgruntled employee,' she suggested, keeping her tone as even as she could. 'Or a business rival.'

He ignored the comment, his green stare sharp as knives. 'Are you afraid of me, Flora?'

This time she wasn't able to hide her shock. 'What? No, of course not.'

'Are you sure? You certainly seemed to be just now.'

Yes, she *had* given herself away. Dammit.

Her control of this situation was slowly slipping out of her grip and that couldn't happen, not when he seemed to be undermining her calm at every turn. She had to do better than this.

She and her mother had been won over by her father, time and time again, when it came to his often grandiose plans for bettering their family. Laura never seemed to learn the lesson, that David's pipe dreams were always just that. Pipe dreams. While Flora had been certain that her handsome, wonderful father would take care of them, just the way he'd promised.

Yet in the end he hadn't taken care of them at all. Apparently neither she nor her mother had been important enough to make him stay, and when he'd died, he'd left them alone. Powerless against the grief…

She would not let herself be so utterly at the mercy of another person again.

She would stay in control of her emotions and herself, and, most important of all, her plans for justice for her parents.

Ceding him even one iota of control couldn't happen, and most especially not given that he was the type of man who wouldn't just take an inch, he'd take a mile and then some.

'You startled me, that's all.' She met his gaze. 'Why on earth would I be afraid of you?'

Again, he didn't answer, merely gave her the same flat green stare. 'It would not do for you to pull away like that when we're out in public together. So, I ask again. Are you afraid of me?'

'No.' She lifted her chin and took a step towards him. 'Do you need me to prove it to you?'

Something gleamed in the depths of his eyes then, something dark and hungry, which sent a hot, electric pulse straight through her. She'd seen that gleam before, when his interest had been caught with a deal, or he'd been issued a business challenge he wanted to meet. He'd never looked at her that way though, not until now, and it stole all the breath from her lungs.

That was a mistake. You've caught the attention of a predator.

Pity there hadn't been any other options. She couldn't let him believe she was afraid of him—even though that might have been the safest course of action—she just couldn't. She wasn't anyone's helpless victim, not any more.

Still, it was too late to do anything about it now.

She *had* caught his interest, and some long-forgotten part of her, a lost, lonely part, liked that. Liked that a lot.

You can't forget what you're here for. Justice.

No, she wouldn't. But maybe there was another way to take back control of this little scenario that he'd stolen from her. A way that she'd initially discarded, because she'd thought he was passionless, and he wasn't.

You could use that interest to get close to him, and if he wants marriage, even better. As his wife you'll be able to steadily drain him dry—

No, perhaps *not* draining him dry on second thoughts. He'd said that if he fell, the company would fall too, and that company employed a lot of people. She'd ruin a lot of livelihoods if she somehow managed to financially destroy him, and her plan was only about him. She didn't want to involve anyone else or make them suffer.

Of course, she should have thought of that earlier, before she'd sent him those pictures, but she hadn't been thinking of other people at the time, only of her own cause.

How else could she see justice served?

Ruin him emotionally, the way your mother was ruined. The way your father was ruined. Break his heart, the way yours was broken...

A cold little thrill wound through her. Oh, yes, why not? She could manipulate his interest in her, potentially using that to seduce him, then make him fall in love with her and then... She'd break his heart and walk away.

A dangerous thought and terrifying, in its way. Firstly, he was an experienced man, who'd taken a variety of lovers, so seducing him might be an issue since she'd had no experience at all, which he'd definitely realise. Secondly, making him fall in love with her would be...difficult, and not least because of that little experience issue. Getting close to him would also put her own secrets at risk, so if she was going to do it, she'd have to be very, very careful indeed.

Definitely something to consider, but right now, the first thing she had to do was make sure he knew that she wasn't intimidated by him.

Inwardly bracing herself, Flora took another step, then another, coming closer to him. He didn't move. His expression was impassive, yet that gleam in his eyes continued to glitter like a fire burning deep in the jungle.

She came to a stop in front of him, her heart beating loudly in her ears as she tipped her head back to look up at him. He didn't take his gaze from hers. His arms were folded across his broad chest and, once again, getting close to him and having his delicious scent all around her made it difficult to think clearly.

'See?' She was unable to keep the faint husk from her voice. 'I'm not afraid.'

He said nothing for a long moment, merely looking down his beautifully shaped Greek nose at her, his tall, dark presence seeming to fill the generous space of the office in way it had never done before.

The moment lengthened, the air around them thickening in ways that made it feel as if all the oxygen in the room had suddenly vanished.

Then, before she could move, he reached out and cupped her cheek in one large hand. The heat of his palm was astonishing, his touch electric. Flora couldn't move, could barely even breathe.

'Does this bother you?' His voice was as cool as water on her hot skin and she had to resist the almost overwhelming desire to lean into his hand.

Her mouth was bone dry. 'No.'

'Good.' Slowly, he slid his hand along her jaw to the back of her head, cupping it gently in his palm. 'How about this?'

Her heart raced, the sound deafening her. His fingertips were pressing into her hair, that gleam in his eyes glittering brighter, sharper. 'What are you doing?' The words came out thick, but she couldn't adjust the sound of her voice.

'Testing you.' His own voice was expressionless, like stone, as if the fact that they were standing so close to each other had no effect on him whatsoever. 'We need to be comfortable touching each other if this is going to work.'

Well. Two could play at that game.

'In that case.' She lifted a hand and placed it on his chest, her fingertips resting lightly on the snowy cotton of his shirt. He felt very warm and very hard, and it was very difficult to keep hold of her usual calm, but she managed to raise a brow coolly. 'Are you comfortable with this?'

His mouth was in its usual severe line and she found herself staring at it, wondering what he would look like if it relaxed, maybe even curved.

He would be astonishing.

Oh, yes. He would be.

'Yes,' he said, his voice as steady as a rock.

Flora swallowed yet again. How was it possible to feel as if she was going to go up in flames, while he was cold as a slab of granite, and just as expressionless? It seemed desperately unfair that he should remain unaffected by her, while for her it was getting hard to think with his hand cradling the back of her head. With the heat of him seeping into her fingertips where they rested on his chest.

So unfair that she didn't really think through what she did next. The only thing that seemed important was that she had to do something to take charge of this, to exert her own power. She couldn't let him have all of it, not if she wanted justice.

So, very slowly, she curled her fingers around his tie, gripping the warm silk like a rope as she made herself hold his dark, green gaze. 'What about this?' she asked.

'Apart from the creases you're putting in my tie, yes.' He didn't move, or betray any physical reaction to her nearness whatsoever.

It incensed her, and before she could think better of it, Flora held on to his tie, rose onto her toes, and pressed her mouth to his.

Apollo didn't like surprises, especially when it came to people's behaviour. He'd never turned his gift for reading people on Flora McIntyre before, because he'd never had to. She was there to do his bidding, and she did it. There was no need to inquire further.

So for her to grip his tie, before rising on her toes to kiss him, was the very last thing he'd expected her to do, and it shocked him so profoundly that for a long moment he couldn't move.

Then, much to his horror, everything male in him woke to full aching life, as a bolt of electricity drove all the way down his spine.

Her lips on his were light as a butterfly and so very soft, so very warm, possessing a sweet hesitancy that grabbed him by the throat and refused to let go.

He'd never felt anything like it in his entire life.

He shouldn't have pushed her about being afraid of him, he knew that, and he wasn't sure why he'd been so insistent. But then she'd lifted her chin in a way she'd never done before, and the primitive beast in him knew exactly what that meant.

A direct challenge. And the most peculiar rush of adrenaline had coursed through him. As if she'd flicked a switch in his brain, or she'd stepped out of the shadows and into the light, and he was seeing her for the first time. A woman, not merely his PA. A woman with a mind of her own, who wasn't merely a blank slate who agreed with everything he said and carried out his orders. A woman with a touch of spirit, probably more than a touch, if that chin lift was anything to go by.

He should have stopped pushing then and stepped back, returned to his usual place behind his desk, but he hadn't. That glimpse of temper had been enough to hold him where he was, to want to know more...

Yet he hadn't thought it would be this, a kiss with the kind of heat that brought a man to his knees.

He'd never denied himself physical pleasure in his quest to rebuild Helios, though his lovers were always chosen with care. Only women who wanted what he did, which was physical pleasure and nothing more.

However, when he'd decided on the next step in his plans for the Constantinides name—the engagement to Violet—he'd easily put all his lovers aside. He'd intended his marriage to Violet to be a real one, though they had not actually consummated their relationship yet. Violet had wanted to wait until their wedding night and he'd agreed. He could control himself; he wasn't desperate.

He and Violet had kissed each other of course, and it had been very pleasant, but this… Flora… This was not pleasant.

This was cataclysmic.

He found himself cupping the back of her head with both hands, his fingertips pushing into the soft thickness of her hair, holding her still as he took control of the kiss.

She shuddered, the taste of her so utterly delicious it was if he'd never tasted a woman's mouth before. Sweet and hot as melted honey, and with something more, something addictive he couldn't quite grasp, which had him shifting his grip to put the pad of his thumb on her lower lip, easing her mouth open to him so he could explore more fully.

She made a soft sound in her throat, but she wasn't pushing him away, so he didn't stop, turning the kiss hotter, deeper. Dimly something was telling him that this was a bad idea, that he'd never felt this way about her before, so why was he now? But he couldn't quite get a grasp on the answer to the question. Because why hadn't they done this before? It seemed ridiculous, when the chemistry burning between them was so hot and strong.

You're her boss, that's why. And this is for the media only. You're not supposed to actually feel this way for real.

Something ice-cold cut through the heat in his veins. That was true. So what the hell was he doing? Flora had never given him any sign she felt anything for him. She'd never flirted, never smiled, never sneaked glances at him while he wasn't looking. Never had her hand linger on his shoulder or anywhere else about his person. Of course, those pictures would seem to indicate that was a lie, but it wasn't. So why was he suddenly kissing her back? The ethical boundaries he'd placed around his business practices were there for a reason and he could not cross them. He could *not*.

With a force of will that took far more effort than it should, Apollo wrenched his mouth from hers and let her go, taking a step back. Only to be brought up short by her small fist still wrapped around his tie.

She was holding on to it for dear life and looking up at him. Her eyes had gone dark as midnight, her cheeks stained with colour. Her mouth full and red from their kiss.

Beautiful. She's beautiful.

The thought came to him without any prompting, the urge to kiss her again was so powerful that he nearly bent his head to do just that. But he knew what happened when he gave into his darker impulses. He ruined people.

Flora had surprised him, and he couldn't allow that to happen again. Honesty was important to him, even if he was going to have to fake a marriage in order to protect her, but control was even more so. Control over his mind and his body, control over his emotions. He couldn't allow his grip to slip, not even for moment.

You're going to marry her, though. So what does it matter if you kiss her again?

He was going to marry her, it was true, but theirs would not be the kind of marriage he'd been going to enter into with Violet. That marriage had been arranged and talked about, every detail decided upon going in, with children part of the mix. An honest relationship based on what each other had wanted, no surprises. No messy emotion to complicate matters.

Which was not anything like marrying Flora. That was a spur of the moment decision, a solution to an unexpected problem, and it would only be on paper. With a quick divorce once the fuss had died down. Any physical entanglements would only make things difficult, and, apart from anything else, he was still her boss, and he had to set an example.

So, no, definitely no more kisses, or anything else of that nature.

Forcing down the heat of desire still burning in his blood, Apollo reached for her fingers gripping his tie, and gently unwrapped them from the fabric. Her skin felt warm against his, though he tried not to be conscious of it.

'I think you proved your point,' he said curtly, releasing her hand and stepping back.

Flora said nothing, her mouth still open, her eyes still dark, the colour high in her cheeks. She looked almost dazed, which gave him a disturbing amount of satisfaction. She'd never seemed anything less than serene, so for his kiss to strip that veneer of calm so completely away from her pleased him on a deep, base level.

Don't turn this into something it's not.

He wouldn't. This was an act, a show to protect Flora from any blowback, as well as for the public to keep his good name and reputation intact.

An act and that's all.

'Don't look at me like that, Flora,' he snapped. 'I'm not kissing you again, no matter how big those eyes of yours get. Do you understand?'

She flushed, a spark of bright silver glittering in her eyes. And, for a moment, he found himself holding his breath, expecting her to fling some spiky comment at him, almost hoping for it. But then the spark disappeared, and her usual serenity settled over her features.

'Yes, I understand.' She smoothed a strand of black hair that had escaped her bun behind her ear. 'So, this draft. What did you want me to include?'

It was admirable really, the way she so easily put her facade into place. Yet he couldn't seem to get that memory out of his head, of her looking up at him, eyes dark, mouth red, all dazed from that kiss. Couldn't shake, either, that very male satisfaction at how he'd ruffled that perfect calm of hers. How he'd made her grip his tie and look at him as if she was dying of thirst and he was a glass of iced water. If she was any other woman, and he a different man, it might have been interesting to play with her a little, find out if that passion he'd caught a glimpse of just before was truly—

But no. He couldn't think such things, not when he had a reputation to rescue.

'Let's go with this,' he said, turning abruptly and striding back around the side of his desk, putting some distance between them. 'You and I worked together, as you said, and our attraction was such that we couldn't fight it. You kissed me after a late-night planning session and that's when we realised we had to make a decision. I'd been going to tell Violet about us, but then the photos were released before I had the chance to do so. But now they're out in the public sphere and we're relieved that we no longer have to hide our passion.'

The colour in her cheeks was still high, the charcoal glint of her eyes still dark. '*I* kissed you?'

There was a slight edge to the question, which again had never been apparent in her voice before. In fact, she'd never questioned him before, full stop.

'Yes,' he said, frowning. 'That part is certainly true, is it not? Besides, it would be worse for my reputation if we said I kissed you first.'

'What about my reputation?' Again there was a brief glint of unfamiliar silver, her temper obviously on a short leash. 'You said you were doing this partly to protect me, don't forget.'

Interesting. She wasn't quite as adept at hiding her feelings as she'd been minutes before. Or perhaps she'd always had this sharp edge and he'd just never noticed? Maybe it was the kiss that had disturbed her...

Not that he should be thinking about that kiss. She was right, he had said he was doing this partly to protect her, and he was. The media was always harder on women, this he knew, and her reputation was as important as his.

'True,' he admitted. 'How about this then? You kissed me, but then you were extremely apologetic and offered to resign. I, naturally, wouldn't hear of it.'

Her gaze narrowed, but she nodded. 'Okay. But we haven't touched each other beyond those photos. We wanted to go public before anything more happened between us.'

Excellent. She wanted to put that kiss behind them too, which was definitely where it should be.

'Agreed,' he said. 'Our relationship has not been consummated. You insisted on waiting until we were married.'

Once again, faint colour touched her cheekbones. 'Do we really need to say that?'

'No, but it's better if we have an answer if the question is asked. And someone will, because the general public is inordinately interested in people's sex lives. Those photos being a prime example.'

'Very well.' Her facade was back in place again.

'Good.' He dug his phone out of his pocket and glanced down at it, scrolling through his calendar. They'd need to be seen together as quickly as possible, and preferably at some major event. 'Tomorrow night I have that gala in Paris. That will be the perfect time to debut our relationship.'

'Tomorrow night?' The edge had returned to Flora's voice, surprise flickering through her dark grey eyes.

Strange that she hadn't thought this through. Normally she was excellent at anticipating and then coping with any difficulties. Then again, perhaps it was because she was personally involved this time. Also, that kiss…

Irritation coiled inside him as the warmth of her mouth on his lingered in his brain. He shoved it away with more firmness this time.

'Yes, tomorrow night. You know how fast and how far gossip travels. We need to release a public statement as quickly as possible, then follow it up with a public appearance together, as a couple.'

This time there was only the slightest flicker of a reaction, before her expression smoothed once more. Whatever control she'd lost, she now had it back in her grasp.

Too late, though. You know who she is now. Who she really is.

Yes, he did, and he would do precisely nothing about

it. Regardless of what act they'd put on for the public, he wouldn't touch her. He was still her boss, and doing anything with her at all would be crossing one of the many lines he'd drawn in his quest to rehabilitate the Constantinides name.

Not to mention rehabilitating yourself, too.

Yes, that also.

'Fine,' Flora said expressionlessly. 'Paris it is.'

Apollo put his phone away and sat down at his desk. 'The situation is in hand then. Get working on that draft. I want it on my desk in an hour.'

CHAPTER FOUR

THE NEXT EVENING Flora found herself standing in front of a full-length mirror in the bedroom of the eighteenth-century Constantinides mansion in Paris's Marais district.

They'd arrived from London a couple of hours earlier. Apollo upsetting Flora's usual organisational routine whenever they arrived anywhere by ordering her to stop fussing, that Madame Choubert, the housekeeper, would be taking over her duties for the remainder of the visit.

She hadn't known what to do then, but a minute after that an officious French designer arrived with a rack full of gowns and Flora was hustled into the bedroom to try them all on, in a quest to find something suitable for the event that evening.

Flora tried to tell Apollo that she'd brought one of the plain black gowns that she customarily wore when she accompanied him to events as his PA, but he flatly refused to even look at it. It wasn't suitable, he told her shortly. She needed to wear something more befitting her new role as his fiancée.

He was right, of course, but as the hour of the event drew closer, all her insides were tying themselves in knots, her palms sweaty.

She only just managed to stop herself from wiping

them on the gown's midnight-blue silk as she stared at herself in the mirror. The gown had small cap sleeves, and a fitted bodice, but the drama came from the skirt, all swathed and gathered on one side at her hip, leaving her pretty stilettos in the same midnight-blue on display, with the rest of it falling away into a dramatic train behind her.

It really was the most beautiful gown. Discreetly sexy, showing a flash of one thigh where the fabric gathered, and highlighting her bare shoulders, neck and cleavage.

She didn't recognise herself wearing it. She looked like a different person. Not the hardworking, colourless PA, who'd dedicated her life to taking her boss's orders and resolutely staying in the background, but a glamorous, beautiful woman, fully worthy of the title of Apollo Constantinides's fiancée.

But you're not worthy. You're lying to him.

Flora ignored the thought as the designer paced around her, twitching fabric here and there, and murmuring *'magnifique'* at intervals.

Yes, she absolutely was lying to him, but she didn't care. He hadn't cared when he'd talked her father into investing every cent of her family's savings into that awful scheme, so why should she?

In fact, now she thought about it, she could see where her mother was coming from when she'd refused to accept Apollo's compensation money. Blood money, Laura had called it, and at the time, Flora hadn't understood her refusal since they'd needed it.

Now, as an adult, she understood. No amount of money could ever make up for the loss of a husband and father, so what did a few little lies matter?

They didn't. Just like Apollo didn't. And so, she was

going to break his heart the way hers and her mother's had been broken, and she wouldn't feel any regret, not a shred.

That will never bring your father or your mother back, you know this.

It wouldn't, but she hadn't spent the last few years of her life working to get close enough to him to put her plans in motion to stop now, not over one little lie.

She'd only be satisfied once he'd felt the same grief and pain she had.

Anyway, she couldn't start second-guessing herself, especially not when she was going to be the centre of attention tonight. She had to be brave, not let the nerves get to her, no matter that she was more used to staying out of the spotlight rather than standing in its centre.

That morning had already been chaotic, with the photos hitting the media overnight, and now global news platforms were full of sensational headlines complete with those grainy shots she'd leaked. Apollo had approved the press release she'd drafted, which had then gone to Violet for approval also, before being sent out to various media organisations in response.

Violet's people had put out a press release of their own, and it had been measured and gracious, with a little white lie detailing how Apollo had been to see her personally and how they'd worked things out. She wished him all the best with his engagement.

Really, Flora couldn't fault Apollo's handling of the situation. He'd controlled things masterfully. He wouldn't allow a dignified silence where other rumours could take root and grow, ordering all requests for interviews to go directly to him. He refused none of them, answering every question with his usual blunt honesty, as well as very real regret, admitting to his love affair with Flora, and acknowledging that this was a bad look given his stance on employer/employee relations and general business ethics.

He did not charm. He did not manipulate. And, as per usual, people liked it, they found it refreshing in a world full of spin, and she just knew he was going to get the entire world on his side again. And as for her...

Flora swallowed, staring sightlessly at herself in the mirror as the nerves returned.

She'd woken that morning to hundreds of text messages and voicemails from the media, all asking for interviews. Which she'd expected. But she'd also hoped that most of the attention would be directed towards Apollo rather than her.

However, given the spin the Helios PR department was putting on the situation—that she was supposedly the love of Apollo's life—she was every bit an object of interest as he was.

Tonight would be difficult, she was under no illusion. Because tonight everyone's eyes would be on her, studying her, whispering about her, wondering about her.

Tonight might be the start of all her secrets being uncovered.

The few flimsy smokescreens she'd put in place to hide her family history hadn't been designed to withstand concentrated scrutiny by journalists, or the internet at large, and it wouldn't take a lot of research to discover that McIntyre was her mother's maiden name. That her real name was Florence, not Flora. That she was the daughter of David Hunt, one of Stavros Constantinides's victims, who'd killed himself after hearing rumours that the

Constantinides scheme was a Ponzi scheme, prompting the police to investigate Helios.

She couldn't risk that happening, not when her quest for justice had only just started.

You're an idiot. Another thing you should have anticipated.

She hadn't though. She hadn't anticipated that Apollo would take her ruination plan and turn it into a triumph, while leaving her at the mercy of the press. Oh, he'd said he'd protect her, but how could he, when he didn't know the secrets she was hiding from him?

She moistened her dry mouth, a headache starting to throb behind her eyes, which she ignored as she glanced at Apollo, standing by the windows.

He wasn't looking at her, his attention was on his phone. He'd wanted to approve the gown, and so far had vetoed all the ones she'd tried on. She didn't know what exactly he wanted, but he hadn't said yes to anything yet.

Light from the setting sun shone through the windows of the bedroom, glossing his black hair and limning his profile in gold. He was already dressed for the evening, all in black, the perfect contrast to his olive skin.

Tall, dark and dangerous.

God, he really was the most outrageously handsome man.

She resented it. Or, more specifically, she resented the way everything female in her was aware of everything male in him, on the most basic level.

It had been that kiss, that was the trouble. That kiss and her reaction to it.

She'd thought she'd be able to kiss him and feel nothing, to use that glint of hunger she'd seen in his eyes to her own advantage. Perhaps unsettle him as badly as he'd unsettled her, and yet, the moment her lips had touched his, she'd been lost.

Heat had consumed her, a hunger rising inside her that she didn't understand. She'd been powerless against it, and then, when he'd started kissing her back, she'd forgotten everything. She'd forgotten that she hated him. Forgotten all her plans for his ruin. Forgotten that her identity was a secret and he could never find out.

Forgotten her own name.

All there had been was the heat of his mouth and the taste of him, wild and dark and raw. The feeling of his fingers pressing into her hair, the heat of his body, and his scent that stole all the breath from her lungs.

It had been a long time since anyone had touched her, not since her mother had held on to her hand the day she'd died in hospital years earlier, and Flora hadn't known how starved she was for someone's touch until Apollo had threaded his fingers into her hair.

She'd wanted his arms around her. She'd wanted his hands on her, stroking her, caressing her. She wanted more than one kiss. And when he'd lifted his head and looked down into her eyes, all she could think was, *Again, please. Kiss me again.*

But he hadn't. And, worse, he'd seen the desire she hadn't been able to hide. He knew exactly how hungry she was for him physically.

She hated herself for it, but there was nothing to be done. She couldn't take it back now.

As if he'd felt her gaze on him, Apollo looked up from his phone suddenly, and their eyes met, and for a second it was like that moment back in his office, after she'd kissed him, the air around them thick with sexual tension.

Then his eyes widened slightly as he took in the gown, and the breath rushed out of her as that dark, predator's gleam caught in his gaze.

He liked the gown, it was obvious.

Unexpected heat washed through her, and while it made the nerves fluttering around inside her worse, it also gave her a measure of reassurance.

Yes, she could do this seduction thing. He'd seemed so unaffected by that kiss, yet was that really true? He'd been very firm when he'd told that there would be no more kisses, but she could change his mind. She would have to. Her revised quest for justice depended on it, after all.

The designer said something in French to Apollo, then disappeared through the door, shutting it firmly behind him.

Flora took a steadying, silent breath as Apollo strode to where she stood, then walked a slow circle around her, scanning her from every angle.

'Yes,' he murmured to himself, his voice a low rumble. 'This is the one. Jacques has really outdone himself this time.'

Flora tried to resist the blush that crept into her cheeks, but there was no stopping it as he lifted his dark green gaze to hers. 'This is much better than the gown you brought,' he said. 'The press will not be disappointed either.'

He sounded cool, yet the look in his eyes was anything but. She wanted desperately to rip her gaze from his, but being coy wasn't going to help her plan, so she ignored the butterflies and stared back at him instead.

'I hope so,' she said, wishing she sounded as cool as he did, not sick with nerves.

'You'll be fine.' He gazed at her a moment longer, then put his hand in his pocket, pulling out a black velvet box. 'I want you to wear this.' Flipping open the lid, he held it out to her.

Flora's heart beat faster, though she had no idea why. It was an engagement ring, and of course it was an engagement ring. She was supposed to be his fiancée, and fiancées generally wore rings.

The ring comprised a single large blue diamond on a platinum band, bright and costly looking as it glittered against the black velvet.

Flora stared at it, the tension inside her pulling tighter and tighter. It wasn't the same as the ring he'd given Violet, and she should know, since she'd organised the purchase of it. He'd chosen it, though, and had spent a good deal of time over the choice, eventually settling on an emerald the same colour as his eyes.

Had he spent time choosing this one? Had it mattered to him which one he bought? Or had he ordered someone to purchase it for him?

But no, thinking about the stupid ring was ridiculous. Of course it hadn't mattered to him, none of this did. The ring was for show, just like the gown, and her attendance at the gala this evening. None of it was real, not even a little bit.

'Please tell me you didn't spend a lot on this,' she said, trying to cover her nerves.

He lifted a shoulder in an elegant shrug. 'I spent enough for it to look like an engagement ring. People will be noting it, so it wouldn't do for it to look like I spent nothing.' When she didn't move, still staring at it, he made an impatient sound and took the ring out, discarding the box on a small side table nearby. 'Here,' he said peremptorily. 'Give me your hand.'

She didn't want to. She didn't want him to touch her, especially given how badly she'd betrayed herself with that kiss the day before. Then again, refusing him now would betray something else, and she couldn't do that either.

Steeling herself, Flora extended her hand and tried to ignore the inevitable pulse of electricity that bolted through her as he took her fingers in his. He remained impassive as he pushed the ring onto her finger, then held her hand a moment, looking down at the ring glittering there.

His fingers were warm, his grip firm. She could feel her skin tightening in response, her breath getting short.

No, this was madness. She couldn't allow him to get to her like this. What she wanted was for him to be affected by her, not the other way around. She hated him. She *couldn't* want him, she just couldn't. He'd ruined her family, destroyed them completely, and she should not be getting breathless just because he was holding her hand.

He looked up, his green gaze capturing hers. 'Do you like it?'

'Like what?' God, she sounded like a teenage girl with her first crush. 'Oh, the ring? Yes. It's very pretty.'

Unexpectedly, he enclosed her hand in his, the warmth of his palm surrounding her, and it was such a shock that she couldn't move. Every part of her seemed to zero in on his large hand holding hers. Long, blunt fingers, his knuckles dotted with a few white long-healed scars. A strong, masculine hand.

No one had ever held her hand the way he was doing so now. Oh, maybe long ago, in the mists of childhood, her parents might have, but not that she remembered. Since her mother had died, all there'd been in her life was rigid determination. She'd allowed herself nothing that wasn't in pursuit of her goal—to get as close as she could to Apollo Constantinides. Now, she *was* close and, in a way she'd never imagined, all she could think about was how good it was to feel someone's hand gripping hers. As if there was not only warmth there, but support too.

Apollo frowned slightly. 'Your fingertips are cold. Are you nervous?'

Briefly, she debated lying to him, but he was looking intently at her now, his focus narrow and sharp, and she knew she couldn't. He'd realise, which would then prompt more questions, and she couldn't face that, not now. So all she said was, 'Maybe a little.'

Strangely, his gaze softened just a bit, as if it mattered to him that she was nervous. 'Don't be,' he said, his voice shaded with an edge of something unfamiliar. 'Yes, the press will likely be in our faces all night, but I'll keep you from the worst of them, understand?'

Another little shock of surprise rippled through her. In the year she'd spent working for him, all she'd seen of him was the cold, ruthless businessman, who was blunt to the point of offensiveness. She'd never seen him be reassuring, not to anyone.

She'd never seen the faint concern in his eyes as he looked at her, or felt the warmth of his grip. She'd never experienced the strange rush of relief that accompanied it either, as if a part of her wanted to believe that, yes, he would protect her.

It had been a very long time since anyone had cared for her or worried for her. Since her mother had died, she'd thrown herself into her quest for justice, and because she'd had to hide her background, she'd allowed no one to get too close.

Bizarrely, the person she spent the most time with was the man standing in front of her now. The man she hated, who was holding her hand, giving her reassurance.

The man you'll be betraying.

Flora pulled her hand from his abruptly, the warmth of his touch lingering on her skin. 'Thank you,' she said quickly, hoping he wouldn't notice how sharp the movement had been. 'As you said, I'm sure I'll be fine.'

Flora was not fine. Apollo was certain of it.

He'd been momentarily robbed of speech just before, as he'd looked up from his phone and seen her standing there, all those delicious feminine curves wrapped in midnight-blue silk. He was so used to her in her PA uniform of white shirt, black skirt and plain black pumps, it had never occurred to him how she might look in a ballgown.

Well, now he had the answer. She looked beautiful. Glorious. Stunning.

He was noticing all kinds of other things about her too, aspects he couldn't remember seeing before. Such as how the deep charcoal of her eyes reminded him of grey diamonds, silvery and dark at the same time. Her full mouth and its gentle pout. The tender skin of her throat, the pale vulnerability of her bare shoulders. The glossy fall of her curly black hair.

They were all physical things, and he shouldn't be noticing them, yet somehow that switch she'd flipped in him the day before was resolutely set to 'on', and he couldn't seem to ignore it.

Perhaps it was merely that for the past three months he'd been celibate and it was wearing on him. He had, after all, been waiting for his wedding night with Violet, and that was now no longer going to happen.

Perhaps you could have one with Flora...

The thought wound through his head, prompting an immediate physical response, though he crushed it before it could fully take hold.

No, he would not be having anything with Flora. He would not cross that line. He was supposed to be protecting her, not taking advantage of her. Yes, after tonight, the world would think that they were already sleeping together, so it wouldn't be as if he was risking anything publicly. But *he* would know.

He'd crossed lines before thinking they didn't matter, and the end result had been a man's death. He wasn't going to do it again. Some of the press might call him rigid, inflexible and lacking in empathy, but he didn't care. His supposed lack of empathy was simply him being too blunt and too honest, and he wasn't going to apologise for that. He wasn't like his father, full of smiles and empty charm. Oh, once he had been. Once he'd been as well known for it as his father had. He'd enjoyed it too, using that charm and his good looks to get people on his side, manipulating them with ease. That had always given him such an adrenaline rush.

But that had been then, before David Hunt had killed himself.

Apollo had been twenty when that happened, which

had been far too young for such a harsh lesson. He'd learned it just the same, though. The recklessness that his father had was in him too. They were both gamblers, enjoying the rush and the thrill when the bets paid off, giving no heed to the consequences.

He had to guard against it, not let anything go to his head, and the problem with Flora was that she did. She was a slippery slope, and he couldn't risk falling down it.

This would merely be a business arrangement between them, nothing more.

Violet had been very gracious about the photos, and he'd even suggested that perhaps, after an appropriate interval of time had passed, they could resume their engagement. She hadn't refused, so maybe the option was still available.

The reaction of the media to the photos had been predictable, but he wasn't concerned. Not now that Flora had agreed to their little sham affair.

What he was concerned about was the pale look on Flora's face and that, when he'd held her hand, her fingertips had been cold. He'd wanted to keep holding that hand, keep it enclosed in his to warm her, but then she'd pulled it away, and quite abruptly.

He studied her, noting the faint wash of colour on her cheeks and the way she was fussily smoothing her skirt, thick dark lashes veiling her gaze. The diamond on the ring he'd bought the night before glittered on her finger. A blue diamond, because it was the biggest and most expensive ring he could get on such short notice. It suited her.

That flush in her cheeks suited her too. Was that him? Because he'd touched her? It was, he was sure. Especially given her reaction to the kiss the day before.

Not that you'll be doing anything about it.

Of course he wouldn't, but still… Had she always felt that way about him? Or was this a new attraction she'd suddenly discovered, ignited by that kiss?

Whatever, they weren't questions he was going to get answers to, so why he kept thinking about them was anyone's guess. What he should be thinking about was the gala they were attending tonight, and how she was going to cope with it. He was used to the public eye, but Flora wasn't. Normally she was his adjunct, not the centre of attention, so this would be a new experience for her.

'You are not fine,' he said. 'And if you pull away from me tonight the way you did just then, you will cause unwanted gossip that we both can ill afford.'

Her gaze flickered. 'I'm sorry,' she said stiffly. 'That wasn't my intention.'

'I know it wasn't.' He frowned, searching her face. 'Just what about this evening is upsetting you? Is it the attention? Because I already told you, I'll protect you from that.'

She gave him a smile that looked so forced it was as if she'd cut it out of a magazine and pasted it on. 'Perhaps I'm…a little concerned, but I'm sure I'll be fine.'

She was lying. He could always tell a lie. But there wasn't much point in pushing her now. They didn't have long before they needed to leave.

'In that case.' He held out his hand once more. 'Come, we should practice a few poses, so we look as relaxed and as natural as possible with each other.'

It was very subtle, but he saw the instant she stiffened, as if she was bracing herself for a blow. This *was* upsetting for her, he could see the apprehension in her eyes.

Apollo had never been a man who offered comfort
to people, or at least not after he and his father had ruined people's lives. Elena had blamed him for the ruination of their family, too, even though it had been his
father who'd conceived and carried out the entire scheme.
Apollo couldn't argue with her, not when he'd been complicit. But after Stavros had gone to jail, his mother had
refused all Apollo's offers of comfort and reassurance.
She'd carried her pain and anger alone, even after Stavros had died, and sometimes Apollo wondered if she'd
held on to it simply so that she could throw it in his face.
He was, after all, the reason his father had gone to jail.

However, it was clear that Flora needed more than
brusquely worded orders. Throwing her into the deep
end of the shark-infested waters of the world's press, and
expecting her to swim, wasn't exactly kind, especially
when none of this had been her fault.

'Flora,' he said, softening his voice. 'It will be all right.
I've already told you that I won't allow your reputation
to suffer and I won't. I won't permit the press to be rude
to you, either, I promise.'

She stared at him for a moment, and he was sure he
saw surprise cross her face. Then she reached for his
hand and he took it, drawing her closer. 'That's it,' he
murmured, staring down into her eyes. 'Keep looking
at me like that.'

Colour had risen once again beneath her skin, the soft
rose making her eyes glimmer, the grey river stones re-
vealing chips of mica that sparkled, catching the light.

She really was very pretty.

The flush in her cheeks crept down her neck and he
could track its path, the midnight-blue silk of her neckline

leaving her shoulders bare, offering a tantalising glimpse of the shadow between her full breasts.

'I was wrong,' he heard himself say. 'You are not just suitable, Flora. You are exquisite.'

Should you really have said that?

Her eyes widened. 'Sir... I...'

Oh, he shouldn't have said it, he definitely shouldn't. But it was too late to take it back. He had to commit to it now.

'Not sir,' he said. 'Not tonight. Tonight, you will have to get used to calling me Apollo. And yes, you should absolutely keep blushing like that.'

He thought she might look away then, but she didn't. She kept on looking up at him, even as he put one hand on her silken hip and brought her nearer, so her body was drawn gently against his. As if they were dancing or merely being close to each other. Enjoying each other's company. Desperately in love...

She felt soft and very warm, and for some reason he couldn't remember the last time a woman had stood this close to him. Ridiculous, when it was probably Violet, and not too long ago either, but still, he couldn't recall the moment. All he could think about was Flora pressed against him, and he hadn't known until now what a revelation that would be. Because that's what she was. A revelation.

The silvery grey glitter of her eyes seemed to brighten as she lifted her hands the way she had the day before and laid them both on his chest. She only pressed lightly, and yet it was as if he could feel every whorl and twist of her fingerprints through the cotton of his shirt. As if he was a lock, keyed to her, and all he needed was her touch to open.

This is madness. What are you doing?

It *was* madness, and yet he made no move to pull away. Because the dark, devious part of his mind, the manipulative part that had led all those investors to their ruin, was already ticking over, noting her response to him, how the chemistry between them was excellent, thinking of ways to make it even more pronounced, so that no one would doubt the story he'd concocted. Wanting to feel once again the rush of seeing people dance to his tune...

He should stop. He should let her go and move away.

But his hand on her hip tightened, the other lifting slowly to cradle her cheek, the way he had the day before, the softness of her skin against his palm. And somehow his heart missed a beat as she leaned into it, looking up at him from beneath thick, black lashes.

How had he never seen her loveliness? How had he missed the tension in the air between them, which he was sure hadn't been there before? Had he been blind? Or maybe he'd deliberately not seen it, because he'd known what a temptation she'd be?

'I'm sorry I kissed you yesterday,' she said unexpectedly, a slight husk in her voice. 'I crossed a line, and I shouldn't have. I should have apologised then, but I... didn't.'

For a second his brain was so fogged trying to discern what delicious perfume she was wearing that he didn't understand what she was saying.

Then he did, and yet it still didn't make any sense. Apologise for that astonishing kiss? Was she mad?

Your sexual harassment policy? That you were very firm about afterwards? Remember that?

Yes. God. And that should be front and centre in his

mind right now. So why was he thinking about her perfume and the softness of her body against his? Why was he thinking about the colour of her eyes?

This was madness and taking it any further was wrong. He'd always thought his control was perfect, but maybe it wasn't as perfect as he'd assumed it to be.

Or maybe it's because it's Flora.

No, he couldn't countenance that. She was his PA. They were going to enter into a sham relationship and marriage, but the operative word was 'sham'. It wouldn't be real. None of this was.

You're really going to endure six months of celibacy for the sake of a sham marriage?

He didn't want to, no, but what other choice was there? He couldn't risk an affair with anyone else, not after those photos had come to light. He had to be on his best behaviour and usually that wasn't a problem, so why it was hard now—in all sense of the word— he had no idea.

'It's all right,' he said coolly. 'I understood that you were trying to prove a point. Now…' With as much calm as he could muster, he took his hand away from her cheek, and released her hip before stepping back. 'Are you ready for our public debut?'

Her hands fluttered a little as he moved away, as if now they weren't resting on his chest she didn't know quite what to do with them. But her expression held its customary impassiveness, the apprehension that had been in her eyes gone.

'Yes,' she said calmly. 'I am. Apollo.'

CHAPTER FIVE

FLORA'S HEART WAS beating so loud and so fast she wondered if she might faint.

The event was being held in a lavish, eighteenth-century palace that had been lit up like Versailles, with lights that mimicked flickering candles. At the front was a set of magnificent sweeping stairs, where the paparazzi had gathered like flies, taking photographs of the rich and famous as they made their way inside.

The gala was for a well-known children's charity and Helios was a major donor, hence Apollo's invite. Normally, Flora would have leaped from the limo first before rushing around, managing his timetable for the evening, checking guest lists and making sure the people he wanted to speak to were available, not to mention also ensuring that the people who wanted to speak to him did so.

But now it was different. Now, she was on his arm, and there was nothing to manage but her own reckless hormones, which was turning out to be far more difficult than she'd ever imagined.

Back in the Constantinides residence, before they'd left, he'd taken her in his arms and she'd been powerless to move. Powerless to resist. He'd drawn her close, one large hand pressed to her hip, the other cupping her cheek, and she hadn't been able to think.

He'd been so gentle with her, that was the trouble, and it was something she hadn't expected. That such a cold, blunt man could ever have such gentleness inside him had been a surprise, let alone him turning it on her.

He would never let the press hurt her, that's what he'd promised, and some part of her very much wanted to believe that. Some part of her very much wanted his protection, and that was insanity. She'd believed her father when he'd told her he'd always look after her, and look how that had ended.

Apart from anything else, he was also the man who'd caused her father's downfall, so how could she want that from him? He could she want him, full stop?

She didn't understand, but not knowing didn't change the fact that she did, in fact, want him, no matter how much her mind told her that it was wrong.

Not that she had much time to think about it, because Apollo had now got out of the limo and was in the process of opening the door for her, letting in a sudden cacophony from outside, people shouting and calling and clapping.

Now was the moment of truth. Now she had to get out of the car and present herself to the world as Apollo's fiancée. Now she had to pretend that she was desperately in love with him, and had crossed all kinds of boundaries to be with him.

Now she had to ignore the fact that this entire situation was of her own making and that if she had anyone to blame for it, it was herself.

Gripping hard to her courage, Flora had no choice but to step out of the limo.

Instantly they were mobbed by paparazzi, all calling out to her and using her name, as if they knew her. She felt momentarily bewildered by the scrum, not knowing where to look or how to respond. Then Apollo's hand came to rest gently at the small of her back, the warmth of his powerful figure beside her as he urged her up the stairs.

'Ignore them,' he murmured in her ear, his breath warming her skin. 'We'll walk to the top of the stairs and then pause to give them a photo op. Relax and follow my lead.'

So she did, allowing the pressure of that warm hand resting at the base of her spine to guide her as she climbed the stairs, hoping desperately that she wouldn't fall flat on her face. It had all seemed so much easier when the attention wasn't on her, when she was merely managing the situation rather than taking part.

At the top of the stairs, she turned around when Apollo did. and when he slid an arm around her waist as the cameras flashed, she let herself rest against his side so the press could get their photos.

She was very conscious of the questions people were shouting at Apollo, such as how did he reconcile his business practices with an affair with his PA? Had they slept together? What did Violet think? Was he worried that he might lose some major investors? Et cetera, et cetera. Then there were the questions shouted at her, such as who made the first move? Was she still his PA? Did she have any comment about the rumours that Violet had stormed into the Helios offices demanding an explanation?

'Ignore those questions too,' Apollo said quietly, somehow making himself heard beneath the cacophony. 'Flash the ring and smile.'

So she did, the smile feeling forced and fake.

'Yes,' Apollo said, answering one shouted question. 'Flora is my fiancée, and we'll be getting married as soon as we can. And yes, Violet has given us her blessing. If you have any more questions, please direct them to my PR people.'

Then, without saying anything further, he turned around and stalked inside the building, ushering her along with him.

Inside it was less chaotic, with music from a string quartet playing, the interior of the old ballroom lit by glittering chandeliers, with bouquets of white roses overflowing from urns and vases and large copper buckets. Wait staff circulated, carrying trays of various drinks and small canapés.

Apollo snagged them both a couple of tall flutes of champagne before finding a quiet part of the ballroom near some stairs.

She was breathing fast, her adrenaline spiking, making her feel as if she'd just taken a trip on a wild and terrifying rollercoaster.

'You did well on the stairs with the paparazzi,' Apollo said, his attention on the crowd in the ballroom. 'Now we have to be convincing for everyone else.'

Flora took a steadying sip of champagne, the dry yeasty flavour exploding deliciously on her tongue. Now she was here, and the initial chaos of the photographers was over and done with, she felt better.

It was fine, she could do this. Her hormones might be all over the place when it came to Apollo, but all she actually had to do was trust in them. She didn't have to hide her attraction to him here. In fact, hiding it was what she *shouldn't* do.

She just had to remember that her very real feelings were supposed to be an act.

You also have to remember that the potential for all your secrets to come tumbling out has never been higher.

The shard of ice that had lodged inside her the day before, when Apollo had told her how he'd solve the issue of the photos, seemed to gain sharp edges.

It wouldn't take much interest from the media to blow her fragile cover, and given the scrum on the way in, the media *would* want to know. They'd want to know who she was and where she'd come from. What exactly was it about her that was enough to tempt a man such as Apollo Constantinides. A man famous for his spotless, impeccable reputation.

But now she was caught between a rock and a hard place, with no choice but to keep going.

She had to hope any discovery the press made about her real identity wouldn't be until *after* she'd gone through with her heartbreak plans. And if it was before? Well, she'd cross that bridge when she came to it. Right now, she had to get through this night.

'Thank you,' she said, a warm glow expanding in her chest in response to his praise, which was silly of her. Then again, he wasn't a man who gave out praise often. For example the most he'd ever given her was 'adequate'.

Wrong. He also called you exquisite, remember?

The warm glow grew warmer at the memory. She'd never even been called pretty before, let alone exquisite, and even though she might tell herself it didn't matter, that she didn't care what he thought of her, a part of her had loved that he'd said it. He wasn't a man who dispensed compliments, so it meant something coming from him.

Stop thinking about this. You can't let him distract you from what you're supposed to be doing.

No, she couldn't. She had to keep her eye on the prize, remember what she was here for, which was to get close to him. Make herself irresistible to him, make him love her. Then break that cold heart of his before anyone found out the truth about her.

Justice must be served.

Justice for her father, for her mother, and for herself.

'Are you ready to brave the rest of the room?' Apollo asked. 'You can let me do the talking if you'd prefer.'

The champagne must have loosened her tongue, because she found herself smiling up at him, and saying, 'Really? With your famous people skills? You hate doing the talking.'

His jungle green gaze settled on her, focusing with the laser intent that indicated she'd said something that had surprised him.

A dark little thrill arrowed through her. Good. That meant she had to keep on surprising him, make sure he forgot all about Flora the PA, who never teased or flirted or disagreed with him in any way. She had to become Flora, his fiancée. The femme fatale who was exquisite and surprising, intriguing and passionate.

A liar...

Flora shoved that thought away hard.

'I'll manage.' His tone was brusque, but the look in his eyes glittered.

Well, the die was cast. She had to commit to her new plan and she had to do it now, when they were on display, even though her experience with seduction was nil.

She was just going to have to wing it.

Taking a risk, Flora stepped closer to him, looking up at him from beneath her lashes. 'I'll be okay, Apollo,' she said, relishing saying his name. 'Thank you for being concerned about me, though.'

He didn't look away. 'Give me your hand,' he ordered softly.

'You have a thing for hands, don't you?' She extended it, feeling the usual jolt as he took hold of it.

'Just yours.' He raised her hand to his mouth and pressed the lightest of kisses on the back of it, his hunter's gaze locked on hers.

Another thrill shot through her at the heat of his lips on her skin, her heart beating even faster.

'I assume that was for the press?' She didn't bother to hide the breathlessness in her voice.

'Of course.' One black brow rose. 'Did you want it to be for you?'

She should say no, of course she didn't want it to be for herself. This was an act, a show. This was pretend. Except what came out of her mouth was, 'Maybe.' And then she added, 'Pull me in closer.'

Something flared in his eyes then, a flame, and abruptly she found it difficult to breathe. He obviously liked this side of her, because he didn't hesitate, tugging her towards him, bringing her so close they were almost touching. She breathed him in, relaxing her tense muscles, because it didn't matter if she allowed herself to revel in his presence, to let her desire show in her eyes. This was all part of her plan.

Then she lifted a hand to his hair, touching the thick, inky softness, brushing a strand back from his brow. A tender touch that a woman might give to the man she loved.

His eyes widened as she touched him, which meant once again she'd surprised him, and that flame lost deep in the jungle green burned higher, brighter.

Flora couldn't look away.

Then he reached out slowly, almost lazily, and slid his fingers into her hair, tilting her head back, before capturing her mouth with his.

Apollo hadn't intended to kiss her. In fact, it was something he'd told himself he absolutely wasn't going to do. All that was needed was for them to stand close to each other, for his arm to go around her waist in a decorous embrace, that was all the touching required.

Except then he'd taken her hand and kissed the back of it, and then she'd touched his hair in a natural, familiar way, and he hadn't been able to stop himself from taking things further and tasting her mouth. Even now, with her lips warm and silky beneath his, he didn't fully understand how he'd got to this point.

Perhaps it had been the way she'd touched him just before, gently, hesitantly, as if he was a work of art and she was afraid of breaking him. No one had ever touched him like that, not even when he'd been a child, and it had robbed him of breath. The silvery glints of mica in her grey eyes had been glittering, and her mouth had had the most delectable curve. He hadn't seen her smile, he'd realised with a small, electric jolt, not even once, and that was clearly a tragedy. Because her smile was a thing of beauty, and he found himself thinking of all the things he could do to get her to smile at him that way again.

It was madness.

Madness to draw her in as she'd suggested. Madness to have her so close, the sweet scent of her surrounding him and making his mouth water. Making him remember that kiss, and how delicious she had tasted.

Madness to kiss her again, especially when he knew how addicted he was to the rush and adrenaline surge that came with doing something reckless.

Yet he just couldn't stop.

He could blame it on the media, that it was part of their performance tonight to convince everyone that they were actually in love, but deep down he knew the truth.

He wanted to kiss her to see if the chemistry that had lit him up inside the day before was still hot, still strong, and yes. It was. It very definitely was.

Yet again, there was glory in her lips against his, silky and soft. She tasted of champagne and strawberries, the kind of summers that contained picnics and ice cream and swimming in the sea under the hot sun. The kind of summers he'd only ever had as a child back in Athens, back when his father was still the hero Apollo had looked up to, not the charlatan he'd turned out to be.

Summers where his mother had loved him and not blamed him for the ruination of their family.

Summers he would never have again.

His fingers tightened in Flora's hair, curling into a fist, holding her tightly as he chased that sweet summer taste, his tongue pushing into her mouth, exploring deeper.

She made a husky, needy sound deep in her throat and leaned into him, her body pressing to his, all heat and softness. There was a hunger to her that he found almost unbearably sexy, because it had been an age since anyone had been this hungry for him. Violet certainly hadn't been. She'd enjoyed his kisses, but he knew she'd been as ambivalent as he was about the thought of actually sleeping together.

Flora wasn't ambivalent. Her blatant desire for him was the purest aphrodisiac he'd ever known, and he wanted to crush her to him, tear the midnight-blue silk from her shoulders and explore the silken curves of her body. Stroke them. Taste them. Bury himself inside them…

But he couldn't. Not here, and not anywhere else either.

She was untouchable. She was on the other side of all the boundaries he'd put around himself, and he couldn't cross over them. He wouldn't. That way lay the slippery slope into ruination, and he'd already been there once before. Someone had died because of him, because he'd grown addicted to the rush, the surge of adrenaline that had hit him whenever he'd talked another person into investing in his father's scheme.

But he'd liked the admiration and approval in Stavros's eyes even more.

Love had led him down that slope, and he couldn't even set foot on it, which meant he had to be on his guard.

With as much gentleness as he could muster, Apollo relaxed his grip on her hair and lifted his mouth from hers. She was delicately flushed, her grey eyes glowing with desire, and he knew it was for him. It was *all* for him. His beautiful PA, and yes, she *was* beautiful. He'd been right about what he'd said to her earlier that day. She wasn't just beautiful, she was exquisite.

His heart was a drum in his ears and there was a tightness in his groin that definitely shouldn't be there. Damn. What had he been thinking? He had to be better than this.

'Come,' he said brusquely, releasing her. 'There are people I need to introduce you to.'

He couldn't bear it suddenly, to keep on looking at her lovely face and the desire in her eyes, so he turned to the rest of the room and took a step towards the crowd. Only to be brought up short as she grabbed his hand, her fingers lacing through his, as if he belonged to her and she was staking her claim.

Strange to be the one who suddenly wanted to pull away. To be the one putting distance between them. Given her earlier responses, he'd expected it to be her, not him, who couldn't bear their physical closeness.

Everything in him wanted to shake off her hand, because the temptation to pull her closer was nearly overwhelming, but he couldn't. Not in the middle of the ballroom with all eyes on them. He'd been the one who'd decided on this lie after all, and changing his mind now would be ridiculous, not to mention an acknowledgment that his control wasn't what it should be.

Shoving away the fierce desire that burned in his blood, Apollo made himself curl his fingers around Flora's, holding on as he stalked towards one particular knot of people.

From then on, the whole evening began to take on the shape of a nightmare.

He couldn't get rid of his intense physical awareness of her. There seemed to be a part of his brain constantly monitoring where exactly she was in relation to him at all times. How close she stood, whether he could smell the sweet scent of her perfume, how the feel of her hand in his made it difficult to think.

Talking to people was almost impossible, since he kept

losing his train of thought, and quite often she had to take over the conversation. And perhaps that was the worst thing—or possibly the best, he couldn't decide—because then he had to watch her smile and chat easily to people, charming them, and not with the kind of manipulation his father used, but with a natural effervescent spirit that he'd had no idea she possessed.

It was like realising a previously insignificant daisy was actually a sunflower, and now it was blooming in all its glory, and he couldn't stop staring.

How was this utterly delightful, beautiful woman the same as his impassive, unquestioning PA? In her boring black-and-white PA uniform? Who did everything he said and never complained, never protested?

He watched her now, chatting to the CEO of a global bank, as if she'd known the woman all her life and not only met her seconds ago. The CEO was smiling and laughing, introducing her husband to Flora, totally ignoring Apollo, standing tall and unsmiling beside her.

No, she wasn't his PA tonight. She was wearing his ring. She was his fiancée.

A lull came in the conversation, and abruptly Apollo couldn't stand being in this ballroom with her so close a second longer. Couldn't stand the lie this was, a lie that held a component of truth he couldn't escape.

He wanted her. It was all purely physical, nothing to do with the brightness of her eyes or the brilliance of her smile. It was simply common lust, nothing special, yet he was having difficulty resisting, and that was an issue. He had to get her away from him as quickly as possible.

Gripping her hand tightly, he said to the group at large,

not caring if he was interrupting the conversation, 'If you'll forgive me, we really must be going.'

His words fell into the glittering edifice of the conversation like stones smashing through glass. His voice had come out harsh and blunt, but he didn't bother tempering it. He *was* harsh and blunt, and people could do what they wanted with it.

Everyone stared at him in surprise, and he supposed he should murmur some meaningless platitudes and smile, but he'd never felt less like smiling.

Instead he turned and strode in the direction of the exit without another word, tugging Flora along with him.

'What's wrong?' she asked breathlessly as they came out of the ballroom and into the glittering hallway.

'Nothing.' Pulling his phone out of his pocket, he texted his driver, even as he kept heading for the front doors, his other hand still holding hers and tugging her along. 'It was merely time to leave.'

'Really? Right now? But we've only been here an hour.'

He ignored her, striding outside, continuing to lead her along as he went down the stairs to meet the limo that had just pulled up.

After they'd got inside and the doors had closed, she turned to look at him, concern in her eyes. 'Are you sure you're okay? That was very sudden.'

'You know I don't like events.' His voice was probably too harsh, but he didn't care. 'As I said, it was time to leave.' He was overwhelmingly conscious of her gaze on him. He'd been conscious of it all night. Every time she looked at him, he'd felt it like an electric shock, and it was slowly driving him insane. 'Stop looking at me like that,' he growled, staring straight ahead as the limo pulled away from the kerb.

'Like what?' She sounded bewildered.

Apollo couldn't stand it. He turned and met her silvery gaze, unable to keep himself from glancing at her bare shoulders where her black hair licked like dark flames over the creamy expanse of her skin, before looking back to her face again. 'How do you think?' He snarled the words like a beast.

There was nothing but puzzlement on her face. 'I'm sorry, did I—'

He reached for her before she could finish, suddenly beside himself with frustration as he hauled her into his lap. She didn't make a sound, didn't protest, and when he took her hair in a fist and pulled her head back, she didn't tell him to stop. And when he took her mouth as if he'd been kissing her for years, as if she was his, she opened it, sliding her arms around his neck and clinging onto him for dear life.

This was a terrible idea, and he knew it. He should stop, take his mouth from hers and put her back in her seat, but he didn't.

He leaned forward instead, still kissing her, hitting the button that activated the screen between the driver and the backseat. Then he kissed her deeper, harder. Sliding his tongue into her mouth and exploring, feasting. She was a delectable treat, tasting of all those long-forgotten summers, and he couldn't stop himself from wanting more. He was quite sure he'd never tasted anything as delicious as she was.

Flora gave a soft little moan in the back of her throat, the way she'd done back in the ballroom, and he dug his fingers into the soft black mass of her hair, closing them into fists. Pulling her head back further so he could taste her deeper.

Her body was pliant as warm wax, no resistance in her at all, as if she too had been waiting for this moment between them, as if it had been inevitable, only a matter of time.

And maybe it was. Maybe this chemistry between them had only been hidden, buried and smouldering, waiting for the right moment to catch alight and burn bright.

You were supposed to keep your hands off her.

He was. Now, though, it was too late. He was crossing boundaries he shouldn't be crossing, the self-imposed boundaries he'd put there for the good of his reputation and to protect people. Protect them from him.

But he didn't think he could stop. Certainly not with her fingers tugging at his tie, trying to undo it so she could get at the buttons of his shirt. She kept shifting her weight in his lap, and the pressure against his aching groin was maddening.

He had to do something to stop this, or else he'd fall all the way down that slippery slope to the bottom.

Gathering all his considerable will, Apollo wrenched his mouth away, holding tight to her hair to keep her still. 'This should not happen,' he growled.

Her eyes were black in the dim interior of the limo, her mouth full and red and open as a flower. 'Why not?' Her own voice didn't sound much better than his.

'Because you work for me. Because I'm your boss.'

'So?' She touched his jaw, her fingertips lightly tracing the line of it. 'I don't care if you don't, and everyone thinks we're already sleeping together.'

The caress of her fingers… It made him want to grab her hand, maybe bite her fingertips, nip them, watch her face while he did it and see if she liked it—

No. He had to stop this and now, while he still could. He'd told himself that he wasn't going to touch her, and if he couldn't control simple lust, then what kind of man was he?

The kind who ruins people. The kind who sold out his own father.

'No,' he said flatly, both to her and the voice in his head.

But she ignored him. 'Apollo.' Unexpectedly, she took his chin in her hand, holding him the way he'd held her the day before. 'Look at me.' Her skin was so beautifully flushed, her hair tangled. She looked like a woman well tumbled already, and they hadn't done more than kiss. 'I want you,' she went on. 'I want you badly. And it doesn't have to mean anything, not if we don't want it to. We could just have one night. Just one. We're not hurting anyone, and the next day we'll go back to pretending.'

She let go of his chin, her fingertips sliding down his throat, to where his pulse beat hard, resting there. She didn't look away from him, her eyes a dark sea he could fall into and drown in. 'Please. Please, don't make me beg.'

His control should have been strong enough to resist her. In fact, it should have been easy. But it wasn't and easy was the last thing it was. His brain felt full of trea-cle, the usual smooth turning of cogs and gears heavy and sticky. It seemed to take a lot of effort to even think why he was supposed to keep his hands off her, especially when something inside him kept straining at the leash he'd put on it, wanting to break free. The wild, reckless part of him, which he'd imprisoned the night he'd picked up the phone and called the police.

One night. What would it hurt? She wanted him. And the way she looked at him, as if she might die if she didn't get to have him, was making him harder than he'd ever been in his entire life.

'One night,' he ground out eventually. 'Just one.'

Her eyes seemed to catch fire then and he couldn't wait. Just couldn't. The leash on his control broke, and he was leaning forward, taking her mouth in a savage kiss before she could speak.

She didn't seem to mind that it wasn't courteous or restrained. She only sighed as if in relief, as if his kiss was cool water on a burn, taking away the pain, making it better. Then her hands resumed their attack on his tie, clawing at the fabric and the shirt buttons beneath it, as hungry for him as he was for her.

She wasn't lying. She *did* want him.

The desire raging inside him had fully broken away and, like the tide, there was nothing he could do to stop it from swamping him. Nothing mattered. Not where they were, not who they were. Nothing except this relentless, aching hunger, and the surge of adrenaline spiking in his blood, flooding him with that familiar recklessness.

He took her hands and pulled them away from him, because that touch of hers was too much, putting them behind her back and imprisoning her wrists in an iron grip. Then he looked straight into her darkened eyes. 'Here,' he demanded. 'Now.'

CHAPTER SIX

HIS GRIP WAS IRON. There was no way for her to break it. And the look in his eyes, black in the dim confines of the limo, was fierce, almost savage with hunger.

He was a starving lion and she was his prey, but unlike a poor antelope, she didn't want to get away. She was already caught, and now she wanted him to gorge on her, feast on her until she couldn't bear it any more.

The world had narrowed to the gleam in his eyes, the warm strength of his hands gripping her wrists, the intolerable ache between her thighs.

Her plans were forgotten—she couldn't even remember why getting close to him mattered—and she didn't care.

She didn't care that he was the man who'd caused her father's death, the reason she'd lost her mother too, and why the safe, contented little bubble of her childhood had been shattered.

She didn't even care that the man who'd destroyed so many parts of her life was going to take her virginity.

None of those things seemed important, not any more.

There was only him. Him and his touch, his kiss, the chemistry that sparked and flared in the air around them.

His body was hard beneath hers, like stone, and her

mouth felt full and sensitive from the effects of that blinding kiss. Her clothes felt too tight, constraining her, and she wanted to be rid of them. She wanted to be naked, basking in the heat he was putting out, sunning herself like a cat.

Here, he'd said. *Now.*

Of course, here. Of course, now. Those were the only logical answers.

'Yes,' she said hoarsely, her voice cracked as old paint. 'Yes, *please.*'

He shifted her on his lap, levelling that fierce stare at her as he adjusted her, easing her knees apart so they were spread on either side of his hips and she was facing him. He didn't let go of her wrists.

'I'm going to hold you like this.' His voice was soft and rough as frayed velvet, his gaze electric. 'You can't touch me, understand? Not yet.'

She swallowed, her mouth dry, her heart beating so hard she could barely hear anything. 'Why not?'

'Because you've got me on edge like a teenage boy,' he said bluntly.

That thrilled her. So, he wanted her *that* much, did he? That made her feel good, made her feel powerful in a way she hadn't ever felt before. He was a billionaire, head of a vast company, a man known for his iron control and his rigidity, and yet here he was, holding her hands behind her back, because her touch was too much for him. *She* threatened his control, and she liked it.

Her heart raced even faster. What would happen if she *did* touch him? What would happen if he lost his hold on that control of his? A shiver chased over her skin, her thoughts tumbling over themselves.

Oh, she wanted to see that. She wanted to see him totally at the mercy of this chemistry between them. She wanted to see him undone by her touch, by *her.*

This is how he can destroy you...

The thought flickered through her head, so fast she barely noted it. Right now all that seemed important was that glint in his eyes, that fire. She wanted to see it burn higher, burn his control to ash and unleash the passion imprisoned by it. Except, to do that, she needed to touch him and he had her wrists in a grip too strong for her to break.

She'd always been wary of losing control, of feeling helpless against the strength of her own emotions, but she didn't feel helpless now. Even with him holding her wrists. He'd let her go if she wanted, she knew that he would, but she didn't want him to.

She wanted sit just like this and see if he would join her where she was, in the middle of all this delicious fire.

Flora lifted her chin and held his gaze, letting him see what he was doing to her, letting him see the depth of her desire, because there was no need to hide it, not now. And deep in his jungle green eyes, she saw an answering desire leap high.

Oh, he liked watching her, he did. And he thought that, by holding her wrists, he was the one in charge here. But he wasn't. She was seducing him away from his control, and he didn't even realise it. All she had to do was surrender to him, and he'd follow.

Moving slowly, he reached behind her, to the zip of her gown, drawing it down in a smooth, measured movement. The blue silk parted, cool air washing over her heated skin, and it felt glorious. Then he slid the little sleeves down her arms before pulling the neckline down, exposing her breasts.

She hadn't worn a bra, not with that gown, so there was nothing impeding his view, and she might have felt horribly self-conscious with another man, but she wasn't with another man. She was with Apollo, and as the fire in his eyes leaped even higher, she knew he was utterly at her mercy.

'I told you that you were exquisite,' he murmured, his gaze roving all over her, looking at her as if he couldn't get enough. 'And exquisite you are.'

And she knew it, felt the truth of it deep inside. Right now, sitting here in the limo, on his lap, in his arms, she felt every bit as exquisite as he said she was.

He lifted his free hand, touching her, fingertips brushing lightly over the pulse at the base of her throat, then her collarbones, and down, tracing patterns on her bare skin. She shuddered, her breathing uneven, the light caresses making her skin tighten and prickle, and the ache between her thighs get even worse.

'Do you like this?' That soft, velvety voice of his wasn't cold any longer, or impassive. It was threaded through with a rough heat, a hunger that seemed only to acknowledge what she already knew, that she had him wrapped around her little finger. He would deny her nothing.

His hand dropped down further, cupping one breast. 'Do you like me touching you?'

The heat of his palm against her bare skin was an intense pleasure, drawing a shudder of delight that she didn't even attempt to hide. Then his thumb brushed over her already hard nipple, sending sparks everywhere, tearing a gasp from her.

'Answer me, Flora,' he said with rough insistence.

'Yes,' she managed, the word ending on a gasp as he pinched her nipple gently, sending a pulse of electric pleasure through her entire body. 'Yes… I… I like it.'

His gaze was a deep jungle pool, emeralds glittering at the bottom like sunken treasure. Such beautiful eyes. She wanted to drown in them.

His fingers wandered, teasing her and stroking her, mapping the curves of her body as if he had all the time in the world. But she could see the leash he held on his hunger, and she knew she was testing it. It was going to break soon, and she wanted it to.

'I'm your boss.' His fingers moved lower, finding the helm of her gown and sliding beneath it. 'Does that excite you?'

'Yes,' she whispered, all her guards down, letting him see the truth. 'But it's you who excites me. You always have.'

He found her bare thigh, stroking her skin, a fine net of sparks radiating from where he touched, prickling all over her. 'Always?' He held her gaze captive as his fingers crept higher, between her thighs, touching her, caressing her. 'Since you started working for me?'

Flora shuddered under his touch, surrendering completely to him. 'Yes,' she whispered. 'Always. Right from the first day.'

An expression she couldn't read flickered across his beautiful face, but there was no denying the glittering flames in his eyes. He liked that she had.

'You hid it well, *matia mou*.' Finding the damp silk of her underwear, he pulled the fabric to one side in a deft movement. 'I would never have guessed.'

She gasped as his fingers found the soft, slick folds between her thighs, exploring, teasing, and the pleasure became so acute the gasp turned into a low moan.

No one had ever touched her there before, though sometimes at night she would touch herself, give herself a fleeting physical pleasure for comfort, when she felt too lonely, the journey she'd undertaken too long. When the quest for justice seemed hollow, like one of those pipe dreams of her father's, and she not worthy, not equal to the task.

What Apollo was doing with his hand, though, was nothing like the feeling when she touched herself. It was sharper and so much more intense that she found herself trembling, on the brink of climax already.

It might have felt too exposing to be so undone by him, to be held helpless like this, trembling under his gaze like that antelope under the paw of a lion, but it didn't feel exposing. And she didn't feel at his mercy or helpless.

No, it was the other way around. *He* was helpless. *He* was at *her* mercy, and she knew it by the savage glitter in his eyes, the way his stare was locked with hers, as if he couldn't look away. As if there was nowhere he'd rather be looking than at her.

He was desperate for her, his forgotten PA. The daughter who hadn't been enough for one parent, and who'd been a millstone around the neck of the other. She had him on his knees with a desire so strong he'd crossed all his own lines, burned his code of ethics to the ground, and overturned his vaunted control so badly he couldn't wait until they got back to the Constantinides residence to have her.

Power coursed through her and she loved it. She loved

that look in his eyes and the way he touched her. She felt like a phoenix, rising magnificently from the ashes, golden and brilliant and beautiful, the object of everyone's desire.

But it was his desire that mattered most to her.

And it was time to unleash it.

He stroked her, easing one finger inside her, pressing her wrists into the small of her back with his other hand, making her spine arch, her bare breasts pressing against the cotton of his shirt. She groaned, her head falling back as the pleasure intensified. 'Please...' she murmured. 'Please...'

'Please, what?' His voice was so deep it was a growl, insistent, demanding.

Flora looked at him beneath her lashes, moving restlessly against his hand, watching as the leash he had on his own desire began to loosen. 'Please, sir,' she whispered.

The look in his eyes blazed. 'Good girl.' He eased in another finger, sliding them in and out, a rhythm that had her panting. 'Very good, *matia mou*.' And he kept on watching as his fingers moved, and the wave broke over her, and she cried out, trembling as pleasure swamped her.

She could see him then, still looking at her, staring at her as if he'd suddenly discovered God, and he was so close to the edge. It wouldn't take much to push him over, and she wanted him to.

He'd stripped her of her control, now it was time for her to strip him of his.

'Let me go,' she whispered, and immediately, his hold on her wrists loosened. She shifted on him, hearing the harsh intake of his breath, feeling the hard evidence of his desire beneath her. Not that she needed either to know how close he was to that edge, not when she could see the bonfire in his eyes.

Flora lifted her hands and took his face between them. 'Now, sir,' she murmured, meeting his gaze. 'Let yourself go.'

Flora had done something to him and he didn't know what it was. What he did know was that he couldn't think, couldn't move, could barely breathe from the intensity of the desire flooding him.

He felt strung out, almost wild, only hanging on to his control by the skin of his teeth. One slip and that grip would break, and he had no idea what would happen if it did.

Yet looking up in her passion-darkened eyes, the sweet smell of her body and her arousal all around him, the top of her gown down around her waist, and her bare skin warm, he was starting not to care.

What did it matter if he did? He'd barely managed to keep it together as he'd slowly uncovered her, unwrapping her like a present, and touching her, caressing her lovely body, had driven him to the edge. Perhaps he shouldn't have told her what she did to him, perhaps he shouldn't have admitted it. Then again, he knew she'd liked his desire for her, knew that it had added to her pleasure, and watching her react to him had been the sweetest gift.

She'd let him see everything, had held nothing back, and something in him had responded to abandon. The reckless, wild part of him that he had to keep under control was fighting to be set free.

She had seen that too, and now with her whispering to him to let go, he couldn't think of anything he wanted to do more.

Apollo forgot about the slippery slope. Forgot that he needed to keep that part of himself under wraps. Forgot everything but the savagery of the desire inside him, and how he needed to bury it in the woman who'd set it free.

There was no time for niceties. No time for gentleness or care. He pulled out his wallet, found himself a condom, then jerked the buttons of his trousers open. It didn't take more than a moment to sheath himself, before he was gripping her hips, positioning her where he wanted her.

He kept his gaze on hers as he lifted her, then eased her down onto him, pushing into the tight, slick heat of her body. Her eyes went wide and her mouth opened, her hitching gasp echoing the limo.

Beautiful, beautiful woman.

He wanted to stay like this, buried inside her, watching the pleasure climb in her eyes the way he had just before, but the demands of his body were too much. He couldn't stop his hips from lifting, couldn't stop his hands from tightening on her, holding her firmly in place as he drove himself into her.

'Sir...' she whispered, the pleasure-soaked sound of the word adding a forbidden spice to his own desire. 'Oh... Apollo...'

Yes, and his name too, spoken just like that... So good...

He couldn't drag his gaze from her face, all delicately flushed, her hair a black tangle around her shoulders, her grey eyes darkened into black. He'd undone her, his unflappable little PA. He'd made her moan, and now he was going to make her scream.

He drove deeper, her gasps of pleasure music to his ears, and yet also loosening his grip on his own sanity. He wanted to make her come again, but he wasn't sure he could hold on long enough. He'd never had that problem before, never.

She will be the ruin of you.

The thought was there and then it was gone before he'd had a chance to fully grasp it. But by then he didn't care. All that mattered was the tight heat of her body, the way she moaned, the endless darkness of her eyes.

Everything had narrowed.

He didn't care that they were in his limo having sex.

He didn't care that she was his PA.

He didn't care about his reputation or his name.

What he cared about was making her come before the climax claimed him too, so he pushed his hand between them, his fingers sliding between her legs to where she was most sensitive, and he stroked her, giving her some added friction.

Flora cried out, her back arching, her head going back as the climax hit her, and he reached for her then, plunging his fingers into her hair and dragging her mouth down onto his, moving harder, faster, his hips falling out of rhythm as the orgasm took him as well. The kiss turned savage and he said her name over and over against her mouth, as the pleasure took him like a building collapsing on top of him.

He wasn't sure how long it took for him to come back to himself. Perhaps an age, perhaps mere seconds, but for a while he was somewhere else. Somewhere far away, where there was nothing in the world but the woman in his arms, her sweetness, her heat, the tight grip of her sex around his. Her soft moans, her needy cries, the abandon with which she'd given herself to him.

He wasn't even Apollo Constantinides, imprisoned on all sides by the boundaries he'd put around himself, or the rigid control he'd kept himself under.

No, he was just a man with a woman he desired, and who desired him in return. Nothing more, but certainly nothing less. And it was a strange thing, but in the afterglow of the most intense climax he'd ever had, he felt as if he'd been suffocating for years, and only now could he finally breathe.

It was Flora. It was all her. How she'd known he'd been holding himself back, he had no idea, but when she'd told him to let go, he had, as if he'd been waiting for the chance to do so all this time and had never dared. Letting the wildness take him and following it wherever it led and... She'd joined him there.

He'd never let himself go like that with a woman before, never ever, and now that he had... Well, now, he felt more like himself than he could remember feeling for a long, long time.

A night, though. That's all you have.

Flora had collapsed forward onto him, her head on his shoulder, and he put a hand to the back of her head, feeling the softness of her hair under his palm. Feeling the softness of her body, warm and relaxed, pressed to his.

A night he'd said, but that had been before she'd completely decimated his control. And she had. Which meant she was a dangerous woman.

Apollo glanced down at her, feeling her soft breaths against his neck. Her eyes were closed, lashes lying softly on her pink cheeks.

He should get rid of her, he knew that. He should perhaps transfer her to a different position in the company, where she wasn't working directly with him, where she could never threaten his command over himself again. And if he hadn't spent years polishing the Constantinides name, making his reputation the pillar upon which everything stood, he might have done just that, ending this pretence of an engagement as well.

But he couldn't.

Everyone thought they were sleeping together, as she'd already pointed out, so maybe they should make that part of it real. That wouldn't break anything. In fact, now that he thought about it, maybe sleeping together would be a good thing. The hold he'd had on himself had been too rigid, but if he could let go with her, within the confines of a bed and, very soon, marriage vows, then that would be a good way for him to let off steam. Indulge his recklessness physically, with a woman who matched him.

Satisfaction gathered inside him as he leaned back against the seat, cradling Flora in his arms. She didn't move, seemingly content to lie there against him.

Yes, that's what he'd do. He'd marry her quickly, make her his wife, and then, once this chemistry between them had burned itself out, they'd go their separate ways, her reputation and his safely intact.

Having sex with Flora wasn't the slippery slope back down to the man he'd once been, it just wasn't. Too many years had passed of him being who he was now, years of having those boundaries around him, years of making sure his moral compass pointed true north.

He would never be that young man again, hungry for his father's approval, proud of his business skills and the way he could charm people, the way he could get them to do anything he wanted. He'd enjoyed bending people to his will back then, seducing them into giving him all their money, it had given him the purest thrill. And then seeing his father look at him as if Apollo was his golden child.

He'd told the police, the media, his mother, he'd told anyone who asked that he hadn't known what his father was doing. That he hadn't seen the signs that his father's investment scheme wasn't as legitimate as it had appeared. That he was just as much a victim of his father's machinations as everyone else was…

But, deep down, there was a truth he hadn't wanted to acknowledge.

He'd known. He'd known exactly what his father had been doing, and he hadn't cared. It had been the first time his father had brought him in, and he'd been too excited to be working with him, to finally be at his side in the family business, that he'd ignored the signs. Ignored the instinct in his gut that had told him there was something amiss.

He'd been chasing that thrill with reckless abandon, loving how his father would drape his arm around Apollo's neck and tell him how proud he was of him. What a chip off the old block he was. All he'd ever wanted to be at that moment in time was his father, his hero.

Now, all he wanted was to be different.

And he was. Sex with Flora wouldn't change things, it just wouldn't.

He wound his fingers into her hair and tilted her head to the side, looking down at her. Black hair covered his jacket, the rosy pink of her cheek contrasting against his white shirt.

Pretty, pretty Flora.

'Are you okay, *matia mou*?' he murmured, the endearment coming as easily as it had before they'd had sex.

She let out a long and very satisfied sigh. 'Yes, I'm very okay.' She glanced up at him, grey eyes still darkened with pleasure. 'You are quite incredible, do you know that?'

'So I've been told. On a number of occasions.'

She smiled, pure amusement glittering in her gaze, and his heart skipped a beat. She was so relaxed like this, lying against him as if she'd done it all her life, looking up at him as if she truly loved him, as if this wasn't a sham at all, but entirely real. She was a woman who was freer and more natural, more passionate and sparkling than his buttoned-up, impassive PA. There was also a mischievousness to her, a glint of something wicked in her eyes, which sparked an answering wickedness in him.

'You're so arrogant,' she said, as if this was an utterly delightful quality.

And he couldn't stop the smile that turned his mouth. A rare smile, since he'd never found that there was much about life to smile at. But he did so now, because she was beautiful, and the way she looked at him made him feel as if there were things to smile about now. 'And you like it,' he said, his fingers playing through her hair, loving the feel of it against his skin. 'You certainly liked calling me "sir".'

Colour swept over her skin, her eyes glinting silver. 'Maybe. Or maybe I just like to indulge your dominating tendencies.'

'That's good, because I have a lot of those tendencies.'

'So I've noticed.' The smile faded from her face slowly.

'So…this is probably a bit late now, but what's going to happen after tonight?'

He shifted her into a more comfortable position. 'Do you want more?' It was a question he thought he knew the answer to, but he wanted her to say it.

'Yes,' she said honestly, obliging him. 'You must know I do.'

'Then you shall have it.' He pushed a strand of hair back behind her ear. 'I propose a wedding as quickly as possible, and then you will move in with me. We'll have a proper marriage for as long as we both want it.'

'Move in with you?' She raised an imperious brow. 'Perhaps you need to move in with me.'

She was teasing him, he thought, but he liked it. He liked it very much indeed. However, he realised, as soon as she said it, that he didn't know where she lived. Or if she lived alone. Presumably she wasn't with anyone, otherwise she wouldn't have had sex with him. No, he was sure she wouldn't, but…

You don't know anything about her.

Something cold penetrated the warmth in his gut, sitting uncomfortably sharp inside him, though he wasn't sure why. Flora had passed all the background checks his HR department did on every employee, and she'd never lied to him. She wasn't a dishonest person, he was sure.

How would you know, when you never paid any attention to her?

His fingers tightened in her hair. 'And where do you live, hmm?' He kept his voice light, matching hers.

'I live in a bedsit. You'd probably find it a bit…small.'

That struck him oddly. He paid her a very good wage, yet she could only afford a bedsit? 'Why?' he asked, abruptly curious. 'I know how much I pay you. You could afford better.'

She sniffed. 'It's a very nice bedsit, actually. But you know, London prices.'

He did know. There were a number of charities he was personally involved with that were trying to tackle homelessness, so he was aware of the issues.

'Yes, but I'm sorry, I'm not moving into your bedsit.' He kept his tone dry. 'You'll have to live with me. At least for the duration of our marriage.'

'Oh, no,' she said plaintively. 'I'll have to move in with my billionaire husband. Whatever shall I do?' The tension had drained out of her, and there was an amused glint in her eye that had his body hardening again.

Pretty Flora.

'A terrible situation indeed,' he murmured, stroking her cheek. 'You might simply have to bear it by lying back and thinking of England.'

Her mouth curved the way it had done earlier that evening, in the ballroom, and he felt savagely pleased with himself that he'd got a smile from her. 'If you have anything to do with it, I won't be able to think at all.'

'That's the plan,' he said, and kissed her.

CHAPTER SEVEN

FLORA WOKE UP the next morning, her body aching in all sorts of unfamiliar places. It wasn't a bad thing, though. In fact, she felt deliciously sated and delightfully lazy, like a cat after consuming a whole saucer of cream.

She rolled over in the massive bed, which Apollo had carried her to the night before, and reached for him.

Only to find the other side of the bed empty.

Frowning, she sat up and looked around the spacious bedroom, but that was empty too.

Thrown across the end of the bed, though, was a swathe of white silk, which on further inspection proved to be the prettiest dressing gown Flora had ever seen. Her clothes seemed to have vanished—she couldn't even remember what had happened to them after she and Apollo had arrived at the house the evening before. Apollo had hurried her from the limo, taking her in his arms the moment the big front doors had closed behind them, and then...

Well, then nothing had seemed to matter, except them both being naked together, with nothing between them but warm, bare skin.

He hadn't been controlled then and neither had she. The leash she'd taken off him in the limo had remained firmly off the whole night, and it had been the most incredible, wild experience she'd ever had. He was an insatiable, inventive lover, indulging her and himself in a few sensual domination games that she'd absolutely loved.

She'd had no idea that sex could be like that. That it could be so consuming, so addictive and, yes, addictive was exactly the word she'd use to describe sex with Apollo. Part of her had wondered if it had been amazing because she'd never had sex before, but then…

It's not that. It's because of him.

Flora closed her eyes, her head full of memories of the night before.

He'd been demanding and hungry, but also gentle, as if he'd been aware of her inexperience. And of course he must have been. He'd had to guide her a few times, and had done so with a patience that belied the hunger he'd shown her in the limo, not to mention a certain tenderness that had made her chest ache.

She hadn't had tenderness from anyone since her mother had died, and she'd had no idea Apollo could be both patient and tender. In fact, there appeared to be a few things about Apollo Constantinides that she hadn't anticipated, and she wasn't sure how she felt about that.

This could end up backfiring on you if you're not careful.

Oh, it could. But she wouldn't let it. Losing control in bed was not the same thing as losing control of her emotions, and those she was holding very tightly.

Anyway, luckily, after the question about where she lived, he hadn't asked her anything else about herself. No, he'd had other things on his mind, and talking was not one of them.

However, she knew he'd probably ask them at some point, in which case she'd better have a few easy lies on hand to give him.

Still thinking about it, Flora opened her eyes again, threw back the sheet and slid out of bed. Then she picked up the dressing gown and wrapped it around her naked body. The silk was cool against her skin, the most delightful indulgence.

She never allowed herself pretty things. Everything she did was in service to her plans. He'd seemed surprised the night before when she'd told him she lived in a bedsit, and given the amount of money he paid her, he might very well be surprised. But she'd put all that money into a savings account; she wanted to have some funds to help her disappear once she'd finished her heartbreak plans.

Tying her robe closed, Flora then opened the door and stepped out into the ornate hallway outside. It was empty, so she went along to the stairs that led down into the main entrance of the house. As she went down them, she heard voices coming from below. One voice was very familiar, and her heart gave the oddest little leap.

Apollo was standing in the entrance way, talking in French to an older looking man dressed in black. Apollo himself was in dark trousers and a white shirt, the sleeves rolled up and his hair slightly mussed, and he seemed to sense her approach, because he suddenly broke off his conversation and glanced in the direction of the stairs where she stood.

His eyes glittered as he took her in, and even though the white silk was very decorous, she abruptly felt as if she wasn't wearing anything at all.

'Good morning, *matia mou*,' he said. 'Come, I want to introduce you to someone.'

She came down the rest of the stairs, and when he took her hand and drew her in close, one arm sliding around her waist, she didn't protest. Then she noticed that the other man was wearing a dog collar.

'This is Father Bayard,' Apollo said. 'He is going to marry us.'

She couldn't mask the ripple of shock that went through her, and Apollo must have felt her instinctively stiffen, because he said something in French to the priest, who nodded and went past them in the direction of the back of the house.

Flora could hear voices coming from that direction too. It sounded as if orders were being given.

'You can't mean we're getting married today,' she said, and didn't make it a question since the very idea seemed preposterous.

One of those addictive, fascinating smiles lurked in the corner of Apollo's mouth. '*Mais oui*. Indeed we are getting married today.'

Flora blinked. 'But—'

'I know,' he interrupted gently. 'I should have spoken to you about this earlier, but I had arrangements to make, and you needed the sleep.' His eyes glinted. 'I was not exactly restrained last night.'

As if she needed the reminder.

'No, you weren't,' she said, her cheeks feeling hot. 'Not that I was complaining. But…a wedding? Now? Today? I thought you wanted a spectacle.'

'I thought I did too. But last night was…' His smile turned warm, deepening that ache in her chest. 'A revelation. So, I thought, like I told you in the limo, that getting married as quickly as possible would be the best thing all round.' He pulled her closer, the heat of his body burning through the silk, making her knees feel weak. 'Also, given the level of media interest in you, the sooner we're married, the sooner you'll be protected. Plus, this will add credence to ours being a grand passion. We couldn't wait to be married, so we had a quick wedding on the terrace outside. I've already got someone from PR to take a few informal photos that can be leaked to the press.'

Flora blinked again, feeling as if she'd somehow got on a rollercoaster and now couldn't get off. No, wait, this had to be a good thing. He was right, it would look very romantic if they had a quick wedding today, and it would certainly be in her interests too. The less time the press had to be curious about her the better, and, anyway, once she was married to him, even if her links to his father's scheme did come out, he might find it difficult to get rid of her. Also, he still wouldn't know her real reasons for getting close to him. If and when he eventually did, with any luck he'd be so wrapped around her little finger, it might not even bother him.

Do you seriously think it won't bother him that you've been lying to him?

No, she knew it would. He'd never made any secret of the fact that he didn't like a liar. But if the sex was good enough, and she'd already managed to get under his guards emotionally, he might, after a few days of being angry, come round. After all, it wasn't as if she knew nothing about how to deal with him. She'd been working with him for a year, and while he wasn't an easy man, she'd developed a few little strategies to handle him.

Apollo frowned all of a sudden and abruptly lifted his hands, cupping her face between them. 'You seem uncertain. Is this too fast? Do you have family that should be invited? I could fly them over here if you wish, and we could wait until then.'

The mention of family caught her off-guard. 'Family?' she echoed blankly.

'Yes. I know this wedding is still a pretence, but it will look strange, I suppose, if your family isn't here.'

Flora took a silent breath, trying to think of an appropriate response. The truth was the easiest. The best lies, after all, were always based on some aspect of the truth. She just wouldn't mention her father's name. she'd tell Apollo he'd died in a car accident or something.

'I have no family,' she said, trying not to avoid his gaze. 'My father died when I was a kid, and my mother died a few years ago. Cancer. I'm an only child.'

Something shifted in his gaze, though she couldn't tell what it was. Sympathy perhaps? It seemed strange to get sympathy from Apollo Constantinides.

'I'm sorry for your loss, Flora,' he said, and yes, it *was* sympathy she could hear in his voice. 'That must have been very hard.'

Inexplicably, the backs of her eyes prickled. It had been a long time since anyone had said anything comforting to her, as if they genuinely felt for her. The nurses at the hospital had been very kind, but also a touch impersonal.

Now, though, with Apollo cupping her face in his hands, understanding in his green eyes… There was nothing impersonal about this. Nothing fake, either. He was being utterly genuine.

Unlike you.

Guilt tugged inside her, unexpected and painfully sharp. He was being understanding and kind, while she was…

Just a liar.

Her chest felt tight, but she pushed the sensation away. She had to keep going. She *had* to. Her father might have done the most senseless thing she could imagine, and she had to acknowledge her own anger at him for that. Anger that he hadn't stayed to be there for her and her mother. Anger that he hadn't kept all the promises he'd made.

But he wouldn't have been in that position if not for the man standing in front of her now. She needed some justice for her father, and Apollo Constantinides's broken heart would have to do.

'It was,' she managed.

'I lost my parents too.' His thumbs brushed her cheek. 'Though I was an adult when they died. It's harder to lose a parent when you're a child.'

Was that grief she saw in his eyes? For his father? Or was it for his mother?

Not that she was curious. His losses were nothing in comparison to hers, and she had to remember that, no matter how understanding he might sound.

'I was ten when Dad died,' she heard herself say, even though she could have sworn she wasn't going to give him anything more. 'My mother and I were left with nothing, so she had to work really hard to keep a roof over our heads. She thought she was so tired was from working all the time, but…it wasn't that at all.'

Apollo frowned slightly.

God, what on earth had made her say that to him? What an idiot she was being. She was supposed to give him a grain of truth and then lie about the rest, not the truth wholesale. She couldn't afford to give him anything more.

'Sorry,' she said quickly. 'That's not exactly great wedding-day conversation.'

'You don't need to apologise,' he murmured. 'I would love to know more.'

That wasn't what she wanted to hear. She needed to change the subject and quickly.

'Later,' she said lightly. 'Don't we have a wedding to go to?'

Apollo's frown lingered, as if he was fully aware of her avoidance. 'We will revisit this, *matia mou.*'

Her stomach tightened. Great. Him being curious about her was the last thing she needed.

'Sure.' She shoved the flutter of nerves aside, keeping her tone easy.

'Good.' His frown cleared and he dropped his hands from her face. 'Come. The priest will be waiting for us.'

Apollo stood on the terrace of his family's French chateau, in the brilliant Parisian sunlight, the roses around the terrace filling the warm air with their heady scent, and watched Flora walk slowly over to where he stood.

She wore the lovely white silk dressing gown he'd bought especially for her—the quickest way he could get a wedding dress—and her black hair was loose around her shoulders. In her hands she carried a bouquet of roses she'd picked from the garden, and a delicate flush stained her cheekbones.

She really was the loveliest woman he'd ever seen.

The night before had been... Well, the best of his life,

if he was being honest with himself, and he always tried to be. In bed, she'd been amazing. Inexperienced, he'd thought, but hungry too, welcoming everything he'd done to her, and then not just welcoming, but issuing her own demands in return. She'd been passionate and honest and generous, holding nothing back from him. He'd never had a lover like her.

He'd woken up that morning with her beside him, and in that moment he'd known that he absolutely had to make her his wife as soon as possible. Yes, it was to protect her, but also—and this he couldn't deny—there was an element of possessiveness in his desire for her. He wanted her to be his wife because he wanted her to be his. His and *only* his.

For a limited time only, of course, but he didn't see why they couldn't start that time as soon as possible.

No one, surely, would raise an eyebrow at a very quick wedding. It would even look romantic if the appropriate story was put in place. They needn't have a spectacle. All they needed was a few leaked photos of Flora looking charming, and himself looking pleased, and that would handle any rumours.

He'd managed to handle the logistics fairly quickly, expediting a marriage licence and getting the rings— simple platinum bands—from a jeweller he did business with. Nothing was a problem when large sums of money were involved.

Breaking the news to Flora had been the most concerning part, since it had only been last night that they'd first slept together, and he wondered if she would find it all a little rushed. When she'd come downstairs as he was talking to the priest—in that white robe and her beautiful hair in a tangle—he'd even found himself thinking that if she said no to him now, maybe he could elope with her somewhere else, take some time to convince her that this was a good strategy.

But he needn't have worried. She'd been surprised but had agreed to his plan, and now here she was, walking to him where he stood with the priest.

She would be his wife.

The thought made something heavy and satisfied shift inside him, in a way it hadn't with Violet. With Violet he'd discussed every aspect of a marriage, and he'd known exactly what it would be. It wasn't the same with Flora, and yet…somehow the not knowing how a marriage with her would be was…exhilarating. Exciting almost. Like a mystery he couldn't wait to start solving.

He knew nothing about her, except what she'd told him about her family, and as they'd stood in the hallway, echoes of an old grief in her eyes, he realised that they had a few things in common. He too, had lost his parents. He too, was an only child.

What more did they share? What other things did he not know? He wanted to find out as soon as possible.

Flora smiled as she came to stand beside him, and together they faced the priest.

He would take things slow, though. He wouldn't demand everything from her immediately. He had two weeks of events and business meetings in various parts of the globe, and Flora would come with him. They could spend time together, getting to know one another, building the facade of a loving marriage to the public, while exploring their physical hunger for each other in private.

It was the best of both worlds, really, and he couldn't have hoped for a better outcome.

The priest began the wedding ceremony and Apollo nodded to the staff member standing with the housekeeper, who was here as a witness. The man took out his phone and began taking unobtrusive pictures.

Soon Apollo was sliding the ring onto Flora's finger and she was doing the same for him, smiling up at him as she did so. And for some reason the fact that this was a sham, that this wasn't actually real, seemed…strange to him.

It *wasn't* real, he knew that intellectually, and yet a current of anticipation was running through him, a degree of excitement that he hadn't felt for a long time.

Perhaps it was the sex. Or perhaps it was that she was his PA and not a stranger to him, that he'd known her and worked with her for at least a year, but it felt as if getting married to her was almost…right.

He couldn't imagine, for example, standing here with Violet.

The priest pronounced them husband and wife, and then it was over. Apollo pulled her close and kissed her, while the designated photographer took some more pictures.

Then he raised his head and dismissed everyone, before taking Flora in his arms and carrying her inside.

'What are you so impatient for?' she asked, laughing as she threw the bouquet of flowers at the housekeeper on their way past. 'Don't tell me, I can guess.'

He approached the stairs and started up them, Flora all warm and silky in his arms. He gave her a wolfish smile. 'I'm sure you can. That is, if you're not too sore from last night.'

She was blushing again. It was delightful. 'Should I be sore?'

They reached the top of the stairs and he began walking down the hallway. 'You might be,' he said as they came to the bedroom. He walked through the doorway, then kicked the door shut behind them. 'Tell me, have you had many lovers, *matia mou*?'

A strange expression crossed her face. 'Oh…uh…not many, no.'

Apollo crossed to the bed, putting her carefully down on the edge of it. She was still blushing and a thought suddenly struck him. Her hesitancy. How she blushed. How he'd had to guide her…

'Flora,' he said. 'Have you in fact had *any* lovers?'

She looked up at the ceiling for a moment, then glanced at him. 'No,' she said at last. 'No, I haven't.'

A ripple of surprise went through him. 'You were a virgin last night?'

She let out a breath. 'Yes.'

Apollo didn't care how many lovers a woman had had. It didn't matter to him. And yet… Flora the night before, in the limo, he'd been demanding, rough…

'You should have told me,' he said, suddenly concerned. 'I would have been more gentle with you.'

'Honestly?' Flora's gaze this time was level. 'I forgot all about it. You made me feel so good that it just didn't matter.'

At that, something in his chest tightened. He wasn't a man who generally made people feel good. He *did* good, but that was different. Doing good implied some distance. Doing good wasn't specific or personal. Just as caring for humanity in general wasn't the same as caring for a person.

He didn't want to care for an actual person. He'd done that once before, and it had led him to make the worst mistake of his life. He wasn't willing to do it again.

Except…it was important for him to make Flora feel good. That *was* personal.

Unless she's lying to you. That's happened before, remember?

Oh, yes, he remembered. The conviction in his father's voice when he'd told Apollo that there was nothing wrong with the scheme. His outrage when it was suggested that the scheme was illegal. The glow of approval in his eyes when Apollo had convinced yet another poor sap to invest his money…

No. That approval was real. And you liked it.

Apollo shoved the thought away. His father was dead and gone now, and he wasn't going to put his suspicions on Flora.

'I'm told it can hurt,' he said, crouching in front of her and scanning her face.

'Perhaps for some people it might. But there was no pain for me.' She gave him a heartbreakingly lovely smile, the truth plain in her eyes. Then she reached out and ruffled his hair. 'Truly, none at all. I wondered if last night was so amazing because sex is amazing, but now I think it was just because of you.'

The tightness in his chest squeezed, a strange kind of ache.

Dear God, he could get used to this. To someone looking at him the way she was looking at him right now, as if he'd performed some kind of miracle for her and her alone. To her touching him as a lover of years might, with gentleness and care, as if he mattered to her.

It shouldn't be important to him. This marriage was all a pretence for the sake of their separate reputations, and yet... She'd done everything he'd asked, going way above and even beyond the call of duty.

She was something special, Flora McIntyre. And he hadn't known quite how special until now.

Reaching up, he took her hand from his hair, turned it palm up and pressed a kiss in the centre of it. 'I will take that, wife.' He rose and gently pressed her back onto the bed, reaching for the tie of her gown. 'Now, let me show you how good I can really make you feel.'

CHAPTER EIGHT

FLORA ROLLED OVER in the massive bed, propped her chin on her folded hands and stared out through the huge floor-to-ceiling windows. An afternoon thunderstorm was moving in over the skyscrapers of Hong Kong.

She and Apollo had arrived late the night before, after a charity event in New York, and had come straight to the luxury Victoria Peak apartment he owned. He had some business with the Helios Hong Kong office that he was going to take care of, before they went on to Athens and his property in Greece.

Two weeks had passed since their marriage on the terrace of that house in Paris, not a long time, yet Flora felt as if the entire course of her life had shifted.

The afternoon after the ceremony, still lying in bed together, they'd drafted various press releases and sent them off, detailing how in love they were, so much so that they hadn't been able to wait to marry, and so had had a quick wedding in the chateau's garden.

That had caused a stir, naturally enough. The press had been full of speculation as to why Apollo had married his PA so quickly, and for a few days there had been a lot of chatter and rumour on social media and in the gossip columns about the possibility of a pregnancy. There were other rumours too and, as she'd feared, they were largely about her. She was a gold digger, some people said, she was blackmailing him, she was a home-wrecker and they'd never give up fighting for 'ViLo'.

There was nothing she could do about that but hope no one enquired too deeply into her background. Apollo, though, had been as good as his word. So far, he'd protected her from the press, shielding her from intrusive questions and instructing his security to make sure the photographers were kept at bay whenever they were out.

She hadn't known he could be so protective, and there was a part of her who loved it. Who loved him holding her hand in his, his tall powerful figure shielding hers as they arrived at whatever event they had next. He was her bulwark against all threats and, even though she knew it was all an act, it made her feel in some small way cared for.

Apollo hadn't broken his promises to her the way her father had. Apollo had told her he'd protect her, and he had.

He'd also done some phone interviews, firmly denying all the pregnancy, blackmail and gold-digger rumours, stating that the hastiness of their marriage was due to love, that was all.

Naturally, she tried to ignore the media circus, but every day she couldn't stop herself from religiously checking websites, message boards and other social media every morning, looking for any mention of her family history. So far, nothing had been said, but she didn't imagine that would last. Someone, somewhere would find out, and she didn't want to think about what would happen then. The now was where she wanted to be, because the now was so good. So...so good.

Since that night in the limo, where she'd jumped into

the deep end of her desire, she'd let herself sink deeper and deeper. And instead of drowning, she'd found that she could breathe. That, in fact, it was her element, that she belonged there, and she belonged there with him, because it was his element too.

He was a revelation to her, his blunt honesty allowing her to be honest as well. In the fragile structure of lies she'd built around herself, there was one precious truth, glowing like a pearl. The truth that she was obsessed with him, that she wanted him. That she might be lying to him, but there was nothing fake about the physical passion he managed to draw from her.

It felt freeing to finally be allowed to have this one thing that wasn't a lie.

He hasn't just rocked your world. He's knocked it off its axis entirely.

She let out a sigh, watching as the rain began to pelt against the glass, the skyscrapers across the bay wreathed in cloud.

Being his wife rather than his PA these past two weeks had been…amazing. And not for the parade of glittering events or the endless supply of beautiful gowns and jewels, the jet-setting around on private planes to different countries, or meeting famous celebrities and important political figures.

No, it was him.

Since that night in Paris, he'd taken the chains off the raw passion that lay at the heart of him, and allowed it free rein. It thrilled her that she was the one who'd managed to unleash it, that she, the blank slate of a PA with no experience of men, had been the one to draw it from him.

Ever since the death of her mother, she'd had nothing in

her life but that one goal—to bring Apollo down. Everything she did was in service to that goal. She did nothing for herself, nothing that wouldn't ultimately get her what she wanted, which was his utter ruination.

She'd been so one-eyed, so rigid in her pursuit, that she hadn't allowed herself even the smallest of pleasures. Yet, for the past two weeks, pleasures both big and small had crept into her days, and it was all due to him.

There were small acts of care, such as the coffee he brought her every morning once he'd discovered she liked a cup before she got out of bed. Strong and milky, with one sugar.

The warm bath he insisted on drawing for her whenever they were in a new city and she was tired and jet-lagged. He'd let her have some relaxation time before her favourite part, which was when he joined her. She loved his hands on her, washing her back and then her hair, which he took his time over, since he liked washing it, as much as she liked him washing it. He'd also figured out her favourite foods and made sure that they were always available, wherever they were.

Those were the small pleasures, ones she hadn't had since she was a child and her parents were still alive. Part of her knew she should tell him that he didn't need to be so solicitous of her, that this wasn't a real marriage after all, yet another part of her was hungry for it. She had been on her own for so long, she hadn't realised how lonely she'd been until him.

Rain fell across the skyscrapers in a glittering veil.

Flora watched it idly, wondering if she could somehow convince Apollo that they didn't need to go to the party they were supposed to attend that evening. That maybe they could stay here and have a private dinner in bed instead.

This isn't real, remember?

No, it wasn't, but part of it was. And she wanted that part to keep on going for ever.

How can it? When all of this, everything you're doing with him, is built on a lie?

Her heart tightened, the threads of guilt that had subtly woven themselves around it constricting painfully. She'd ignored those threads, told herself she didn't feel them, told herself she was justified in what she was planning to do to him, and yet…

Those were lies too.

But what else was there for her? She could tell him the truth—and part of her desperately wanted to, yet, if she did, it would render the entirety of her life since her mother had died, meaningless. Her parents' deaths meaningless too, and she couldn't let that happen. What was the point of anything otherwise?

Apollo came into the room just then, completely naked and carrying a tray, and Flora forgot about the guilt aching in her heart, watching him instead. He was so much more fascinating, especially when he wore nothing but his smooth, velvety olive skin.

A sigh escaped her. The man truly was the personification of the god he was named for. Broad-shouldered, his chest powerful, his stomach flat and hard, not an ounce of fat on him. Then lower, his narrow hips and muscular thighs, and the glory of that very male part of him.

He put the tray down on the edge of the bed, and she saw he'd brought her a little tasting plate of different cheeses, crackers, grapes and nuts, along with a couple of flutes of champagne.

A traitorous warmth expanded in her chest, the way it always did when he brought things for her, tugging hard on those threads around her heart, deepening the ache. She didn't want to feel this way about him, she couldn't. It was dangerous, and yet she couldn't seem to stop herself from feeling it.

And the more time she had with him, the more of him she wanted, because a curiosity had taken root inside her. About the reasons he was so rigidly controlled on the outside, yet so passionate and hot on the inside.

A forbidden curiosity. She couldn't ask him about himself, because then it might prompt him to ask questions about her, and that she couldn't allow. Lies were all she had for him, and she didn't want to tell any more, not when the weight of the ones she'd already told were getting heavier by the day.

It was a pity, because he was such an intelligent man, and they'd had some fascinating conversations. Their topics had ranged from global politics to books, art and then onto philosophy, and from there his charity work and how the rate of scientific progress should be used to improve the lives of everyone, not just the few. He had a voracious curiosity, his mind full of knowledge on the most obscure topics, and she loved talking to him about them. It was a little depressing that she couldn't reciprocate with her own interests, because she really didn't have any. Her life had always begun and ended with her quest for justice.

'For me?' she asked, glancing at the tray of food and smiling as he sat down on the bed beside her.

'You have to keep your strength up for the event tonight.' He slid a propriety hand into her hair and gave her a hot, slow kiss before releasing her, desire still glittering in his eyes. 'Not to mention for afterwards.'

She'd never get tired of that look, or the hunger in it, the desire that was for her and her alone.

Will he still want you when he finds out who you really are?

Flora shoved the thought away, along with the feeling of foreboding that came along with it. She should have spent this past week putting a plan in place for what she'd do if and when the truth came out, how she'd deal with it, or more specifically how she'd deal with him. But she hadn't. Some part of her simply couldn't bear to think about it, because she just wanted this for a little while. Someone's touch on her skin. Someone's hand to hold. Someone to hold her.

No, not someone. Him.

If you're not careful, it won't be his heart you break. It will be your own.

Apollo frowned, studying her face. 'Are you all right, *matia mou*? You've gone pale.'

She forced another smile, hoping he wouldn't press the issue. 'Only a headache.'

He reached out and cupped her cheek in one of his large, warm hands. 'Shall I get you some painkillers?'

The warmth inside her turned bittersweet. He was a naturally caring man, and very protective, and his concern was absolutely genuine. Yet it wasn't specific to her, she suspected. He would do this for anyone.

You want it to be for you, though.

No. No, she didn't. He was the enemy, and she couldn't lose sight of that.

'No,' she murmured, unable to resist leaning into the warmth of his hand. 'I'm fine, honestly.'

But his frown didn't lift, his gaze narrowing as he scanned her face. 'The last two weeks have been something of a whirlwind, I know. Once we get to Athens, it'll be better.' His thumb brushed her cheekbone gently. 'You could probably do with some rest.'

She hadn't asked him much about what was going to happen after this. He'd mentioned her moving in with him back in Paris, but they hadn't discussed it since. In fact, they hadn't had any practical discussions at all. 'And after that?' she asked, shivering a little as he caressed her again.

'After that, we'll have some time in Greece, then we'll go back to London, and I'll arrange for you to move into my residence there.'

She should leave the future to take care of itself, not ask him anything more, and yet she couldn't stop herself. 'What will happen then? Will I go back to being your PA? Or will you hire someone else?'

His frown deepened. 'Being my PA won't be appropriate now, even with the marriage. I know I promised you that your job wouldn't be affected by our arrangement, and it won't be. But perhaps you might feel more comfortable in another position?'

She hadn't thought of a different job, not when her whole life had revolved around her mission. She hadn't given any thought to what would happen after she'd completed it, either.

You haven't thought about a lot of things, have you?

Ignoring the voice in her head, Flora concentrated on him. 'Such as?'

'There are a few positions vacant in the London office, and a couple of them would suit you very well, but...' He paused a moment. 'It wouldn't be a good look for me to appoint you without going through the proper procedures, especially considering you're my wife now.'

It didn't matter. She was closer to him as his wife, more than she'd ever have been as his PA.

'You're very rigid about your reputation,' she said without thinking. 'Why is that?'

His hand fell away abruptly, leaving her skin feeling cold. 'You must know why, Flora. Because of my father.'

She froze, watching his face. He'd never mentioned his father before, or his past. 'You mean, the investment scheme collapse?' she asked carefully.

'Yes.'

'It's been...what? Fifteen years? Surely you don't have anything left to prove now.'

'It doesn't matter how many years have passed. My name will always be linked to that scheme, and the misery it caused so many people.' His voice had flattened, all the warmth that had been in it leaching out. 'And, as such, my behaviour and that of my company will always be measured against what happened back then. I must be above reproach at all times, you know this.'

The lines of his face had hardened along with his voice, and inside her something hurt. It shouldn't, yet it did. Because looking at this caring, protective man now, it was becoming more and more difficult to see him as the man who'd ruined lives back then. The man she'd thought was ruthless and hard, manipulative, who merely paid lip-service to being a good employer and an upstanding businessman.

Except…she'd been wrong. She knew that now. He genuinely believed in all the good things he was doing—everything he'd done to protect her, for example—and certainly it was belief that shone in his eyes now.

'It must be hard,' she said impulsively. 'To feel that you have to be above reproach all the time.'

Something flickered in his gaze, as if he hadn't expected the statement. 'It's not…easy, no,' he admitted after a moment. 'But it's important to me that I set myself apart from my father. To do the right thing, be a better man than he was. I want the Constantinides name to be associated with helping people rather than destroying them.' There was a glow in his eyes now, fierce and hot, and for once it had nothing to do with sex. 'I will not be my father, Flora. I will never be him. I refuse.'

Apollo wasn't sure where his need to make Flora understand that he wasn't his father had come from. He'd spent his life setting himself apart from Stavros, and most people knew now that he was a completely different beast, and yet it felt very important that *she* know that.

Her opinion had never mattered to him before. She was his PA, she did what he told her, and he'd never thought beyond that. But somehow, at some point in the course of the past two weeks, her opinion had begun to matter.

She had begun to matter.

She was lying in his bed, a white sheet twined around her naked body, with her black hair in a tangle over her shoulders. Her eyes were the same dark grey as the thunder clouds outside, and she'd never looked more lovely.

Your wife.

A deep satisfaction stretched out inside him, that she was his.

Marrying her that day had been a very good decision indeed, especially when even the past two weeks of having her in his bed every night hadn't eased his hunger for her. In fact, if anything, having her constantly at his side had somehow made it even worse. Two weeks, and he was still just as obsessed with her as he'd been that first night.

Even right now, despite the fact that they had another event in a couple of hours, all he could think about was pushing her over onto her back and taking her mouth, hard and hot and hungry, then feasting on her body, making her scream, and then, and only then, thrusting into her, giving both of them the pleasure they craved.

It was madness. Somehow he'd gone from being in complete control of himself to being totally at the mercy of his need for Flora. Her and only her. No one else would do. No one else had managed to get under his skin so completely that it felt as if she'd always been there.

She'd released something in him, opened the door to the cage that some part of him had been trapped in, and she hadn't been ruined by it. No, if anything, he was the one who'd been ruined, and he couldn't bring himself to care.

Flora's clear grey eyes met his. 'You're not anything like him,' she said, as if she was well acquainted with Stavros and his foibles. 'You're not.'

This was a line of conversation he didn't particularly want to follow, but she'd told him the day they'd got married that she'd lost her parents. It hadn't been easy for her—he'd seen the grief in her eyes—so he could hardly shy away from telling her about his. Anyway, she'd have heard all about his father's infamous misdeeds. Many people had, especially after the suicide of one of the investors. Perhaps she had questions, and, if so, he had to give her the opportunity to ask them. He was her husband after all, and she should know what kind of man she'd married, even if the whole thing was a sham.

Not that he'd ever shied away from what his father had done or his own role in it. As he'd told her, he had his standards, and they were honesty and transparency at all times. He wasn't a hypocrite.

'You didn't know him,' he said bluntly. 'He used to tell me how like him I was, and there was a reason for that. I'd always wanted to be employed in the family business, follow in his footsteps, so when he said it was time for me to learn the ropes, I couldn't wait. I loved it.' He didn't look away, didn't bother to make the words sound better than they were. It was the pure, unvarnished truth and she should hear it. 'He wanted me to recruit as many people as I could into that damn scheme, so I did. I enjoyed it too, charming people out of their money. I believed it was for a good cause. A few things didn't add up, of course, but I ignored them, because I thought my father was a brilliant businessman, and he must have dealt with any discrepancies.' He paused a moment, then added, because he didn't want to sugarcoat it. 'I think deep down I knew the scheme was wrong somehow, but I loved my father and I wanted his approval. I wanted him to be proud of me.'

Flora's face had paled. Understandable really, considering what he was confessing. 'Apollo,' she began.

'No, let me finish. I hold myself to these standards

because of what I did. Because I gave the worst parts of myself free rein. Charming people, convincing people to hand over their money, manipulating them… I loved all of it. But the pride Stavros took in what I'd done, I loved most of all.'

Flora said nothing, only looked at him.

'So now you know the truth,' he said into the heavy silence. 'I was complicit in my father's crimes, and that's why I have to set myself apart from them now. Why my reputation must be spotless. And why I can't ever lower my standards, not even once.'

A strange expression crossed her face then, one he couldn't read. 'You enjoyed it?' she echoed.

'Yes.' He didn't flinch away, didn't pretend it was something other than what it was. 'I liked the challenge. The rush I got when someone, who hadn't been interested, now suddenly was, because I'd convinced them.'

Her lashes fell, veiling her gaze, and she picked up the edge of the sheet, slowly pleating it with her fingers. She had tensed. 'So…when did you realise it was all a scam?'

He could remember it still, so clearly. First, a call from one of the investors, David Hunt, whom Apollo had brought on board personally, asking if there was any truth to the rumours that what Stavros was running was a Ponzi scheme. That had been news to Apollo, so he'd reassured Hunt that of course it was no such thing. Stavros would never do anything so terrible. A week later, Hunt had killed himself, and subsequent enquiries into his financial dealings had revealed he'd invested everything in the Constantinides scheme.

The rumours got louder and the authorities got involved, and still Apollo had thought the whole thing was a media beat-up, defending Stavros to anyone who would listen. Then one day he'd come into the office to find his father in the process of shredding files. Stavros had thrust a pile at him and told him to destroy them, and it was in that instant he'd realised. That everything they'd been saying about Stavros was true. His father was a liar, a cheat, a fraud. His scheme had led to the death of someone, and he'd involved his own son in it.

Apollo had felt then as if the world had collapsed around him. He'd refused to shred the files, had demanded Stavros tell him why he'd done what he did, and Stavros had rounded on him in a fury, saying that Helios needed money and how else was he to get it? That if he truly loved this family, Apollo had to help get rid of the evidence, like his father had told him to.

Stavros hadn't cared that he'd stolen from people. He hadn't cared he'd led a man to his death. He hadn't even cared that he'd made Apollo complicit in the whole thing by lying to him about it. Apollo had been furious with his father, but had saved the worst of his fury for himself, for how he'd let his love for his father blind him to the truth.

He hadn't destroyed what remained of the evidence. He'd gone straight to the police with it and turned Stavros in.

After Stavros had gone to jail, his mother had refused to speak to him, blaming him for not standing by his father when he'd needed him. The company collapsed into ruins, all their friends abandoned them, and he was left with nothing but blind fury and a crushing sense of guilt.

He'd had no way to deal with any of it, except to force it all down and do better. Remake the Constantinides name, get the business back on its feet. Make reparations to those who had lost money in the scheme's collapse, and then do everything he could to put as much good in the world as he was able.

So that's what he'd done, and what he continued to do.

'The first I heard was when one of the investors called and asked me if I knew anything about the rumours that my father was running a scam,' he said. 'I told him no, because I was sure my father would never do anything like that, but...' He didn't want to talk about this, not with his beautiful wife naked in his bed, not when there were other, far more pleasant things to be doing. But he forced himself to go on, because he'd promised himself all those years ago that he would be honest. 'A week later, the news came through that the man I'd spoken to had taken his own life. Subsequent investigations revealed that he'd sunk his life savings into my father's investment scheme, and that there were...irregularities.'

Flora nodded, but didn't look at him. Her fingers that had been pleating the fine linen of the sheet in a nervous movement had stilled. She seemed even more tense.

And why not? This was difficult to say, and probably worse to hear.

'The authorities wanted to investigate my father's dealings,' he went on. 'And one day I came into the office to find him in the process of shredding files. I'd refused to believe the rumours that he was crooked, but that day... I realised they were all true. That a man had died because of him.' Apollo paused and the corrected himself, because he had to be honest. 'Because of me.'

Her hand closed convulsively on the sheet, bunching it up in her fist. Yes, this was a terrible thing he'd done. No wonder she'd gone so pale.

'Does it bother you?' he asked, after a moment, not knowing why it mattered to him, only that it did. 'My past? What my father did? What *I* did?'

'No,' she said.

But there was an edge in her voice that made him reach out and grip her chin, tilting her head back so he could look into her eyes. 'Flora,' he said softly. 'Don't lie to me. You know how I hate that.'

Shadows clouded her gaze, and there was a complicated expression on her face that he couldn't interpret. It looked as though she might speak, but then she leaned forward suddenly and her mouth was on his, kissing him hungrily.

There's something she's not telling you.

The thought occurred to him, clear as day, then her hands were on his shoulders, pushing him down onto the bed, and her mouth was tracking kisses down his neck, to his throat, over his chest, down to where he was hard and ready for her, as he always was.

Another thought occurred to him then, as her hot mouth closed around him, a belated thought, that she was trying to distract him. That what he'd told her *had* bothered her, but she hadn't wanted to admit it.

But then, as her tongue began to explore him, and her hands clasped him tight, in just the way he preferred, the thought went straight out of his head.

And there was nothing more but the exquisite pleasure of her mouth around him and the firm grip of her hands.

CHAPTER NINE

THEIR AFTERNOON INTERLUDE almost made them late to the party that evening, held in a rooftop bar in one of Kowloon's sky scrapers.

Flora—in a silvery, clinging cocktail dress that Apollo had bought for her, and her hair loose—tried to ignore the kernel of ice that sat in the pit of her stomach. Even the heat she and Apollo had generated in bed that afternoon hadn't managed to get rid of it.

She hadn't expected him to even mention his past, let alone talk about his own role in his father's scheme, or the moment he'd discovered that Stavros was a crook. Every word he'd said had been weighted down with regret, and it had been in his eyes too. The toll it had taken on him had been obvious, just as it had been obvious that he'd meant every word he'd said. He'd enjoyed deceiving all those people, her father included.

But he'd been deceived in turn. By Stavros. It had happened a long time ago, so he'd have been young, and like all young men he'd have wanted to prove himself to his father. And naturally, if he'd loved Stavros, then he'd have believed everything Stavros had told him.

It had all made sense to her.

She'd been a child when her father had died, and her

mother had never gone into the details. She hadn't known that David had heard rumours surrounding the scheme, nor had she known that he'd called Apollo to ask if the rumours were true, or that Apollo had told her father everything was fine.

In the years after the scheme's collapse, Apollo had never made a secret of his own involvement in the scheme, or his regret for what had happened, but as she'd worked towards her goal of ruining him, she'd told herself that he must have been lying. That his regret and admissions of guilt weren't sincere, especially when he'd been given immunity for turning his father in.

Then, as she'd got to know him as a boss over the past year, his cold, brutally honest manner had seemed like dispassion, making her sure that he was only paying lip-service to feelings of guilt and regret. He didn't actually feel it. He didn't seem to feel anything at all.

Now though, after listening to him explain what had happened, she'd heard the pain in his voice. Heard the regret and the guilt, and, somewhere inside her, that icy effigy of him that she'd built up in her head, already undermined by the past two weeks of glorious passion, cracked right through.

Of course he cared. The man who held her in his arms every night, making her gasp and shudder and shake, wasn't some cold, unfeeling statue. He was honest, yes, but that honesty came from a genuine desire to tell the truth. To not lie to other people the way his father had lied to him.

And not only that, but he'd been affected deeply by the death of that investor he'd mentioned. An investor that could only have been her father.

She hadn't been able to look at him when he'd spoken about that, hadn't wanted to look into his eyes and see the truth, that the man she'd spent her life wanting to bring down had been as much a victim of his own father as hers had been.

Apollo had answered her questions with the same unflinching honesty that he answered any questions. Yes, he'd convinced her father to invest his money. Yes, he'd told David that there was nothing wrong, the scheme was totally legitimate.

Yes, he'd made a mistake and he regretted it. He blamed himself for it.

You were wrong about him. All this time you were wrong.

Flora's throat closed, tears prickling behind her eyes, no matter how hard she tried to blink them away. He was a good man, and she'd known it for a while now. Honest, protective, kind. He was everything the media said about him. More, he was also passionate, feeling things on a deep level. His heart was true.

Unlike yours.

The limo opened its doors into the sultry Kowloon evening, with the inevitable gathering of the press pack outside the skyscraper party venue.

Despite the humidity, Flora felt cold. She'd felt cold all afternoon, the knowledge sitting inside her that it wasn't him who was the liar and the cheat, it was her. She was a con woman who'd taken in a good man, and not only was she lying to him, she was lying to herself.

Telling herself that it didn't matter if she lied to him. It didn't matter if he was hurt. That her parents deserved some kind of justice for how he'd ruined their lives.

Except he'd been ruined too, and by his own father.

How can you continue with your plan now? His heart has already been broken once, and you're intending to break it again.

Her throat closed, anguish collecting inside her. The thought of hurting him now felt like a knife in her side, and she knew all those doubts she'd had—that this plan had the potential to break her heart too—were true. It would.

In ruining him, she'd ruin herself.

The thunderstorm of the early afternoon had long gone, but the streets were still damp, neon staining the puddles everywhere. Cameras flashed and the press pack shouted questions as she and Apollo exited the limo.

He held out his arm to her and, even though she should have been used to seeing him in black tie by now, she was still caught by how devastatingly handsome he was. How her heart instinctively leaped whenever he turned his jungle green gaze on hers, glittering still with the remains of their afternoon passion.

This was the man she wanted to ruin. To cause him the same kind of pain that her father must have felt when he'd taken his own life. The same kind of hurt and betrayal she and her mother had experienced after David died.

She'd wanted to break him, yet now she knew the man behind that incredible gaze and list of accomplishments a mile long. The man who brought her coffee in the mornings and shielded her from the media, and who held her at night. The man who'd talked to her about everything under the sun, and who'd been nothing but honest with her...

She couldn't do it. She just couldn't.

She'd thought he was the villain all this time, but he wasn't.

The villain was her.

Flora clutched Apollo's hand as they walked up the steps to the building's entrance, tears filling her vision, her legs feeling unsteady. He glanced down at her with some concern, obviously spotting that she was in distress, which was a bad thing. He'd want to know what was upsetting her and, if he asked, she wasn't sure she'd be able to lie again.

She was so tired of lying.

What about justice for your parents' deaths?

But was it really justice to intentionally hurt someone? To cause them pain, simply because you yourself were hurting?

She knew the answer to that. It had been there all along, she just hadn't wanted to see it. Of course it wasn't justice. It was mean and petty and cruel. It was revenge, and there was nothing just about that.

Apollo had done what he could to mitigate his father's actions, and his own. He'd apologised and he'd paid out compensation. It wasn't his fault that her father had chosen the path that had caused the most pain. It wasn't his fault that her mother had refused that compensation in anger, before becoming ill with the cancer that would kill her.

None of that was Apollo's fault.

You need to tell him the truth then.

Yes, she did. Her mouth went dry at the thought of admitting that, for the entire year she'd been employed by him, she'd been hiding her background. That she'd planted those cameras. That his reputation was being called into question because of her. That she was the daughter of the man who'd killed himself...

She didn't know what he'd do when he found out the truth, but she did know one thing. He hated a liar. And there would be no more lazy afternoons in bed with his hands on her, making her feel beautiful and giving her pleasure. No more coffee in the morning, or little tasting plates. No more warm baths and him washing her hair.

No more of him at all.

He'd be furious with her, and he'd have every right to be.

As they reached the top of the steps, someone from the media pack yelled, 'What do you know about your secretary, Apollo? Do you have any comment to make about the rumours that she isn't who she says she is?'

Flora's blood turned to ice, and for a second she froze, completely unable to move. Apollo gave no sign of having heard the question, merely glancing at her, the concern in his eyes deepening.

Pull yourself together.

She gripped his arm, forced herself to give him a nod to indicate she was fine.

'Apollo!' The same person shouted again. 'Ask your wife about her background!'

Apollo's dark head turned in the direction of the media pack, and Flora wanted to tell him to keep moving, to go inside and get away from the questions, to find a quiet place where they could talk. But she didn't want to draw any more attention to herself than she already had.

'Flora!' someone else shouted, taking advantage of their pause at the top of the steps. 'Does your husband know about your family?'

Apollo's head whipped around in the other direction. Flora gripped his arm even tighter, feeling sick. 'Can we go inside?' she asked urgently. 'Please, I'm not feeling well.'

He glanced at her again, then nodded, ushering her into the building. The door slid closed, shutting out the clamour.

Inside was a vast marble foyer with lifts at one end, and Flora felt as if she was traversing a mountainside, her heels clicking on the floor and echoing in the silence.

Apollo said nothing as they came to a stop in front of the lift that would take them to the rooftop bar. A man in evening clothes waited outside the doors. He smiled and greeted them, then pushed a button, opening the lift doors and gesturing at them to step inside.

The ice inside Flora wouldn't go away as the doors slid shut.

The interior of the elevator was large and mirrored. She could see herself standing there in her glittering silver dress, Apollo tall and darkly beautiful standing beside her. Her face was pale, and there were dark circles under her eyes.

In the mirrored doors, she met his gaze, and felt her stomach drop away.

'Is there something that you're keeping from me, Flora?' he asked.

Her fingertips had gone cold, her heart beating hard and fast, but that didn't matter. What mattered was telling this man the truth she'd been hiding from him all this time.

He will hate you for it.

He would. And she would deserve that hate.

Her father had taken his own life for a reason, after all, and it hadn't just been because of the money. It couldn't have been. None of the other investors caught up in the scheme who'd lost everything had, so why had he?

You weren't enough for him. You never were.

The words whispered in her head as she looked helplessly back at Apollo, hoping desperately that the lift would finally stop, or maybe even plummet back down to the ground, and this terrible moment would end.

But neither of those things happened.

Say it. Tell him. Now.

He turned and his hands were heavy on her shoulders, turning her to face him. There was concern in his eyes and worry, and she knew it was for her. Because he cared.

And in a sudden flash of insight, she suddenly understood why this moment was so hard, and why the thought of telling him made her feel physically sick.

Why, in the end, there was no other option for her but to give him the truth.

Because, despite all her justifications to herself about how this was only physical, that her heart wasn't involved, that she was perfectly in control, she wasn't.

She was in love with him and had been for the past two weeks, and if there was one thing this man deserved, it was the truth.

'Flora?' His eyes narrowed. 'Flora. Answer me.'

His grip on her was firm. There was no escaping his gaze.

No escaping this moment either.

She swallowed, her mouth bone dry, and made herself hold his gaze. She couldn't be a coward about this. He deserved the same honesty that he'd given her.

'Flora McIntyre is my legal name,' she said in an unsteady voice. 'But it's my mother's maiden name. My father was David Hunt. The man your father convinced to sink his life savings into that investment scheme. The man you told that the rumours were unfounded, and there was nothing to worry about.'

For a moment, Apollo just stared at her, as if he hadn't heard what she'd said. Then it must have penetrated, because his eyes widened in shock, and he dropped his hands from her shoulders, then took an unconscious step back, staring at her. 'What? What are you talking about?'

Flora forged on. 'Those statements the press were throwing at us… It's going to come out at some stage, but I hid my background from you. When I took the job at Helios, I didn't want you to know my history.'

He said nothing for a long moment, his expression still one of shock. Then, like water in a lake slowly freezing over, his expression hardened, his eyes becoming cold chips of dark green glass. 'And why would that be?'

Flora's fingers curled into fists. 'Because I've been planning to ruin you.'

Apollo couldn't move. Shock had frozen him where he stood. All he could do was stare at the woman in front of him, the same woman he'd married and had spent the last two weeks exploring every inch of. The woman who'd relaxed with him and laughed with him. Who'd unleashed her passion onto him every night and hadn't been afraid to have him do the same to her. Who was the only person he'd ever met who hadn't treated him either like a criminal or a paragon, but just as a man.

The woman who'd apparently been lying to him all this time and he hadn't known.

She'd been his PA for an entire year and had given no sign that she was anything but the woman he'd hired. Unflappable, calm, serene. He'd known nothing about her, but at the time he hadn't thought he'd needed to. Then, when he realised he *did* want to know more about her, he'd thought he'd take it slowly, since she hadn't been very forthcoming with details about herself.

Except, there was a reason she hadn't been forthcoming.

If what she'd just said was true—if indeed he could believe anything she said—then she was David Hunt's daughter. The man who'd killed himself over the loss of his life savings. It had been years before Apollo had managed to get Helios into a position where he could give compensation to the victims. He'd located Hunt's family, but David's wife had refused any money, and nothing he'd been able to do had changed her mind.

It had been one of his life's biggest regrets.

Yet now, the daughter of that man was standing right in front of him, telling him she'd been lying about who she was all this time, and all because she wanted to ruin him. Lies of omission were still lies.

'Why?' He managed to dredge the word up somehow.

Flora had gone pale, yet her chin was held at a determined angle, and her grey eyes were clear. 'Because you ruined my parents' lives,' she said simply. 'So I was going to ruin yours.'

The shock echoed, ricocheting inside him and rebounding like a rock bouncing down a mountainside.

'How?' Apparently he'd been reduced to one-word questions.

'I wanted to get close to you,' she said. 'I spent a few years, actually, working towards getting hired by Helios, and then becoming your PA.' She swallowed then, the first sign of tension she'd shown, apart from her pallor. 'I was going to start with your reputation, and then I was going to ruin you financially, too.'

He stared at her, still trying to process what she'd said. 'You really thought you'd be able to ruin me?' he asked, because he couldn't get his head around it. 'By being my PA.'

'Yes.' Her voice was flat, as if she was having to force out the words, and he noticed that her hands were in tight fists at her sides. 'But then the photos came out and you offered to marry me instead of Violet, and... I decided financial ruin would affect too many other people, so I thought if I could get you to fall in love with me, then I could...hurt you. I could leave you, break your heart, the way my mother's and mine had broken.'

She used you the way your father used you, and you didn't see it. You only saw what you wanted to see, because you were obsessed with her. Just like you were obsessed with gaining your father's approval.

Something twisted inside him then, something else that had nothing to do with the present moment, and more to do with the past. A bitter grief, an endless guilt at what he'd done and the consequences that followed. But he shoved that aside, because the anger he felt about his own actions was a bottomless pit he couldn't afford to fall into.

Far better to be angry with her and her lies, at what

she thought she could do to him, make him fall in love with her. As if he'd *ever* be so stupid.

Aren't you, though? You thought she was something she wasn't...

The rage inside him grew, at her for lying to him. For being so beautiful and passionate, and so accepting of him and his demands. For making his heart skip a beat every time he walked into a room. For smiling and laughing with him, for teasing and flirting with him. For being too good to be true.

And no matter how hard he tried to avoid it, he couldn't escape the fact that he was complicit in this too. For believing what she'd told him. For thinking that she was honest, that there was nothing manipulative about her. For baring parts of his soul to her, and not even realising that all this time, she must have hated him for it.

Yes, and for letting his heart take control when it should have been his brain. And he knew, deep down, that no matter what he told himself, it *had* been his heart that was involved, tthough how deeply, he didn't want to think about.

Because he should have been able to laugh this off. Fire her and put in place more stringent HR guidelines for Helios. Divorce her and send her away, never see her again, or take her to this event and pretend nothing had happened. Act as if it didn't matter.

Except he couldn't seem to find his usual cool veneer. His measured manner. There was only a blinding, hot rage, and a sense of deep betrayal.

'So all of this was a lie then?' he demanded, his voice much rougher than he wanted it to be. 'Every night we spent together, every time you called my name. That was all an act?'

Something flared in her eyes then, something that looked like anguish. 'No,' she said hoarsely. 'No. None of that was a lie. That was all real, I promise.'

'Promise?' The word was acid on his tongue. 'How can you give me promises when you've been lying to me for months?'

'I know.' She swallowed yet again. 'I just didn't know—'

'Didn't know what?' His voice was as sharp as a whip-crack, and he didn't bother to temper it. 'That I hated liars? That I thought what we had together was something special, something different? That I thought *you* were different?'

She'd gone white. 'I didn't know you thought that. And I didn't know that you were everything people said you were.'

'So you thought that I was being insincere, did you? You thought that I was a liar, even though—' He bit the words off, swallowing them down. They were in a lift going to a party, and this was neither the time nor the place to have this confrontation.

Then he realised something else. She was the daughter of David Hunt, and once that came out, there would be interest in his past again, in the collapse of his father's scheme, in what had happened all those years ago. Tongues would wag, and he knew how it looked. He'd seduced the woman who'd been one of his father's victims—one of *his* victims…

There will be no divorce. Not yet at any rate.

Further down, beneath his anger, was something else,

something that felt like pain, but he didn't want to acknowledge that. He didn't want to acknowledge anything at all except rage, and that he forced away, because he couldn't give into it, not here, not now.

'So,' he said finally into the heavy silence, 'I suppose I have you to thank for those photos?'

She was the colour of ash now, but he told himself he felt no sympathy. She'd brought this on herself. 'Yes,' she said faintly.

This time there was no shock, not even any surprise. Of course she'd engineered the photos. Of course. She was the reason he was now in this position. It was all her fault.

And you believed it, don't forget that. It was your idea to marry her.

Oh, he wouldn't forget. How could he? When the ring on her finger and the dress she wore was his?

'So this is revenge?' he asked.

She didn't flinch, and he would have admired her courage if he hadn't known that the only reason she was telling him all this now was because the press had somehow found out.

Another silence fell and still she didn't look away, her shoulders squared, as if bracing for a blow. 'I thought it was justice,' she said. 'What I told you in Paris was true. My father did die. He took his own life, and it broke my mother's heart, and mine. Mum didn't want the compensation you offered, she was too angry, so we had nothing. We had to sell the house, and then we were on the breadline. She had to work two jobs to keep us solvent, and then...' Her voice faltered. 'That's when she got sick. I lost her a couple of years ago.'

He'd felt sorry for her back in Paris when she'd told him about her parents. But he didn't feel sorry for her now. She'd had the opportunity to tell him the truth then, and she hadn't. She'd lied to him. She'd done exactly what his own father had done.

'My father went to jail,' he said, fighting to keep his voice level. 'My mother and I were left with nothing, also. Was that not justice enough?'

The look in her eyes flickered once again, darkening. 'You were the one who convinced him to sink all his money into that scheme. And you were the one who told him there was nothing to worry about.' She blinked, and he saw then that there were tears in her eyes. 'But that was before I…before you told me about…' She stopped.

Before tonight, he might have taken her in his arms and kissed away the tears. But it was tonight, and she'd dealt him a mortal blow. She'd hurt him knowingly, in the one place he was vulnerable, and he was too furious to care about her feelings.

Furious, and getting more and more so by the second.

The lift chimed, having reached the rooftop, but he put his hand on the button, keeping the doors closed. 'You worked for me for a year,' he snapped, unable to help himself. 'Did you not think, even for one moment, that I might have been a victim of my father, just as yours was? Did you really think that everything I've done to put right what he did wrong was a lie? That I didn't mean any of it?' His voice had risen, but he didn't try to quiet it.

Flora was still facing him, her chin high, but she was starting to tremble now and a tear had escaped one eye, slowly tracking down her cheek.

He was too angry to care about her tears. If she was hurt then good. She'd hurt him.

'I'm sorry,' she whispered. 'I was wrong.'

He didn't bother to ask himself why this mattered to him so much, why *she* mattered to him so much. He didn't bother to question why the sight of that tear made him feel an obscure kind of pain.

He only knew that he was angry, and there was an event they needed to get through, and none of what was happening between them could be allowed to show in public.

'It's too late for that,' he said coldly. Then he reached out and grabbed her hand, holding it tight within his.

She stiffened. 'What are you doing? You can't want me to go with you now.'

'No, I don't,' he said, brutally honest. 'But if your background comes out, what do you think people will say if I divorce you? If they think you seduced me, charmed me into believing you were who you said you were, I'll be a laughingstock. And if I get rid of you, I'll be the bastard who kicked one of the victims of my father's scam to the kerb. Either way, my reputation will suffer, so, yes. You'll have to come to the party with me, just as I'll have to pretend I knew who you were all along.'

He took his finger off the button and the doors slid open.

'Come,' he said brusquely. 'We have a party to go to.'

And he stepped out of the lift, into the noise and lights of the bar beyond.

CHAPTER TEN

FLORA FIERCELY BLINKED back the tears as he tugged her into the bar. Her heart hurt, everything hurt, but what he'd said in the lift made sense. She could plead a headache and go back to the apartment, but she was the one who'd created this mess. She was the one who'd lied to him, deceived him. Put at risk everything he'd worked for, and betrayed the growing understanding between them.

It was the least she could do to attend a bloody party, even if looking like she was enjoying herself was the hardest thing she'd ever done.

She couldn't believe he'd thought that everything that had happened between them in the past two weeks had been a lie. Surely he must know that it had been real. Surely… Then again, she could understand why he didn't. Everything else had been a total fabrication, so why wouldn't he think that?

Except her feelings for him weren't a lie. They were deeply and distressingly real, and they hurt. They hurt so much, because she had hurt him, and that was the worst part. A month ago, she'd believed all those untruths she'd told herself, believed the worst of him, based on nothing more than her own anger and pain. And in the space of a couple of weeks, everything had changed.

She'd fallen in love with the man she was supposed to hate, the man she was supposed to ruin, and what might have been the start of something wonderful was now in ashes, and she only had herself to blame.

She'd broken his trust, and he was never going to forgive her.

She was never going to forgive herself.

Before, whenever they'd arrived anywhere, he'd shortened his stride to match hers, but now he strode ahead without slowing, his hand still securely holding hers, leaving her to trot in order to keep up with him.

Her throat was tight and she wished with all her heart that she'd never decided on this little revenge plan of hers—and yes, it was revenge. Cold and petty and mean.

She didn't even feel a sense of relief that he knew about it now. No, all she could see was the flaring shock in his gaze and the look of betrayal that had crossed his face. Then the fury...

She'd come to love the distinct emerald glow in his eyes that was a sign of his passion. But the vivid emerald she'd seen in the lift had been nothing but rage.

Perhaps she should take some comfort in the fact that, if he'd been so furious, it must mean he felt something for her. But she wasn't comforted. All she knew was that she'd hurt him terribly, and she hated herself for it.

The bar had soaring ceilings and massive floor-to-ceiling windows, which gave magnificent views over the city and the harbour. The decor was very minimalist, the seating upholstered in black, the carpet too, with drama and colour brought by gold light fittings.

A beautiful space, but Flora couldn't appreciate it. All she was conscious of was Apollo's tall figure, tension radiating from him, as he stopped by a small group of people and glanced at her. His gaze couldn't have been colder if he'd tried, but she forced a smile on her face anyway. She would do this, she would bear it. It was the least she could do for him.

Apollo introduced her to them, even as the names sailed straight out of her head. All her attention was on him, watching him talk, his green eyes glittering. He was smiling, but she could see his rage. It was seething in the air around them, making it difficult to breathe, much less think.

She kept the smile plastered to her face, tried to act as if nothing was wrong, but it was. Everything was wrong and it was her fault.

You're just like your father, giving out empty promises you had no intention of keeping. Betraying the people you care about because of your own pain. You're selfish, just like him.

Something ached deep inside, something sharp and edged, cutting away at the core of who she was, hurting, bleeding.

A woman she'd just been introduced to was looking at her with some concern, and Flora knew she'd been asked a question. But she couldn't remember what the question had been, and she couldn't get any words out anyway, and now everyone was looking at her.

'You look very pale, dear,' the woman said. 'Are you quite all right?'

Flora could feel Apollo's gaze on her, the pressure of his anger pushing down on her, squeezing the life out of her, and abruptly she couldn't stand it anymore. She'd been pretending for too long, the course of her life directed towards a goal that had now been revealed to be a hollow, pyrrhic victory.

She'd wanted to ruin him, and yet all she'd done was ruin herself.

Flora wrenched her hand from his and turned, making her way blindly through the knots of people until she found the doors to the rooftop terrace. She pushed them open, and stepped outside, the humid air instantly wrapping itself around her.

The massive city stretched out below her, the glittering neon turning Hong Kong into some kind of science fiction fantasy.

There was no one else on the terrace, so she stood there for a time, looking over the magnificent view of the city and the bay, struggling not to let the tears fall, feeling as though someone had ripped a hole in her chest.

'Flora.'

His voice came from behind her, deep, rough, and she turned around sharply, swiping a hand across her cheek to make sure there were no tears. She didn't want him to see how awful she felt. It was her problem to deal with. She didn't want to make it his.

His face betrayed nothing, his gaze level and flat. 'What are you doing out here? We need to show a united front, remember?'

'Yes,' she said, trying to keep her tone as even as his. 'Of course. I just…needed some air.'

His cold green gaze swept over her, studying her as if she was a stranger, which was of course what she was to him now. 'Why are you upset? You were the one who put us in this distasteful situation. Deal with it.'

His voice was like ice, and her heart ached for the

warmth and the heat that she'd had for the past two weeks. The little displays of care and concern that had made her feel so good, the desire in his eyes that had made her feel beautiful.

You don't deserve any of it. You never have.

No, she didn't, she understood that now. And he didn't either. He didn't deserve what she'd done to him, and that whispered apology in the lift hadn't been nearly enough.

She turned to face him. 'I'm sorry,' she said starkly. 'I'm sorry I lied. I'm sorry I put you in this situation. I should have known the kind of man you were when I first started working with you, but… I didn't. I shouldn't have done it, but…'

He said nothing.

She took a breath, and went on, wanting him to understand that the problems were hers, not his. 'I loved my father. I loved him so much, and he always promised that he'd take care of Mum and me. That we were the most important things in his life. And then…he left us. He broke all those promises he made, and left Mum and me with nothing, nothing at all. She had to go out and work two jobs just to keep a roof over our heads. And then…it was six years after Dad died that she got cancer. I don't know if it was the stress or what, but… It was incurable.' Her throat was tight and she had to swallow to even breathe. 'When she died, I was all alone.' Somehow there were tears on her cheeks, even though she hadn't known she was crying, but she didn't bother to wipe them away. 'After they were gone, I had nothing and no one, and I was just…so angry. Angry at Dad for leaving us the way he did, for not even thinking about the effect it would have on us. But he was gone, and you and your father weren't, so… I blamed you instead.' She stopped, her throat aching. What was the point of telling him this? Why would he care? It was justification after justification, and she knew it. 'I'm sorry, Apollo. I didn't know what kind of man you were until…'

He took a step towards her, the lines of his beautiful face hard. 'You think I care about any of that? When you lied to me? When you put me in a situation where I had to go against *everything* I believed in, and lie too? After I've made my entire life about transparency and honesty.' He took another step. 'You made me a liar, Flora. You duped me, the way my father did, then you turned me into a liar like him.'

Rain had begun to fall again, a sudden and thick tropical downpour.

Flora ignored it as her dress soaked through, his words like stones being thrown at her, causing an abrupt protective anger to flicker to life.

He had a right to his anger, but there were some choices he'd made that had turned the whole situation into something more complicated than it had needed to be.

She took a step towards him, the rain making her dress stick to her skin. 'You didn't have to lie,' she shot back. 'This marriage was your idea in the first place. There were other things you could have done. It didn't have to involve—'

'You?' He was standing right in front of her, as soaked to the skin as she was, his emerald eyes blazing. '*You* involved me, Flora! You put at risk everything I worked for. Everything I—'

'You destroyed my family!' She shouted, uncaring who heard, all the pain and rage overflowing inside her.

'My father *died* and so did my mother, and I was left all alone. Dad didn't care what would happen to us after he was gone and, as for Mum, I was nothing but a millstone around her neck that she didn't need!' She kept on shouting, the hurt demanding some kind of outlet. 'I lost everyone I loved and everyone who loved me, and all because of you!'

Apollo was so close, staring down at her, the look in his eyes electric, blazing. 'Don't act as if this was something you were forced into, Flora,' he bit out. 'It's all about choices. Your parents had choices, and if you didn't like them, that's got nothing to do with me!'

His tall figure was wavering in front of her, and she wasn't sure if it was due to the tears in her eyes or the rain. Even now, even like this, hurling yet more painful truths at her, he was the most beautiful man she'd ever seen.

She took an unsteady breath. 'I know,' she said, in a voice thick with tears. 'I know. I believed him. I thought he'd take care of us, that he'd never let anything bad happen to us, but I was wrong. I was wrong about *everything*.' She swiped her hand over her face again and turned away, not wanting him to witness the breaking of her heart, but then a firm hand gripped her shoulder and she was pulled around to face him again.

He was breathing fast, the lines of his face taut. Then he glanced up at the sky, muttered a curse, grabbed her hand in an iron grip and strode towards the doors, pulling her inside.

Unable to break his grip, Flora had no choice but to run behind him to keep up. He shouldered through groups of people, apparently not caring that they were soaking wet and everyone was staring at them.

He led her down a short hallway, before finding a door and opening it, dragging her inside and kicking the door shut behind them.

It was a small powder room, with a couch and an armchair, and a mirror above a little vanity along one wall, not that Flora was taking much notice.

She was soaking wet and shaking with emotion. Fury and guilt and a pain so sharp and raw it felt as if someone had taken a scalpel to her soul. She opened her mouth, to say what she didn't know, but then Apollo was reaching for her, gripping her shoulders and pushing her against the wall.

His hair was soaked, licking across his forehead like black flames, his eyes a dark blazing emerald. Her heart kept tripping over itself just looking at him.

The grip he had on her verged on painful, every inch of his magnificent, powerful body tense with fury. 'I don't care what you lost,' he said through gritted teeth, his Greek accent becoming pronounced. 'I was only trying to protect you, that's all I was ever trying to do with this farce of a marriage. And as for breaking my heart... You'd never be able to do that, not in a million years. How could I ever love a woman who lied to me?'

She was shivering now, but it wasn't because she was cold. Not even with her wet dress plastered to her and the air con in the room. No, it was because of him, because the heat of his body was radiating into her like a vast, dark fire, and all she could think was how had it come to this?

He'd been the target of her anger for so long and she'd told herself she hated him. Except she didn't, it was the opposite, and now the tables had been turned. She was now the object of his anger, his hate, and the thought that she'd broken his trust so selfishly made her feel like the worst person in the entire world.

She wanted to say something, offer another apology, but he saved her from answering by bending his head, his mouth suddenly on hers, and it felt as if the very air around them caught fire, ignited by the heat of their connection.

It was a raw kiss, fuelled by rage and pain, guilt and hunger.

He bit her bottom lip hard, making her gasp, and then she was kissing him back, trying to bite him the way he was biting her, draw blood, take out this aching swell of emotion on him in some way. But he wouldn't let her.

He grabbed her wrists and forced them down to her sides. 'I can't divorce you,' he said low and rough. 'No matter how much I want to. We have to stay married for six months to a year in order for the blowback about your background to die down. But now you owe me, Flora. For all the months you lied to me, and for those ill-advised photos. For the trust you betrayed. Do you understand?'

She was breathing very fast, her mouth full and sensitive, her whole body wanting him desperately. She wished she could tell him that he was wrong, she didn't owe him, but she couldn't. She couldn't lie any more.

'Yes, I understand,' she said hoarsely, because what else could she say?

'So here is how our marriage is going to be.' He gripped her wrists tighter. 'I want something in return, and that will be you, in my bed every night, because as much as I don't want to want you, I do. You will act on the outside as if you've never been happier than to be in

my presence. You will give me anything I want whenever I ask, and you will not refuse.'

She swallowed. 'Why?'

'Because I never gave you any reason to doubt me,
and yet you did, this whole time. So this will be your
apology. You will give your trust to me without receiv-
ing anything in return.'

'And if I don't want to?'

'Then leave. I won't stop you. But you will never see
me again if you do.'

Flora knew she should take the escape he offered, run
away and never see him again, that it would be kinder
to both of them if she did. But she couldn't, she already
knew that. The thought of leaving him was even more
unbearable than the thought of staying with him.

'Okay,' she said hoarsely.

'Your agreement,' he bit out. 'Say it.'

'Yes, I agree. To everything.'

The look in his eyes flared. 'Now, I want you. And you
will let me do anything I want to you, right here, right
now.' There was a cruel twist to his mouth. 'But you will
get no satisfaction from it, understand? If you come before I say so, you will be punished.'

A quiver ran the length of her body. The tattered rem-
nants of her pride wanted to push him away and walk out,
but it was too late for that, far too late. All she could feel
was his heat, the smell of rain and his aftershave were
making her dry-mouthed with desire. He still wanted
her, that was something, and so she would give herself
to him. She couldn't do anything else.

She would give him anything and everything.

She stood there as he dropped to his knees in front of

her, pushing her wet dress up to her hips, before grabbing the fine lace of her underwear and ripping it away. She was trembling by then, her knees weak, the ache between her thighs almost as needy and raw as the ache in her heart.

He looked up at her, his gaze fierce. 'You will not touch me. That, you'll have to earn.' Then, without waiting for her to speak, he put his hands on her thighs and gripped them, then used his thumbs to delicately spread the soft folds of her sex. Then he leaned forward and covered it with his mouth.

A raw bolt of electric pleasure lanced through her, making her gasp as his tongue began to explore. She'd learned over the past couple of weeks that he was extremely good at this, and now he used his knowledge of her to devastating effect. Licking, teasing, stroking her so that her knees became so weak only his hands on her thighs were holding her up.

It was all she could not to grab his shoulders or thread her fingers through his hair, touch him the way she was desperate to, but he'd forbidden her. She didn't have to do what he said, she knew that, but he'd made it impossible for her to do otherwise.

She *did* owe him.

She loved him and she'd broken his trust, and now all she wanted to do was make it up to him.

He did something with his tongue then that made her shake like a leaf, and she had to put her hands over her mouth to stop the cries. She tried to think unsexy thoughts, anything to stop the relentless drag of pleasure, but nothing seemed to work. She wanted to prove to him that she didn't doubt him by doing what he asked and hold back her orgasm, but she didn't think she could. And then his tongue sank deep inside her and she closed her eyes, screaming against her own hands as pleasure exploded around her and she was lost to it.

Apollo felt her tremble, heard her hoarse, muffled scream, tasted the flavour of her orgasm as she came, so sweet it pierced his soul. He didn't understand that sweetness, didn't know why it still had that effect on him, even knowing now what she'd done to him.

He was still furious, too. As furious as he'd been the moment she'd lifted her chin and told him that she'd been lying to him. That she was nothing but a con woman and a charlatan, just like his father.

Perhaps that's why he was so angry. Because of what Stavros had done to him all those years ago, duping him the way Flora had duped him. Perhaps the sense of betrayal had nothing to do with her specifically, but was only an echo of that long-ago breach of trust his father had committed. Because yes, he'd trusted her—he'd had no reason not to—and she'd broken that trust.

He shouldn't be here now with her. He should have continued walking through the party, pulling her along behind him. They could have left via the back way, out of the bar, without anyone being the wiser, then gone back to his apartment where he would have left her in the bedroom alone.

He hadn't needed to drag her into this room. He hadn't needed to tell her exactly how their marriage would proceed from now on. All he'd needed, to continue this farce, was her presence in public, not in private.

Yet, as he'd stood on the outside terrace in the pouring rain, watching her eyes go silver with fury as she'd told him about her anger, about how she'd lost everyone she'd ever loved and that he was to blame, all he could think about was how much he wanted her, even now, even after what she'd done.

Beneath his own anger, there had been the ghost of something softer, something that had ached for the pain he'd seen in her eyes, but he'd ignored it. He hadn't wanted to feel sorry for her. He'd tried hard to hold on to his control then, but even standing amid the shards of his broken trust in her, somehow she managed to get under his skin. She'd been standing there in the rain with her wet dress plastered to her, the neon skyline making her look as if she'd been dipped in molten silver.

She was so beautiful, and all his fury, looking for an outlet, had been alchemised full force into breath-stealing desire before he'd even been aware of it.

All that seemed to matter was having her, pouring out his rage into her willing body, punishing her for what she'd done to him by giving her pleasure but no release. It would all be on his terms now, not hers. She'd given up the right to that when she'd forced him into this lie of a marriage.

'*You didn't have to lie...*'

The words she'd flung at him on the terrace outside, about the choices he'd made himself, echoed in his head, but he ignored them. He was too angry with her to accept his own culpability in this mess, and now he was too hard to think about anything but having her.

She was shaking as he rose to his feet. He didn't touch her, didn't bother to adjust her dress. Instead, he reached into his pocket, got out his wallet and found a condom.

'You disobeyed me.' He'd planned to sound cold and brusque, but his voice came out hot and rough instead. 'You came when I told you not to, which means you don't deserve to have anything more. This is for me, Flora. Just for me.'

She didn't move as he ripped open the condom packet, then unzipped his trousers. Her eyes darkened even further as he dealt with the protection before stepping closer to her. He slid a hand down the back of her thigh and behind her knee, then he hauled her leg up and over his hip, spreading her open. She gasped softly, arching back against the wall, damp black hair tangled over her shoulders.

'Do you hear me?' He positioned himself before thrusting hard and deep, pinning her. 'It's my turn.'

'Yes,' she whispered on a gasp. 'Oh…yes…'

He pushed deeper, holding her pressed to the wall, grey eyes gone ever darker, nearly black, staring into his as if he'd mesmerised her. 'Why you?' The words escaped before he could stop them. 'Why can I not stop thinking about you? Why can I not stop wanting you?'

She shuddered as he began to move, a deep insistent rhythm that made her arch and her mouth open, soft panting breaths escaping. 'I…have hated you,' she said softly. 'I hated you so much, and yet…it changed. I didn't know…that it would.'

Pleasure had him in a vice, even as he felt her inner muscles tighten around him, holding him, giving him the most exquisite friction. 'This could have been something.' He slid the strap of her dress roughly down, uncovering one beautiful breast. '*We* could have been something, Flora. But you ruined it.'

A shiver rocked her as he toyed with her nipple—her lashes lowering, her pallor gone, washed away by the flush of pleasure staining her skin. 'I'm sorry,' she whispered. 'I'm so selfish. I hurt…the people I love.'

Through the building heat, he could hear the note of pain in her voice.

'Look at me.' He pinched her nipple hard, making her lashes lift abruptly, her gaze coming automatically to his, and he could see the same pain in her eyes too. 'What are you talking about?'

She swallowed, her breath coming harder, faster. Watching him as he moved inside her. Her eyes were reddened and a tear slid slowly down her cheek. 'I…l-love you, Apollo, and I hurt you. And you will never know how sorry I am for that.'

The strangest bolt of electricity went through him then, part pure physical pleasure, part a surge of what felt like joy, and over the top, another flare of anger. Because why tell him this now? After she'd conned him. Broken his trust and betrayed him.

'Liar,' he ground out. 'How will I ever know if you're telling the truth?'

'I told you,' she murmured, another tear sliding down her cheek. 'The past two weeks…it was all real. My feelings for you are real too.' Her eyes were wide and dark, and he thought she was telling the truth, but again, how would he know?

Now wasn't the time for this discussion, though, so he didn't speak. Instead, he leaned forward and licked her tear away, then covered her mouth with his.

He kissed her with raw passion, and a savagery he hadn't thought was in him, pouring all his anger out and into her, and she didn't pull away, didn't protest. She didn't touch him either, as he'd told her, only moved with him.

He wanted to take his pleasure first, to leave her hungry and wanting and desperate, but even in the depths of his rage, he couldn't quite bring himself to do that. So, as the orgasm began to take him, he slid a finger between her legs, down to where they were joined, and felt her body convulse around his, a cry of release escaping her.

Then he was moving harder, faster, until the rising pleasure blinded him, swamping him utterly.

Afterwards, he leaned against the wall, crushing her against it, her body soft and warm despite the fact that they were both damp from the rain. She felt small and fragile, and she was shivering, and the protector in him wanted to gather her up and hold her close, to soothe her somehow.

He crushed the urge.

She's still your wife, though. There's no point in being needlessly cruel.

He'd never been a cruel man, and he wouldn't be cruel now. But things wouldn't go back to the way they were before all of this had happened either. He'd given her the new terms of their marriage, and had offered her a way out, and she hadn't taken it. Which meant this was their marriage now. He still wanted her, and he'd be damned if he was going to spend six months to a year being celibate, but she'd get nothing else from him.

She'd betrayed him. The same kind of betrayal he'd felt when he'd walked into the office that day and found his father shredding documents, and realised that the man he respected and loved had been lying to him. Had charmed him and manipulated him into doing the most terrible things, and all for his own gain.

Flora was just like that. Charming him, manipulating him, causing him to go against everything he believed in, and all because she was angry.

He couldn't forgive it, as he'd already told her. And he never would.

Pushing himself away from her, he dealt with the condom and adjusted his clothing. Then he turned back to her and, without a word, helped her cover herself. Her hands were shaking as she drew the strap of her dress back over her breast, and again he had to crush the part of him that wanted to hold her.

Instead he held out his hand. 'The party is waiting for us.'

She pushed her hair back and glanced at the door, then back at him. 'You can't mean to go back to it. After that?'

'Yes. As I've already said, it's even more important we look as if we're together and madly in love now, especially with your identity in question.'

She blinked, her eyes dark. Some of her mascara was running and her mouth looked red and full, as if she'd bitten it. 'But my dress…your suit…'

'We'll tell them we got caught in the rain, which we did. That at least I don't have to lie about.'

She flushed. 'I'm not wearing underwear.'

'You can go without.' He held out his hand more insistently. 'It will make it easier to avail myself of you later.'

She took his hand, which felt small in his. 'I…don't think I can do this.'

He tightened his grip and gave her a feral smile.

'You've managed to deceive everyone beautifully until tonight. Just keep doing that.'

Her father took his own life and she lost everything, don't forget. That's what she said.

Yes, he remembered. But he was in no mood to hear about her past or her reasons for lying to him. His well of sympathy had run completely dry.

Flora had no answer to that, so he turned and pulled open the door, stalking back into the party.

It was a nightmare, the way that first party they'd gone to had been a nightmare. Of her, in her damp dress, with her black hair in a tangle, her mascara running and her mouth still full and red from his kisses. Knowing he'd ripped her underwear away and she wasn't wearing anything underneath. Of still wanting her despite everything.

He smiled at people, made light of their damp clothes, pretended he was still as in love with Flora as ever, yet it had never felt more like an act. He'd never felt the toxic combination of rage and desire more strongly than he did right now.

They moved through the crowd, Flora barely saying anything, the smile on her face more a rictus than anything else, and he didn't want to feel sorry for her. God, he'd even told her all about his betrayal that afternoon in bed. About how he'd found out what his father had done, and what he'd done after it. He'd talked about her father's suicide too, and how that had affected him.

He'd bared a part of himself to her and her response hadn't been to tell him the truth, but to distract him with sex. Well, that was fine. She'd get nothing but sex from him now.

He made them stay another two interminable hours

before he finally called the car to take them back to his apartment.

He'd been planning to have her as soon as they got home, but one look into her silvery eyes told him that she was expecting it, that she wanted him just as much as he wanted her.

Too bad. He didn't want to give her what she wanted.

'Go to bed,' he said brusquely. 'I'm too angry for anything more tonight.'

Then he turned on his heel, strode down the hall to his study and shut the door behind him.

CHAPTER ELEVEN

FLORA SAT IN the shade of the bougainvillea, on the terrace of Apollo's beautiful Greek villa. It had been built high on a hill above a little fishing village with the sea stretched out below her, a swathe of measureless aching blue.

They'd arrived from Hong Kong a couple of days before, and while the villa itself and the surroundings were heart-wrenchingly beautiful, Flora hadn't been able to appreciate any of it.

Apollo had withdrawn from her completely. It was as if he was a stunning island that she desperately wanted to visit, yet had no way to cross the vast gulf of the ocean between them.

The only attention he paid her was at night, in his bed, where he turned from ice into flame in a matter of seconds, drawing pleasure from her again and again. As she'd promised, she denied him nothing. She'd thought he might do as he'd vowed back in Hong Kong, leave her desperate and wanting, without any satisfaction, but he didn't. He'd never been a selfish lover and he still wasn't, not even in the depths of his fury.

In a couple of days they were supposed to be giving interviews about their great love affair and marriage, and there was to be a photoshoot too, and she was dreading it. Yes, she'd spent a year pretending to be someone she wasn't as his PA, but the thought of pretending there was nothing wrong between her and her husband made her feel exhausted.

Her husband. Was he even that now? Apart from the sex, he ignored her even more than he had as her boss.

Regardless, she didn't want to keep pretending, keep lying. That's why she'd told him she loved him back in Hong Kong. Maybe that had been a mistake—he'd certainly looked anything but happy at the declaration—but she'd wanted to be honest with him. She couldn't bear the thought of lying to him yet again.

But you'll have to keep lying.

That was true. The rumours about her background had been swirling since that night in Hong Kong. And so, to keep ahead of any misinformation, Apollo had issued a statement saying that he'd known all about Flora's family history right from the first, and he'd been keeping quiet about it to protect her. Of course he knew that she was David Hunt's daughter, but that hadn't factored into their marriage.

He hadn't run the statement by her first, he'd simply issued it without her approval, but she didn't protest. How could she? She'd keep lying to the public, pretending she was deliriously happy, just as he did, but she would not lie directly to him. Never to him. Never again.

There were yachts out in the bay, scudding across the waves, and the air was full of the smell of salt and dry earth, and the spice of some nearby flower.

She wished she could enjoy it, but her heart hurt too much. What she wanted, now that the initial shock of her deception had passed, was to tell him everything. Not for the sake of unburdening herself, but so he had some context at least. Then she wanted him to tell her about his past, about his father, about how he blamed himself for her father's death, because he did. She knew he did.

Of course, whether he told her anything at all was up to him, she had no right to ask, and she had no right to ask him to listen to her, either. But still. She wanted it.

After that, well. She didn't know. They'd have to stay married, but did he still want her to move in with him when they got back to London? If so, he hadn't said.

She didn't have to stay in Greece. She could leave, go back to London on her own, try and pick up the remains of her life somehow, but… That would leave him having to clean up the mess of their marriage and she couldn't do that. And as for the remains of her life… What even was that? She'd spent years aiming for this one goal, the complete ruination of Apollo Constantinides. and she'd cut out everything that hadn't directly related to that goal. And now, as she wasn't pursuing it any more, what was there left for her? An empty bedsit and an empty, directionless life.

Isn't that what you deserve?

Probably. She'd made him feel like he was his father, that's what he'd hurled at her that terrible night in Hong Kong. She'd taken him in, duped him, just as his father had, turning him into something he hated. a liar. So, yes, she did deserve it.

She'd hurt him where he was most vulnerable, and when she should have told him the truth, that afternoon when he'd bared some of his soul to her, she hadn't.

Now, though, every night in his arms, she bared her soul to him, trying to show him what he meant to her. Without words, because at least her body had never lied, but whether he understood that or not, she didn't know. He didn't speak at night and, in the mornings, she always woke up alone.

Her heart ached as she glanced along the stone terrace towards the white villa. The dark wood-framed doors were steadfastly shut, as they had been the few days she'd been here, even though she kept hoping he would push them open and come and join her. But he hadn't.

Maybe you should be the one to go to him.

The vice around her heart tightened. She could, but he might not want to see her. He might not want to listen to her, and then what would she do? All the people she'd ever loved had left her. First her father, by making a choice she was still furious about all these years later. and then her mother. Cancer hadn't been a choice, but her mother hadn't fought it. She'd succumbed quickly, as if she had no heart to keep on living.

No one wants to stay for you.

Her throat closed, more stupid tears were wavering behind her eyes. No, no one had. And the one man who might have, had she not ruined it the way he'd said back in Hong Kong, had cut himself off from her.

So what? Yes, life dealt you a crappy hand, but that's all you'll ever *have if you don't go out and fight for him. You had the determination to ruin him, now find that same determination and love him.*

A small electric shock bolted through her, stealing her breath.

It was true. that stubborn determination to follow her goal had led her to his point, and nothing had really changed except the goal itself.

She loved him. She wanted him. She wanted this marriage to be real, but if she was going to make that happen, she couldn't sit here wallowing in self-loathing. She couldn't keep obsessing over her losses and miring herself in fury.

There was no way to change the past, what had happened, had happened. But she had the power to change her future.

To let go of her anger and choose love instead.

She had to go to him, talk to him. Tell him what she wanted, which was to spend the rest of her life making it up to him, because a life loving him was better than a life alone, with nothing but her rage to comfort her. And if he didn't want that then…well, she'd have to deal with it.

Flora let out a breath, and with it she finally let go of the anger that had been fuelling her for years, the anger at her father's choices and the unfairness of life that had taken her mother too, burning like a flame in her heart. Yet the flame didn't flicker and go out. It began to burn. Brighter, more intensely, as a far more powerful feeling took its place.

It was sweeter and it ached, but it was right. It was true. It was love.

Flora pushed herself from the chair and walked across the terrace to the doors. Inside was the cool stone of the floor of the living room and its heavy-beamed ceilings, with lots of couches and low armchairs all upholstered in white linen.

Apollo would be in his office, so she went down the hallway, pausing outside the door to take another breath to calm her nerves, before pushing it open.

It was empty though.

She searched the entire house without finding him,

only to hear the sound of splashing coming from the pool on the other side of the house.

The pool area was built into the side of a cliff, with an infinity pool overlooking the sea, and a white stone terrace scattered with sun loungers.

Flora came out through the doors, stepping onto the warm white stone.

In the pool in front of her, one powerful olive-skinned arm rose and fell, as Apollo pulled himself through the water.

She stood for a moment, her heart full and aching in the cage of her ribs, watching him. He was graceful in the water, and strong, sleek as a shark.

Eventually, gathering her courage, Flora walked over to the edge of the pool and waited for him to notice her. He did another couple of laps before finally lifting his head from the water, raising his hands to push his wet hair back from his face. His green eyes were cold, no hint of welcome in them.

Flora's mouth went dry, a combination of nerves and appreciation at how the water sheened his skin, emphasising every hard, cut muscle of his chest and abdomen.

'Yes?' he inquired imperiously. 'What do you want?'

She swallowed. 'Can I talk to you, please?'

'I'm swimming.'

'I know.' She held his gaze, willing him to soften, even just a little. 'But this is important.'

He said nothing for a moment. Then he put his hands on the side of the pool and pushed himself out, in a demonstration of effortless strength. The water streamed off his magnificent body, making him look more like Poseidon than Apollo, and the ache in her heart deepened.

How to measure her love for this man? How to encompass his beauty? Words weren't enough and they never would be. Yet words were all she had.

He strode to one of the sun loungers and picked up the towel lying on it, then began to dry himself off. 'Make it quick,' he said curtly. 'I have things to do.'

Flora steeled herself. She had no idea what he felt for her, if he even felt anything at all after Hong Kong. But she knew what she felt. That was real and she had to trust it. She had to trust herself and her love for him.

She had to cross the gulf between them, because if she didn't try, she knew she'd regret it for the rest of her life.

'Apollo,' she said, as he wrapped the towel around his lean hips and stared at her. 'What I said back in Hong Kong was true. I'm in love with you.'

If the words made an impression on him, he didn't show it. 'And?'

Maybe he doesn't care.

He sounded so cold that it might very well be true. But then, if he didn't care, why was he still so angry? A person only got really mad if they cared a great deal, didn't they?

'You're angry still.' She had to fight to hold his gaze.

His mouth was a hard line. 'Yes,' he said flatly. 'I am.'

Well, that was the one thing she could count on with him, at least. He was honest. He'd never lied to her.

'I can apologise again if you like,' she went on determinedly. 'I can apologise as many times as necessary.'

'The first time was already more than enough.'

'And yet you're still angry.'

'Did you really expect my feelings to change just like that? Because you offered me an apology?' There was a distinct icy glitter in his eyes. 'I told you that I won't forgive you. I meant it.'

Was there really no way for her to bridge this space between them? Was there really no way back to him? She had try. She'd come this far.

Flora took a soft, silent breath. 'My dad loved Mum and me, but he was never good with money. He was always into these get-rich-quick schemes, and Mum loved him so much she was blind to his faults. When he told her what he was doing, that the returns were too good not to invest everything, she supported him. He wanted to better our lives, to take care of us, that's what he promised. Then he just…betrayed that promise. He betrayed us. He…didn't care enough about us to stay, to help us through the devastation. He took the easy way out.' She didn't bother to hide her bitterness. She was going to be nothing but honest from now on. 'So, I told you that we had to sell the house, and Mum had to get two jobs. It was all she could do to earn enough to keep our heads above water. I kept thinking how much easier it would be for her if she didn't have me.'

Apollo didn't say anything, but he didn't move either, the expression on his face impassive.

'She had no time for me,' Flora went on, clasping her hands together to stop them from shaking. 'She had no time for anything except work. I was in high school when she got sick. It was cancer, and I think she just gave up, because it was quick in the end. But I was so angry about it. I think… I was really angry at her for refusing the compensation money, and that if we'd had it, she wouldn't have worked so hard and got sick. But being angry at her was unfair, and I felt it so very deeply, I had to have some outlet and so… I blamed Dad.' Somehow she'd lost a little of her courage, so she turned to stare across at the ocean, since that was easier than looking at the stony expression on Apollo's face. 'I had no one after she died, only this anger at the unfairness of it all. Dad was gone, I couldn't direct it at him, and I just felt…powerless. Eventually, I found myself reading everything about the collapse of your father's scheme, about all the people involved. I saw that you'd been the one who'd convinced Dad to invest all his money. And I read that you'd turned your father in and escaped prosecution.'

The breeze lifted her hair on her shoulders and she wanted to turn around, to see if he was still there, still listening, but she didn't. This was all the olive branch she could offer him and, if he refused to take it, that was his prerogative. 'Your father had died in jail, so I couldn't touch him anymore. But I could get to you. I could make you pay for what happened to my family, and so that's what I set out to do.' She watched a boat zigzag across the blue water. 'I told myself it was justice, but it wasn't. I was just so blinded by anger in the end. So sure of the truth. That you were a liar, a master manipulator. I was sure that you were only paying lip-service to all those good deeds you did, that your bluntness was coldness, ruthlessness. That you didn't care.' Had he gone? Was she only talking to thin air?

'I wanted you, though,' she forced herself to go on. 'Even then, even when I told myself I hated you, I wanted you so badly. And then…' Her voice cracked. 'That two weeks we spent together was the happiest of my life. I didn't know who you really were until then, and I didn't realise that I'd been lying to myself. I wanted to believe that you were a terrible person so badly, because the only alternative was admitting that I was the terrible one. That I wasn't important enough for my father to make a different choice, and my mother not to fight her illness.'

Apollo stared at Flora's still figure. She wore a loose, tiered dress of white linen, held up by ties on each of her shoulders, and her black hair lay glossy and thick down her back.

He wanted to be angry with her. He wanted to turn his back on her and walk away. The past week since Hong Kong had been so difficult, even though he'd tried not to let it be. He thought pouring all of his anger and betrayal into her more-than-willing body every night in bed would help. He'd even told himself that he'd leave her wanting and unsatisfied, in punishment for what she'd done to him, but when the time came, he could never do it.

In bed, undone and abandoned in his arms, was the only time he knew she was honest with him, and the orgasms he wrung from her were always real. There was nothing fake about her response to him, and so he could never stop from proving that to himself.

Her background had come out now, and, as he'd thought, the media had driven itself into a frenzy over how he'd married the daughter of David Hunt, the victim of his father's scheme, who'd killed himself over it. Apollo had issued a statement as soon as the first rumours had gathered momentum, informing the public that she'd taken an assumed name to escape publicity. There was still some speculation about them, but at least other, more important news was now starting to take precedence.

What he'd hoped was that, as the rumours ceased, his

need for her would also cease. That he'd become tired of her, that the endless, aching desperation and obsession with her would fade, that his fury would fade along with it, and yet...

He couldn't stop looking at her, couldn't stop the response of his body to her, and something in his chest wouldn't stop aching. He wanted be angry with her still, but the fierceness of that fire seemed to have burned itself out, leaving only glowing embers behind.

Anger wouldn't help him anyway. Anger wouldn't help the ache or the need or the hunger. It wouldn't help the sense of betrayal that had cut to the heart of him. Being cold to her had only left him feeling hollow inside, as if in shutting her out, he was shutting out some vital part of himself that he needed for his very existence.

For the first time since that night in Hong Kong, Apollo tried to see her without the red haze of anger, and sort through what she'd told him.

Was it the truth, what she'd said about her parents? About how she'd lost everything? Or was it simply a tissue of lies to gain his sympathy? And all these protestations of love... Were they lies too? Did she mean it? She wanted him, oh, he knew that for certain, because her body didn't lie, but love?

Well, he knew about love. He knew how it blinded you, how it stopped you from seeing the truth. After all, it had blinded him to the truth about his father, had made him believe all the lies Stavros had fed him.

If she loves you, then she's blinded too. She won't see your faults.

That was true, and he had many of them. He was, after all, his father's son, and it was him who had led her fa-

ther to his death. She must see that. She'd told him she
was angry about the choices her father had made, but if
he hadn't been around, her father would never have made
those choices in the first place.

Slowly, Flora turned around, her dark, grey gaze meeting his. She was pale, her hands still clasped tightly in
front of her, but she didn't flinch from him.

'There,' she said. 'I've told you everything about me.
Those are the reasons I did what I did, but they're for
your information only. They're not meant as justifications.' She took another breath. 'I'm sorry that I made you
lie. I'm sorry I took you in. I'm sorry I turned you into
your father, but I'm not sorry that I fell in love with you.'
She lifted her chin in that determined way, because after
all, she was a very determined woman. 'You'll never be
him, Apollo. Everything you do, everything you are, is
his polar opposite. You're kind, protective and you care.
I was stupid not to have seen that earlier. I let my anger
blind me, but... It was love that made me see who you
truly are. The most amazing man I've ever met.'

He hadn't expected that, just as he didn't expect the
glow in those lovely grey eyes of hers. The glow of conviction. She believed what she'd said. She wasn't lying to
him now. She believed every word was the truth.

His heart tightened. He hadn't known what that would
mean to him, that she saw him in that way. That she didn't
see the man who'd been complicit in a scheme that had
brought so many people to ruin. The man who'd believed
his father's lies, who'd let love blind him to the truth.

'I know you believe that,' he said. 'But you're wrong,
Flora. It's got nothing to do with anger. I loved my father, and that love blinded me to who he really was. A

charlatan and a fraud. And I think it's blinding you to
who I really am too, because I'm none of those things.'

He expected her to turn away, but she didn't. Instead
she took a step forward, then another, slowly crossing
the distance between them, until she was standing right
in front of him. 'I loved my father too, and I felt the
same way about him when he died. It felt like a betrayal.
As if love had blinded me too, but now… I think that's
wrong. Love is making me see clearly for the first time.'
She tilted her head back and looked straight at him, then
she reached up and put a cool palm against his cheek.
'You're all of those things, Apollo. I know you don't think
you can trust me and I understand why. But you need
to trust this, trust what I'm saying right now. You gave
me the happiest two weeks of my life, and if that's all I
ever have—'

'I killed your father, Flora,' he interrupted hoarsely.
'You can't excuse—'

'No.' Her voice was firm, and very certain, as her
thumb brushed along his cheekbone. 'You didn't kill him.
You told me in Hong Kong that he made a choice, and
you're right. He did. I thought it was a selfish choice,
and it caused me a lot of grief, a lot of heartache, but… I
loved him. And maybe he thought that was his only option. I don't know. But what I do know is that I can't do
anything about it now, neither of us can.'

'If I hadn't—'

'Don't, please,' she interrupted once again, though this
time her voice was gentle. 'Don't do that yourself. Don't
take the blame for what Dad did. You were young, and
you wanted to please your father, and you didn't know
what Stavros was doing.'

Her touch on his cheek was soft, tender. He'd missed that touch. He'd missed it so much. 'I should have known… I should have seen it.'

'No, you shouldn't. Like I said, you were young and—'

'I wasn't young with you.'

Regret settled on her delicate face like a weight. 'You weren't to know that either. You employed me, and you trusted me, and I broke that trust in the worst way possible. You'll never know how sorry I am for it.'

She was sorry, he could see that now. There was something in her eyes, something that looked like…hope.

'Why are you looking at me like that?' he couldn't help but ask.

'I thought you'd walk away, I thought you wouldn't listen to me, but…you stayed.' She took a breath, then dropped her hand. 'You're a better person than I'll ever be.'

A better person… He wasn't, he knew that, but she'd said all of that was in the past and there was nothing they could do about it now.

His father was dead and so was hers.

And she loved him…she *loved* him…

Was it true what she said about anger and love? Was it anger that blinded you? Was it love that made you see clearly?

Deep in his heart, Apollo felt something shift, begin to uncurl, to stretch out. To bloom.

He had lived in his own anger for a long time, had made it his familiar. It dogged him everywhere, at his heels wherever he went. It had made him make an effigy of his name and reputation, yet one made of glass that could shatter at the slightest breath. It was rigid and unbending. Unforgiving…

Flora had left that anger behind. It was obvious from the open and honest way she looked at him, letting him see everything in a way she'd never done before. Letting him see her vulnerability, her soul.

Was it that easy? And did he want to do the same? Could he lay his own anger at his father and himself aside? Was it worth it? And if he did, what would be there instead?

Apollo lifted a hand before he could stop himself, pulling an end of one of the ties holding her dress up, and then the other. The soft white cotton fell slowly from her body and she made no effort to stop it, simply looked up at him, the dark charcoal of her gaze clear and open.

She was naked beneath the cotton, her body still every bit as lovely as it had been the first time he'd seen it, her skin honeyed and golden in the sun.

'Apollo,' she murmured, lifting her arms to him, and he needed no more invitation than that. He got rid of his own towel and then, because after all there was still a piece of him that wanted to punish her a little bit more, he picked her up and took them both into the cool water of the pool.

She gasped and when he pulled her into his arms, pressing her back against the pool wall, she twined her legs around his waist as if she'd been doing it all her life.

'Apollo,' she repeated breathlessly as he looked into her eyes, watching the familiar flame of desire leap high.

She was wet and slippery and he was too, and he thought he could probably look into her eyes for ever, watching them darken in response to her desire, and his.

She'd left behind her anger. Admitted her pain. Had

come to him and apologised for what she'd done, and he
believed her. Her regret was real.

But he had a choice to make. He could either let his
anger and hurt win, shut her out for ever, believe her
to be a con woman, the way his father had been a con-
man. Or...he could let the past go. Let his father go, let
his anger go.

*You know what's there, underneath all of that. You
know.*

Perhaps he did know. And perhaps it had been there
for longer than he'd cared to admit. This obsession with
her, this need for her... It wasn't only physical. It had
never been only physical. It was far more than that, it
went deeper...

'I have never believed in love, *matia mou*,' he murmured, brushing kisses over her forehead and nose, the
petal softness of her cheek, and then, finally, her mouth.
'I always thought it was a lie. It made you blind. Told you
things that weren't true.'

'I don't care if you don't feel the same way,' she said
huskily. 'I just want you.'

Apollo kissed her for a long time, then he lifted his
mouth, positioned himself and thrust inside her, easily,
naturally. She moaned softly, shuddering against the pool
wall.

'Tell me,' he whispered against her mouth. 'Tell me
everything about you.'

He didn't make it easy for her, with the insistent press
of his hips against her, but she tried, he'd give her that.
Telling him about her lonely childhood and how she'd always longed for siblings. How after her father had died,
she'd pass the time when her mother was out by reading

anything she could get her hands on. She didn't flinch about her quest for revenge, and answered every question he asked without protest.

The gentle thrusting he was doing as she submitted to his questioning might have had something to do with that, but there was no denying her honesty.

She held back nothing.

And somewhere, in the pleasure that gripped them both, Apollo let go of his past, let go of his guilt and, most important of all, his anger, because he knew what lay under all of those things, and it was wonderful.

It turned out that Flora was right. It was surprisingly easy to let go of all those things, and once he had, he could see truly for the first time in his life.

This was what he wanted. Them, together. Flora in his arms. Flora as his wife. Flora as his future. It had never been his reputation or his good name. It had never been the accolades and nominations, all the awards and good press.

It began and ended with her.

And once he'd let love fill his heart, a powerful tide sweeping all his preconceptions and certainties aside, he could see the new landscape that it made. And it was beautiful. A new certainty. One to build a life on.

'Your turn,' she said, her voice breathless and gasping. 'Tell me everything about you.'

But by then it was becoming impossible to think, so he only took her mouth as the climax gripped her, muffling her scream of release. Then he was following her, and this time he pressed his forehead to hers, looking into her eyes as the pleasure detonated inside him.

'Oh, *matia mou*,' he murmured roughly, when he could

speak. 'I was wrong about love. You're right, it doesn't blind. It doesn't lie. It helps me see the truth.'

Her breathing was starting to slow, but her grip on him didn't loosen. 'What truth?'

He looked into her eyes. 'That I love you.'

She stilled, shock rippling over her lovely face. 'What?'

'I can either stay angry at you for ever, or I can let it go.' He leaned forward and kissed her softly. 'So I'm choosing to let it go. I'm choosing to trust you. I'm choosing to love you, Flora Constantinides.'

He didn't need anything else, in that moment, because in that moment he knew.

All he'd ever needed was her.

EPILOGUE

'"Apollo and Flora's baby joy!"'

'Baby joy?' Flora looked at her husband as he began to read aloud from the magazine article underneath the headline. 'Really?'

It was a photo spread Apollo had approved, of them and their new baby. One last, final bow to the media. At least, that was what Apollo had promised her.

His green eyes glinted with a wicked humour. 'Certainly. We have a baby and it is joyous, correct?'

Flora looked down at said baby, the newly minted Elena Laura Constantinides, and smiled, her heart full of the most intense, almost painful love. 'Yes,' she said. 'Yes, that's true.'

Apollo put down the magazine and came over to where his wife sat on the couch with Elena in her arms, sitting down beside her. He bent and kissed the top of his new daughter's head, then he kissed his wife. 'You know what else is true?' he asked, settling back in the couch, an arm around Flora so she and their baby were nestled against him.

Flora glanced up at him, into his jungle green eyes, every part of her thrilling to his presence. She smiled. 'Tell me.' It was a little ritual they had.

'That I love you,' he said, and gave her his beautiful, amazing smile.

'And I love you too,' she said, because she always had and she always would.

Love was the bedrock that they'd built their lives upon. No word of a lie.

* * * * *

Were you captivated by Newlywed Enemies?
Then you're certain to love these other
intensely emotional stories
by Jackie Ashenden!

Enemies at the Greek Altar
Spanish Marriage Solution
Italian Baby Shock
The Twins That Bind
Boss's Heir Demand

Available now!

MILLS & BOON®

Coming next month

RUSH TO THE ALTAR
Abby Green

As if being prompted by a rogue devil inside herself, she blurted out, 'I couldn't help overhearing your conversation with your solicitor earlier.'

Corti's mouth tipped up on one side, and that tiny sign of humour added about another 1,000 percent to his appeal. For a second Lili felt dizzy.

'What was it you heard exactly?' He folded his arms now, but that only drew attention to the corded muscles of his forearms.

Lili swallowed. 'About how you have to marry and have an heir if you want to keep this villa.'

'And this is interesting enough for you to bring it up…why?'

The night breeze skated over Lili's bare skin, making it prickle into goose bumps. She was very aware that she was wearing just a swimsuit and a tiny towelling robe, her wet hair streaming down her back. The sense of daring fizzled away. She was being ridiculous.

She shook her head. 'It was nothing. I shouldn't have mentioned it.'

'But you did.'

There was a charge between them now. Something that felt almost tangible. 'Yes, I did.'

Continue reading

RUSH TO THE ALTAR
Abby Green

Available next month
millsandboon.co.uk

COMING SOON!

We really hope you enjoyed reading this book.
If you're looking for more romance
be sure to head to the shops when
new books are available on

Thursday 22nd May

To see which titles are coming soon, please visit
millsandboon.co.uk/nextmonth

MILLS & BOON

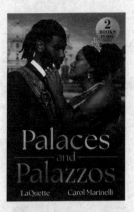
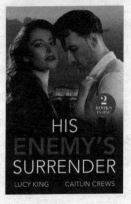
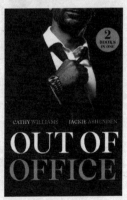

afterglow BOOKS

Afterglow Books is a trend-led, trope-filled list of books with diverse, authentic and relatable characters, a wide array of voices and representations, plus real world trials and tribulations. Featuring all the tropes you could possibly want (think small-town settings, fake relationships, grumpy vs sunshine, enemies to lovers) and all with a generous dose of spice in every story.

♪ @millsandboonuk
◉ @millsandboonuk
afterglowbooks.co.uk

#AfterglowBooks

For all the latest book news, exclusive content and giveaways scan the QR code below to sign up to the Afterglow newsletter:

SCAN ME

LET'S TALK

Romance

For exclusive extracts, competitions
and special offers, find us online:

f MillsandBoon

𝕏 @MillsandBoon

⊙ @MillsandBoonUK

♪ @MillsandBoonUK

Get in touch on 01413 063 232

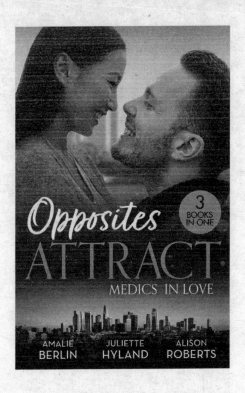